JEM SPEARS

PAPER ROADS

Paper Roads

An International Love and Misadventure novel

Copyright© 2026 by Jem Spears. All rights reserved. No part of this book may be reproduced or transmitted in any form or by any means, electronic, mechanical, photocopying, recording, scanning, or by any information storage and retrieval system without the written permission of the publisher, except where permitted by law. It is illegal to copy this book, post it to a website, or distribute it by any other means without permission.

www.jemspears.com

This is a work of fiction. All of the characters, organizations, and events portrayed in this novel are either products of the author's imagination or are used fictitiously.

NO AI TRAINING: Without in any way limiting the author's and Spear Stone Press's exclusive rights under copyright, any use of this publication to "train" generative artificial intelligence (AI) technologies to generate text is expressly prohibited. The author reserves all rights to license uses of this work for generative AI training and development of machine learning language models.

Printed in the United States of America.

Spear Stone Press | Cincinnati, Ohio

First Edition

Editor: May Peterson

Cover illustration: Amanda Lander

ISBN 979-8-9929810-1-8

Library of Congress Control Number: 2025913907

Also by Jem Spears

The International Love and Misadventure Series:
Starlight and Cinnamon
A Courtship in Quarantine

Content Guidance

It's a short one this time! This book contains the mention of parents' deaths, food poisoning and its associated consequences (not detailed), and a briefly missing child.

For everyone willing to give love a second chance.

Contents

1. October 2022   1
   Rin
2. October 2022   7
   Luke
3. October 2022   14
   Rin
4. September 2021   22
   Luke
5. October 2022   29
   Luke
6. October 2022   32
   Rin
7. March 2020   42
   Rin
8. October 2022   51
   Luke
9. October 2022   58
   Rin
10. May 2020   65
    Luke

11.	October 2022 Luke	76
12.	October 2022 Rin	89
13.	April 2020 Rin	99
14.	October 2022 Luke	106
15.	June 2020 Luke	116
16.	October 2022 Rin	126
17.	October 2022 Luke	140
18.	September 2021 Rin	152
19.	October 2022 Rin	161
20.	June 2020 Luke	174
21.	October 2022 Luke	181
22.	October 2022 Rin	194
23.	October 2022 Luke	212
24.	October 2022 Rin	228

25.	October 2022 Luke	240
26.	October 2022 Rin	250
27.	October 2022 Luke	257
28.	July 2020 Luke	271
29.	October 2022 Rin	285
30.	October 2022 Luke	294
31.	August 2020 Rin	304
32.	October 2022 Rin	309
33.	October 2022 Luke	324
34.	October 2022 Rin	331
35.	October 2022 Luke	339

Epilogue: November 2022 Rin	351
Acknowledgements	357
About the Author	359

Chapter 1
October 2022
Rin

I saw Luke from the road, several houses the color of winter grass between us and the salt from the sea peppering all of my senses, but his sandy hair was unmistakable even under cloud cover, and a year apart wasn't enough time to bury the memory of his smile deep enough to forget. With that memory, all the others followed, and I stopped in my tracks—legs weak and heat flushing my body despite the autumn breeze—suddenly filled with a yearning I was sure I'd overcome.

Hell of a way to realize I was still in love with him.

What was he doing in Scotland, anyway? What were the chances that I traveled ten thousand miles from home just to end up bumping into a neighbor and ex?

Slim. Unless it wasn't chance at all.

I turned away, hoping he didn't see me and pretending I didn't see him.

"Matalina Redgrave, you sweet, American muppet, what did you do?" I muttered, fighting with the uneven weight of the golf bag as I got my phone out of my pants' pocket. I scrolled to Mattie's name in my recent calls list and poked it aggressively. Usually there was math involved, calculating our different time zones between San Francisco and Auckland, but she was in London and should have been expecting this call if, as I suspected, she was behind this setup.

"Violence," she croaked when she answered. "Calling me so early. Rin, why?"

"Oh, Mats. I think you know why." Silence, on her end. Sea birds cried overhead, some kind of gull I couldn't name.

Luke would know what they're called.

Shut up, you.

"Mmm. Is it Saturday?" Mattie coughed the gravel out of her voice. "You must be at golf. You're welcome. Are you surprised?"

Mats and her sister Daphne were my best friends, and they were ride-or-die. They would—in the past, they had—set me up with a "seemingly chance but actually meticulously orchestrated" meeting with a crush. But they'd never meddled with an ex. Certainly not with a Big Ex.

"Shocked," I answered flatly, unzipping pockets of my bag and shoving my hand in as though I were looking for something. In case Luke had seen me and wondered why I stopped, it would look like I had a legitimate reason.

"We knew Luke would be filming up in Stromness, so when you said work was sending you to Kirkwall, we thought it would be a fun surprise. You're only a half hour away from each other."

"We live practically a half hour away from each other."

"Yeah, but not in Scotland." A pause. Mats gathering again, hopefully, and then a sigh as she figured it out. "Rin-Rin, you didn't want to see him, did you?"

I took a slow breath and snuck a glance behind me, towards the clubhouse. Luke was still there, all tall and tailored and tan and blond, turned and talking to someone in a black puffer jacket. The feeling in my legs was coming back, my heart letting up on its marathon pace.

What were my choices? Run or stay? Working in hospitality meant I was well used to managing unpleasant situations, and I liked sports enough that golf would be fun either way. It wouldn't matter if he smelled like summer and hiking through a forest, or he looked at me with eyes the color of a cloudless dawn and sparked memories of waking up beside his warmth and bulk...

"I expected to see him," I said, fake focus back on the golf bag. "It would have been unavoidable at the premiere."

Mats grunted in disapproval, which thanks to years of friendship I understood was disapproval in herself, not me. "I'm sorry, Rin. You've seemed fine together in our online producer meetings, so I thought this would be a good idea."

Was there any point in the last two years where it would have been a good idea to meet Luke again unexpectedly? First, there was the pandemic, sudden and brutal and upending, then wearying. The aftermath months of the family business slowly dissolving. All while navigating my evolving gender, my progress in boxing, the changing world. When, in all that, would I have liked to reconnect with Luke Maston?

"I usually turn off the video," I admitted. "I haven't *seen* seen him in a year."

Did he know he would see me today, or would it be as much a surprise for him as for me? Did he want to? My stomach answered with a little flip, an unhelpful reminder of the butterflies I'd get when I was in his physical space. Damn him for being everything I wanted.

"Fuck," Mattie said, her voice softening. "You're not over him."

Apparently not. "I thought I was. I tried to convince myself I was."

"But then you shut off the video."

"I shut off the video."

"You could have told me," she said gently. I imagined her biting her lip.

"You know I like my romances private. Also, I've had a lot going on, so it was never in the front of my mind."

Everything was still too complicated. Luke didn't deserve my mess, and even if he said he didn't mind it, I wasn't at a place where I could trust him to be the kind of partner I needed.

"I'm sorry I added to your stress. I know you didn't need any more. But I have a plan." Mattie sounded so confident. She always had a plan. Good plans, for the most part, but I wasn't sure I was in the mood for hijinks.

"I would consider an HMA plan, but I make no promises."

"Not Honest Mischief Alliance, dear, just a Mattie plan: turn around and walk away. If Luke brings it up to me or Raphael later, I'll say I had a little meltdown and only you could help me. Saves face for you, and he doesn't take it personally. Can I arrange a driver for you? Do you need a place to stay? I'll call some hotels."

I couldn't blame Mattie and Raphael for this situation, even though Mats did try to build a narrative from coincidences. I might be able to blame it on work. The company—The International Travel Source (yes, TITS, I know)—had been trying to buy my family's North Island Pinnacle Leisure (yes, NIPL, believe me, I know) since the early 2010's, and we always politely refused. Then, my mother died in 2018, my father in 2019, and my good luck in 2020, when the pandemic hit the travel industry so hard I could no longer successfully run the business that was as old as I was.

I tried. I pivoted. I pivoted again. I sold assets. I took out loans. But in July of this year, it was time to come to terms with the new reality, and TITS bought us out. They were nice enough about it. Offered me a job, which I, in my broke and broken state, couldn't refuse.

I'd requested this week off to visit Mats and Raph and Daphne and Cinnamon in London for a bit before our documentary premiered, but once the boss knew I was going to the U.K., he asked if I'd work a few of those days, go to a conference in Inverness and get some insider tips for traveling to Scotland. I needed the money. Driving a business into the ground will do that to a person. I went to the conference and decided to head up to Orkney, see and do whatever I thought could be considered a business expense, golf included.

So I wouldn't even be in the position of seeing my ex on a Scottish golf course if work hadn't sent me here in the first place. But if I acted like I was only golfing as research for work, and tried to do that job well, that might be enough to distract me from the whole Luke thing.

The wind picked up, scent bringing me back to the present, a mild low tide, and clay, and something being fried so close I could almost taste its golden deliciousness. I looked out to the water, steely grey and placid, and the hills beyond that, panning my gaze back towards the little town with its narrow streets and blocky buildings. So different from home, from Auckland. Part of the reason I loved to travel. Could I not set aside discomfort for a few hours and enjoy this new and lovely place? I'd faced worse.

"Thanks, Mattie, but I think I'll stay. It'll be fine with Luke. I'll have to shift around some feelings and whatnot, but it'll be fun. No worries, you did good."

"It will be fine with Luke," she agreed. "It'll be fun. And if nothing else, you'll get to whack at things with sticks, and that should be cathartic."

"Remind me to never take you golfing," I said. "You might like one of those rage rooms, though."

"You know me so well. Call or text if you need anything from me. Love you, Rin."

"I will. I love you too, muppet."

I ended the call, put the phone away, and checked my bag one more time, to zip anything I'd unzipped during my pantomime. When I turned to face the clubhouse, every intention of keeping my gaze down for the rest of the walk there to feign surprise when I caught up with Luke, he was no longer standing outside, and I couldn't see where he'd gone.

Well enough. I let out my breath all at once. *Focus on the work. Pay attention to your senses and surroundings. Luke is, if nothing else, a friend and an ally, and he doesn't want this to be weird, either.*

I shouldered my bag and continued my slow walk to the man whose heart I reluctantly broke.

Chapter 2
October 2022
Luke

The similarities between Scotland and New Zealand should have been a comfort. I found familiarity in the horizon, the smells on the air, even in the cows. It was close, but not close enough. Like an uncanny valley of valleys and mountains, off just enough to remind me this wasn't home, but somewhere foreign and unknown to me.

Luckily, I had a failure-proof way of dealing with discomfort, and that was to pretend not to care.

Easy. I was already pretending not to care that I wasn't as good at golfing as the two buddies who took me to the green today. I was also pretending I didn't care about my documentary premiering in a week, or that my best friend's life had improved since our co-quitting two years ago while my life had only gotten worse, or that I missed my daughters an annoying amount, or that I was starting to feel very lonely and wondering if I was going to indulge in an ill-advised midlife crisis.

I wondered if I would be able to recognize a midlife crisis, or if it would simply blend into all the other crises.

"Oooo," a nearby bird called, offering a sarcastic commentary on my broody musings.

"Eider duck," I said under my breath, and it didn't coo again. Like naming it had shamed it into silence.

A tap on my arm, and I turned to Suraj offering me a cigarette. I didn't think I'd gotten into the habit, but I'd taken one every time the production assistant had offered. My theory was the man could sense when someone's nerves were about to shake them apart, like a dog predicting an earthquake.

"It's just golf, mate," Suraj muttered, bringing out a lighter. "Supposed to channel your frustration to the game, not add to the running tally."

"I'm not worried," I lied, finding a concerning amount of relief in that first tobacco-filled breath. "Friendly game. I imagine you and Will have played here enough to learn its secrets. Friends would share those secrets." I gave them my best, seductive smile, to no effect. Working with good-looking actors had steeled the two of them against manipulation via beauty.

"And rob you of the joy of discovering them yourself? Go on with you." Will pulled his set of clubs from the car's boot and shut the lid. "Now then. We're a bit early. They've got a local cider worth trying while we wait for your friend. Unless they're already here?"

I glanced around the parking lot, but we were the only three people I could see—not just at the club, but in any direction. The sun threatened to make an appearance through the clouds, and it would have been the first time in almost two weeks. Either nobody cared or the locals all knew the possibility of a nice day was only a tease. "I don't know if they're my friend."

"You've invited an enemy, then?" Will asked. "Bold."

"No, no. Well. Maybe?" I frowned. "Raphael only told me he sent someone to be our fourth. Didn't say who. He loves a good prank, it might even be him."

"Ah, yes," Will said, picking up his bag and nodding for us boys to follow him to the clubhouse and the promise of cider. "Raphael

Callan. Movie star, heartthrob, philanthropist. Way out of your league, friend-wise."

I thought so too, once. "Well. He is a bit of an *arse*." I leaned into the word, and the Scots took it the way I intended, as a dig at the well-liked Englishman. "But otherwise, he's ok. He wouldn't have sent an enemy, but he's definitely playing at something."

Which Raph only had the forethought and fortitude to execute because I had taught him everything he knew about pranks. I snorted to myself. Current-Me in a predicament once again thanks to Past-Me.

The cider was refreshing but nothing special, and I wished I'd waited until after the game. It was going to slow me down, and I wasn't exactly proud of my skills to begin with. Ten minutes before start time, I got up to wander around outside for a smoke and keep watch for our mysterious fourth golfing partner. No new cars had arrived. I was beginning to wonder if the joke was that there was no fourth person to wait for when I saw someone with a large, black bag walking up the street towards the clubhouse.

"That must be your mate," Suraj said, startling me. "Wonder they didn't drive."

I smiled at the approaching figure, slightly too far away to discern their features. I wanted to squint, but it would look too close to a frown, and if I knew this person as well as Raph insisted I did, I'd rather not look unwelcoming. Who on earth did he send? Raph himself would have had a car or taxi. Walking with a golf bag meant very, very local, or skint enough to take the bus—

"Oh. Shit," I said aloud. The figure stopped and turned away, looking through their bag. Something in my stomach danced (the cider, but also, nerves), and I felt the blush rise into my cheeks (also the cider, but also also, memory).

"An enemy after all?"

"An ex."

"A bad one?"

In a way. Bad for my heart, this ex, because I hadn't wanted the relationship to end. Bad for my mental health, because I was still thinking up ways we could have made it work. And today, bad for my game, because I was not going to be able to concentrate on anything but them.

"Only because I'll never be over them," I finally answered. When was the last time we saw each other? We had heard each other for the documentary's Zoom meetings, but their video never worked. I suspected it was deliberate but here they were, somehow walking towards me at what felt like the ends of the earth. That was a choice.

"So," Suraj said. "A really bad ex."

If I didn't already have years of experiencing first-hand the sneakiness and dramatic lengths to which my friends would go, I would wonder how my New Zealand ex had found their way to Scotland, to Orkney, to Stromness, to this particular golf course at this exact time to join me in a game of golf after not seeing each other for a year and barely speaking for two.

The figure seemed to finally fix whatever was wrong with their bag, and I took a step back to hide behind the fence before they could glance up and see me.

What am I doing?

Coward.

Suraj sidled over until he, too, was hidden from view. "I don't mind hiding, if that's what you have to do, but I do prefer to know the name of the person I'm hiding from."

"Right," I said. It was already getting harder to pay attention. I could hear my blood rushing, and the easily distracted part of me wondered what my pulse rate and blood pressure were, if they were getting close to dangerous levels. I peeked out at the road. It wouldn't be long before they were at the clubhouse, and what would my move be then?

"Rin. Rin Butcher. New Zealander, like me. Owns a luxury travel business. One of the six in our Alliance."

"Alliance?"

"It's a game, a dumb game my mates and I play sometimes. Never mind."

Suraj came closer and took his own peek beyond the fence. "We can leave if you'd like. Don't need to speak to her."

"Them," I corrected automatically, suddenly appalled by the cigarette in my hand. I ground it into the gravel with my heel and hoped Rin hadn't seen. "Rin uses they/them pronouns."

"Oh, aye," Suraj said, nodding, his eyes following the path of the dropped and smooshed cigarette. "And they don't like you smoking, do they? Perfectly good ciggy, could have shared."

September 2021. That was the last time I'd seen Rin. Cinnamon's party was in San Francisco, which was too far away from the problems I was then in the middle of, too much of a distraction from said problems, and too costly, despite Raphael's offer to pay. Ended up going only because some "anonymous" do-gooder (I was 99.9% sure it was Raph) paid off the defaulted loan on my mum's house, which was the most major problem sorted.

Since Raph and I righteously walked off a career-ending film project in 2020, I'd had a hell of a time finding work beyond what was already lined up. But the bills kept coming anyway, and mum was retired, and my girls should have had the opportunity to stay kids as long as possible, so it was *my* responsibility I kept failing at. Raph's career was as unaffected as his generational wealth, and I tried not to hold it against him. Especially if he was the reason my family wouldn't be homeless.

So it was with renewed optimism and a lighter heart that I accepted the plane ticket from him and went to party with my best friends. I was even ready to look for a romantic relationship again. Until I got there, saw Rin, and knew I wouldn't be happy with anyone else. Not yet. A year wasn't enough time to get over them. And seeing them now, after a year more, I wondered how long it would actually take.

Across the parking lot, Rin's hair was the same auburn as always, dark and somehow shiny even without the sun. They never dyed it, as far as I could tell, and kept it in a slick, low bun or loose to their shoulders depending on their gender mood. For golf, it was a bun. No glasses today, so either contact lenses or they'd gotten corrective surgery on their watercolored eyes.

Rin strode towards the clubhouse, gaze focused on the front doors, and I almost blew my cover. When we'd first met, Rin had been boxing for a few years, and they must have kept it up, because they looked like a powerhouse. I suddenly remembered their tattoos, the little scar behind their left ear, the tartness of the sweat between their breasts. I laughed under my breath, realizing my attraction to them had also become stronger. Just what I needed.

"We should meet up with them now," I mumbled, watching Rin enter the building. I was already shuffling towards them, my feet giving me no choice.

Suraj squinted at me and took another drag on his cigarette. "Mate, you want to cut your smoke break short, that's your business. I'll meet you at the starter."

I barely heard him. I regained control of my feet and walked faster. Rin probably didn't know that our friends had manipulated the situation and they'd be seeing me for the first time in a year. Which meant, thanks to an unfortunate recent uptick in U.K.

transphobia, Rin must have prepared themself for the possibility that the strangers they got paired with would be hostile to them. And if I knew Rin at all, a friendly-but-awkward ex was infinitely preferable to a dangerous unknown.

Chapter 3
October 2022
Rin

The clubhouse was nice enough. A few modern amenities were retrofitted into an older building, though not as old as the medieval structures in Orkney. Instead, it had the sharp angles and beige stucco popular in the 1960's. The worn green carpet smelled of a mild cleaner. So. Nothing for my clients to brag about, besides the remote location. And view, of course. The plains, the hills, the bay. It would be stunning on one of the island's few clear and sunny days.

I've never golfed with Luke. I bet he makes it easygoing and chill.

Zip it. I need the details so work will pay for all this.

The map on the back of the scorecard was adorable, drawn like a colorful cartoon, with a squiggly Loch Ness-style monster in the blue w's of the bay. The attendant pointed out the gear for sale, the hallway that would take me to the snack corner and restrooms, and the door that led to the beginning of the course. The clubs for sale were passable quality but significantly overpriced. Island. Scarcity of resources. My clients would bring their own and if they didn't, wouldn't have a problem buying a throwaway set for the day. They'd never rent.

I nodded thanks to the attendant and headed towards the door to the course. The too-loud sound of a TV turned to some kind of sport gave me a better idea of where the lounge was. I would have to try the food while I was there, but at least I didn't have to rent my clubs. Mattie had Raphael ship up one of his sets from London, and it had been waiting for me at the hotel when I got to Stromness: one less purchase to hope my employer would cover.

"Rin?"

For a moment, my attempt to block out anything not work-related was successful. So it wasn't until the word hit whatever part of my brain kept my precious things that I stopped walking. After all these months and years, my name in his voice still sent a thrill through me. I took a breath and closed my eyes long enough to centre myself before turning to Luke Maston.

Of course he was just as gorgeous as the last time I saw him up close like this. Only a little taller than me, blond hair floppy and shiny and probably soft as always, undeniably a white boy but still tanned. Blue eyes somehow both a window to his soul and a mirror reflecting whoever was lucky enough to have his attention. The same blocky black glasses would look nerdy on anyone else but made him look stylish and approachable.

The most recent installment of the *Knuckletracker* movies had resumed filming the previous year, but Luke had lost most of his character's bulk since they wrapped, to the point where I was closer to his character's physique than he was. His lean, bare forearms should have been illegal, they always put me in a state, and the mint-green polo hung off him. He must have bought it during filming and kept it because, well, he was frugal. The jeans, though. They fit perfectly.

His face was open, smiling in a half-grin that had me doubting the uncertainty I'd heard when he said my name.

"Luke." My heart gave a pinch and I took a quick breath. Couldn't stand there all day looking like an idiot. I smiled back and walked to him, meeting him halfway and throwing my free arm around him. Not as bulky as he used to be, but just as solid. He smelled like summer, coconut and citrus, and a bit of cigarette smoke, too. He must have been anxious lately.

"Mats and Raph send you?" He murmured into my hair and I couldn't suppress the chill it sent down my spine.

"Who else?" I pulled away and adjusted the bag on my shoulder. If we stuck to small talk, there was a chance I wouldn't feel too embarrassed. "What are you even doing up here?"

Luke stuck his hands in his pockets and beamed down at me. Small talk or no, having his undivided focus was always disarming. "Work. We've been in Stromness this week. Now I get a week off to make a quick run to London and the premiere of *Shutdown*, then it's back to New Zealand for another month, and that should be the end of it."

"Lena and Cassidy will be glad to have you back."

"My daughters are on their own personal eighth wave of feminism, so at the moment, I'm more of a nuisance. Does it get easier when they're full teens? It has to, right? Because this tween stage is so unpredictable."

I gave him a pitying look and clapped my hand on his shoulder, trying my best to ignore the solidness of his body beneath the shirt's silky texture. "Sure, bro. Teen girls are famously more stable than their younger counterparts."

"Excellent." His smile said he was in on the joke. "They're doing great, but I'm sure that doesn't surprise you."

It didn't surprise me at all. Luke and I had only dated a few months, but it was at the beginning of the pandemic and we were sort of joyfully forced into each other's company, and that included his daughters. They were curious and brave, clever and mischievous and thoughtful. Just like their dad.

"I'm glad," I said, a little more wistfully than I meant to. The past four years had been hard for me in every way possible, but those weeks together with the Mastons made me think that having a family wasn't totally beyond my reach. "Make sure you give them my love."

"Ah!" Luke held up a finger. "Great news: you can tell them yourself at the premiere." He paused and lowered his finger. "If you're going, of course. You are going, right?"

"I am," I confirmed. "And I will tell them myself. Are they flying in just for the film? Such a long flight."

"Their mother and step-dad are bringing them from California. We all missed the Auckland and Los Angeles premieres, but since they're in the movie, I thought we should try to make it to one of them." He grinned even wider. "And I'm hoping the thirty hours of travel temporarily dampens their sense of adventure until they're old enough to pay for it themselves. Do you know how expensive it is to visit all the Florida theme parks now?"

His smile faltered, a quick thing I wouldn't have caught unless I was staring directly at his mouth (*pull yourself together, Rin*). Our friends had never stopped updating me about him, and I knew he had been having financial problems. Hell, who wasn't? I opened my mouth to change the subject, but Luke got there first.

"Anyway," he said quickly, "how does Rin Butcher find themself so far away from Auckland? Was this totally coordinated by Mattie and Raphael, or was their manipulation minimal, and our meeting serendipitous?"

Luke always got a little more articulate when he was flustered. A way to deflect what would otherwise be uncomfortable for him.

"A bit of both," I answered. "Mattie found out I'd be in Inverness for a work conference before the premiere, and she urged me to come up to Orkney first. Told me she got me into a golf course and sent up some clubs." I shrugged. "I'm not regretting it yet."

"Of course you're not regretting the fun part. And it must be nice to travel for work. Is NIPL going to expand overseas? Or was this like, a general conference for holiday rental businesses and tourism?"

My cheeks flushed, and my throat closed a little.

Now I was starting to regret this trip.

Luke gently grasped my arm, steadying me, his expression growing more concerned. People assumed he was flaky and self-absorbed—a byproduct of his easygoing act—but he was more astute than he let on. He had read me correctly and he would ask follow-up questions, given the chance. That was one of the things I always liked about him. In any situation, his actions might seem inexplicable, but he always had a good understanding of what was going on and what his friends needed.

Even without knowing the details, sympathy shone in Luke's eyes, which darted behind me to someone knocking on the glass door to the course. I followed his gaze to a short guy with warm, chestnut skin and a black beard trimmed close to his face. A black knitted cap hid his hair, but the puffy coat couldn't disguise his slight frame. He nodded to Luke and pointed to his watch with the stub of a cigarette, then walked away.

"Friend of yours?" I asked, glad for the excuse to change the subject. Luke gave me a look that said he knew what I was doing. He gave my arm another encouraging squeeze before letting go and indicating we should follow the man in black.

"Suraj," he said. "He/him. One of the PAs. Then there's Will. He's another actor. They're local and refuse to give me any clues about what I can expect on the course."

He opened the door for me, and I held up the scorecard as I walked through. "If this map is accurate, eighteen holes and possibly a sea monster."

"An entire sea monster? In this economy?"

I barked a laugh far too loudly, which got Luke going, too. He had a little giggle when he was genuinely amused, and I felt an ache hearing it again. With one disaster after another, I'd almost forgotten how to laugh. And I'd deliberately tucked away the memory of his. It didn't and couldn't work out between us, and it hurt too much to remember all the ways I loved him.

"Hey mate," someone yelled, and I turned to see Suraj getting into a golf cart with another guy. A second cart stood empty except for a navy-blue coat and a set of clubs that must have been Luke's.

"I can't race you there fairly if you don't get into the bloody cart first," the driver yelled, waving us forwards. When we got close enough, I slid my clubs beside Luke's, and Suraj threw Luke the key to the second cart.

"Rin," Luke said, "This is Will Ambergris, he/him. Suraj Batwal, he/him. Lads, this is Rin Butcher, they/them."

Suraj nodded and lifted his cigarette in greeting. Will, sporting that classic English strawberries-and-cream complexion with a mop of golden brown hair, gave me a once-over that I had experienced a thousand times before. Was it my height, this time? Muscles? Was he trying to figure out what equipment I had underneath my clothes? Was I going to have to choose between enduring an unwelcome gaze all day or not playing at all, a choice I'd already had to make too many times in the past?

"Are you a stunt performer?" He asked.

My prepared response stuttered in my mind. Well. That was a new one. "Uh. No," I answered.

"You fight?"

"Boxing."

"You looking to switch careers?"

Was my misery and its source so obvious?

"Boxing is the only thing that loves me back," I admitted.

"Will," Luke said, the word sharp.

The other actor raised his hands in surrender. "Sorry, Rin, I'm short on charm, and I thought Luke might know you from work. But I shouldn't have presumed your situation." He lowered his hands and frowned. "How's your golf game?"

"Excellent, actually," I said. The change of subject didn't do anything to assuage my fears, and I had to get a better idea of what the dynamics here would be. Hoping Luke would have my back regardless of the fallout, I asked, "Are you going to be ok playing with someone who's nonbinary, or will I have to use those boxing skills today?"

Will's face split into a grin, and he pushed on Suraj.

"Out, Suraj. Rin is my partner now. You have to be with Luke."

"For the love of Christ," Suraj muttered as he left one cart and sat in the other.

"Um," Luke said, glancing between us with what looked like a little bit of panic in his eyes. "There are no teams. Well, there's one team, and we're all on it."

"Nope. Two against two. And they're on my team. Come ride with me, Rin. Help me win this and I'll buy lunch. Hope you like fish and chips."

I hadn't gotten picked first for a game…ever. Suraj seemed naturally reticent, Will seemed accepting at the very least, and I could count on Luke if it turned out I misread the situation. This might actually turn out to be fun.

I gave Will my own dazzling smile. "I love fish and chips. You're on."

Chapter 4
September 2021
Luke

"Is this your first time?"

Raphael leaned in to be heard above the music and laughter, chocolate-colored eyes flirting with me in his flawlessly ochre face and giving me his damn rakish smile like I hadn't been immune to it for years. It had only worked the one time, the first time, over a decade ago, and it hadn't worked since. I knew him too well now.

And he could guess my answer to whatever it was he was talking about. First time in San Francisco? Yeah. First time at Cinnamon and Daphne's house? Yep. First time at an adult party that was mostly tabletop games? Also yes.

"Don't suppose you'd be able to show this old dog some new tricks?" I met him grin for grin. "Teach me that gaming and wine won't destroy this ancient body the same way a night of dancing and vodka would?"

He clapped one hand on my shoulder and the other on my chest. "I've got you, bro. Right this way."

The girls' place was cute. The dark-blue two-story craftsman that had survived a number of earthquakes was one hundred percent not Daphne's style. The interior was cozy with earth tones and good lighting for the several tables of board games taking place in the living room and kitchen. I'd imagined Daph's style to be closer to her personality: chaotic and loud but making it work for her. The understated order must have been Cinnamon's touch.

The house smelled like a bakery, bread and cheese, something sweet, with individual perfumes rising faintly and fading away just as quickly as I walked through the rooms. Raph steered me among the tables, the instrumental music (moody and probably from some fantasy soundtrack) low enough to make introductions easier when the guests weren't completely absorbed in their games. Others stood in small groups or sat on the couch, talking and laughing. I knew some of them from Cinnamon's monthly online RPG night, which I'd participated in off and on since April of 2020, before she and I had met in person. Raph tried to get me into another campaign, but doing one thing I sucked at a month was my limit, and also, Rin was currently in that other group and I wasn't sure how to feel about it.

"If any games pique your interest, I'm sure they'd make room for you."

"Is there an Uno table?" I asked.

"Not interested in building roads or waging space wars?"

"Did I come here to work or did I come here to party?"

The birthday girl was in the kitchen playing a board game that looked about fifty steps too complicated for me. My daughters would have loved it.

"Luke! Luke is here!" Daphne launched herself out of her seat to give me a hug. "Cinnamon, look, it's Luke!"

"Hey Daph," I said, kissing her forehead before she danced away. Mattie waved from where she sat, and Cinnamon rose from her chair infinitely more decorously but no less enthusiastically than her wife. I kissed her cheek as she leaned in for her own hug.

"Happy birthday, C."

I'd met Daphne when I met Mats and Rin, early 2020, when they were in New Zealand for a wedding. Cinnamon had stayed behind in the States because Daph didn't want to subject her to her and Mattie's otherwise awful family, the Redgraves. I saw that awful family first-hand and though Daphne might not always make good decisions, protecting her wife from those people was definitely one of her greatest. So was marrying her in the first place.

I didn't meet Cinnamon Cheung until after the pandemic shutdowns, months later, when I was in Los Angeles for work. The couple flew down from San Francisco to spend time with me, and I finally met the sixth member of their Honest Mischief Alliance, which is what they called themselves and what they initiated me and Raph into with our own code names once we proved to be just as clever and chaotic. Of all of us, Cinnamon seemed to be the most put-together.

"It's so good to see you," she said, squeezing me. "Don't tell me you traveled all this way just for me. Gaming with strangers isn't a good enough reason to hop on a fourteen-hour flight." She brought her face closer to my ear and whispered, "Especially for someone who doesn't enjoy board games."

"Generally, no," I agreed. "But *you* are always worth a fourteen-hour flight." I reached in my pocket and handed her a small, purple package. "I know my presence is a gift in itself, but I also brought you something to unwrap. Unless you wanted to unwrap me?"

Across the room, Daph shouted in a low and fake-angry voice, "Hey, that's my wife!"

"I love you, Luke, but only Daphne does it for me."

I shrugged. "Never hurts to ask. You don't have to wait to open it. The wrapping paper, not me."

Cinnamon's shriek of laughter as she shucked the last bit of wrapping brought Daphne flying to her side, and Mattie stood up to see, too.

"It's art," she said, tilting the picture frame towards them. It was a sketch of her behind a computer desk, working away, while Daphne as Batman perched in the window. The balloon above Cinnamon said, "Not until I get more intel…" and there was a black scribble of frustration over Daphne.

"Aw, because she's Oracle!" Daph gave me a look full of her watery doe-eyes. "And because she keeps me from making bad impulse decisions."

"It's perfect, thank you, Luke." Cinnamon tapped her fingernails against the frame thoughtfully. "I know it's *my* birthday, but I would love to be able to offer you something just as meaningful."

Hmm. For someone whose birthday it was, that sounded suspicious. I squinted at her, and she blinked all innocently. Her maturity compared to the rest of us had lulled me into a false sense of security. She was just as crafty, but better at masking it.

"Rin is in the backyard, if you want to see them."

While I processed that information, Daphne's innocent grin turned into a playful smirk, Mattie raised an eyebrow, and Raph tried to cover his laugh with a cough.

I blushed.

Children, the lot of them. True, I had never said I didn't want to see Rin again. It was also true that I may have, in fact, told one or two of them I *did* want to see Rin again. I couldn't blame them for my indecision. I wanted both. To see them if we could be at least friends, to not see them if they wanted nothing to do with me.

We'd only been together a few months, under unusual circumstances, as the country shut down and we couldn't go to work and in some cases, had to quarantine. Everything had been in flux, but

I'd been attracted to them since before I even met them (thanks to Raph's description of their form absconding in the dark). My desire increased tenfold when we met, and I immediately felt less alone in the new, unstable world. Still, when they broke it off, I understood. We both had to go back to our lives, lives that looked completely different from the other's and completely different from before the pandemic. It was a lot to handle.

The sounds of the party wound their way into my senses again, and I looked down at Cinnamon, who patted my arm.

"No pressure," she murmured, "but the opportunity is there if you want it."

I wanted it. But my well-meaning friends had seen too much of the feelings I'd been trying to hide, so I stayed inside with them and chatted until my exit to the backyard seemed more from boredom than eagerness.

I'd packed wrong. I was used to L.A. weather and didn't realize California was so big it encompassed several different climates. So I thought the steam rising from the heated pool was deliberate, a moody addition to the fairy lights to achieve a kind of ethereal atmosphere. Of course I went out there to see Rin, and of course it was too cold for my shorts and tee.

There were only a dozen people outside, most of them gathered around a fire pit, and that was where I found Rin. Their tawny skin glowed in the firelight like they were lit from within, warm and golden. Black boots propped on the lip of the pit, dark leggings and jacket appropriate for the weather. Hair loose, and wearing new tortoiseshell glasses similar to the ones I remembered from the year before. They sat in a camp chair close to a beautiful Black man I didn't know, laughing at something he said, and I suddenly wanted to lick the entire inside of Rin's mouth.

Do I really want to do this?

They've moved on.
Say something, idiot.
You missed your chance.
Be cool. You love them. That's for you, not them.
"Luke?"

I'd spent too much time thinking. Rin stood up and maneuvered around the chairs with a huge grin on their face, and I took a deep breath and mirrored them.

"Rin Butcher," I shouted, holding my arms wide. It was hard to breathe, but that was from the cold. The shiver when I saw them, the numbness turning to warmth in my body: also from the cold. My thoughts glitching and words no worky? The cold. Good thing I knew all these symptoms were from the frosty evening and not, say, a medical emergency, or realizing I was still foolishly in love with my ex.

They came in for a hug and I held them tight, the smell of chocolate poofing out of their coat and hair. I was never able to figure out where the confectionery scent came from, whether a perfume or their soap, or if it simply saturated their flesh from eating it so often. I'd never seen anyone eat chocolate in the quantities and with the frequency Rin did, and I had two daughters.

"Been a while," they said, pulling away. "How's everyone back home?"

Small talk. I could do small talk. The chocolate scent and their smile and their soft skin and strong arms and earnest eyes weren't doing anything to me that I couldn't act past.

"Oh you know, the usual. Robust. Chaotic. Loud. Well fed."

"Yeah? Everyone healthy? Everyone safe?"

A weird way to phrase it, and they seemed a little squirrely, not meeting my eyes. Raph must have told them I'd been having money issues and almost lost the house, and Rin felt they weren't close enough to ask about it outright. Hell, Mattie had told me that Rin's family business was doing badly, and I wanted to ask Rin how that was going, so I understood how they felt. No worries.

"The Mastons are all in a good place right now," I answered. *Thank you for asking and also, I still love you.* "How about you?"

"Good," they said, nodding. "Better now."

Better now that you saw me?

"You should stop by sometime," I said. "Everyone misses you." *Especially me.*

"Oh, I miss everyone too. Text me when you're home from all your work travels and I'll see if I can swing by."

They led me to the campfire and made introductions, but we didn't get a chance to talk again that night. And of course, when I got home, I didn't text them. Beyond feeling uncomfortable, I was worried I would blurt out that I still loved them, and things would get awkward, and I'd have even more trouble trying to get over them. It was looking more and more like distance was what I needed to finally keep the past in the past and move on.

Chapter 5
October 2022
Luke

If I had any doubts about whether Rin would feel comfortable with Will and Suraj, they disappeared before the first swing. And by the turn, the three of them were friends. Rin would never admit they were good at social interactions, but the usually quiet Suraj opened up for them once they got talking about rugby, and Will was just happy to play with someone who could keep up with him.

Their makeshift team won by an amount I'm too embarrassed to say, with Will in the lead by a few measly strokes. Before we got the promised fish and chips, we stayed for a quick, celebratory cider at Rin's insistence. They claimed they had to make note of the food and drink offerings for "work," a subject they had successfully sidestepped throughout the game.

I didn't know exactly what was going on with their "work," but I knew their business had never recovered from the hit it took in the first year of the pandemic. If their North Island-specific travel company needed them to research Scotland, it was for reasons I couldn't fathom. Something was wrong. And they didn't want to talk about it.

For lunch, we sat in the corner of Will's favourite pub, its booths made of dark wood, deep scratches in the table varnished over, old beer adverts on the walls. The seat padding was flat, and the whole establishment smelled faintly of mildew, but the food was worth it.

"Mmm, yup," Rin said around a mouth full of fried fish, grease and salt coating their fingers and running down their arm. "That's sweet as, thanks for bringing me here. And for the game."

"Our pleasure," Suraj said, and I blinked back my surprise. It had taken weeks for him to be that friendly with me.

"You're always welcome to join us," Will added.

"You've been tremendous," Rin said, wiping their fingers on a bundle of paper napkins. "And it's been fun, but I'm not sure it's been day-and-a-half-of-travel fun."

Will considered this, taking a sip from his pint. If he was already trying to secure plans with them, he must already like them. A thread of something strange moved through my emotions.

"Well, if Luke puts in a good word for us, we could join him on a project in New Zealand. Then it would only be a car ride's worth of travel for you to experience a day-and-a-half-of-travel-worthy fun."

Suraj perked up at that, and Rin spared me a glance, their greenish-blue irises almost vibrating with amusement. I swallowed the unexpected urge to shout *No! Mine!* Because that would be a whole thing.

"Sorry mate," I said instead. "Haven't you heard? I'll never work in this town again. 'This town' being any film project of note."

"Oh, come on," Will lowered his glass in exasperation. "You're here, aren't you?"

Yes. And that was the problem.

"Where's here, again?" I asked, attempting to keep it playful. "Is this Los Angeles? London? Bollywood? Vancouver?"

"It's work." There was a finality in Suraj's words that shut me up, beyond the feeling I'd never get another cigarette from him.

It was work. I should have been grateful. But wasn't there a world where I got that work more frequently, or something higher paying, or higher profile? Hell, if I was looking into alternate realities to explore, I could definitely find one with both the career I wanted *and* Rin as my partner.

"It must be difficult," Rin said, their voice soft. They twisted their pint glass around on the coaster, watching the beads of sweat smoothing as it turned. The rest of us looked up at the change of tone.

"It must be difficult," they repeated, "to work in an industry that's so unpredictable. Where you have the talent and the drive and skills, but don't know if you can make a living with them because there are so many variables. I'm not familiar with how a production assistant's career works, exactly—" they smiled at Suraj, who nodded encouragement. "But I know Luke recently finished the last *Knuckletracker* movie, which was a constant for him for years, and it must be stressful not to know what happens next." They shook their head. "I would want more stability, too."

The lads were nodding, likely finding truth in Rin's words, and my gratitude fanned the affection that had been rekindling all day. But the last thing struck me.

If I had to summarize the reason for our break-up in one word, "stability" would be it. Our careers had been in flux and neither of us could be an anchor for the other. The world was changing rapidly, and there was fuck-all either of us could do about that, too. Not much had settled, but maybe two years was enough time for us to adapt. If we got together now, maybe it would be different. Better.

Once outside the pub, I asked Rin if they'd like to have a late dinner with me. They had some work to get done that afternoon—that elusive "work" I'd have to ask them about later—but they agreed, and we parted ways. A few hours apart wasn't bad. At least it wasn't a few years.

Chapter 6
October 2022
Rin

Of all the things I didn't expect today, sitting down to dinner with Luke was number one on the list. Even after the surprise of him, golfing together, sticking around for cider, snacking on fish and chips. Dinner was simply out of reach for my imagination.

We'd seen each other last a year ago. He'd invited me to visit the next time we were both home in New Zealand, then never texted. I can't say I would have responded, even if he had reached out. Seeing him at Cinnamon's party had been rough. He reminded me of a time when I thought everything could still work out for the better.

For those few short months we were together, NIPL could still "pivot," like so many businesses were doing in 2020. Luke would be out of work for a while—a nice break for him—but he had a couple future projects already set up, so there wouldn't be a huge disruption to his income, which he worried about. I loved his family, his mom, his daughters. I'd just started asking people to use gender-neutral pronouns for me, and I was feeling more and more comfortable about it. It wasn't his fault everything fell apart. But when I saw him across Cinnamon's backyard a year later, so many of those problems had become so much worse.

It also didn't help that I was there with a date. The first since Luke. Mal and I had known each other for years and had hooked up more than once. We cared for each other, but with lives in different countries, it could only be casual.

Seeing Luke again made me want something more than casual. Both that night in San Francisco and again when I saw him this morning in Stromness. But even if that yearning was genuine, I didn't know what to do about it in the long run.

For tonight, though, we'd decided on dinner at my hotel, since it was convenient for me and they consistently got good reviews online. Between the conference in Inverness, traveling up to Orkney, and the many hours of buses, trains, and ferries ahead of me to get down to London for the premiere, I was already burned out. So my recommendation to clients was going to be the place I could stay in the building for. I hoped it was decent.

I shut my notebook and looked around the restaurant. It was off-season, with weather quickly turning to cold, and the few diners were preoccupied with their own conversations. But when Luke walked in, every one of them turned to stare.

He'd changed out of the baggy mint polo and into a fitted navy-blue sweater. The collar of a light-blue button-up poked above his dark pea coat, the one I'd made fun of him for two years ago, asking if he'd just come back from time-traveling through the 90's. It was worn but patched. Luke didn't have the luxury of buying new things whenever the old ones got a little damaged. Even if he did have the money, it was more his style to mend what still functioned. And the coat fit him well enough to draw every gaze in the room, so ultimately, it was a good choice.

He found me. I waved. He smiled. My heart did that stupid little dance, and I cleared my throat and fiddled with the menu. He kissed my temple, said hey, and slid into the seat opposite me.

And then it was just us.

I didn't know what I expected. It had seemed easier—fated, even—when there had been other people around. When I didn't have his undivided attention and I could pretend he didn't have mine. We stared at each other, smiling like idiots, and I opened my mouth to speak but closed it fast. How to start again?

Luke seemed almost as lost as I was, but as he cleared his throat and took a breath, the server appeared and asked what we wanted. *To be able to interact with Luke as easily as I did two years ago. Not on the menu? Then I'll take the stew.* We ordered quickly, then we were right back to sitting in silence.

This was dumb. I could do this. Luke was my friend, and there were reasons I liked him so much.

How about honesty?

I laughed and shook my head. "Ok. It seems like this is as awkward for you as it is for me." He inclined his head in acknowledgment, and I continued. "We haven't seen each other in a while, but I'm assuming our friends have kept us both informed about what we've been up to, so what would you say to jumping right into the present and...enjoying the moment?"

Luke was already nodding. "Done," he said. I smiled. *Could it be that simple?*

"But." He held a finger in the air. I guess it couldn't be that simple. "If you don't want to talk about what's preoccupying your thoughts, you'll have to tell me what it is, so I don't ask about it."

I squinted at him. He made sense. And if Luke said he wouldn't bring it up again, he wouldn't bring it up again.

"Work," I said, hating the blush creeping into my cheeks. My self-imposed deadline for telling my friends about NIPL's demise was a few days away, and I hadn't done anything at all to prepare for it. A month before the first premiere of *Shutdown*, our executive producer called me for a life update to add to the epilogue.

When I hesitated, he said the others wouldn't see it until the premiere, and I told him the truth. I figured, if I couldn't get my shit together and tell my friends before then, it would serve me right for them to find out by watching the film.

I lightly tapped my water glass so all Luke's attention wasn't on me when I answered. "It's different from before and...overwhelming. I might bring it up in response to something you say, but please don't go digging."

The weight of his stare was like a caress, and stupid me leaned into it. He nodded, slowly, having seen what he needed to. "You can talk to me about anything, and I'll do whatever I can to help. But until then, you can trust me not to mention it."

I nodded, blinking back tears. Damn. That wasn't even him helping with my problems, just acknowledging he saw that I struggled. He always did see me.

"And you?" I asked. He might not bring it up again, but I didn't want to linger on it. "Any topics you'd rather I avoid?"

Luke blew a breath out slowly, the stream catching a strand of his hair and flopping it upwards. He sat back in his chair and looked across the restaurant. How was he so handsome in profile?

"Uh. Raph?" He winced as he said it.

"I'm Rin, dear."

"Well, Rin, I'd rather we didn't talk about Raph tonight."

My jaw dropped. "Raphael Callan. Your best friend." *Wow*. "Ok. Ok, yeah, I'm sure I can do that."

He shifted uncomfortably. "We're still friends, or we will be again. Right now, the thought of him makes me irrationally angry, and I can't imagine how much worse it'll be when I see him in London."

"I am *completely* intrigued." I leaned forwards to rest my chin in my hand. "And yet I'm oath-bound not to ask you anything more about it."

Luke laughed, and I sensed the tension leaving his body. A thousand questions pushed to the front of my mind. None would help him, but the drama they'd unearth would help me forget my own problems. Raph and Luke had famously been best mates for years, long before any of the members of the Honest Mischief Alliance met them. If they'd had a falling out, I would start to question everything I believed in.

"I'm gonna hold you to that," Luke said with a smile.

I managed to not mention Raphael and he didn't ask about work for the whole two hours of conversation over lamb stew, Orkney crab tart, vegetable biriyani, and a local cheese plate. I'd almost forgotten I had to pay attention to the food for work, though if I'd been alone, it would have been easy. It wasn't dinner's fault that Luke could effortlessly command my attention, even when competing with the best pecan pie I'd ever had.

We caught up on the major events of each others' lives (with a few omissions, of course), gossiped about our friends, then moved on to Luke's current film project in Scotland, which brought us to the documentary premiere later in the week.

"Do you have more filming this week before heading down to London?" I sipped at my whisky, its spicy warmth daring my body to submit to languidness, but I was already considering what I would say if Luke wanted to stay the night with me and didn't need alcohol's encouragement.

"No, no," he answered, licking his spoon of the last bit of lemon posset. My eyes followed his tongue in a way I'd be embarrassed about if I were completely sober. "I'm done until after the premiere. Then back home for a few days and up to Miramar for pick-ups on another project. How about you? Any plans between now and London?"

"Sleep," I said with a shrug. "I was going to try to catch the ferry tomorrow, then buses and trains and whatever other public transportation is necessary."

"Sounds more like an economical Rin decision than research for posh clients." He looked up at me and grimaced. "That's a comment on your skill at traveling on a budget, not anything having to do with—" he glanced around and lowered his voice. "W-O-R-K," he spelled.

He meant it playfully, I know he did, but my stomach still froze at the mention of my clients. I took a longer sip of whisky to smother the cold in my gut.

"I know what it spells," I said. "And it is what it is."

His blue eyes searched mine, probably gauging whether he'd fucked everything up, or needed to apologize, or if he could skate past the mistake and keep the rest of the evening as lighthearted.

"I have an idea," he said.

In the past, that had meant everything from "let's make s'mores" to "time to crash a wedding" to "I'm going to make a phone call and get a domestic terrorist deported," so without context, it was impossible to guess where his mind was going.

"That could mean anything," I said with a smirk.

"It could," he agreed, returning a grin. "But in this case, it means I have access to a car and several days to drive approximately one thousand kilometres."

"That's less of an idea and more like, just, facts?"

"We'll go together."

"What?"

"You and me, we'll get the car and start driving." Luke shifted around in his seat, more animated as he told me his spontaneous plan. "We can wander off path and find cool sights, take our time getting there. Split the cost of staying at B&Bs. It would probably come to about the same amount as buses and trains, but less lonely."

Several days stuck in a car with Luke. I could think of worse experiences. I stared off into the distance, listening to my mind's warring arguments. Bus would get me there in a day or so, but a car would let me explore, which would be better for my job. Also, I could count it as a business expense. Luke wanted to spend more time with me, but if he still had feelings for me, he could have said something—anything—in the past year. It shouldn't take a road trip to get it out of him. And then there was the problem of his total lack of planning skills.

Luke thrived in a mode we called Order Panic. The further out something was, the less likely he would be able to commit to it. But if something came up unexpectedly, he could make a decision in a snap. Waiting in line at a fast food place, he'd waffle over what he wanted until it was his turn to order. Hence, Order Panic.

But being "less lonely"...was he lonely? I brought my gaze back from afar and really looked at him. A divorced father of two who traveled a lot for his career. That career introduced him to dozens if not hundreds of people every project, and carried his face to movie theaters around the world. He met people all the time, and fans adored him, but those were still lonely relationships. Who in his life knew him? His kids, who were less friends than dependents, even if they were all on the same team. His retired mother, who lived with him and took care of his girls. Raphael, who he apparently had some kind of falling out with. Me and the rest of the squad, who he rarely saw. Yeah. Yeah, I could believe he was lonely.

And wasn't I lonely, too? Co-workers at a place I despised, estranged family, two best friends living in another country. No boyfriend or girlfriend or partner. No prospects and no desire to make time for them if they did exist.

I hated that all signs pointed to yes.

"An interesting idea," I said slowly. "What would it look like? What were you thinking?"

"You. Me. Car. Whoosh—" he weaved his hand between the empty plates and glasses, more like a swimming fish than a swerving car, and jabbed his finger at an empty spot of table between us. "London!"

The nervousness I thought I saw in him before was replaced with boldness. That was what usually happened, like his discomfort got to a tipping point and he had no choice but to transform it into false confidence. But that confidence was still all ideas and no plans to make those ideas real.

"How many hours of driving each day?" I prompted. "Where will we stop, where will we stay the night? What sights are there?"

Luke shrugged, still grinning like this was the best idea he'd ever had. "We'll figure it out!"

I closed my eyes and pinched the bridge of my nose. Order Panic only worked for single, immediate decisions, not a multi-day, 24/7 offensive requiring strategy and forethought.

"We wouldn't need to plan everything down to the minute," I said, "but we do need to have a destination in mind, and some historical or geographical locations so we don't miss something and regret it later. Map it out."

"It won't be that difficult. There are signs everywhere. We can jump into the car and go."

If there was any chance of me accompanying him, the trip would have to be much more structured than that. And if I had any hope of work paying for it, I'd need a comprehensive itinerary. And to get it, I would have to be the one to structure it.

Was it worth it? Organization came easy to me, but it sounded like Luke's participation would end with acquiring the car, and that imbalance of tasks bothered me.

"We can absolutely decide stuff ahead of time," he said, holding his palms up, in either surrender or agreement. "I'm at Will's tonight, so you and I can meet up tomorrow morning and start planning it then?"

If we were going to do this, I didn't want to wait. I might lose my nerve.

Plus—if I was being honest with myself—I'd missed him. A lot. But there were no concrete markers for this kind of thing with him, only vibes, and I always hated that.

"I was originally planning to leave tomorrow morning." Anxiety be damned. "If that doesn't sound too rushed to you, it'll give us more time to explore. If we become bored, we can get to London early to spend more time with Mattie and—and our friends." I cleared my throat to cover my stutter, which in turn was covering the fact that I almost named Raphael. Once we got started, it was so effortless to talk to Luke that it was hard to avoid the topics most sensitive to us.

"I'm all in," he said with his easy smile. "Let's hash it out tonight. We can go up to your room. Or you can grab your laptop and come back here for coffee. I'm sure they'll let us stay."

"Um." Luke coming up wasn't a good idea. I wanted him, and that would always win over us trying to collaborate on a program of travel. That, and my proficiency would be butting heads with his carefree attitude. "Us taking a car and driving to London, I love it," I said. "I'm in. But can I work out the how and where and when by myself tonight? You can show up with the car and drive us, but

I'll feel better knowing there's a plan to follow and a backup plan if that fails. You can text me if there's somewhere specific you don't want to miss, and we can review it all tomorrow on the ferry and change what doesn't suit you."

"Yes!" He yelled, all grin and nearly bouncing out of his seat. "Yes," he said more quietly. "I trust you and I know you need that bit of control. If there's anything you need from me—before or during—or ever," he added with a hand wave that tried to downplay the word's importance but only emphasized it, "you text or call me. Day or night. I have you set up to ring through even if it's in Do Not Disturb."

Oh did he? Interesting. And it was strange hearing him frame my need for control that way, like he remembered it as something to be accommodated and not one of the things that drove us apart.

"This will be fun," I assured him, remembering Mattie saying the same thing to me earlier when I was freaking out about seeing Luke again. Maybe it was time for me to put more faith in my friends.

A whole road trip's worth of faith.

Chapter 7
March 2020
Rin

Tell me you like mischievous, handsome men.

I'd read Luke's text to me a hundred times if I'd read it once. My phone battery blinked a critical red from unlocking it so many times to read that one, audacious, sexy-as-hell demand. Not the rest of the conversation. Just that one line.

It did things to me I didn't know words could do.

Raphael had only had our numbers a few hours before starting a group text that included him, me, Daphne, and Luke. The Redgrave wedding—much like the Redgraves themselves—was driving Mattie to her absolute limits, and Raph had already fallen for her by then, despite their separate quarantines and not being in each others' physical space yet. His plan was to get our four brains together to think of ways to help her. It was sweet. And his earnestness did a lot to convince me he genuinely cared about the girl who had been my best friend since grammar school. If he was putting that same energy into the letters he and Mattie were exchanging, it was no wonder she was equally smitten with him.

Hell, with one text, I was ready to fall for Luke Maston.

The power of the written word.

The four of us had chatted in the group text but didn't come up with any solutions, only mitigations to harm that could occur. Mats was the most stubborn person I knew, and she would find a way to slip past all our objections and do what she felt was right and necessary, no matter the cost. If that meant causing a scene at her brother's wedding, then that's what she'd do.

A stupid muppet, but I loved her dearly. If I didn't love her so much—or her sister Daphne just as much—I wouldn't have rearranged my schedule to accompany them to so many of the wedding-related events. But someone had to remind them that they were loved as they were. Because their relatives were going to make them feel like nobody did.

And that was how I ended up sitting outside an outrageously posh private meeting room at the Billingstead Hotel, waiting to whisk Daphne away from some family meeting that all her wiles and whines and baby-of-the-family pleas couldn't get her out of. There was no way to know how long it would last, but I had plenty of emails to get through, so that was my evening sorted, until Daph was released and we could go to dinner.

Well. I *meant* to read through and respond to emails. But once my phone was unlocked, I went straight to my text messages. Straight to the private conversation between me and Luke.

Me:
Are those your only standout traits? Clever, cute, and confident?

Luke:
Did I need more? It's worked so far. Something tells me you're not so easily won over.

Me:
Mats is the one all aflutter over love letters. I need something more solid.

Luke:
I assure you, I'm solid.

Me:
Like, thick-headed?

Luke:
I'm sure some people think so. I'll let you judge for yourself.

Me:
Difficult to do through text.

Luke:
Great, I'll pick you up at seven. Take you to my local, if you drink. If you don't, there's a cart in town selling meat pies that are sweet as. And if you don't do meat…well, we'll figure it out together. No worries.

Me:
I don't have any dietary restrictions, including alcohol, but we're not going out tonight because I'm busy supporting Daph.

Luke:

Luke: Ah. Wedding stuff?

Me: Some family meeting thing.

Luke: "Family meeting" = everybody gets together and gossips about Mattie?

Me: You're close to the truth there.

Luke: I've been in the same hotel as them for only a few days and I already know they're the fucking worst.

Me: I've known them since childhood and can confirm.

Luke: So you'll be at the hotel tonight?

Me: Meeting starts at 7. No outsiders allowed, so I'll be hanging around somewhere nearby while I wait for Daph to make her Great Escape and we can get the hell out of there.

Luke: Maybe I'll see you tonight after all.

Me: Why does that sound more like a promise than a possibility?

Luke: Because you already know you can count on me. See you tonight.

It was five past seven. Daphne had walked into the room ten minutes ago, the doors had shut five minutes after that, and still no Luke.

Have you already got a crush on a boy you've never met because he's flirty and you've seen his dumb, perfect smile on the big screen and felt like he was smiling specifically at you? Oh god, are you a Mastondon? Are you entertaining a fantasy shared by thousands of other fans? Jesus, pull yourself together, Rin.

I turned off my phone and set it face down on the table. It was so stupid, getting myself worked up like that. But a part of me liked that fantasy: being the special one to catch the eye of the beautiful, successful person who was admired by the masses. And the chances of it happening were only slightly better than winning the lottery. I had to get the idea out of my head for good before I got hurt. And if I didn't, I had no one to blame but myself.

"You're Rin."

I jumped at the voice and turned towards it, already recognizing its cadence from the minutes and hours I'd watched him in movie theaters. Tenor, I'd guess, and his original Auckland accent flattened slightly, as though he'd spent time in Australia or the States. Which, film-making, so that made sense. I was familiar with the sound of him, even if his presence at that precise moment was unexpected.

Even more unexpected was the desire I felt simply looking at this man in person. He was tall enough that he wouldn't feel insecure about being seen next to my nearly-six-foot-tall frame. Sneakers, dark jeans that fit really well at his narrow hips, a purple-and-black striped tee just starting to strain across his chest, like he'd bought it before he started building up muscle. For those

Knuckletracker movies, most likely. He was probably the main reason women watched them with their kids so frequently.

His smile caught me like I knew it would, and he held up two unopened bottles of beer.

I meant to respond. To smile back (did I not smile back?) and gesture to the empty seat at my table, but besides my initial thoughts of *wow he actually showed up* and *oh no he's beautiful and he's smiling at me*, my mental capacity maxed out on one important detail.

You're Rin. Not a question. I assumed he'd looked through my photos on social media, but the confidence in his words felt like he already knew me. Not just how I looked, but like he saw the heart of me, the thing that always took so long to show people because I hated being vulnerable. The thing that I was only starting to understand and accept myself, and, even more recently, asking people to acknowledge. This man showed up out of nowhere, took one glance at me, and confirmed for me, with absolute faith, that I was, in fact, exactly who I was.

Even I had never been so sure about me.

"Rin," I said, my mouth knowing I should probably say something, and with my galaxy brain and jump-started heart, my name was the first and last thing I could form. "I'm Rin," I repeated, clearing my throat. "Luke, I presume?"

His smile deepened and he took the seat across from me, placing the beers on the table. "The one and only. I thought I might keep you company while you kept Daphne company. When Raphael told me about your adventures in bringing Mattie a bag full of contraband, I knew I had to meet you."

"It was a group effort," I said. Damn it, I could feel the heat rising in my cheeks.

"Don't be so modest." He brought out a key chain with a bottle opener and opened our beers. He handed me one and I took it, letting my fingers touch his. "From what I hear, you were the brains of the operation."

"Daphne has brains. She just lets impulse win out."

"I heard that, too. And something about a bow and arrow?"

I rolled my eyes and took a sip of my beer. Hmm. The man picked out a good lager. "That's the impulse," I explained. "Though it did solve the problem of how we were going to get the end of the rope onto Mattie's top floor balcony."

Luke leaned forwards and put his chin in his hand, like he was listening at story time. "Suction cup," he said.

"Suction cup," I confirmed with a nod. "Sounds like you already know all about it."

"I have Raph's account. We can talk about something else, if you like. I just wanted to hear you speak."

"You can check that off your list." *God, Rin, what's wrong with you? Did you forget how to talk to attractive people?* "You didn't have anything else to do tonight?" I asked, changing the subject.

"Well, thanks to the egregious oversight on both our parts of not asking any questions before we agreed to make this film, most of my time is occupied with thinking of ways to get me and Raphael out of making said film."

"A full-time job in itself." I gave him a rueful smile, meeting his eyes over the lip of my bottle.

He shrugged and settled back in his chair, looking relaxed. "I would say it should be Raph's job, since he's the one in quarantine and has the time, but I know he's busy romancing your best friend, and I can't ask him to abandon that. You know, I can't remember the last time he pursued someone like this. He's never been so enamored and sure."

Luke squinted into the distance. "That doesn't sound like something I should be telling other people. Don't tell him I told you."

I laughed. He sounded like Daphne. "I don't snitch, Luke. And besides, if we're going to help them get together, we have to pool our resources. Including information."

At the mention of working together, Luke perked up. "That will cut into my 'how to stop a film production' thinking time, but it would make Raphael happy. And if he's released from quarantine with a new girlfriend, he'll have more incentive to do whatever it takes to get released from this stupid job. And since my ideas fall anywhere between harmless pranks and terrorism, we need his brain to come up with the good stuff." He nodded, coming to a decision. "I'm in. But before we do that. I came here for you, and I want to hear more about you. Our friends can wait."

So I told him. Not everything, of course, I'd never do that on a first date (was this a date?). He told me about himself, too. It was obvious he was passionate about his work, loved his kids, and thrived on chaos and charm. When we'd been so honest that we started to get shy again, the conversation came back to Mattie and Raph. I told him Mats needed someone who was a real partner to her, and he said Raph always took care of the people he loved.

We lost track of time. We both jumped when Daphne burst through the doors in a cloud of frustration and stormed past us. Her brothers called her name from inside the room, exasperation in their voices for having to talk sense into their baby sister once again.

"Rin-Rin," Daph growled, already a good three metres beyond our table, and we stood to follow her, leaving the long-empty beer bottles behind.

"Oh shit." One of the Redgrave brothers had followed her out of the room and finally noticed the two of us waiting for her. "Luke Maston?"

For all that Luke was known for being charming and accommodating, he completely ignored the man who had put his already-friend Daphne into a state. Luke jogged up to join her, making it clear he wasn't going to interact with someone who upset his friend, and the three of us left.

When I thought about it later—months later, but hours later, too—I pinpointed that reaction as the moment I loved him. Even I would argue that it was far too soon, but it's true. It was the first time I saw his values in action. Over the course of that week, he would make that same decision, again and again. Choosing the people he cared about when it came down to that or societal expectations, or looking good, or doing what was best for his career. And if he ended up loving me—a long shot, a fantasy, and my most foolish wish—I already knew I could rely on him for the support I always needed but never thought I could ask for.

Chapter 8
October 2022
Luke

After accidentally implying the afternoon before that the birthplace and beloved home of Suraj was incalculably inferior to international big cities, I was sure he would (understandably) retract his offer of loaning me a car. Of course, I didn't think about that until after I told Rin that I'd already procured said vehicle and would love their company on the drive to London.

Rin said they were going to take a bus and all I thought was, "but I want to spend more time with you," and what I said before any doubts or logistics or facts could interfere was, "I HAVE A CAR I WILL DRIVE YOU."

Technically, I did not have a car. Not yet.

I called Suraj in a panic the moment I left dinner with Rin, apologizing and offering him everything from guaranteed work on any future films of mine to anything in my wardrobe to his choice of props I'd "acquired" through the years. I would have offered him my first-born, but Cassidy was basically me in teen girl form and would have been more curse than gift.

When I thought he was still going to refuse, I started talking about Rin. How much they loved the girls, the many ways they supported and even loved me during those shaky months together. How this was the perfect opportunity to see if we could potentially be partners under normal circumstances instead of extraordinary ones.

And it worked. Suraj told me where to meet him to pick it up, first thing the next morning. *Look at what love can do*, I thought, ending the call and smiling like a fool. *Anything is possible. The world is good. My luck is changing.*

And then I saw the car.

That early in the morning, the sunrise still but a rumor, I didn't trust my eyes. And I couldn't believe my co-worker would be sending me on a hundreds-of-kilometres trip with a vehicle that looked like it would have trouble traveling hundreds of centimetres.

"What am I looking at?"

Suraj finished pulling off the car cover and I swear I saw moths fluttering away. I imagined them disgruntled at being evicted from a warm home that had been theirs for decades. The tiny, boxy Ford looked like the car every child draws when they think of a car, harsh angles and straight lines, the stick-figure drawings in it oversized in an—at least with this car—unfortunately believable way. It had been blue, once. It still was, I guess, though faded from a bolder shade to a light one, and inconsistently, with patches of white among the light blue and, of course, rust. Silver duct tape outlined the passenger's door and held foggy plastic in place where the window should be. The duct tape matched the number plate's shiny digits, which stood out from the black background.

Will, my early-morning ride to Suraj's house and never unprepared when it came to finding the right words for something, simply grunted.

"Mate," I groaned, rubbing my face with both hands. A day's worth of stubble scratched me back. I'd gotten up too early to trust myself with a shave. All so I could get this car early, so I could be on time for Rin and not look irresponsible.

"Mate," I repeated. "You're taking the piss."

Suraj gathered the cover into a ball and tossed it to the ground in front of the garage door. "Here I was thinking you wanted to drive it, not marry it. She may not be braw but she'll get you on your way."

"All the way to London?"

"Aye, I reckon."

I shuffled closer, peering at the tires and expecting them to wither under my scrutiny. The bonnet sat askew, a headlight bulged out of its socket, and I didn't know what Rin had in the way of luggage, but if it was anything more than a wallet, it wasn't going to fit in the two-doored clown car.

How had I already fucked this up?

"What else have you got?"

Suraj rolled his eyes and put an unlit cigarette to his lips. "You've mistaken me for Colin Gregg," he said, cigarette bouncing as he tried to light it.

"I don't know who that is."

He closed his eyes and took a breath, visibly relaxing. "I'm not a fucking car dealership, mate. It was my dad's, and my mum never sold it when he died. It's time to get rid of it." He glanced up at me, seeing suspicion in my face. "It'll make it to London, but it won't make it back. Park it wherever you like. It'll get stolen or towed and either way, I don't have to see it again. I'm doing you a favor, and you're doing me one in return."

I glanced over to Will's car, a sturdy sedan that had behaved admirably over the weeks we'd been filming, and had the added bonus of being built this century.

"Oh, I don't fucking think so," Will said with a smile. "If you need money to buy Rin and yourself bus tickets, I'm happy to lend it, and extend to you my good wishes for a very emotionally and physically fulfilling reunion with them. But your charm can't buy its way into my driver's seat, mate."

It was useless to argue. And I'd promised Rin a car.

The sky was lightening. I didn't have a lot of time. And I didn't have any other options. I turned to Suraj.

"Give me the keys."

***

Rin had texted around midnight with the detailed itinerary of our first day of driving. It was better than anything I could have come up with, but I was still torn about not participating in its creation. I sprung this road trip on them with no further thought in my mind beyond "together??" And Rin may have had a knack for travel planning, but that didn't mean it should always be their responsibility.

Against all odds, Mr Bean (I named the car) had started immediately, if a little unsteadily. I tried to ignore the flash of worry in Suraj's eyes before the engine leveled out and the earnestness in his voice when he wished me luck.

But I'd made it to Rin's hotel, and that was farther than I expected.

"Good job, Mr Bean," I murmured, hesitating before shutting off the engine. I sent a silent prayer to whoever was listening that it would start up again. "Please don't embarrass me."

I hadn't decided how to react when Rin saw the kind of vehicle they had to trust for four days. Pretend I didn't see anything wrong with it? Give a shocked, "Why, it wasn't like that when I got it!"? Chagrin? The very true emotion of embarrassment? Most likely I'd fall back on what I usually did: acknowledge it was not an ideal situation, shrug, and not worry about any problems until it was something that absolutely couldn't be ignored.

Before I could lose my nerve, I got out to meet Rin in the lobby. They were working on their phone, and I breathed a sigh of relief when I saw that the entirety of their luggage was one backpack and small duffel bag. A master traveler, that one. So much so that a clunker like Mr Bean wouldn't even break their top ten travel transportation failures. They'd had to take an overnight train with overflowing toilets. They once had to sleep at a Lima bus station for two nights in a row when all the hotels and buses were booked full thanks to an international football match. No, no, this ancient piece of vehicular technology wouldn't faze them at all.

When Rin saw our chariot, their face fell.

I glanced at the car again, hoping the brightness from post-sunrise would somehow paint it in a literally better light.

It did not.

"Um," Rin said, fiddling with the backpack straps. "I..."

They didn't have to find the words. I saw it all on their face. Surprise, disappointment, worry, calculating what it would take to abandon the plan and return to the original idea of busses. Wondering why they trusted me.

"Here," I said, stepping up and reaching for the duffel. "Let me store that for you. The boot doesn't open, but one of the back seats is missing, and it's a surprisingly convenient shortcut."

Rin let go of the duffel with some reluctance.

"Luke. There's no window."

"Oh," I said, jiggling the passenger door handle until it opened. "Sure there is. This is a luxury plastic, see? Glass, you know, that's infinitely recyclable. But if you're rich enough to discard the world, you want plastic windows. Bonus: the wind whistles through it like a banshee. Or whatever the Scottish equivalent is."

I put Rin's duffel next to my messenger bag. My carry-on was small enough to fit through the seat/boot hole, where it slid around in what I hoped was an otherwise empty space. I'd asked the production team if they could post my larger suitcase back to Auckland, since I wouldn't need anything in it before I was home.

I stood back from the car and gestured towards the open door.

"Gentlethems first," I said with a flourish.

Rin groaned and put their head in their hands. "Oh no, Luke."

"Hey." I walked over to put a hand on their shoulder. "Hey, no, it's fine." I looked back at the car and put my other hand on my hip. Ok, it wasn't great.

"Ok, it's not great," I admitted. "But this is classic Honest Mischief Alliance antics! And it will be an amazing story if we live to tell it, which we will, because I'm with you. And together, I know we can tame Mr Bean and make it to London, and we'll have a brilliant time at the premiere—"

"Who the fuck is Mr Bean?"

"The car, bro, do try to keep up."

"You named the car Mr Bean and you want me to believe we'll get to our destination with zero problems?"

I gently turned them to look at me. "Maybe we can't trust Mr Bean, but you can trust me. Whatever situation we find ourselves in, I'll do whatever it takes to get us back on track. Even if it means calling up Raphael and asking him to send a helicopter or whatever it is rich people do. So let's go on an adventure and see the countryside and those stone circles and that lake and the cute B&B you booked and if we get stuck, I'll get us out. But don't worry about it until then. Now, please get in the car. Your seatbelt works."

They looked at me and I could see the gears turning in their head. I gave them a half smile, half grimace, and they laughed, shaking their head.

"Goddamn it, Luke. Get in before I change my mind."

I squeezed their shoulder and jogged over to the driver's side. Mr Bean sputtered but pulled through, Suraj's blessing of good luck holding, and we made our way to the ferry that would take us back to mainland Scotland.

Chapter 9
October 2022
Rin

Mr Bean The Car had, shockingly, started without complaint and gotten us onto the ferry. I wasn't any less concerned about how it might behave in the future, but as of now I could still catch a bus if the car lived up to expectation.

There was free Wi-Fi, and I wanted to do some planning for day two of our trip, so I had gone straight to the restaurant on board and parked myself at a table by the windows. Luke had followed me, but without something to focus on, he was restless. He took a selfie of us and sent it to his daughters and the squad. I'd already told Mattie and Daph about the road trip and they responded with teasing and speculation. There were plenty of things for them to do in London before I got there and I could be certain they would do none of them if it meant they got to harass me during my several-day road trip with my ex.

When Luke finally stood up with a suspicious gleam in his eye, I assumed he was going to find some chaos to cause to keep him entertained. But he returned a few minutes later with breakfast and beers for each of us. Looked like he needed me to entertain him.

"I know you said you were comfortable winging it, but was there anything specific you wanted to see or do? Today is Scrabster to Lairg, tomorrow is Lairg to Edinburgh, the next day is Edinburgh to Leeds, and the day after is Leeds to London. Not too rough, about four hours of driving a day. Plenty of time to explore."

He looked at me with that big grin on his face. "It's totally up to you," he said. "You'll find the best things to see, the best places to stay. My job is to get us there."

Then he went right back to being bored. His fidgeting was distracting, but him staying still was also distracting. He could attract my attention doing anything at all. I fidgeted myself, thinking of how I'd like him to fill my hours.

I'd have to be proactive and entertain him with a story from one of our Honest Mischief escapades. Luckily, I had just the tale.

"Speaking of boats. Did we ever tell you the story of when Daphne got stuck on a yacht?"

That drew Luke's attention away from his ocean view, but it didn't stop him from bouncing on the balls of his feet. "Daphne doesn't do boats. She gets motion sickness too easily."

Two and a half years ago, Luke wasn't anything more to me than a pretty face I occasionally would spend a few dollars and a few hours to watch in his latest film. So much had changed since then, I sometimes forgot he was a movie star and I worked in tourism, and it was wild when I remembered he knew me and my best friends well enough to assume Daphne wouldn't make choices that aggravated her illness, and he knew what that illness was and how severe.

"Oh," I said, "she was properly motivated."

Interest piqued. "What could have motivated her to voluntarily embark on a journey that would, without fail, make her sick to her stomach?" He thought for a moment. "Did she get sick? Or was this before she knew she would get sick?"

"She did, and she knew," I said, typing more search terms into my browser. I didn't need to stop my trip-planning to tell the story—I knew it by heart. I had been around for the whole thing, from the moment Daphne met Cinnamon through their courtship and breakup and then Daphne's endeavors to get her back. All in all, the whole thing had taken about a week, which Daphne assured me was equivalent to about nine heterosexual months.

Luke stared over my head. Now that he had something to fidget with in his mind, he stopped bouncing his leg. It was a trick I had used on Daph many times.

"It was for love," he said, leaning back and looking at me all smug. "That's the only reason I would do it, and nobody loves love as much as Daphne."

"Sound reasoning," I said. "But what does love have to do with a boat?"

Our back-and-forth held his interest for a while, as I finalized our route and B&B for the next day. Then I shut my laptop and told him the story. Or, as much as I could. Daphne had trespassed, and the Coast Guard was brought out to rescue her under false pretenses, and sensitive information had been stolen, and Mats and I helped her steal it, and it all started because of Daph's work as a secret corporate spy, and for many reasons, I couldn't tell Luke all of that.

It was compelling nonetheless. And that kind of dedication and commitment and deciding to risk so much in the name of love made me feel inferior for not doing the same. I hadn't been serious about a romantic partner in a long time. I dated. I hooked up with people. It was fun. But when I thought about letting those people get close enough to know how stressed I was over family, career, and gender stuff, I made sure to keep them an arm's length away.

Luke had been good to me, first as a friend, then as a lover. But those first few months of the pandemic, my business took a hit it would never recover from. It was a lot to deal with, and it didn't seem fair to ask him to devote his energy to my problems. I knew he would be like Daphne in that situation, devoting every moment to helping me in active, actionable ways, while disregarding his own life, career, and safety.

That was too much to ask of someone I'd known just a few months.

Even worse, I didn't have any extra energy to deal with him and his issues. His easygoing attitude was charming to a point. After that, it felt like laziness, like he didn't want to have to think about anything he did ahead of time. I saw it as immensely privileged and not a little immature and imagined a future with him that looked like me doing most of the work most of the time, interspersed with unpredictable bursts of him making his own grand gestures. At a time when I needed stability and reassurance, that sounded like a nightmare.

It sucked. I loved him.

Daphne knew she would get seasick and she snuck onto the boat anyway. But I wasn't even willing to put in the effort to see what worked best for me and Luke as partners. And if I wasn't willing to put in the minimum effort, even if my stress was caused by situations completely out of either of our control, it didn't feel fair to continue our relationship.

Luke stared at the table, drumming his fingers against it absent-mindedly as I finished the story.

"I'd like to be that kind of person." He said it so softly, I wondered if he knew it had been out loud, and if he'd read my mind.

"I think you are," I said. "I've watched you choose the people you love, even when it jeopardized your career. You take risks most people wouldn't, and for good reasons."

His half-smile didn't do much to hide his sadness, or disappointment, as he glanced up and caught my eye.

"But not *successfully*."

Because he didn't walk away with a partner? Oh. He counted me among his failures.

"That's not your fault," I said, willing away my deepening blush. The words came easy. They were true. "Besides, do you know how many times Daphne wasn't successful before the yacht thing? She was a walking stereotype, and we loved her dearly, but she had never been serious about anyone before. If she succeeded this last time, I am one hundred percent sure it had everything to do with Cinnamon. That was a variable Daph couldn't control. So. Until Cinnamon, it wasn't her fault. Just like it isn't your fault."

He looked at me for a long moment, and my stupid blush didn't go away. Sure, it was a roundabout way of saying, "it wasn't you, it was me," but it *was* me. Without literally everything else going wrong in my life at the same time, I might have had the mental capacity to explore what Luke and I could have been together.

"You're saying I need a Cinnamon."

"I'm saying you need *your* Cinnamon."

"What if," he said, and I could hear the gears turning in his head. "My problem isn't one of who, but when."

A gentle wave of sensation broke through me, pins and needles and a cascade of fading coals. Did he still have feelings for me? Seven hundred sunrises later? Couldn't be. He was charming and flirty and I was attracted to him, and that warped my perception. And if it were true, it would be very bad for him, because if I was a mess two years ago, I was a fucking garbage patch now.

Was Luke still messy, too? Distant and joking in serious situations, unwilling to work for a solution when he could slide on a pair of sunglasses and act like it didn't bother him? That version of him was completely incompatible with my anxiety. Four days in a car together should be enough time to know whether he'd changed at all, whether I could believe in him as an equal partner. If that was even something we wanted.

"Well, I don't think Cinnamon would have fallen in love with you even if you'd gotten to her before Daph did." For both our sakes, I had to be willfully obtuse and skirt the topic. "For one, I'm not sure she's attracted to men in that way, and for another, you would eventually compete with Daphne. You're a force to contend with, Luke, but have you ever stolen a monkey from a lab to impress a girl?" I paused, long enough for him to catch up but not so long that he could respond, and pretended to shift my attention to the laptop.

"So tonight," I continued before he could answer, "we're staying in Lairg. It's a two hour drive if we go nonstop from Scrabster, but there's a farm along the way with highland cows and tours and heather honey, then standing stones farther on. I know it's impossible to go anywhere in Scotland without seeing standing stones, but these were only discovered a few years ago. The story is fascinating. I won't bore you with it now, but I intend to info-dump every detail once we're in front of them."

Luke still looked serious, though he'd stopped staring directly at me. He had to know what I was doing, but the question was whether he wanted to be candid about the heavy stuff this early in the trip or table it so our time together flowed more smoothly.

"We have highland cows back home," he said, meeting my eyes again. He'd chosen peace. "As well as all the other cows."

"You don't want to see them in their natural habitat?" I asked, smiling. Avoiding emotional confrontation was one of my favourite things, but his earnestness and disappointment had me second guessing myself. I could be bright, too. Easygoing. I had been, as a kid and teen. Growing up had made that freedom feel unsafe.

Luke is the most safe. You don't have to put all your vulnerability in his hands, but it's ok to trust him with how you wish you could be again.

"This is going to be fun." I nodded definitively. Things became true when repeated enough, right? "I've got the bare bones of a plan in place, you got the car, and the open road is ours for the taking."

"As long as the weather holds," Luke added, crossing his arms in front of his chest.

A weird thing to say in Scotland in October. "What happens if the weather doesn't hold?"

"Unclear. But according to Suraj, Mr Bean doesn't like rain."

"Of course he doesn't. What does that mean?"

"I have no idea. Honestly, I was afraid to ask."

Was it too late to take the bus? "The forecast said rain every day this week."

Luke shrugged. I shifted in my seat. "Let's hope it means the clingfilm window leaks," he said, "and not a catastrophic breakdown in the middle of nowhere."

Chapter 10
May 2020
Luke

After five weeks of being cooped up at home, we were chocka with ennui. The adults found plenty to do to fill our sudden free time, from remote work to all the home improvement projects we'd put off for years to cleaning out closets and junk drawers to catching up on shows and movies we'd missed. But the eight-year-old and the ten-year-old didn't have any home they were responsible for improving, and they liked the state of their closets and drawers, and all they wanted to watch was *Frozen* on repeat forever because their love for it was as limitless as their imaginations.

Turned out, their imaginations' limit was about a month.

We'd been taking them over to the Redgrave sisters' rented cottage a couple times a week to give them a change of scenery. They loved their Uncle Raph, grew to regard Mattie with a shockingly mature respect, and if I caught Lena and Cassidy in the middle of making some kind of mischief, there was a fifty-fifty chance Daphne had put them up to it in the first place. They liberated clothes from everyone's rooms and put on a fashion show, nearly got lost in the woods behind the house, and sang and danced around the campfire by the lake.

Once novelty began to bore them as much as familiarity did, we had to take drastic measures. Rin and their lifetime's worth of tourism skills found a petting zoo an hour away. All the pens were outside, they were only letting a certain number of people in at a time, and everybody was expected to maintain two metres between themselves and anybody not in their household group, or pod, or whatever they were calling it when a bunch of people braved the shutdown in the same house.

Rin had made all the plans, called the zoo to confirm hours and prices and rules, mapped the route. Bought snacks and car games for the road. The day was clear and sunny and not too chilly. Everything was perfect and we were ready to leave.

So of course we couldn't find Lena anywhere.

"Cassidy, where's your sister?" I asked with a sigh. Pranks I was used to, but I couldn't see how making us late for an appointment to pet pigs—a dream come true for both girls—was playful.

Cassidy gave me a wide-eyed look, fingers absentmindedly playing with her pin-straight, unbrushed hair. She shook her head like I had asked a ten year old to explain string theory. Though to be fair, she might have been able to explain it. Most of the time, their did-you-knows encompassed facts I was embarrassed to not, in fact, know.

Mattie, Raph, and Daphne were already at the house, and after I couldn't find Lena in any of the obvious first places to look, they and mum joined in the search. Mum checked the backyard and Lena's favourite trees to climb. Raph braved the crawlspace and Rin went in the opposite direction, climbing on top of the roof to check there and to get a better view of the grounds.

The Redgraves looked in places I was sure my youngest could never fit or didn't have the strength to maintain. They went into the closets and frisked all the clothes, because Lena might have crawled up into a coat to hang on the hanger. They checked the clothes hanging on hooks on the back of the doors and in the front hall for the same reason. When they saw that the girls' rooms looked like tornadoes had hit, they checked all the piles of clothes as well as the drawers.

"One time, all us siblings were playing hide and seek and Daphne won when we couldn't find her for a full day," Mattie told me. "She had emptied one of her dresser drawers, scattered the clothes around the room so they blended in with the rest of the mess, crawled into the drawer, and somehow shut it. Even when our father started bellowing through the house: nothing, no Daph. She said later that she'd fallen asleep, but I think she liked making our parents worry. Not that I think that's what Lena's doing," she added.

"She's eight," I said with a shrug. "I wouldn't put it past her and I wouldn't blame her. But she's holding all of us up, and that's plain rude."

After an hour, I circled back to Cassidy. She had been far too quiet, sitting in the living room playing with a hand-held electronic Little Mermaid game that had been my sister's when we were young. When Rin said they were going to climb onto the roof? Mermaid game. When Daphne started looking in both the bottom and top cabinets in the kitchen? Mermaid game. When Mats was throwing around clothes and stuffed animals, making even more of a mess? Mermaid game. Only one reason my eldest wouldn't be interested in that kind of anarchy.

"Cass," I said, squatting on the footstool opposite the big chair she liked. Her bare feet kicked the air, her head tipped back near the ground, lounging upside-down in a position that made me dizzy just to see it. The game beeped out a simple but driving melody, the noise tinny where it used to be entertaining, and she didn't take her eyes off it.

"Cass," I repeated, more firmly. "Game down. I'm serious."

"There's no pause," she explained. "If I stop, I die. Just like a manta ray. Manta rays can never stop swimming cause if they do, they die."

"Ok," I said. "We can wait until you lose."

"Yeah. I never got this far before." She scratched at her nose. "It's a personal record."

"You don't say."

Five seconds later, the music shifted to the familiar three-note melody of defeat, and I grabbed the game before she could start another round.

"Hey! I wasn't done!"

"Game over," I said, sliding the console under my butt so she couldn't get to it. "You think I don't recognize the music of failure?" I sang the little song, doing my best robot impression. "I've only been listening to it for thirty years. I've beat that game a hundred times and it took ten thousand deaths to do it. Tell me where Lena is, and you can have it back."

Cassidy pouted and crossed her arms, then crossed her legs that were still resting against the back of the chair. Her hair dragged on the floor as she shook her head. "I. Don't. Know."

"No? And you don't care? You don't care if your sister is safe, or if she's hurt, or got stolen?" She knew, and Lena was fine, and Cass was getting more enjoyment out of it than Lena was, I was sure. If Cass honestly didn't have any idea where her sister was, she would be freaking out. Despite whatever was going on today, and whatever arguments they had, they loved each other, and I made sure they knew how important it was to show it.

"She's not hurt and she's not stolen. She's just a ratbag."

"Prove it." Nothing. "No? Ok. Not a problem. Let's see. Let's make this interesting." I rubbed my chin, thinking. "If Uncle Raph or Mattie find Lena, you can't go over to their cottage anymore.

No more beans on toast." I had no idea why Raph had fed her beans and toast, of all things, and no idea why she liked it better than chocolate or cake or crisps, but it was decent leverage.

"What?!"

"If Grams finds her, you can't go with her to the sewing shop for six months. She'll take Lena and leave you behind with me, and you'll clean your room instead."

Her jaw dropped. This was all inconceivable and incredibly cruel.

"If Daphne finds her, I'll send Lena to San Francisco to visit her and Cinnamon without you."

Cass huffed and squirmed her way into an upright position, glaring at me.

"If it's me, I'll buy Lena gifts at the petting zoo shop, but you won't get anything. I bet they have little sheep and pig toys. If Lena appears on her own, you'll be grounded for a month." I paused. "But if you tell me where she is, you'll only be grounded for a week."

"A *week*?" She sighed with her whole body in the way only a child could. All the injustices in the world were nothing compared to the trials I put her through.

"Yeah," I said. "Because Rin planned this whole day for us, and they put a lot of work into it, and now we're late. They're sad that their plans are ruined." I shrugged. "Maybe that's Lena's fault, but if you know where she is and didn't tell us for almost two hours, then you have to share the blame, too. You hurt Rin's feelings."

She chewed on her lip and kept giving me the side eye, considering.

"Oh, and I almost forgot," I said, remembering something Cassidy liked even more than Rin. "If Rin finds Lena, I'm taking away all the *Frozen* movies for a year. You won't be able to watch any of them."

There we go. If looks could kill! Cass slid off the couch and stomped in place before stomping out of the living room and towards the front door.

Before we even made it that far, Rin was yelling from the front yard.

"I got her! She's ok!"

I broke into a run, past Cassidy and out the door. My legs were suddenly watery, and my throat constricted. I couldn't let myself be afraid while I was hoping Lena was safe. Only after knowing she was, would I let the fear in.

And there she was, dressed in the clothes I'd put her in myself a few hours before, holding onto her little backpack, looking utterly confused. I dropped to my knees and grabbed her, holding her in the tightest hug that wouldn't crush her.

"Where were you? We were looking everywhere. You scared us."

Lena burst into tears, and I pushed her hair out of her face. She may have been a chaos agent like the rest of us, but that didn't mean she wasn't sensitive.

She stammered, "Cassidy said—" *Of course Cassidy said.* "—that she was going to ride with Daphne and Uncle Raph and that I couldn't ride with them, and I wanted to ride with them, so when they got here I went into their car and buckled up so I was there first and they couldn't kick me out."

"You've been in their car this whole time? Didn't you see us looking for you? You didn't hear us calling?"

"I, I, I..." she blew a snot bubble and wiped it across her face with the palm of her hand. "There were blankets and I fell asleep."

"Oh, sweetheart," Rin said, putting a hand against Lena's back.

I pressed my hands to either side of her head, and my forehead against hers. "You're not in trouble," I assured her. "But we were all very worried. You have to always tell an adult where you're going, ok? Me or Grams or Rin. Cassidy doesn't count. Understand?"

Lena sniffled and nodded, and I heard the beginnings of a wheeze.

"Where's your inhaler?" If she had had an asthma attack while we couldn't find her and didn't have her inhaler...I shoved the thought out of my mind. She was safe now, and I didn't need the adrenaline that more panic would activate.

She held up her backpack. "I packed it."

"Good," I said. "Good." I kissed the top of her head and turned to Rin.

"Thank you."

They smiled. "Don't need to thank me, mate. Just glad she's ok."

Behind me, everyone else had come out of the house, but kept their distance as I talked to my daughter. Cassidy had creeped out, too.

"Lena, go to Grams and take your inhaler and get washed up. You still want to go to the petting zoo? Rin, is there still time?"

"Of course," they said. "I always schedule some buffer time for unforeseen circumstances."

"Go on to Grams," I repeated to Lena. When she was on her way, practically stumbling into her grandmother's arms, the other adults turned to go back into the house, and I turned to Cassidy. Her arms were crossed over her chest and she played with her lower lip, staring at the ground so she wouldn't meet my eyes.

"I told you she wasn't hurt or stolen."

I had never wanted to hit my kids. I still didn't. I never would. But her mocking tone, the disregard for the worry she caused, the lack of regret for the whole thing—I had started fist fights with men my size over less. That was the language they understood, and I was happy to communicate my displeasure in whatever way they would most take it to heart.

Cass was ten. Her language was freedom, food, and *Frozen*.

Rin must have sensed I was gearing up for an uncomfortable talk with my daughter. "I'll make sure everything is all set for us to leave," they said. "Whenever you're ready."

"A moment, if you don't mind, Rin. You see, once I realized Cassidy knew where Lena was, she and I had a heart-to-heart. I told her if she told me where her sister was hiding, she would only get grounded for one week. If anyone else found her, she would receive a punishment related to whichever person that was."

I waited, looking at Cassidy. She would remember that all of the options were bad, but did she remember which one Rin triggered?

Her eyes got wide and she blew air out of her nose like an angry bull. Ok, so she knew.

"I told you where she was!" She yelled.

"No you didn't. Rin found her."

"That's not fair. I was *bringing* you to her. You said if I found her, I wouldn't get grounded, so I had to go get her."

"I know you have to test my memory," I said with a smile that was halfway between pity and smirk. "But I haven't forgotten what I said. If you told me where Lena was, you'd be grounded a week. And if Rin found her first..." I shrugged like it was out of my hands.

"What would happen?" Rin asked, shifting uncomfortably. Maybe I shouldn't have involved them in this.

"No! Dad!" Cassidy said. "I was in the middle of telling you where she was, with my feet!"

"I said no *Frozen* for a year." Rin grimaced.

"No!" Cass said again. She turned to Rin, tears in her eyes. "Rin-Rin, can't you tell my dad I—can't you talk to him?"

Rin's face softened, and they glanced between Cass and me. They didn't have kids. It wasn't because they disliked children, or imagined their perfect life without them, though either of those were perfectly reasonable. After all, I had over a decade of experience defending Raphael's decision to be childfree to people who were, largely, unworthy of the response.

When Rin had taken genuine interest in my daughters, I was relieved, and again when they got along, and when the three of them seemed to form their own squad, mirroring the one Rin had with Mattie and Daph. I'd been divorced for four years, and while my focus was always on being the best dad to my kids, a part of me still wanted, very badly, to find a partner that would fit perfectly into this life that I loved. More than once in the weeks I'd known them, I thought it could be Rin.

They cocked their head, like they'd had an idea.

"Luke, could I talk to Cassidy for a minute?"

Interesting. This felt like teamwork. This felt like something a partner would do.

"Sure. I'll be right over there." I gestured to the house. Everyone else had gone inside, but I was going to eavesdrop. Rin nodded and turned to Cassidy.

"Here, Cass, will you sit with me a minute?" They sat on the ground and patted the bit of earth next to them, and I watched from a little distance away as my daughter flopped onto the spot, legs crossed.

Neither spoke for a minute. Rin was gathering their thoughts, I'd wager, finding the right thing to say. They were good at that, as long as they weren't in the middle of a plan of their own that was unraveling disastrously.

It wasn't a long conversation. Rin told Cass about how they didn't have any sisters, how they were lonely as a child until they met Mattie and Daphne. How they loved those girls and would do anything for them. A few stories about the three of them getting into trouble and how much fun it was, and how it wouldn't be the same without them. They hoped Cassidy and Lena could think of each other like that, too. Become best friends. Value and love each other beyond sisterhood.

I watched Cassidy tell Rin about a time she saved Lena from a lizard, and how she always gives her younger sister the wider popcorn bowl on movie nights because Lena eats it by sticking her whole head in the bowl and picking up the kernels with her tongue. I heard Cass crying, saying she didn't want her sister to be hurt and didn't want to be mean to her. Rin comforted her and said it was hard sometimes, but the trick was to remember they were a team, standing against the world, together.

I wiped my own tears away, and the two of them stood up, hugged, and came over to me.

"I'm sorry," Cass said, and I gathered her into a hug. "She was bugging me all morning and I wanted to trick her. It was mean. And it was mean to make everyone look for her."

"I'm glad you could see that," I said. "I forgive you. But you have to apologize to Lena, too. And everyone else, for wasting their time."

"Ah," Rin said, clearing their throat. "Since Cassidy's punishment was specific to *me* finding Lena, I would like to advocate on her behalf and say *Frozen* shouldn't be withheld from her. If you want their sister-bond to be strong, you need to let them experience positive stories about sisterhood without restrictions."

I narrowed my eyes at them over Cass's head. It made sense, but it still felt like I was getting bamboozled.

"That's a fair point," I grumbled. "What do you think, Cass?"

"If I controlled winter, I would *never* use it to hurt Lena."

"Not quite what I was looking for, but good to know. Fine. You're grounded for a week, which means no movies at all, but after that, no new restrictions. Ok, are we still up for petting zoo? Let's find the others and get on our way."

Cass ran ahead of us into the house, shouting for her sister. I pulled Rin to me and held them, not knowing words that were adequate to thank them, or that encompassed all the love I had for them. The best I could do was squeeze them tight, and show them with actions all the gratitude and affection that were impossible to express in any other way.

Chapter 11
October 2022
Luke

Mr Bean didn't let us down. We got in the car as the ship docked, and when I went to turn the key, Rin grabbed my arm.

"Should we—" They frowned and sounded out the next word like they were unsure how to pronounce it. "P-pr-pray? Should we pray?"

I laughed. It felt good to be silly together again. "It couldn't hurt, as long as we pray to the right thing."

"Damn, I was going to suggest Loki."

"Absolutely not. I'm the wheel of fortune's favourite show to watch. I'm not going to court disaster by demanding the attention of a trickster god. What about..." I trailed off, thinking.

"I've got it," they said. "We pray to all the travelers whose names we don't know because they never encountered any problems or extraordinary circumstances? The people who succeeded at the same task as us with no unplanned interruptions."

"Dear successful people," I said, closing my eyes and pitching my voice like a preacher calling down brimstone. Rin giggled and squeezed my forearm where they still held it. "We beseech you today to look upon us and bestow the same fortune of fair weather, no obstacles, and incorruptible health upon our selves, auto, and roads. May we arrive at every destination unmolested, on time, and in high spirits. In the name of the wind, and whisky, and Mr Bean, amen."

"Amen." I opened my eyes and Rin let go of me and nodded.

The car started without a hiccup.

First things first: petrol and snacks. Rin had a couple granola bars and bags of crisps that they had gotten when they thought they'd be taking busses all the way down to London. It didn't seem like enough food for a full day of travel, but it had been emergency-only. They didn't have a lot of wiggle room to fit more in their two small bags. But now we had four days of travel and a whole car we could fill with Starbars and Twirls.

Just off the ferry, I pulled into the closest petrol station and sent Rin on the mission to find a dairy. For the first time in weeks, I didn't have to explain that a dairy was a corner shop or convenience store. It was nice to be in the company of another Kiwi again.

Once the car had a full tank, I started it and began toggling all the switches to see what worked and what didn't. Headlights did, surprisingly. Its lazy eye pointed in a too-far-down direction, but it technically worked. Windscreen wipers, check. Or rather, wiper, as in one. Passenger's side. I got back out and tried to figure out how to remove it and reattach it on the driver's side, but it stumped me. Brake lights yes, heater no, seat belts yes, boot latch no, and radio no.

So we'd be fairly safe, not exactly secure, probably uncomfortable, and if we ran out of things to talk about, awkward. That radio would have been doing a lot of heavy lifting if we got shy.

Enough time had passed that I began to worry Rin was lost. I was about to go hunt them down when I saw them turn the corner. Their auburn hair shone in the sun, aviator sunglasses glinting in the light. I wondered if it was the first time their whole trip they'd had to wear them. Their purple winter coat wasn't so puffy that I couldn't imagine their physique, and besides, their leggings showed off every curve, every muscle. They glanced towards me, making sure I was in the same place as when they left, and smiled.

And I wanted to run my tongue along their jaw, down their neck, across their clavicle, and bite that firm trap muscle between their neck and shoulder.

My face flushed, and so did the rest of me. This always happened. Even if Rin and I had been bingeing shows all day, or hiking together, or spending the afternoon attempting math in a way that might save their business. Even after seeing them for hours, sometimes I would look up and get this sudden, sharp desire. And once I knew they were keen on me too, I acted on it.

Being intimate with Rin was different from anything else I'd experienced, in the sexiest way possible. Thanks to society, we were expected to just *know* what to do with a romantic partner. There had always been little, if any, direction, so of course I always asked for clarification. It surprised me that a lot of my partners didn't like that. Or maybe they would have, but they had expectations that included not having to ask for it. It felt like a guessing game I was always losing.

Totally different with Rin. No guessing required. Being intimate was an opportunity to explore. Each other and our own pleasure. We wanted to do what the other liked, and that required communication. Consent. Honesty. Trust.

It was, in the truest sense, sexy as fuck.

For not only that reason, I would have followed them to the ends of the earth. But our lives started changing in ways we couldn't control and Rin didn't feel comfortable relying on me as we went through those separate life issues. I blamed myself for a while. Wondered how I could have been more reliable, someone they could have planted roots with. I knew it wasn't the sex. If Rin had been able to be as honest and vulnerable with their private and emotional life as they were with sex, I doubt we would have broken up.

"Got some Flakes," Rin said, sliding into the passenger's seat. I cleared my throat and shifted in my seat, trying to both hide and make comfortable the burden that had grown between my legs, while they listed the provisions they had gathered for us.

"Waters, juice, chocolate, pretzels, Cheetos, crisps, and chocolate."

"Wait, did you get any chocolate, though?"

Rin rifled around in the reusable bag they'd brought. "Let's see…oh, yeah, and chocolate. Almost forgot." They pulled out a Starbar with a flourish.

"My thanks, my liege," I said, taking it and putting the car in drive. "Where am I going?"

"Excellen queshion," Rin said, mouth already full of candy bar. They put the bag of goodies on the floor of the backseat (a questionable choice—I'd only checked the buttons and couldn't be sure that part of the car even existed; sorry, snacks), and brought up their phone. "Let me answer your question with a question: are you hungry for a meal yet?"

"Awways." Like Rin, candy bar in hand immediately became candy bar in mouth. "Buh I'm gooh for a why."

"Good for a while, got it. In that case, our first stop is Shallow Creek Farm. It's about an hour away. I'll give you turn-by-turn directions as we go, but here's the overall route. Pretty easy."

They turned the phone to me and I adjusted my glasses. All paved roads, not many turns. Mr Bean had this in the bag.

"There are also castles and distilleries nearby, if you wanted to check out anything like that."

Rin had made a great itinerary, and I trusted they'd mapped out the best route to hold our attention. Four days of travel, just the two of us sitting side by side in a cozy car. Three nights of sleeping in the same room even though there would be a chasm of space between our beds. Skipping interesting stops during the day wouldn't make the nights arrive any faster. When we were ensconced in the room together, no stops or detours or following any preordained path, their eyes off the map and mine off the road and our minds able to wander back to each other, that would be my pick of things I wanted to do.

"If there are that many castles and distilleries, I'm sure we'll bump into some along the way. And I assume we'll be sampling local spirits at any of the restaurants and pubs on your list."

"You know me so well."

They turned the phone back to them, told me to take a right out of the petrol station, and we were off.

***

The Scottish Highlands were absolutely stunning in October, fields mottled in greens and browns, lochs and puddles reflecting a steel-grey sky. The hills were, as oft and accurately described, "rolling." Soft and sharp, pastel green and deep russet, the land told a story in many voices, its song dynamic and hypnotizing. I could have driven through it for hours.

My phone had been vibrating in the cup holder since we embarked—normally a distraction, but this time, superseded by the novelty of the view and Rin sitting next to me. After the sixth or seventh time Rin shot a glance at the buzzing device, I caved.

"Can you check it for me?" I asked. "Doubt it's an emergency, but."

They hesitated. "I'm—I don't think I can. What if it's personal?"

"It's not," I said.

"If it's your mum and something private?"

"It's not," I repeated with a sigh. "And there's nothing in my life I don't feel comfortable sharing with you, so go on."

They pursed their lips and eyed the phone. "What if it's, uh, photos of a personal nature?"

It took me a moment to translate what they were saying. I snorted. "You think someone is sending me dick pics?"

"Well..."

"No one is sending me dick pics. Or anything like."

"But how can you be sure? I don't want to intrude."

I took my eyes off the road to risk a long look at Rin. "I haven't had anyone who would potentially send me 'photos of a personal nature' in two years. Trust me."

I stared at them until I saw the blush creep into their cheeks and I knew they'd done the math. *No one since you, mate.*

Sure enough, there were texts from Suraj and Will, Raphael, Daph and Mattie in the squad chat, and my girls, who reminded me to send them pictures of all the things I told them we'd be seeing on our drive to meet them in London.

No dick pics. As I suspected.

First stop on Rin's itinerary was a large, family-run farm that offered tours of their vegetable gardens and livestock. Sure, we had cows in New Zealand, but all cows were adorable. Lena and Cassidy always loved animals, but had only recently discovered where hamburgers came from, and for the past month had refused to eat any meat. So we decided to go vegetarian as a household.

It was easier than I expected because I wasn't the one making meal decisions or cooking. When we first moved in to my mum's house, right after my divorce, she refused to let me pay rent. So I employed some Rin-level sneakiness (even though it would be a number of years before I even met them) and calculated the hours of work she put into supporting me and the girls—cooking, cleaning, brushing hair, home repair, lawn care, etc. I presented my findings to her and announced I would be paying her $200,000 a year to cover all those jobs.

I'd never seen mum so angry. She wasn't doing it for the money, this was what family did for each other, she wanted to be a part of her grandchildren's lives. I told her she would always be a part of our lives, and she didn't have to perform unpaid labor for it. We went back and forth for a while until she finally agreed that we could pay rent for a fraction of what I offered to pay her for her services. I also insisted on splitting up the chores. Mum insisted on cooking for us.

So: vegetarian, thanks to mum. And I'd kept it up outside the house because I told the girls I would.

After the highland cows were the other animals, classic barnyard stock, and I was reminded of the day we went to the petting zoo near Ōhura. Bees next, and finally the gift shop. Rin bought their smallest jar of heather honey. They were going to bring it to work to try so they could get reimbursed. And if they couldn't, at least it wasn't too expensive a treat.

Not knowing if we still had an embargo on talking about their work and Raphael, I simply moved the conversation along by asking if the attached restaurant had vegetarian options. They realized I'd ordered vegetarian last night at dinner, and I told them the story of how this new facet of my life had come to pass.

But in the background, my brain kept pestering me to ask about Rin's job, and it was unrelentingly distracting. Something had changed, in a big way, but what? How? Why? And why would such a specific local tourism business send them all the way to Scotland?

I tried concentrating on the conversation, but it was a struggle. A struggle I had to relinquish halfway through lunch, when Rin began to suspect I wasn't paying attention. I'd pulled myself together by the time we were on the road again, and when we arrived at the next stop, I was completely present.

If I hadn't been, the enormous circle of dark, looming monoliths would have snapped me back anyway. I'd visited the ones in Stenness, stark but maintained. These were wild, a coven of misshapen stones sprouted out of a hill to gather for the new moon, in a circle easily fifty metres wide. Smaller rocks dotted the centre in a pattern I couldn't discern from a distance.

Rin started talking the moment we got out of the car, and I started taking and sending pics just as quickly. The site's history was as full of twists and turns and mysteries as any Shakespeare play: mistaken identity, inheritance, murder, twins, noblemen (if not kings themselves), mystical influences, a god or two. It was moody, feral, and mysterious.

"They should have used these as the model for the ones in *Outlander*," I said, running my hand over the rough surface of one of the bigger menhir. Lichen bloomed across it in greys and yellows.

"Nobody knew about them at that point," Rin said, hiking over the long, umber grass to stand beside me. The vegetation crushed under their boots released the smell of the field, dirt and loam and somehow the idea of autumn. "It was on private land that was in the middle of a property dispute. If anyone still remembered they existed, they weren't out here telling people about it."

Their eyes skimmed over the stone, and they gently brushed the divots and edges, like they were trying to memorize it.

I never thought I'd be jealous of a rock.

"You know, I auditioned for that role. The main guy in *Outlander*."

Rin's attention turned to me. *Ha, take that, ancient mysterious boulder*!

"Oh yeah? I didn't know." They smirked. "Did you get the part?"

"Yes," I said. "That's why I'm super rich and in high demand with all of the biggest studios in the world, and why I flew us to London in my private plane instead of driving some shitbox through the wop-wops of Scotland."

Rin tsked. "Mr Bean The Car hasn't done anything to deserve our scorn. He's not pretty, but he's functional."

"He's missing a backseat, a windscreen wiper, a lock, a window, and almost your entire door."

"Well, I kind of like the high-pitched whistle every time we hit third gear." They crossed their arms and looked down their nose at me. "It's like the car is singing a little song for us."

"A swan song," I muttered, looking back towards the offending vehicle.

"I'm sorry you lost the part."

"Oh, no, I didn't lose it," I said with a grin. Here was where I'd really impress them. "I had to bow out of the running. It was in the middle of one of the last rounds of *Outlander* auditions that I got the call I was going to be Wisdom Connor in the *Knuckletracker* franchise."

"No kidding?"

I nodded, all pleased with myself, and started walking towards the next stone. "I know what you're thinking. Why would I commit to something many people would call a kids' movie—at the time, you remember, anything superhero or based on comics was considered immature—when I could be the lead in a serious, romantic series that would probably demand as many years of my life?"

Rin had followed me and caught up quickly. "I could guess," they said.

I shrugged. "Well, you're brilliant and you'd guess correctly, so go ahead."

"No, no. I want to hear the story the way you tell it."

I could hardly feel the chill anymore, my happiness warming me right up.

"Location," I said. "Scotland versus Australia. Cassidy and Lena were babies, and I didn't want to be so far away from them. Especially for so long. Their mother hadn't gotten her big break yet, so she could have stayed with them alone while I was off working. But I didn't want to do that."

In 2013, Mia was still a year out from getting hired in Hollywood (costume design, it was her dream job in her dream location), and three years out from divorcing me.

"Still another country," Rin said thoughtfully. "Was there any animosity?"

Rin asking me to share something with them more personal and private than I had since we broke up? A good sign. I adjusted my glasses and ran a hand through my hair. A good sign, but still a tender subject.

"I realized later that Mia had some...resentment. From my getting hired on a big production before she did. From having to stay with the kids while I was working. We didn't have the money to do it any other way. If I had known she wanted a career more than she wanted children, I would have offered to stay home. But it was more than that. She wanted a completely different life, and she wasn't going to be happy with anything else.

"I couldn't hold it against her. Sometimes we don't know what we want until we're waist-deep in the thing we're quickly realizing is exactly *not* what we want. It sucked, my family changing in a way I wasn't expecting, but it was for the best. Mia is happier now, confident, and self-aware, and she could never have achieved any of it in our old life. It's better for the girls, too, because they know when their mother sees them, it's because she genuinely wants to see them. When she tells them she loves them, they know it's because she really does."

During the few months I was with Rin, I had never wanted to mention Mia. I had to, of course, when talking about the kids, but there was no reason to get into the past like that. The most I had said at the time was that we had wanted different things. Irreconcilable things. I'd left out the details, and I was still leaving out plenty of details.

Rin had plucked a long blade of grass from the earth and was folding it like an accordion, a gentle and rhythmic rustle and snap.

"The girls have people who love them," they said, looking up across the plain. "People they can count on. And that's all that matters."

"Yeah. There's no animosity now. Just a sort of vague disappointment. For me. Feeling like my family isn't one hundred percent complete."

"Did it ever feel one hundred percent complete?"

"Not with Mia."

Only with you.

"I know what you mean," they said. I startled, thinking for a second that they had read my mind.

"When I was staying at your place," they continued, "it felt like I was part of a family again. Since I lost my parents, my family was Mattie and Daphne and Cinnamon. Then Raphael wrote his way into Mattie's life and dragged you all too willingly with him." They looked down and scuffed a boot into the soil. "It meant a lot. Being included. Feeling...seen? I guess? And looked after. I'd nearly forgotten what being part of a family was like."

My heart opened so wide I almost fell in. Yes. Yes, this was what I'd wanted. For Rin to feel like a part of my life, my family.

What if I had said, right then, that I missed them and wanted them back? We didn't need to catch up first. They were always Rin, and I was always me. I could cup their face in my hand and pull them in for a kiss. We could stand there in the middle of this ancient circle, reconnecting, reaffirming our affection, as though those two years apart had never happened.

It would be incredibly romantic, and Rin deserved romance. But we had only reminisced about what made us great together and not the reasons we broke up in the first place. And how much had it changed, when it sounded like they were dealing with even more stressful career problems, and I continued to default to an infuriatingly laid back attitude and humor to deflect my anxiety over things I couldn't control?

I saw them, which they needed, but I had to prove to them I could be someone to rely on.

"Sometimes," I said, "family doesn't see each other very often. But they're still family." My voice cracked on the second "family" and I turned to face the stone. Too vulnerable. "Hell," I said, knowing I was saying something too flippant as I was saying it, "we fought like family."

Beside me, Rin went still, and I cringed. *Still saying the wrong thing after all this time.* When I glanced back at them, ready to apologize, they stared at the ground and crossed their arms.

"At the time," they stammered, "I was—there was—a lot of—"

"No, no, you don't have to explain, Rin. I was there, and I understood at the time, too. I—" *Luke, you muppet.* "We were being vulnerable and I got scared and so I made a dumb joke. Like I always do. Would it help to know that I get flustered around you?"

They glanced up at me, a sly look on their face. "Maybe."

I grinned. "Rin, you've got me all atwitter. Always have."

Saying it as a joke was still saying it, but without the seriousness that would make me feel exposed. I was generally charming, but I didn't flirt with just anybody. Rin knew this, or I hoped they did. Now it was up to them whether they felt the same way (pretty sure they did) and whether they wanted to do anything about it (because I sure did).

As they opened their mouth to speak—to say, obviously, that they felt the same way and let's go make out in the car—thunder cracked above us and we jumped, searching the sky that was a more sinister pewter than when we arrived.

"It was going to storm," Rin muttered.

"Mr Bean doesn't like rain," I reminded them. Their eyes went wide. "Back to the car!" I said, already sprinting towards the road. It was another half hour to the B&B, but if Mr Bean was going to act up, I'd rather he did it when we were parked at some warm accommodations and not on the way to those accommodations.

Chapter 12
October 2022
Rin

When someone traveled as much as I did, they picked up a lot of stories. The flights they were sure would be their last, the missed connections, nights spent in the shallowest slumber because the bus or train was delayed overnight and the hostels were full and a dirty corner of the station was the best available place to rest. Or simply existing as a femme-presenting person in an unfamiliar territory on their own. Traveling could be fearful.

Trying to get to our Lairg B&B before the rain started because our car was made of cardboard and vibes was more stress I'd felt while traveling in years. If either of us had known what the consequences were or how much precipitation, exactly, it took to get to that point, I wouldn't have been so worried. But my door was attached with duct tape, and a suspicious breeze beneath my feet meant there was a significant hole in the floor somewhere, but I was too afraid to look.

Luckily, much of my anxiety from this particular problem was overshadowed by picking apart what just happened at the standing stones.

When Luke and I had been a couple, circumstances out of our control accelerated what would have otherwise taken years to tell each other. I knew Luke and his ex-wife were friendly, though he would get quieter when he talked about her. I thought he was still in love with her.

But now, it sounded more like envy. Mia got to have the kind of family experience she wanted—her career above all, a new husband who supported but didn't interfere or expect much, children when she wanted to see them and never when she didn't. It meant Luke didn't get the family experience that *he* wanted: kids and a partner tied for first place in his life. Was he unable to get over the fact that Mia could never be that person for him?

Between what he said at the standing stones and what he said on the ferry about finding the right person but not the right time, I was getting the impression it was me he wanted as a partner. Like he felt that rare certainty that he'd found the person he wanted, even though he'd technically only been in a relationship with them for a few months, and that was two years ago.

Until we were safely settled in London, the best I could do was keep acting like we were friends. We *were* friends. And if he wanted to flirt, that was fine. I could match him for it. But if he wanted to go past that, we'd have to have a conversation.

Fuck, we would have to have a conversation either way.

What were the chances neither of us would push the issue before then?

***

Against the odds, we got to the guest house before the rain caught up to us, and I wondered in an off-handed way if we had used up all of our travel luck. I said a quick thanks to the unnamed travelers we prayed to earlier in the day, just in case.

Lairg was a small village, and the loch was even smaller. At first glance, there didn't seem to be any reason for me to end our day here. It was a popular local holiday village, though less so in the fall, like a smaller-scale Rotorua. With less volcano. But one odd attraction stood out, and there wasn't a chance in hell I would let Luke drive through this stretch of Scotland and not visit it.

"I'll check us in," I told Luke as we turned off the road and into the driveway of the guest house. "But it's already pretty late in the day, so if we want to see the museum, we should head over there as soon as we have the room key. We can bring in the luggage after."

"It's special enough to rush over there so we don't miss it, but not so special that you tell me what it is," Luke said, narrowing his eyes at me.

"It is so extraordinary, I could never rob you of the joy of seeing it for the first time in person." I was ready to tuck and roll out of the moving car to save time, but Luke brought me right to the door instead of parking first.

The building was a two-story home with several different styles of additions tacked on. The front room had been turned into a lobby, and I checked in with the person behind the little desk.

"I'm Marnie," she said, smiling. "You need anything, ring me or Callum, numbers are on the card. We have a full house tonight, but they're an odd sort, so you might not see them."

"Is that…something I should worry about?" I asked. My hair was down and I probably passed, but I didn't know Marnie's flavor of bigotry and "odd sort" could mean anything from my fellow Rainbow Mafia to Travellers to people who wore a different style hat than she liked.

"Bugs," Marnie said. "Some new species of insect discovered nearby. They'll likely tell you all about it, if you can find them. Came down a few days ago and have been waiting for rain to bring out the bugs. You're in the North Room. Upstairs, take a right, last room on the left. I can show you, if you'd like?"

I blushed, embarrassed to have thought the worst of her. Nerds. She was describing nerds. "Oh, no, thank you. I'll find it. We have to be somewhere now, but if I have any trouble finding the room when we're back, I'll let you know."

Luke was still waiting at the door when I came outside.

"Park it," I said to him through his open window. "We're walking, it's only a few blocks."

When he'd gotten it into an empty spot, he waved me over. "Help me with this shield against rain destruction." He unfolded the car cover with a snap, and I helped him shroud Mr Bean.

"Will we make it to your secret destination?" He asked when we started walking.

"They close soon," I admitted. "But they'll let us stay as long as we like."

He frowned. "Rin, are you banking on using my fame for leverage against these unsuspecting people?"

"Yes," I said. "But they'd want me to."

"Rin."

"You have to trust me, Luke."

Three minutes later, we stood outside a door that led to the basement of a normal-looking house in a residential neighborhood.

"Why do I feel like we're thirty seconds away from starring in a real-life Saw movie?" He regarded the door warily.

I cleared my throat and pointed to the hand-written sign hanging on the wall at eye level. Luke leaned in to read it, and sucked in his breath.

"I wouldn't have brought you here if it was unsafe," I said, putting a hand on his shoulder. "And I wouldn't have brought you here if I didn't think you'd have a good time. We don't have to go in if you don't want to risk either of those things, and I won't be upset. But I think we should at least check it out."

His reaction made me more uncomfortable than I expected. We'd just been talking about grand gestures, how he wished he was the kind of person to successfully execute one. This wasn't a grand gesture, and I wasn't saying I loved him or asking him to take me back, but it did require a lot of trust, and only someone who knew him like I did would be sure it was a good idea.

Emotions warred in his eyes, until finally he closed them and nodded.

Almost there. I said, "To quote some of our best friends, 'I need verbal confirmation.'"

Luke opened his eyes. "Let's do it."

***

"Hello?" I called out as I knocked and opened the door. I pulled two face masks from my pocket, handed one to Luke, and put on the other. A sign on the door said it was required, but I'd already read it on their website and came prepared. A long, well-lit hallway rolled out in front of us, framed movie posters lining the walls.

"Hello, come in!" Someone called from another room. "Welcome to the *Knuckletracker* Museum of Lairg!"

"Oh, these are from all over," Luke said quietly, positioning his mask and pointing to several of the posters. "That's U.K., that's Hong Kong. Italy."

I walked ahead and around the corner to pay our admission. At the makeshift booth sat a kid, giving the impression of late teens but they could have been younger, their forearm crutches propped against the wall. Despite their face mask, I could tell they were smiling, radiating enthusiasm. Next to them was an older man, their father, I guessed, by the same eyes, and he jumped up when he saw me.

"Hi there," I said, reaching out to shake the kid's hand. "I'm Rin, they/them. I'm so excited to visit your museum."

"Connor," he said. "He/him."

"Connor? Really?"

"Really," Connor's dad said, also taking my hand. "For nearly twenty years. Mitchell Thompson, he/him."

"Dad," Connor whined. "He makes the same joke every time."

I laughed. "Well, it's a good joke."

"We're always happy to meet more *Knuckletracker* fans," Mitchell said, sliding his hands into his pockets. "There's no set price for entry, it's pay-what-you-can, but we do give tickets, to keep track of the number of visitors. And all proceeds go towards Cerebral Palsy Scotland."

"I love that. Two tickets, but would you tell my friend about the charity, too? I'll go get him."

I poked my head back into the hallway. Luke was only halfway through it, stopping to look at every poster.

"Hey, mate," I said softly. "Looking isn't free. Come pay the admission with me."

"Do we leave the same way?"

Oh, he and Connor were going to have a lot to talk about. "I promise you can come back to look at them."

"And they're not closing soon? I don't want to be a bother."

"Ask them yourself."

With a sigh, he tore himself away from the memorabilia and joined me.

"This is my friend Luke Maston, he/him," I said. "This is Connor and Mitchell Thompson, both he/him."

I thought the Thompsons' eyes would pop out of their heads. Luke assessed the situation immediately, with the kind of insight that takes years of practice from thinking on his feet, ready for any change at a moment's notice.

"Wisdom Connor," Connor whispered.

"Connor Thompson," Luke replied, taking the kid's hand in both of his. "I'm absolutely honored that I have the opportunity to visit your museum. Please forgive me for arriving so close to closing time."

"Mr Maston, you can visit whenever you like," Mitchell said, wringing his hands, almost as starstruck as his son. "We'll open it for you, even in the dead of night."

"Luke, mate. Call me Luke. I'd say you could call me Connor, but that might get confusing." He pulled one hand away from the kid Connor and placed it on Mitchell's shoulder. "Rin here has only given me the barest of details about your museum, because they wanted me to be surprised. Tell me all about it, and if it's possible, I would love a private tour with your personal commentary."

For two hours, Connor and Mitchell showed Luke their collection. Connor had been eleven when the first *Knuckletracker* movie came out, and it resonated with him in a way nothing else had. It helped that he shared a name with the main character, but the story was just as important. The themes of never giving up, always having hope, taking care of each other. The limitations of one's body, testing them, acknowledging them, accommodating them. After he saw the first film, he started reading the comic books and collecting franchise memorabilia.

Thanks to social media, people around the world found out and began sending him whatever *Knuckletracker* stuff they could get their hands on. It had been a private collection until about six months ago, when Connor asked his parents if he could turn it into a museum and donate the money to charity. Luke had missed all of this because he wasn't often online. He had visited young fans before, both as his character and himself, and if he had known about Connor's collection, he would have sent in autographs or props or himself or whatever else he wanted. Mitchell explained that his son didn't want to take Luke's time away from his daughters or even the other sick kids he visited.

It was a testament to Luke's acting skills that he didn't break down and cry when he heard that. Hell, I was trying to keep a little bit of distance both physically and emotionally, and I still got misty-eyed. I well knew what it was like to believe that Luke Maston had better things to do than spend time with me.

Mats had told me Luke wasn't getting as much work lately, and she suspected it was thanks to the director he'd pissed off when he quit *Broke* in 2020. I heard the same thing from Daphne later, though she framed it as, "isn't this an interesting thing I read about our friend in the gossip magazines and has nothing to do with your relationship with him or how I think you should go comfort him in a number of fun and intimate ways I'll now list for you."

And obviously, beyond what our friends told me, I had been known to click on his IMDB page or watch his interviews on late-night shows. And despite his charming smile and easygoing attitude, I always sensed a deeper sorrow in him. It could have been projection, on my part. But it wasn't projection when Mats noticed it, or Cinnamon, or Raphael. And if they told me about it, it was because they thought I could do something about it.

Well, this was me doing something about it. Luke loved making kids happy, and showing an interest in Connor's collection would bring him joy. But Luke also loved *Knuckletracker* as a fan, and the opportunity to get into it with someone who loved it as much as he did would lift his spirits. He also needed the reminder that he made good work that people recognized and appreciated. So it was a win-win-win.

We stayed so late that the Thompsons invited us to have dinner with them, and there was no world where we declined the invitation. The food was hot and filling and perfect, especially after a week of restaurants, fast food, and snacks. Afterward, Luke autographed every single thing they asked him to sign and took a thousand photos with them. He asked them not to post any online for two days, so they didn't give away his current location.

Before we left, Luke took out his wallet and gave Connor the Wisdom Connor ID card he'd carried around with him since the first movie. Then everyone *did* start to cry. It was the perfect way to end our visit.

On the way back to the B&B, we passed the lake again, and Luke stopped to look across it. Lights dotted the far shores, and between that and the chilly night air, it reminded me of our time at the Billingstead, and the campfire by the Redgrave's cottage. I wondered if he was reminiscing, too.

"It—means a lot to me," he said, his voice gravelly, like he was still trying not to cry. He cleared his throat. "It means a lot to me that you found this place and brought me here. I feel reconnected. To something I didn't realize I had lost. I don't know who else would have been able to do this for me."

I linked my arm in his and rested my head on his shoulder. "I thought you might like to meet the only person in the world who's a bigger fan of *Knuckletracker* than you are."

He chuckled and squeezed my arm in his. We walked the rest of the way back like that, holding each other and in a comfortable silence. It had rained a bit, but the car cover seemed to have protected Mr Bean. We grabbed our bags and made our way to the room. For a full day of travel with a lot that could have gone wrong, we were lucky everything had gone right. No breakdowns of the ferry or auto or human variety, everything we'd wanted to see had been open and easy to find, and we'd gotten everywhere on time.

So of course when we finally got to our room, we discovered there was only one bed.

Chapter 13
April 2020
Rin

The three outfits I'd laid across the bed for comparison mocked me. They were obviously a metaphor, and if they were a metaphor, I knew which one I should pick: the one that represented my current, indecisive state. But I was trying to practice listening to my body, and I wasn't sure if that meant going with my first gut feeling or analyzing it for hours. Usually, I would ask Daphne to help style me. Her sense of fashion was bold and she would make sure I didn't embarrass myself. But she liked all my choices and I wanted to pick for myself, like an adult.

I'd bought the dress months ago, once I received the invitation to the Redgrave wedding. I doubted Mattie and Daphne's brother Kyle remembered who I was. My guess was that some Redgrave saw my name in the adverts I'd taken out for North Island Pinnacle Leisure on billboards and bus stops from Auckland to Wellington and it rang a vague bell that reminded them of Mattie and Daph's best friend since childhood.

Dark-purple satin dress, bodycon style, sleeveless with a square neckline. It would show off my shoulders and arms, which were looking deliciously buff. It came with a short, matching cape that Daphne loved. She said it would make a striking silhouette, and the transformation from cape to no cape would be dramatic. I liked the idea of being able to hide a little if my confidence started retreating into its shell.

On the other end of the bed was the pantsuit. I ran the risk of looking like a politician, but the expensive fabric, custom tailoring, and eggplant color did a lot to deflect that assumption. Pants felt much more secure than a skirt. Leggings would have been perfect, but the Redgraves were the poshest people I knew, and I rented holiday homes to rich people for a living. No leggings at a Redgrave wedding.

I'd found men's dress shoes in my size and they were surprisingly comfortable. I could picture myself in this outfit as easily as the dress. Besides the jacket being a little snug around my upper arms, it was a good fit overall. I'd bought a binder to smooth the front of the white button-down, but hadn't worn it yet. Today might not be a femme day, but it also didn't feel quite masc enough to require flattening my chest.

That left me with the Goldilocks outfit: a shiny, butterfly-sleeve jumpsuit in maroon (I looked great in purple). It was the perfect combination of secure pants and sleeves that would give my arms room to breathe. Bathroom would be a nightmare. I had a theory that jumpsuits were invented by vampires, because nobody who'd ever had to pee in a public restroom would happily wear a garment requiring nakedness for the task. But Luke and Raph both had rooms at the Billingstead, so I had a way to manage it in private, if it came to that.

So why didn't I pack it up and be done with it?

Luke.

He hadn't done anything to make me think he wouldn't accept me in all of my forms, in the whole week-ish that I'd known him. He'd also only seen me in my usual accidentally nonbinary outfits, the ones I didn't know I was building when I just wore what was most comfortable. But would he think the same of me in a binder? In a push up bra?

What if I brought the clothes I liked now, changed into them tomorrow for the wedding at the Billingstead, and five minutes later realized it was wrong?

Then you'd come back and change, stupid.

And draw more attention to myself.

Look, if the Redgraves do what the Redgraves always do, nobody at the wedding is going to even notice you. It's about the bride. And the gaudy display of wealth.

Luke would notice.

Yeah, he's been noticing you all week, you could show up in a potato sack and he'd think it was the hottest thing ever.

I rolled my eyes at myself. Always this war between confidence and cowardice.

"I'm going to the car," Daphne called from downstairs. "We're taking yours because the Spider doesn't have a trunk. Or backseats. It barely has front seats. So I'm going to your car, and I'm bringing the meat tray. Ha, meat tray."

"Right behind you," I said. I grabbed the jumpsuit and its associated underthings and shoes and put them in my duffel bag with the rest of my overnight stuff. Luke had offered his room in a way that made me think he wanted me to stay the night, but he wasn't super clear, and I could have heard what I wanted to. And what I wanted was to be prepared for any eventuality. Just in case. And if I put on the jumpsuit tomorrow and hated it, I would drive back here and pick another outfit. Or drive back here and stay. I'd have to see where my mood took me.

***

Luke let me change in the bathroom while he changed in the bedroom. The heels felt right, but the hair didn't, and I spent a lot of time slicking it back into a bun that made it look like a boy's short haircut from the front.

I was donning my wedding guest outfit sixteen hours early. This was exactly the type of "any eventuality" I was planning for when I packed my bag. Did I know Mattie was going to crash the wedding rehearsal to call out her childhood bully in front of everyone because the wedding the next morning might be canceled due to immediate covid-related restrictions? I did not. I only knew that when the HMA was involved, anything could happen.

With the wedding status up in the air, the rehearsal was the only time Mats could warn everyone about the bully-turned-hate-group-leader, and the only time we could all wear our fancy outfits.

I put on some eye makeup and a little bit of lip stain. Face was looking good. A few wisps of tattoos visible around the neckline. I struck a pose in the mirror to show off my biceps: the loose sleeves gave them plenty of room to do their thing, while still being a little fluttery and girly.

Butterfly sleeves, butterflies in my belly. I was matching all over the place.

"I'm ready," I said through the bathroom door. "Are you dressed? Is it safe to come out?"

"Those questions aren't mutually exclusive," Luke said from the bedroom. "But I am dressed, and it's as safe here as it was when you went in there."

I opened the door slowly. Luke faced away from me, towards the mirror, tugging at the sleeves of his jacket. The suit was the darkest black, and smooth, and cut absolutely perfectly for him. It only had one button, low, and the fit accentuated his narrow hips. He'd opened the top few buttons of the crisp, white shirt, collar falling open to a flirty but not audacious depth. Instead of dress shoes, he wore black loafers, no socks, in case anyone doubted he was a Kiwi, and the whole thing somehow worked.

He looked up in the mirror and caught my eye, and his physical presence shifted. His shoulders relaxed, and the frown of frustration smoothed out to look like...hope? Surprise?

I gave him a half-assed curtsy and put my hands on my hips. "Sorry I couldn't rise to your level of class, mate."

Instead of replying, he turned on his heel, closed the distance between us, and swept me up in a kiss. One arm snaked around my waist, pulling me against him, and his other hand started against the back of my head, but in a moment had slid so he was holding my mouth against his by the crook of his elbow.

Yes. This.

My hands moved against him without thought, grabbing just to feel him, to somehow get him even closer to me. He laid kiss after kiss after kiss on my lips, too slow and too fast, I couldn't decide. Either I wanted all of him immediately or I wanted to draw it out and savor it. Both, at once, and I blazed at the crossroad.

He made a noise, a moan, a whimper, almost too soft to hear, and that was it. I was his. I needed him.

A knock at the door, and we paused, breath heavy.

"We're heading down, mate," Raphael called.

I darted in to steal another kiss, bringing my fingers around to trace the outline of his jaw.

"Stay with me tonight," Luke whispered. The words struck me like an arrow, marking their claim on me. I repeated them to myself, in a chorus, until they reverberated through every cell of my body.

"Yes," I breathed.

"Mate?" Raph again.

"We'll meet you there," Luke growled. I giggled against his cheek.

"You'll never find it! You need to follow me!" Daphne wasn't kidding. The Billingstead campus was massive—hundreds of acres—and it would be impossible to find any single room in the main building, let alone one of the dozens of outbuildings.

"What do you think? Ten minutes?" Luke whispered behind my ear, and the shiver it caused almost dropped me to my knees.

"I'm only worth ten minutes?" I asked. He ran his lips across my temple and kissed my forehead.

"Rin, you're worth a lifetime."

"You need a map for this!" Daph yelled.

No, I thought. *This is the kind of map Luke and I will make together.*

"Two minutes," I croaked to Luke. "To fix my hair."

He brushed his fingers across my cheek and tugged at a strand that had come out. "Was this not deliberate?"

I sighed. "Two minutes for my hair, and five for Mattie's. I told her I'd make her a messy bun."

"If it's a messy bun you want—"

"Hello, are you alive in there?"

"Daph," I yelled, "give me a few minutes to finish my hair, then you can all come in and I'll do Mattie's. Just. Hold tight."

"Hold tight, messy buns, why do you have to make everything sound so sexy?" Luke nuzzled then bit my neck, and when I yelped, he laughed.

"We will pick this up where we left off," I promised, holding up one finger. "Once we've prevented Mats from getting bullied, bruised, or murdered."

He perked up at that. "She has my axe. And by axe, I mean fists."

"Fix yourself then let them in," I sighed, giving him a once-over and turning back to the bathroom. It was going to take every bit of strength I had to focus on supporting Mattie for the rest of the evening, and I cursed every one of the people who had forced her into this situation. She deserved to be free of their manipulation and scorn, and I deserved to make out with Luke Maston. Hopefully I could get both done tonight.

I'd have to wait and see.

Chapter 14
October 2022
Luke

"This is wrong," Rin said. My heart sank.

And it had an extraordinary depth to sink, too, since our visit to the *Knuckletracker* Museum of Lairg had my spirit soaring for the first time in I don't know how long.

"What's wrong about it?" The bed. It had to be. So they hadn't booked it deliberately to seduce me. They had wanted separate beds and still did.

"The website said this room had two single beds." Rin bit their lip, scrolling through their phone. Looking for the confirmation email, I'd wager. "I wouldn't have—I wouldn't have done this to you, Luke, that would be so sleazy. I'll fix it. I'll call Marnie."

"Oh." I tried to keep the disappointment out of my voice. "Well, I'm sort of drained. All the travel, all the emotions of the museum and the Thompsons. It's not like you and I are going to stay up for hours gossiping or staring into each others' eyes."

I looked up at them, trying to catch their eyes to demonstrate what we might have done.

"Not picking up," Rin muttered, tapping at their phone. "Nobody in the lobby, either. Shit. I'm sorry, Luke. I can find another place to sleep. There are couches downstairs."

"Rin, it's just a bed. I'm knackered and I'm sure you are, too. And you don't need to put physical walls between us if you don't want to be intimate. You know me. Say you're not interested, and I'll respect that."

They glanced up at me and I could see their mind working.

Oh? They *were* interested? But unsure. Ok, then I'd take the lead.

"I'm going into the dunny to change into sleep-appropriate clothing," I said, pointing towards the door of our en-suite toilet. "Then I'm going to climb into bed, meet sleep before my head hits the pillow, and spend all night happily unconscious and less happily snoring, and I apologize for that last part. You will join me at some point, but I won't know it, because I'll be asleep. You'll fall asleep, be unconscious of the whole world, then it'll be morning, and we'll both arise unmolested. I know it isn't your original plan, but is it an acceptable substitution?"

They considered it for a minute before nodding. There was definite relief in it, but if I wasn't mistaken, there was a little bit of disappointment, too. *Sorry, love. I know what your enthusiastic yes looks like, and I won't accept anything less.*

"I should go over the itinerary for tomorrow," Rin said. "Make sure I didn't fuck up anything else. And I need to write up travel tips and organize the receipts from today and email them to Bea."

Rin had mentioned work in vague terms several times since asking me not to. They hoped the journey from Orkney to London would be reimbursed if whatever they discovered was of use to...someone. Their clients? Did they have a new co-owner? Did they sell NIPL and have a boss now? My curiosity was piqued as hell, but if Rin kept getting more comfortable with me, they'd tell me at some point. Before getting to the room, I was emotional enough to talk about Raph, if Rin had brought him up.

I did as I said I would, changing into pyjama pants and a tee and getting into bed. Rin was on their laptop at the tiny desk.

"Night, Rin," I said. "If you need me awake, throw cold water on me. Not sure anything else will be strong enough."

They laughed, and a knot in my chest loosened. "If it comes to that. Sleep well, Luke."

Turned out, I couldn't do that. Not because of the dim desk lamp across the room, or Rin's tippy-tappy on the keyboard, or even thinking about the possibilities these next few days together could lead to. Rin was planning things, like they planned the trip to the museum for me because it must have been obvious that I needed to be reminded I was good at something. And that led me back to Raphael and my irrational yet understandable professional envy.

Some days, I thought the only people I could entertain were kids and their moms. Kids needed to be entertained, I knew that before I contributed to the creation of two demons of my own, and becoming a super hero for them was fulfilling and fun. The adults, though? Most of the time, I thought they liked my character, but they projected that onto me with an enormous helping of lust, which made me uncomfortable and was something I wasn't allowed to publicly suggest was inappropriate.

It was especially tough with *Knuckletracker*, because it was a superhero comic book I loved even before getting the role, and I didn't think it was just for kids. Or kids' moms. Nerds like me, lovers of stories, would appreciate it too. And they did! And I loved them for it. But with the franchise coming to a close, I'd started looking for what was next for me, and I found...not much.

It was unfair to compare my career to Raphael's. But he'd always been a soulmate, and the reason I couldn't get work now was that I'd followed his lead and quit *Broke* in 2020. We'd walked off together, but he wasn't getting the same snubs I was. Stir in his family's wealth and my financial problems, and the fact that he paid off my mum's house even though I told him not to, let it cook for two years, and I successfully baked a delicious Jealousy Cake.

Rin might not have known what exactly was bothering me, but they knew something was. I'd always felt we were connected in a way that transcended time and distance and the need to speak things aloud. How would they have found and taken me to the only location that could heal my soul otherwise?

Knuckletracker's number one fan. I wish I had known about Connor and his love for those stories earlier. He was a kindred spirit, and if he felt starstruck at all, it passed quickly, and we got right down to our favourite characters and lines and scenes and fan theories. His enthusiasm gave me permission to be the geek I always had been.

It didn't feel like enough, being there, autographing everything he asked for, taking pictures. He'd returned something to me I didn't know how to restore, and now I was all upside down and emotional about it. And when one emotion got stirred up, they all did.

I turned to the wall and adjusted the pillow, sliding my arm under it. Maybe my mind would settle down once I was sleeping. The laziest option wasn't always the worst option.

***

When I awoke, the room wasn't much different than when I fell asleep. Quiet, dimly lit—though now from the small window by the desk instead of the lamp—and the bed empty but for me. When I'd told Rin I wouldn't wake up during the night, I was trying to make them feel more comfortable about sharing a bed with me, but I guess I hadn't been joking about being exhausted. Last thing

I remembered was thinking about Rin and what it would look like to get together with them again. Woke up with them still on my mind.

The first time we kissed was the first night we slept together. Anyone outside of our relationship would think it was fast, but I'd been interested in Rin since Raphael had first described them to me. He'd been three storeys up and the sun hadn't risen yet, so there was a good chance his recollection of them included not a little of his imagination, but something about how he talked about Rin made me want to get to know them.

So we met. I made it happen. And I'd been right: immediate connection. And even though I knew I would like them, nothing about Rin was what I had been expecting. In the months after we broke up, I figured out that, while I had an idea in my mind of what they would be like, I ended up loving who they actually were even more, because they could surprise me.

Like the night we'd escorted Mattie to her brother's wedding rehearsal to support her when she confronted her lifelong bully. After Mats had said her piece, after the celebratory dinner to replenish the energy that adrenaline had consumed, and before going back to our rooms, Rin said they needed to take care of something real quick. I assumed it was related to work and the new travel restrictions due to the sudden covid lockdowns. Rin had been nonstop busy and I was happy to have even a few hours with them. But when they came to my room later, hair down and knuckles bruised, I immediately knew what they'd done.

Tired of watching Mattie do things her own way and get hurt doing it, Rin had tracked down that fucking guy and punched him in his stupid face. I asked them and they admitted to it. They said watching me stand up in the chapel and put my body between

Mattie and danger was not only the hottest thing they'd ever seen, but made them want to punish the guy physically, too.

It made me want them even more.

I thought about that night a lot. I thought about that next morning, too. Waking up entwined with someone I trusted and wanted and adored, for the first time in years. I'm no scientist, but I'm pretty sure that night changed my DNA.

Bringing my mind back to Scotland, I glanced at Rin's empty side of the bed and saw they had written me a note.

Went to run and grab breakfast. 2 hour drive to next destination, so shower and pack as soon as you're up. -Rin

I touched the words on the paper, wishing I'd had the chance to wake up one more morning in Rin's arms. There were two more nights until London. Before I said or did anything, I had to be sure. Sure I wanted to try it again with them. Sure I could give them whatever I hadn't been able to before. Sure that Rin wanted that, too.

I got up and did as the note said. When Rin returned from their run, it was with a whole tray of breakfast foods they'd gotten downstairs. We ate, finished packing, and checked out. Mr Bean started right up, Rin gave me an overview of the route, and we were off.

***

"I knew we would end up at a castle sooner or later," I said.

"Well, this is the ruins," Rin said. "So we've visited half a castle."

I picked up on a bit of exasperation in their tone. "Yes, ruins, but on Loch Ness. That gives it some extra credibility."

Rin took a few more photos of Urquhart Castle with the lake in the background. "Credibility isn't a substitute for half a castle."

They'd been distant all morning. Distracted. Had sharing a bed gotten them thinking about how we'd shared a bed in the past, too?

Whatever the reason, it certainly wasn't helped by the recognition I was getting. Even in October, supposedly the off season, the villages hosted a lot of tourists. While I never expected everyone to recognize me, the more people I encountered, the more likely I'd be approached for a picture. And after the restoration of my faith in fans and myself from meeting Connor the night before, I felt I had to oblige. I was grateful for them. And as much as I liked visiting notable castles and ruins and lakes, my connection with people was more important.

I took a photo of Rin frowning at their mobile and sent it to my girls. *Leave it to Rin to spend their time at Loch Ness worrying about how to get your dad to the next stop on the list,* I texted. *You can't take me anywhere!*

"Ok." I stepped closer to Rin. "What's gone wrong now?"

They looked at me, surprised. "Nothing. We're here. Castle. Yay."

"Wow. Ok. Come with me." I grabbed their arm and gently guided them down a side path to the water. They put their phone away and didn't complain or resist.

"Can I put my arm around you like a boyfriend?" I asked. "People are less likely to intrude if it seems intimate. Though they will take more pictures of us." They shook their head, but smiled, and got me in a side hug so I could put my arm across their shoulders. With only a few inches of height difference, we fit against each other perfectly.

We found our way to a viewpoint on the shore and sat at an empty bench.

"I didn't realize it would be this busy." Rin sighed. "The *Knuckletracker* Museum was different. I should have called ahead, here. They might have offered to give you a private tour so you'd miss the crowds."

"This is fine," I said, making a turtle face. We'd dated during the lockdown, so Rin had no frame of reference for what it was like to be out with me in public. They'd seen it with Mattie and Raphael, though, and they weren't a stranger to being a public face, even if being in adverts in Auckland was slightly smaller in scale. "Better than I would have expected, for a tourist attraction. And everyone's been kind. This is just what it's like. You shouldn't stress about it."

Cold lake breeze hit us, and Rin snuggled against me. "I know," they said. "But also, there's so much to do. I didn't know. I didn't plan for more than a few hours here. If we had driven through to Drumnadrochit yesterday, we would have had last night and most of today to see everything."

And that would have solved the bed situation.

This was familiar. Rin would get in their head over the way something went wrong, and there wasn't anything I or anyone else could do to help them find a balance. Luckily, our friends were good about sending mental health reels and TikToks to our group chats, so I felt prepared. This was what happened when one hundred percent of a friend group were, as the kids said, neuro-spicy.

"I'm happy to spend time with you, Rin," I said, adjusting my sunnies that were meant more for curbing recognition than rays. The sky looked like it was going to rain again at any moment. "The castle is fun. Loch Ness is cool. I'm going to pick up some Nessie souvenirs for the girls. But more than that?" I shook my head again. "We could stay an hour on this bench talking or staring at the water in silence, appreciating the beauty of where we are, and the day would be perfect. So it's up to you, love. What do you want? Out of this place, this day. Me. And don't lie. Don't say what you think I want to hear. What I want to hear is what the inestimable Rin Butcher would choose to do today."

Rin shifted in their seat, and I eased my hold on them so they could get comfortable. The lake-and-fallen-leaves smell, stronger at the shore, was briefly overpowered by Rin's consistent but inexplicable scent of rich cocoa, and I was simultaneously soothed and aroused. Comforted and intrigued.

"I know it isn't the most exciting option," they said, interrupting my growing memory, "but I like sitting here. With you." Couldn't help it, my chest might have puffed up from the praise. "There are so many other things to do, but I'm getting overwhelmed. So, here for a bit? Then the museum? Food? Gelato?"

"Sure," I said. "Anything you want, dear."

When Rin was given time and space, the cluster of their thoughts could spread out. They'd see more clearly, breathe more easily, and generally avoid a meltdown. They were good at managing stress. But only to a point. That they seemed to be hitting that point faster now was troubling.

If Rin still hadn't told me all of their major stressors by tonight, I'd text Daphne tomorrow and bribe her into telling me. It wouldn't take much. She'd been the first to want us to get together and had never stopped her doe-eyed, unsubtle hints that we should get back together. All I'd have to say was "Rin is very stressed…" and Daph would fill me in on all the details.

Without our conversation to drown it out, birdsong filled the silence, and I listed to myself what I saw and heard: grey wagtail. Bullfinch. So many ducks. I flooded my daughters' phones with pictures. They'd tease me about it when their California time zone emerged out of bed time.

After a while, Rin opened up. Not about work or anything immediately relevant, but skipping right over the small stuff and heading straight to existential ponderings. I loved that Nessie had brought them to this place, and that Rin and I could talk about both little and big ideas without feeling self conscious.

"It's necessary to believe in something magical or unlikely," they said, "but the Loch Ness myth is so pervasive, and people keep using scientific instruments to try to find it, and that all seems like a waste of time."

"Not for the people who launched those experiments," I said. "That myth, that rumor inspired them. And if they didn't find anything this time, they still walk away with the skills to investigate other unlikely but interesting rumors, and maybe they'll find something somewhere else. It also brought in a ton of tourism. Money and business and everything needed to support it. I know you understand that part."

Not wanting them to dwell on tourism in general—a topic that would lead their brain to work and career and then spiral from there—I quickly added, "Plus, all the science in the world can't shake belief. Obviously, that can be problematic. But when it's believing a dinosaur survived and is living in a small Scottish lake? That's the definition of magic."

"What if it's not magic? What if it's just nature?"

It was a trick question, and one we both knew the answer to, having experienced it firsthand in New Zealand. "Nature is magical. And we should let it remind us of its wonder, if only to put our own, small problems in perspective."

Chapter 15
June 2020
Luke

"You've brought me here to kill me."

I put the car into park and rolled my eyes.

"That sounds like a lot of extra work when I already live on a secluded lot with a whole forest to hide a body," I told Rin. "I would have to pack up the weapons and shovels and a tarp. Then there's the risk of being seen. I know I don't come up with the most successful plans, but do give me some credit."

To be fair, I had told them our destination was a surprise. We had driven for a while and half of it was through side roads neither of us had ever traveled before. The car park was little more than a turn-off, the dirt-packed rectangle fenced off with sagging wooden beams. There were only two other cars there when we arrived, and I wondered if there was a different entrance or if we would be sharing the equivalent of a national park with two other families. No signs indicated where, exactly, we were, but plenty of posters in a multitude of warning colors reminded us not to leave any valuables in the car, as this was a high-theft location.

Where the thieves came from or hid when they got here, I had no idea. I'd lived in this region for all of my four-ish decades and had never heard of it until a few days ago. Rin had lived farther away but was in the tourism industry, and they hadn't heard of it, either. I begged them not to look it up online. There was a chance the site wasn't as awe-inspiring as the internet had led me to believe, so we left the girls at home with mum in case they'd be bored. But if it turned out to be worth it, I wanted it to be a "me and Rin only" thing.

"What's a Blue Spring, anyway?" Rin asked, glancing around the car for any valuables to put in their knapsack. "Is this going to be like that waterfall we tramped for hours to reach, and then it was the dinkiest little thing and obviously a trap to discourage tourists from reaching the actual good stuff?"

Late afternoon sun streamed through their hair, which was down, surprisingly, and shone like a dark garnet. They turned to unbuckle and the resulting puff of chocolate-scented air made me smile. At least they'd worn hiking-appropriate clothes and boots. I had tried to prepare for this outing and still ended up in jeans.

"From what I hear," I answered, "this place seems like the real deal."

Rin nodded. "Grab your valuables, mate, I heard this place is chocka with burglars."

"What?" I patted my pockets. "I didn't hear that. Are you sure?"

"What I've been told."

"Grab my valuables. Ok then." I reached over and got my arms around them. I tried pulling them onto my lap, and it wouldn't have worked anyway, but they were laughing too hard to be anything but dead weight and ended up sprawled across me. I was laughing too, the warmth and heart of the moment encompassing me. When they'd wiped their eyes and could breathe again, I rested a hand against their cheek and kissed them.

An awkward angle, so it didn't last long. Seeing them happy made me want to show them how they made me happy, too.

"We should go," they said, "before they add public indecency to the list of crimes regularly committed here."

"They should be so lucky."

For a June day, the weather was perfection. Sunny with a smattering of the platonic ideal of clouds instead of crowded rainclouds. The hills blocked whatever breeze there might have been, though the shadows they cast plunged us into a noticeable change in temperature.

We followed the dirt path to the end of the fence and the one, huge sign saying "Welcome to the Blue Spring." The image was a painting rather than a photo of the river, and we skimmed the history blurb and the bid for us to help keep this natural treasure intact.

"Well, the painting looks beautiful," Rin said, nodding towards the placard. "How far up the path is it?"

The trail cut through someone's farm, it looked like, animals out and grazing in the tall grass, birds picking their way through the mud. It turned, eventually, hugging the curve of one of the hills and disappearing into thicket.

"We've got our hiking boots," I said. "Let's tramp it and see."

"I've got *my* boots," they said. "I don't know what you're doing."

Old sneakers, as our U.S. friends called them. Obviously. I turned one out to show them off. "They're my emotional support shoes. The sign says to stay on the path anyway, I can't imagine we'll be going off-roading here."

They scrunched their face, probably thinking that I didn't plan very well, though instead of saying it, they shrugged and led the way to where the dirt trail became better defined with small grey pebbles.

I walked behind them for a bit, which was a bad idea, because I was probably missing some incredible nature while staring at Rin's incredible natural assets. Spending time together like this, exploring life side by side (or one in front of the other), was something I loved. But every time I looked at Rin, I wanted to grab them and lead them into the closest private space and explore them and us and forget about the rest of the world. Balancing the physical attraction with my desire to experience regular, everyday, mundane adult human things with them was tricky.

"Huh. Do you feel that?" We had passed the curve of the trail and were on the other side of the hill, farm and parking lot shielded by earth and dense shrubs and trees. Rin had stopped on the path, still in shadow, hands out at their sides. "It was like walking over a threshold," they said.

I came beside them and stared ahead, taking a deep breath. It was quiet in the way the forest was, sometimes, when there was water nearby and no other people. Different from my forest, though. I got chills. Whatever it was, whatever we were feeling, was specific to this place.

I had two daughters. Of course I believed in magic.

"The world we left behind is now beyond our ken," I said, channeling some dramatic wizard energy. "The world towards which we strive is wild, and fragile, our steps a heartbeat we make together, human and nature, soul to soul."

I placed a hand on Rin's shoulder, intending to punctuate the joke with a playful squeeze, but my own words got to me. Somehow I'd hit on a truth, or enough of a truth to turn me serious. Rin caught my eye, and I knew they'd sensed it, too.

"I'm ready if you are," they said.

Rin saw it first, a glimpse of movement through the brush, down below. Streaks of emerald and topaz, and low shrubs crowding the far bank all the way down to the water. They looked about to crawl through the parting of verdure like Alice in Wonderland, and I caught their elbow.

"There's a bridge ahead," I told them, pointing. "Boots or no, crushing all those plants to get closer is a bad idea."

As much as we wanted to see it (and as much as Rin was ready to throw themself down a steep hillside to get to it quicker), we didn't hurry. Part of that was knowing we didn't need to. The river was there, waiting for us, and we had no competition. The atmosphere was an invitation to match the tranquil pace.

We stepped onto the sturdy but faded bridge in silence. The river wasn't very wide, a few car lengths at most, but it felt wrong to compare something so pristine and untouched by capitalism to cars, of all things. I'd always been incapable of gauging distance and it was the best I could do.

The water was crystal clear, and we could see all the way down to the bone-white riverbed and bright green plants beneath the surface, long fronds like dill swaying gently with the current. Vegetation layered through the water and above it in different colors and textures, and that, with the water's clarity, the sun, the sky, and the angle it was viewed from, dictated whether the stream appeared clear, or bright blue, or peridot, or all at once, like the facets of a gemstone. Islands of dry, fuzzy and frilly leaves interrupted the flow, and enormous trees grew right at the water's edge, keeping it hidden from everything but the river itself.

We were mesmerized.

"This is unreal," Rin whispered. "It's so..."

"Quiet?"

"Yeah. Peaceful. Soothing."

"Restorative," I added. People were always saying that going out into nature was a healing experience. I figured that meant mentally and physically. Being away from industrialization. Appreciating birdsong and beauty. Trekking through it, working up a sweat. I'd never felt an emotional connection to nature like I did at Blue Spring. It was a psychic healing, which was an unexpected thing for me to think, because my only experience with psychic damage was in Cinnamon's online roleplaying game. Perhaps, like magic, it was based in a more inscrutable corner of reality.

"There's more to see," I said finally, taking my eyes off the flowing water. Pine needles littered the ground, but glimpses of pale gravel pointed the way on and up, a significant hike, with the walkway widening at the top of the hill. Tall evergreens dotted the high clearing, their trunks too big to wrap my arms around, but I had to try.

The river wound its lazy path below us, dividing us from the hill on the other side, the one whose shadows we walked through to travel to this sacred space. The golden afternoon light illuminated its sweater-fuzzy, impossibly green grass and spiky trees, huge white cliffs poking through like teeth. It looked like the models they'd made for *The Lord of the Rings*. All it needed was a scattered flock of white sheep. The word "idyll" snaked through my head and I thought of the light before sunset on a perfect, ancient Greek day.

The water ran faster, or so it looked from this height. The jungle pushed in on its banks and all the bright earth colors would have run together if it weren't for the stark changes in texture.

"I feel like I fell into another world," Rin said, standing beside me and taking my hand. It grounded me, their skin and heat, the small muscles pulsing to pump twice. "Like, how does this place even exist? The colors are so bright. And the water?"

"It reminds me of a jelly aquarium," I said. "Did you ever have that, as a kid?"

"No, but it sounds disgusting."

"Well yeah, as an adult. It's a dessert, too complicated to make except for special occasions, like a birthday party. A clear container filled with light-blue jelly, and different sweets stuck at different heights, like Nerds or jelly beans for sand, gummy fish and sharks swimming in the middle. Sometimes a stray gummy bear or worm for an underwater explorer or electric eel."

Rin raised an eyebrow. "That's what this place reminds you of?"

"We can see everything in the water, every little leaf on every piece of kelp, or whatever that is. It looks frozen in time. But then you look closer, and it jiggles a little, and everything moves."

"I think it looks like a dreamscape," they said. "Something that someone painted but is too beautiful to actually exist. A little bit of surrealism."

It did feel surreal. And overwhelming. If it really existed—and it obviously did—it made my dumb little human problems seem absolutely insignificant in comparison.

The river went on, and its surroundings and the path, but didn't beg interaction. It wasn't a place for climbing, or running, or setting roots. It wasn't a place for argument or violence. A yell wouldn't be out of place, as long as it was one of joy, the exuberant celebration of being alive, the blood in our veins an unplanned sympathetic magic to the constant but unhurried spring.

It was a place to witness. A place to stand and let wash over us, in its unbothered pace, like the river flowing through and around the lengths of plants, leading them in a dance that had gone on for ages and if left undisturbed would go on for ages more. And like the plants, we were cleansed, by the caress of its always-moving energy.

"Maxfield Parrish," Rin said. We stood on a wooden walkway jutting out over the water, farther on, once the hill on this side swooped back down to water level. Birds darted close to us, fast and blue, upset we trespassed into their territory, and me only a little upset I couldn't identify them. The tui and fantails I knew, and a pūkeko that I would have taken a hundred photos of, if I hadn't wanted to keep this place just mine and Rin's.

"That's funny," I murmured. "I thought it looked like Greece, even though I've never been there and I'm sure this place is unlike anything else. But now it reminds me of—" I broke off. This was a land of natural beauty and wonder, and so far I had compared it to autos, a kid's dessert, and now, a cartoon. I sighed. "*The Little Mermaid*. In the lagoon."

Ducks on the far shore quacked, like they could hear me and took offense. Paradise shelducks. Rin laughed, and it echoed over the river. "I see it," they said.

"I like your comparison better."

They took a deep breath and stretched their arms out over their head. "It's fantastical, isn't it? A holdover from when the world was new."

They looked up to the sun, close to setting but not quite there yet. "I know I said I felt something when we first got here. I thought I'd have shaken it off by now, but it's only grown. This all feels…ancient. I think you named it when you said it was restorative. It feels right, and big, and puts my life in perspective. Not in a scary way. But in a, I don't know, a hopeful way? If that makes any sense."

Yes. "It feels like I was called here, to remind me to slow down and that most of my problems aren't that important, in the grand scheme of things."

Hours had gone by, and we had passed them quietly, not even taking photos, or videos that definitely would have made it into the documentary. We felt innate respect: whatever drew and kept us here was powerful, a force of nature, and we sort of forgot about everything outside the boundaries of this place once under its spell. Not completely, not one hundred percent, but when a thought came, I let it go with the current. It felt like what people always wanted me to do in meditation but I could never figure out.

Rin must have felt similarly, because they were more relaxed than I'd ever seen them. Posture open but strong, sure of themself. No lines of worry creasing their face—though I loved every line, I hated what caused them—no stress bunched in their shoulders, no thoughtless fists.

First time ever I was jealous of a damn *location*. I wanted to make Rin feel that way. Not just in the middle of nowhere, with awe-inspiring scenery, no responsibilities, and zero other people. I wanted them to feel this secure, this confident and happy, every moment of their life. Whether watching a movie or in the middle of a shitstorm at work. They were smart, and compassionate, and could think on their feet, and I needed someone like that. And I wanted to be that person for them.

I took a breath to speak. If I told them I loved them, would they think it was the charm and novelty of this place, influencing my emotions? We hadn't known each other that long. Would they think it was too soon for me to feel this way?

"And somehow we're alone," Rin said, before I could say anything. "So whatever magic called us here must be keeping others away."

Yeah, I was influenced by the magic, but I was influenced by Rin's magic more. "It turns away the eye of Sauron," I said instead. *Coward*.

They snorted and wrapped an arm around my waist. I hugged them back. "You're such a nerd," they said, a mischievous glint in their eye that I recognized from so often having the same glint myself. "Hey. Wanna recreate that lagoon scene?"

"Without boat but *with* kissing?" I moved my hand up to cradle the back of their head.

"Mmm," they answered, "right here with what we've got. I think that's enough."

I grinned and guided their other hand around my hips, leaning in to kiss them. "What we've got is perfect."

Chapter 16
October 2022
Rin

By the time we closed in on Inverness, I knew the day was a bust. I had suspected as much at Loch Ness, but Luke distracted me from my gut feeling by reminding me that none of our problems were life-and-death (yet—we still had a ways to go, and Mr Bean could cark it at any moment). We were feeling pretty good when we got back on the road. With a three and a half hour drive to Edinburgh, barring disaster, there would be a healthy buffer of time between arriving at the hotel and the dinner reservations I'd made. The hotel was booked, and with two single beds this time, for sure. I had called them and confirmed.

Sharing a bed with Luke was terrible for my emotional state, but great for my physical comfort. That was part of why my emotional state was so fragile.

Luke's phone pinged in the cup holder, but he didn't seem to hear it. He peered ahead, down the line of brake lights, drumming his thumbs against the steering wheel. So far, none of the texts he'd gotten had been romantic in nature, which I'd feared, which was stupid of me because if I wasn't going to claim him, I had no right to be upset someone else might. Once again trying to apply logic to my heart. I should have known by now that it never works.

"You want me to check that?" I asked.

"Huh?" He turned to me with a smile.

We're stopped, you should climb on top of him and kiss him like you've missed him for two whole years.

"You got a text," I said, blushing.

"Oh. Was it Cass?"

"I didn't answer it. Since the car is stopped, I thought you might want to look for yourself." Was he bored? Was I boring him? Was he upset about the traffic? "What were you thinking about?"

He stopped drumming long enough to pick up his phone and look for himself. "Hmm," he mused. "Lena got up early and surrounded Cass with watermelons in her bed. Couple of weirdos."

He turned the phone to show me the photo. Cassidy was asleep, curled up completely under the covers except for her hair splayed and tangled cross her lavender pillow. Seven mini watermelons nestled close around her. The minute she moved, watermelons were going to start splatting against the floor.

"Clever," I said. "Shows dedication to her craft. What time is it there?"

"God, I don't know. They're in Los Angeles with Mia and Hank. Five? Six in the morning?" He slid the phone back into the cup holder. We progressed a few car lengths just to stop again.

"Do you think monkeys are happy?"

It took a moment for my mind to switch over from Los Angeles and time zones and the kids. "What?"

We pulled forwards again. "You asked what I was thinking about. I was wondering if monkeys are happy."

"Like, in general?"

"Yeah. Obviously not the ones in captivity. But the ones out there in the jungle or natural habitat, chilling, living out their little monkey lives without human interference."

It was a silly question, and a serious one. Luke did that a lot. It may have started as a passing thought, but it had stuck in his mind well enough to become a mild hyper-fixation. A curiosity he shared with his daughters, and if it was sometimes annoying, it was more often endearing. People shared a lot of themselves through these kinds of random thought experiments.

So we talked about monkeys. And the traffic dispersed. Before we escaped from the outskirts of Inverness completely, Luke asked if I was sure I didn't want to stop there.

I shook my head. "I spent five days here for a conference before making my way up to Kirkwall. It's a lovely city, but tainted with the memories of work."

He glanced at me like he was waiting for me to say more. I would have loved to look out my window and away from him, so he couldn't try to guess my emotions by looking at my face, but the plastic sheet subbing for the glass wasn't exactly transparent. I could look out the rear side window, but that required reclining my seat, and I was told there was a chance it would never get back into an upright position once it got a taste for the horizontal life.

I'd never related to a car more.

Luke inhaled weirdly, like he was considering saying something. I'd asked him not to bring up my job, and he'd been respectful of it so far. Thing was, if he asked me, I would tell him. Everything. And I would cry, and be totally vulnerable, and he would be sweet and understanding, and then I'd try to kiss him and we both knew where that would lead.

"I'll tell you," I said, surprising myself. Surprising him, too, by the look on his face. "Not now. Not while we're driving. But it keeps coming up, and I know you're curious, and it feels unfair to keep it from you if I'm going to be mentioning it. It's hard not to, you know. Work is a major part of our lives."

It shouldn't be, though. More and more, I thought I shouldn't have put all of myself into the business. Years and energy. It shouldn't have taken time that I could have given to family. I wondered a lot what my life would be like now if I had sold NIPL as soon as it started to collapse. It was scary, at the time, to think about having to start over. And to lose something that had been so important to my parents.

But if I'd done it, I could have lived off the profit for a couple years. Committed to Luke and the girls, if that's what I wanted (*yes, that's what you wanted*). Learned a new skill. Maybe gone back to school. At this point, I felt too old. And I'd made all the wrong choices, lost two whole years, all my savings, and an entire goddamn business.

"Work is a major part of our lives," Luke agreed. "And your job seems to include travel, and we're traveling, so it's hard to avoid. But it upsets you. And I don't want to do that."

"I know you don't."

We jumped back on the A9 after taking a detour through town, and the shift from city to country was stark. We had hardly left behind the dense, dark buildings before we were driving past flat fields of grazing sheep. The grey of the sky deepened, and we had a good ten minutes of panic where we thought it was going to downpour, but fortune favored us, and we once again avoided the mysterious consequences of Mr Bean getting caught in the rain.

Three hours of driving required food and bathroom breaks, and when that time was extended by unexpected traffic, those breaks were even more necessary. The drinks and candy bars from Scrabster were getting low and we hadn't picked up more, but I had thoughtfully included a food stop between Inverness and Edinburgh. It wasn't much more than a little roadside stand, but it had a bathroom almost as highly rated as its meat pies, so it was perfect.

Or, it would have been perfect.

Technically, it was off-off-road, a slight detour from the highway that wouldn't add much time to the drive. Dense trees stood on one side of the street, a clearing on the other, empty except for the small building that was little more than a shed. A level patch in front of it was paved with gravel and empty of cars. The sign by the road should have been illuminated, which would have been helpful in the growing gloom, but there was no power to it.

"Uh," Luke said as he turned into the car park. "Did you bring me here to murder me?"

"Shit," I said, unbuckling even though my gut told me it was useless. "They're supposed to be open. I'll take a look around."

"I'm going with you," he said, putting Mr Bean in park.

"Because you're afraid you'll be murdered if you stay alone, or because you're afraid I'll be murdered if I go alone? Is this a *Jurassic Park* situation?"

He gave me a look as he unclicked his seatbelt. "It's *always* a *Jurassic Park* situation, bro. That's the whole point of the film."

Once we investigated the darkened shed, I almost wished there were dinosaurs. Would have beat driving out of our way for nothing. The running would have been a good way to stretch, too. Get some energy. But all we found was the little building, all closed up, for an emergency or for the day or for the season, I didn't know. The bathrooms to the side of the storefront were locked, but after all that time sitting in traffic, it was either break in or use the scary forest on the other side of the road.

"Are there cameras?" I asked, looking around. I didn't see any. I would slide a fiver through a crack in the door anyway, in case they had to replace the lock.

"Got it," Luke said. He stood up and pushed the door open, using his phone's flashlight to peek inside.

"Did you just pick that lock?" I asked. I'd been prepared to do it myself. Better for me to be caught than Luke. He had a family to provide for and a career requiring a decent reputation. Then again, I thought of all the well-known actors who committed breaking and entering, drunk driving, domestic violence. Forced entry to use a bathroom without destroying any property might not even make the list.

He smirked. "One doesn't fraternize with Daphne Redgrave without picking up a few tricks. Besides, how else am I going to impress you, if not for my espionage skills?"

I don't know, maybe with literally everything else about you?

"I'll go first," he said. "In case this is the reason they closed for the day."

"Because of dirty toilets?"

"Or they're inoperable and couldn't be fixed. I'll let you know. You stay here and watch for dilophosauruses." He disappeared behind the closing door.

"A lookout for dinosaurs," I muttered. "Sure." I'd played this role before, but it was usually for security guards or another human who might snitch. I checked my mobile, but the one tiny stub of a bar wasn't enough to connect to anything. Without that distraction, I turned my pee dance into squats and stretches while I waited.

Luke returned moments later and gave the place his stamp of approval. No electricity, but otherwise perfectly functional, clean, and not scary. He was supposed to be my lookout in turn, but when I exited and clicked the lock back into place, he was standing by the ordering window, writing on something at the counter.

"In case there are cameras we missed?" I asked.

He shook his head. "No." The note said we used the toilets and were sorry to have missed their meat pies, and he folded it around a ten note and pushed it under the crack in the window.

I laughed. "I was thinking of doing something like that, too."

"Of course you were," he said with a smile. A strand of his hair had escaped and fell over his eyes, reminding me of a nineties heartthrob. He flipped it back out of his face with a shake of his head. "You love keeping the scale balanced. And if it means taking care of people, all the better."

Is that what I did? Luke was the one leaving the money, did that mean he also tried to act fairly? How similar were we, exactly?

"Well, thanks for the assist, then," I said. "On the balancing act. With the money. But I'm afraid I've failed the taking care of people, what with the lack of food."

A shrug I should have expected from Luke. So easygoing. Arguably too easygoing.

"You said you made dinner plans. I can wait. Or there's always petrol station snacks."

I grimaced. "I don't know if I can do any more Starbars."

"Then let's go." He pushed himself away from the counter and walked towards the car. "Get to Edinburgh fast. See if they can seat us early."

We did not get there early. We did not get there on time. Whatever had caused the traffic earlier in the day had continued it, and on our exact route. Three hours after the detour to no meat pies, the app said we were still over an hour away from our destination.

Luke wasn't showing any sign of irritation. The cellular connection was good enough for him to get a couple texts from his daughters, and I was happy to relay his replies. Mia texted once, asking for details about the premiere Thursday night. Luke asked me to forward an email to her and let her know. Raphael texted a couple times, and since Luke told me not to reply at all, he started texting me on my phone.

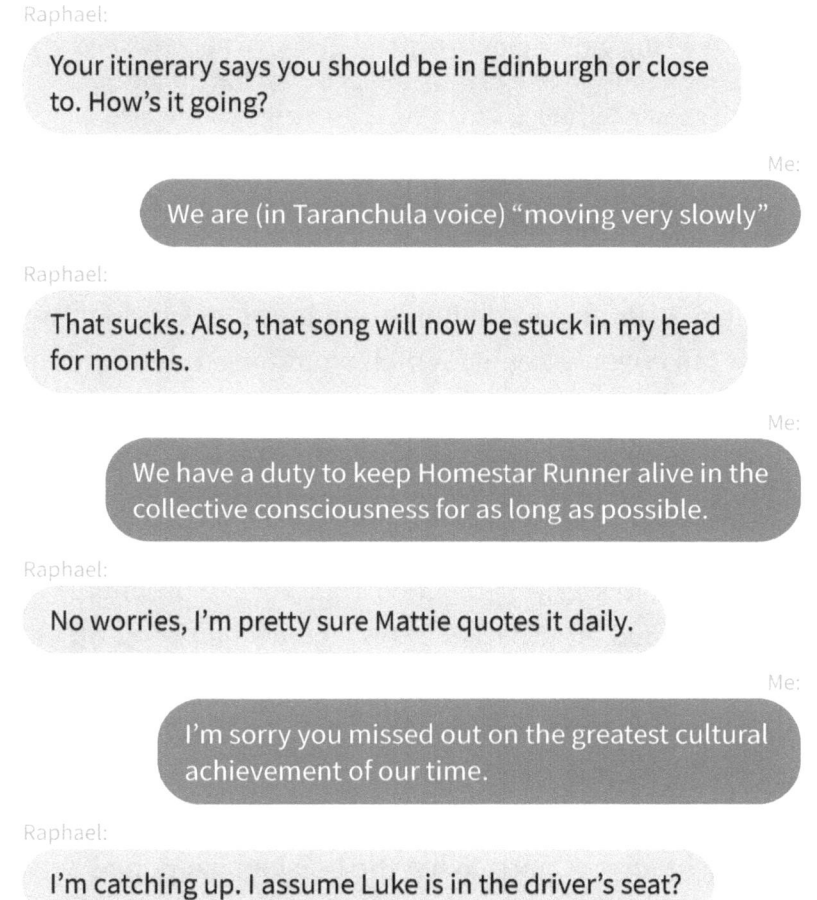

Raphael:
Your itinerary says you should be in Edinburgh or close to. How's it going?

Me:
We are (in Taranchula voice) "moving very slowly"

Raphael:
That sucks. Also, that song will now be stuck in my head for months.

Me:
We have a duty to keep Homestar Runner alive in the collective consciousness for as long as possible.

Raphael:
No worries, I'm pretty sure Mattie quotes it daily.

Me:
I'm sorry you missed out on the greatest cultural achievement of our time.

Raphael:
I'm catching up. I assume Luke is in the driver's seat?

I glanced up at the man in question. The radio didn't work, but he was bobbing along to whatever was playing in his head. I wondered if it was somehow the Taranchula song.

> He is, and he's doing a commendable job. Did you need to talk to him?

Raphael:
> I texted him, but he didn't respond. Not an emergency. Just wondering if he has something to wear for Thursday or if I should tell my guy to bring some options in his size.

If Luke hadn't wanted me to respond to Raph's texts before, there was no reason to believe he'd want me to now. The difference was that Raphael was bothering me to get to him, or that was how Luke would see it. Which would make him even more irritated at the unsuspecting Englishman.

But if I was going to open up about my number one problem, I would want Luke to do the same. He could only do that if I gave him the chance.

"Raph wants to know if you need a suit for the premiere," I said. We were stopped on the road again, like we had been off and on all afternoon. Though it was getting into evening now.

Luke shifted in his seat and looked to his phone, still in the cup holder. "Is he texting *you*, now?"

"You haven't answered him. I told him you're driving and can't."

He thought for a minute. What the hell had happened between them? Raphael didn't even seem to know Luke was upset with him. He was a good enough actor to fake it, and a good enough friend not to try.

"I don't need his help. Don't text him that." Luke ran a hand through his hair and sighed. "Tell him I'm all set."

Me:

> He's got it covered. But personally I think more options would be nice. As long as it doesn't cost anything extra. Don't tell him I told you to do that. You know he doesn't like accepting help.

Raphael:
> Yeah, sounds like someone else I know.

Me:
> I'm working on it.

Raphael:
> We do it because we love you.

Me:
> Ug ok dad, I know.

Raphael:
> Should I ask for some options in your size, too?

Me:
> I may have packed light, but I packed thoroughly. I am well prepared and have an outfit, but thank you.

Raphael:
> Sure, let me know if you change your mind. Hey unrelated topic. Have you noticed Luke acting strange?

Bold of him to think I would know. Raphael had to have seen Luke more recently and frequently than I did. But. This was an opportunity to try to get the story from Raphael. I didn't spend my whole life solving mysteries and causing mischief with my friends to not investigate.

Me:
Yes. But I haven't seen him in a while. How do you think he's been acting differently?

Raphael:
Well, for one, he's not answering my texts.

Me:
He's driving.

Raphael:
When he's not driving. Or if it is only when he's driving, he must have a new job as a long haul trucker, because he very rarely replies.

Me:
Work?

Raphael:
He replies to Daphne. And Mats. And his mum.

Me:
You've asked Ann about it? Must be serious. What did she say?

Raphael:
I expected his mother to act like mine and be overprotectively suspicious, but she seems to think he's worried about money and getting good work. Same things he's been worried about for years.

Me:
That sucks.

Raphael:
It does. Good thing some kind-hearted person paid off their house, huh? One less thing to worry about having money for.

My stomach did a little flip. Did he know for sure it was me? Nobody was supposed to be able to trace that money trail. I doubt Raph figured it out all by himself. Daphne would, if anyone. People thought she was flighty and impulsive—and she was. Oh, she was. But she was also very good at her investigative job. The question was whether she had shared her suspicions.

Raph hadn't come out and accused me. Just hinted at it. Which meant either he wasn't one hundred percent sure, or he wasn't sure he was supposed to let me know that he knew. I'd have to use that to my advantage.

> Me:
> We get it Raph. You're rich and you're a good friend. Don't suppose you want to pay off my mortgage, too?

> Raphael:
> Send me the details. It'll be fully yours by tomorrow.

I should have known better than to ask him for something so meaningful that he could easily make happen. Luke had been talking about how I like to keep the balance. I'd sold my house a few months after I paid for Luke's, for funds I was sure NIPL would soon regain but never came. I lived in a cheap flat now, but the idea of owing someone the cost of a house made me uncomfortable. What would it take to repay someone not only the dollar amount, but the emotional value of that feeling of security?

Hell, that was why I paid for the Mastons' house as anonymously as possible. Shell corp in an LLC in a DBA or something like that. My real estate wizard at the time had set it up, and I didn't know the details, but it was some kind of Russian-nesting-doll style business venture. I was assured it would take a *lot* of digging to trace it to me, and I was counting on Luke's ADHD to make sure he didn't get that far.

Because if he knew it was me? He'd feel like he owed me. And I didn't want to wonder, any time he was kind, if he was doing it because he liked me or because he wanted to even the score.

Also, I loved him. That didn't stop when we broke up. He didn't deserve my love any less just because we were apart. He was going to lose the house. I wasn't totally financially stable, but I had savings, and what else was I going to do with it (*oh sweet, younger me, if you only knew what the future would bring*). I didn't regret it. I only wished my own situation had turned out differently.

Me:
> I know you're serious, and I appreciate it. But I think you know I can't let you.

Raphael:
> It's all good, mate. I have a decade of practice getting rejected in this kind of thing by Luke. You know you're infuriatingly similar, yeah?

Me:
> So I've been told.

"Are you still talking to him? What's he saying?" Luke craned his neck to see my screen, and I jumped.

"Yeah. He was talking about the premiere and then you and then your mum."

"He's talking about my mum? What's he saying?"

"Nothing bad, just that he talked to her the other day."

"Why is he talking to mum?"

I rolled my eyes. "Because your friends care about you and they like your family and they're very personable and charming, and you should be used to it by now."

He settled back with a huff.

"But you're right," I said. "I'm being rude, texting him and ignoring you, when you're the one doing all the work right now. Let me say goodbye and then I can give you my full attention."

"I'm getting off the next exit," he said. "I need to eat something, and we might as well fill the tank. Who knows how long this hour drive to the city will take? We might live on the highway now, so we should stock the pantry."

I texted Raphael that I was going to put my phone away and asked him to let me know if he could think of any other reason why Luke would be distant with him. With my itinerary getting bulldozed by a traffic jam, I had other things to worry about. There'd be plenty of time later to get to the bottom of what was bothering Luke.

Chapter 17
October 2022
Luke

I'd rarely seen Rin out of emergency mode in the hundred and forty-six total days we'd been in each other's physical presence, and today was no different. The trip wasn't going as planned. Not a huge problem for me, whose idea was to just get in a car and drive, but slightly more frustrating for Rin, who needed to feel a modicum of control over any given situation.

I wondered if it would help if I let them take the wheel.

But then I wouldn't have an excuse not to text Raphael, and even though nobody would know it but me, I would rather not have to lie.

He and Rin had texted for a while. Was it paranoia to think they were talking about me? Well, no, because Rin said they were. But what *about* me? Pretty sure neither of them knew what was upsetting me. Ah, so they were speculating?

Come on, bro, let it go.

Rin saying they'd tell me why they were so upset about their job was shocking. Trying to get information out of them was practically an Olympic sport. The verbal acrobatics, strategizing, body mirroring. I nearly broke a sweat any time I thought something was bothering them. They were worth it, but the trick was in making *them* believe in their worth as much as *I* did.

One of those tricks was making sure they were never too hungry. I'd like to credit that one to having children and needing to predict what might send them into a tantrum, but honestly, it came from looking within and taking note of what I needed to not pack a sad myself. Most of the time, it came down to snack or nap. Neither of those were enforceable, but I could make sure Rin had the options available to them.

And that meant getting off the highway-turned-car-park and throwing ourselves at the mercy of the unknown.

Or, in this case, a petrol station.

I'd been on the lookout for one for close to an hour—or, thanks to traffic, about six kilometres. I couldn't see what was causing the backup, and Rin couldn't find anything on their phone about it. I wasn't the only one who was impatient, hungry, or low on petrol, and we pulled into a crowded four-pump BP with a dairy only slightly larger than the abandoned meat pie shed.

"You can run in and grab something to eat," I said as I pulled into the queue. "I'm off the *Knuckletracker* diet, so I'm not picky."

"It's my turn to pump," Rin muttered, eyeing the cars in front of us. "Looks like everyone had the same idea."

"We've been idling for hours. I'm surprised there's any left. In Mr Bean and also for sale. Oh god, what if there's no petrol left to buy?"

Rin huffed and leaned over to look at the gauge. "Half a tank. Enough to get us to the next station if there's none here, which, doubtful. Cars would leave immediately and we wouldn't be waiting for an empty pump."

"And where is the next station?"

"Far away," they conceded. They pursed their lips and adjusted their glasses. "It'll be fine."

It'll be fine? Ok, they must be really hungry, if they stopped caring about the details. One less schooled in the ways of Rin might think this was a hack, a shortcut to mellowness. It wasn't. It was a trap. And on the other end: Phase Two. That anxiety that seemed to be defeated? Returned, bigger and badder than ever.

"You're right," I said with award-worthy enthusiasm. "It will be fine. All of us will get fueled up and we'll be in Edinburgh in no time. The absolute worst thing that could happen is we run out of gas and have to sleep in the car. Nothing a short phone call can't fix. It's not like we're lost in the woods with no mobile service or shelter. Look at all the people around us!"

I gestured towards the world awaiting us out the windscreen, including the now-empty spot I pulled into. "I'll get us food," I said. I put the car in park, unbuckled, and grabbed my phone. "You get us petrol. Meet back here in a few minutes. Go team!"

I didn't stay to hear their response. I needed to provide for my Rin. I was on a quest.

The overflowing car park should have been enough of a clue to what I would find inside the shop. But I had been thinking of too many things at once, and neither that nor my eventual hyperfocus left any room for new information. So I walked in expecting to find some bags of crisps, lollies, a sandwich or two. What I found were clerks so harried and shelves so empty it could have been a reenactment of the post-apocalyptic pilot I'd done a few years back.

Unfortunately, I had been trained to fight zombies in this situation, not regular Scottish humans who were far too polite and sentient and not thirsty for brains to use any of the moves I knew.

What I should have done was left. Instead, I took photos of the mild carnage and a video of myself in front of the empty shelves, pretending my voice echoed in the cavernous space. That one went to the girls, and I giggled as I sent it.

Rin was sick of Starbars. All for the better, because there were no Starbars left. It was fate. I grabbed a couple of chocolate bars with dried fruit in them, and a chocolate bark whose wrapper hadn't been updated since the 60's (or the dairy had been trying to sell that one bar since the 60's). Cola in abundance. The only crisps left were pickled onion or masala, which sounded interesting but they must have been the only ones left behind for a reason. I picked up two bags.

We were going to miss the dinner reservations. Eventually, we would eat, unless Rin ate absolutely nothing between now and then, in which case they would choose sleep over food, and I hated to think of them so downtrodden. So, with what would turn out to be far less scrutiny than the situation demanded, I also scooped up two sad-looking egg sandwiches and a tray of sushi.

"You're so popular today." I gave the clerk my best smile as I laid my hard-gathered food on the counter. She was not impressed. Eh, sometimes a little bit of charm can brighten someone's day. Other times, it's a retail worker who's underpaid and stressed to the point of tears, and they need something much stronger and longer-lasting than a wink from Luke Maston.

Back at the car, Rin stood by the passenger door. We tried not to open or shut it more than necessary, since we didn't know how much work the duct tape was doing to keep it attached. I offered them my shirt-basket of goodies, and they eyed everything warily as they took my scavenged treasures one by one and stashed them in the reusable bag we'd been keeping the snacks in.

"Sushi?" They asked, holding it up and shaking it for emphasis.

"And sandwiches, and the least gross chocolate I could find. I don't want you to go hungry, and, as you said, everyone had the same idea, so the choices were this or nothing. Literally. I'll show you the photos I took."

"Of course you took photos." They got into the car with a grumble and I shut their door—not too forcefully, not too softly—and returned to the driver's seat.

"It might be better if we take a less direct route," Rin said, sounding as if they were admitting defeat.

"No worries, mate. Take me on the Tiki tour."

And that's how we ended up arriving in Edinburgh four hours late. Four hours, two detours, one almost-not-gross bag of masala crisps, two egg sandwiches, one fruit-filled chocolate bar, and one tray of sushi (that one was all Rin) before arriving at the very normal-looking hotel that did have—at Rin's insistence—two very single beds.

I understood why they wanted separate beds. They were still in love with me, obviously. Obvious because I was still in love with them, and they were acting like I would if I were Rin and in love but with a whole lot of baggage. Not to say I didn't have baggage. But mine made me reckless. Rin's made them cautious.

Being settled for the day did wonders for Rin's mood. Since we'd eaten on the way, there was no rush to get a late dinner, and the first thing they did was bust out their laptop and review what our drive to Leeds tomorrow would look like.

"Traffic was from protests," they announced. "Organized, though. So we shouldn't run into the same delays tomorrow."

"No, we'll have all new ones."

They leveled a stare at me.

"*Jurassic Park*," I explained.

"I know." Rin closed their laptop with the sigh of the long-suffering.

"We don't have to go out," I said from my bed. I had laid out and was texting with Cassidy and Lena, mostly. Four of the watermelons from that morning had exploded when they rolled off the bed, and the weight of them and the noise startled Cass so she tried scrambling out of bed and ended up slipping in the watermelon guts. She was fine, besides a few bruises and a new vendetta against her younger sister. Raph had messaged to ask if we made it to the city yet, and I'd told him yes but barely. He started asking more questions and I had to cut him off by saying we were going out to get dinner finally and I'd see him in a few days. *No worries, bro, travel safe*. He'd said. *Can't wait to see you*. His kindness was so irritating.

"I know that too," Rin answered, running a hand through their hair. They leaned back in the desk chair so they could cross their socked feet on top of the desk. For a minute I thought they meant they, too, well knew how frustrating Raphael's friendship was. "I wish we had more time here. There's so much to do."

"Could we spend another night?"

"We could. I hate to say it—especially after only two days of relatively easy travel—but I'm sort of already burned out on the whole planning thing."

I sat up straight, my phone falling out of my hand. "Rin. Are you saying you want to—" I tapped my fingertips against my chest and glanced around the room for eavesdroppers. "—*leave things to chance?*" I stage whispered the last part.

"Let's not get ahead of ourselves," they said with a laugh. Hearing them so at ease did something to me. Something in my belly and cheeks and in my soul. "We still have a plan. But I'm tired of trying to force things into a shape they can't be."

This was certainly new. I wondered if they were feeling ok. I scooted to the end of the bed and swung my legs over the side, right near their desk chair.

"For the trip?" I asked, setting my elbows on my knees and adopting a very relaxed but interested position. "Or for life in general?"

They looked at me, straight on, for the first time in maybe a year. Every other glance had been at an angle, coy, guarded, or a stare that clearly meant "be for real." Now, they looked right into me. It felt like judgment. I suppressed a shiver. They might be shit at assessing their own strengths and shortcomings, but they sure as hell could pinpoint them in everyone else, with an accuracy, depth, and speed that would have gotten them burned at the stake in a different century.

"Both," they eventually admitted, with a quick smile before glancing away. "Might be my only option at this point."

I believed them. They would have already tried everything except accepting that they couldn't control what was causing them stress. My bet was on NIPL, and Rin seemed almost comfortable enough to tell me about it.

"Did it ever get better?" I asked. I looked at the floor as I spoke. Rin could only let themself be vulnerable in one way at a time, and if I wanted answers to their emotional state, it would help if they knew I wasn't physically perceiving them.

I doubted they'd talked to anyone about it, because if Mattie or Daphne knew that Rin was this upset, they would have brought me and Raphael into a conversation to brainstorm how we could help them. We were all pretty shit at caring for ourselves, but by god, we knew how to rally for each other.

"For a while. It got better for a while." They started picking at the corner of a notebook on the desk. "Then it got much worse."

I'm sorry, I wanted to say. *I could have been with you, even if I couldn't have helped, tell me everything.*

"Actually, I—" they cut off suddenly and moved their feet from the desktop to the floor. "Oh."

"What?" A revelation? A memory? They looked nervous. Pale. A haunting?

"Oh. No." They stood up and put their hand over their belly. "Egg sandwich was a bad idea."

I rose, too, and reached for their shoulder. Those sandwiches did look sus, and who the hell gets sushi from a petrol station? Panicked me, that's who. Should have stuck to crisps and chocolate. "It's ok if you have to throw up. It's nothing to be embarrassed about." I'd taught my daughters that too well, and they had no shame vomiting wherever they happened to be. "I've seen it all. I can hold your hair back."

"I'd rather you go far away and put on headphones." They were sweating now.

"I have no gag reflex, grew up with dogs, and have two children prone to illness and eating things they shouldn't. I'm not going to leave you alone to chunder."

"Worse than that," they said, before running to the toilet and shutting the door.

"Rin," I said from the bedroom, trying to talk over whatever sounds they might not want me to hear. "I'm gonna stay right here in case you need anything from me. My offer to hold back your hair still stands. Glass of water, something to settle your stomach. I can even go out and track down some medicine or ginger chews or peppermint. You can text me instead of yelling, whatever you—"

Something deep in my abdomen churned, and it was like flipping a switch from totally fine to vomit sweats. Except it was too deep to be just vomit.

I looked around the room, frantically, like there might have been a second toilet I'd missed. It was the egg sandwich after all. I had been betrayed.

"Text me, I'm going out," I yelled, my voice way too high to cover up my panic. There was a single toilet by the front lobby, and I grabbed my phone off the bed on the way out the door. By skill or by luck, I made it in time, but it didn't take long for me to realize I wouldn't be able to make it back up to the room for a long while.

Me:
So. How's it going.

Rin:
please tell me you haven't heard a damn thing

Me:
I have honestly heard nothing.

Rin:
Thank you. If you want to go out, don't feel bad about leaving me behind.

Me:
Bro, I too have been betrayed by our snacks. Who could have known that dodgy petrol station sandwiches were a bad idea?

Rin:
Oh no. Wait, where are you?

Me:
Toilet by the lobby.

Rin:
yikes.

Me: I'd cross my fingers that nobody recognized me and nobody's waiting for this toilet but trying to do anything besides sending a little message to you and remaining upright is too much effort.

Rin: Lie down, mate.

Me: That sounds like admitting defeat.

Rin: Embrace it. Hold on

Me: I'm confused, should I hold on to my dignity or embrace lying on the floor?

Rin: …

hold on because I needed to do something else for a minute. I'm too exhausted to care what you do.

Me: I'm glad we can text. Then we know we're not alone.

Rin: Even though we can't do anything about it.

Me: I'm going to keep this in mind if we ever need to get information out of someone. Leave out a mayo based sandwich for a couple days and bam. The most effective torture. I'm willing to tell you everything, all my secrets, just to make it stop.

Rin:
this sounds like an opportunity I shouldn't miss, and yet I have no energy to pursue it.

Me:
Good news for you, then, because I would tell you all my secrets anyway. No torture required, all you have to do is ask.

Rin:
Remind me when I'm not crook and burning the candle at both ends.

Me:
That's not what the saying means but maybe it should be.

Rin:
I knew this trip was going too smoothly. We were due for a disaster.

Me:
It's just a setback. At least we're in shelter and Mr Bean hasn't broken down.

Rin:
Why would you jinx us like that.

Me:
If you and I can get through shared food poisoning, a little roadside trouble is nothing.

Rin:
You're trying to make me feel better, but knowing you're in as much pain and discomfort doesn't inspire the relief you think it does.

> Me:
> Well it should. Camaraderie. Now if you'll excuse me, I'm in the middle of a date with a toilet bowl and I don't think I'll be home until late, so don't wait up for me.

> Rin:
> changed my mind, I am relieved that this is happening to you too

It was a nice text, and the last one I saw before another round of sickness and several hours of absolute exhaustion that couldn't be alleviated because of my apparently bottomless stomach and intestines and my body's desire to completely clear it out over the course of a night and not all at once. At some point, I fell asleep on the floor, and I didn't wake up until Rin called me the next morning.

Chapter 18
September 2021
Rin

"Luke might lose his house."

Daphne said it so casually, between sips of her Mexican mocha milkshake, like it was some petty celebrity gossip and not a major crisis affecting one of our closest friends. Mattie rolled her eyes, indicating through sisterly shorthand that that wasn't an appropriate way to break the news to someone, but Cinnamon watched me closely to gauge my reaction.

I looked down at my own shake, a triple chocolate concoction I dreamed about whenever I wasn't in San Francisco. Deciding to visit was usually fifty percent the Honest Mischief Alliance (Redgrave sisters and Cheung) and fifty percent Shake & Quake. Late morning sun illuminated the window-side half of the booth and the sisters' similarly pale skin, and glinted in the reddish-gold highlights of Mattie's hair and the enormous blue gemstone on Daphne's finger. I'd arrived in the States the day before and my lingering jet lag made me irritable and emotional, my senses sticking on some details and blurring the rest.

"God, that sucks," I said. Cinnamon narrowed her eyes at me. "I assume the lot of you have come up with some kind of plan?"

Next to me, Mattie sighed. "Oh, we've come up with several plans."

"But we always run into a big problem," Cinnamon added.

"Yeah and his name is Luke Fucking Maston," Daphne yelled, before I could ask.

That sounded about right. That man was constantly giving of himself and aggravatingly unwilling for anyone to give *to* him. "What have you tried?" I asked.

"Raph wants to cover it. These two said they'd pay it off." Mattie pointed towards Daphne and Cinnamon with the condensation-covered glass of her milkshake. Snickerdoodle, her usual. I could smell the spices even though it was a cold drink. "He said he doesn't want anybody's charity."

"Well, he's gonna have to take it if he wants his daughters to be living in a home and not on the streets!" Daphne was all worked up. The situation must have been serious.

"Hey, Starlight, take a breath." Cinnamon rubbed Daphne's back. "We all want what's best for Luke and his family. Now we've got Rin on it too. It'll work out. Here, breathe with me."

She led Daph through a series of breaths, which seemed to calm her down.

"What happened?" I asked Mattie. I was trying to keep my own breath even, despite the pit of grey nerves lumped in my belly. Ann, Luke's mother, owned the house where he and the girls lived. Luke on his own would be fine, he could couch surf and charm his way into any other living arrangement. But if the four of them were out of luck, the whole family, that was a different story.

"Apparently, Raph and Luke were talking and Luke hinted at being…what's that word? British for broke?"

"Skint," Daphne said. Her breathing had evened out. "Because neither of them want to hear the word 'broke' ever again. It'll always be the name of that stupid, stupid film they quit. Stupid film."

"Right," Mats continued. "So Luke kind of says something off-handedly and Raph gives him the opportunity to say more about it, which of course he doesn't."

"Of course he doesn't," I muttered.

"Of *course* he doesn't!" Daphne threw her hands up.

"But that doesn't bother Raph at all. He's had like, fourteen years or something to figure out Luke. So he calls his mom."

"Raphael called Luke's mum?"

Mattie nodded, a sly little smile on her face. "She's his second mom. They talk a lot. It's very cute. So he calls Ann, and Ann tells him they've just run into a spot of trouble. She's retired—well, you know." She cast me a glance, not knowing if she should bring up that Luke and I dated. Whatever. It was unavoidable. I tried not to be weird about it, so I inclined my head. Yes, I knew.

"And she takes in some sewing now and then, but that's basically the beginning and end of her income. So after the lockdown, Luke wasn't getting any work, besides the *Knuckletracker* movies he was already contracted for, which themselves were delayed because of the pandemic. Income stops, but bills don't."

Yeah, and I knew all about that. I had implemented every idea from all my friends and coworkers, and NIPL was only afloat now because I had let my fellow milkshake-drinking muppets "invest" what I needed to cover a few months of lost income. Since then, I had also sold a painful number of our properties and dipped into my personal savings. Government-sponsored loans helped a bit, but it was like treating a gunshot wound with a butterfly bandage. At the very least, we were more stable than the year before, when the future had been totally unclear. Things were, tentatively, looking up.

"If I had to accept all your investments to keep me housed, Luke should have to do the same."

Cinnamon tapped the side of her glass with her fingernails. "Luke, for all his charm and easygoing attitude, is low-key the most stubborn of all of you."

"Hey," Daphne said, pouting.

"You're the most obviously stubborn," she clarified, and Daph beamed.

"But we can bypass him," I said. "Go straight to Ann."

"His hard-headedness didn't come from nowhere," Mattie said.

"But this is his house. His kids live there."

Mats gave me a look. This was The Problem they kept running into.

"So we need to bypass Luke and Ann," I mused. "Ok. What about Daphne's, uh, work contacts?"

I hesitated to bring up her secretive job as a corporate spy in public, but I was subtle compared to Daphne's big personality.

Daph stared into the distance. "I might have someone who could hack into the loan servicer's website. Make it think there were extra deposits. I don't know how it would work, exactly. Wipe the debt completely."

"Always straight to the illegal options with this one," I said.

Mattie, ever the practical one, uncharacteristically shrugged. "Where he won't accept charity, perhaps he'll accept chaos."

Perhaps. "Cinnamon?" I asked. "What do you think about this?"

"I would consider it, but only as a last resort." She lowered her voice. "White collar crime might be rarely punished, especially for white women—"

"I'm trying to use my privilege for good!" Daph interrupted.

"And I know," Cinnamon stressed, "we might be willing to do jail time to help a friend out of a life or death situation, but there are many, many avenues to explore first, and ultimately, if Luke is refusing all help, he might have a plan of his own that he isn't under any obligation to share."

Daphne huffed. "I hate that plan."

"Me too," I said.

"Yes, me too, we all do." Cinnamon stabbed her straw into her raspberry sorbet smoothie, getting her frustrations out in the motion. "But, for instance. Rin. Is there any way to put him and his family up at one of your properties?"

It was a good idea. I had plenty of empty houses. But it still only solved the future problem of possible houselessness, not the immediate problem of trying to not lose a house.

"In a heartbeat," I said. "He has a safety net. And I think, when things get right down to the wire, when the consequences become inevitable instead of theoretical, he'll make the right decision and accept our help either way."

"But if we can do something so he doesn't have to get to that point..." Mattie trailed off, blinking back tears. She was a sensitive soul, and her friend being in trouble was upsetting to her.

"Money," Cinnamon said. "That's what it comes down to. Or, yes, Starlight, crime, I didn't forget."

Daphne shut her mouth, her frown indicating she was about to remind her wife of exactly that.

"Which we have, and Luke won't accept," Mattie said. "Unless...could we do it anonymously? Is that possible?"

The three of them looked at me expectantly. "Why are you looking at me?"

"You buy houses all the time," Mats said. "You're the closest thing we have to an expert here."

If that was true, we were in trouble. The last property NIPL bought was in the spring of 2018, a few months before my mom died. Then my dad got sick and passed away the following year, then covid hit the following spring, and I never got the chance to buy any properties on my own. I'd had my hands full trying to keep us solvent even before the pandemic—as much as I hated to admit that Luke had been right about my parents running the business on a knife's edge of possible ruin, he was absolutely spot on.

I knew at the time he was right, and I was embarrassed, still, a year later, that my reaction to his very keen and correct observation was so volatile. The only good thing to come of my outburst was deciding to break up with him. I didn't want him to be a victim of my emotional dysregulation, and with everything happening in the world and with my company, I didn't see any way to protect him from it besides distance.

"I haven't actually bought any houses on my own," I admitted. "I have someone I can ask, though."

"Can you ask them now?" Daph was practically bouncing with energy. She didn't need caffeine, but she always had a shot of espresso in her milkshakes anyway.

"Sure. It's..." Mathing while jet-lagged. "Eight-ish there now. Let me see what I can do."

To her credit, my real estate advisor was absolutely game. Lizzie loved puzzles and numbers as much as Daphne did, but where Daph's love was pattern recognition in profit and loss statements, Lizzie loved the housing market and all its ups and downs and intricacies. As someone who ran their own business that had a lot to do with real estate, I wished I had half as much interest in either of those things as either of them.

Over the next hour, as the four of us got another round of shakes and some fries that counted as lunch, Lizzie retrieved all the information about Ann Maston's house. Like, so much information. It was astounding. I asked her if it was possible for a third party to pay off the loan anonymously to the Mastons. She said yes. And asked if I wanted to do that. She could have the whole thing wrapped up by the next day.

That left one problem. If Raphael contributed, he wouldn't be able to keep it from Luke. He was a successful actor for a reason, but he was open and honest with his friends and would want Luke to know how much he cared about him. Mattie didn't have any money, though she and Raph were solid partners and I considered all their belongings shared. Cinnamon wouldn't tell a goddamn soul except Daphne, but Daphne, like most comic book villains, needed people to recognize her cleverness. She would drop hints here and there and Luke wasn't not insightful.

But.

There was one way.

I checked my savings account, knowing what I would find. If I did this, I'd be left with a few thousand dollars, and that was it. I would have to work harder, make sure North Island Pinnacle Leisure started turning more of a profit again. But Luke and Lena and Cassidy and Ann would keep their home. And none of the friends he regularly talked to would have to lie, so he couldn't get upset with them.

Besides, what else was I going to do with it? I owned my house and didn't have any other personal debt. If NIPL tanked, I would have to make some excruciating decisions, but we were doing better now, and as Mattie always said, we had to have hope. And what was money for, if it wasn't to help our loved ones out of situations like this?

I texted Lizzie to do it. She emailed me what she needed and I gave it to her. She said she would have everything sorted and would send me all the confirmations and contracts necessary.

The entire time, I had been typing in silence. Mats and Daph and Cinnamon had carried on their conversation, letting me do what I could in whatever way I could, and they knew that way usually involved uninterrupted focus. When I finally slid my phone into my pocket with a sigh, they all stared at me.

"We will never speak of this again," I said.

The three of them waited a beat before talking all at once. Mattie's "Jesus Christ" overlapped with Daphne's "What the fuck," and Cinnamon's simple but wary "Rin?"

I held up my hand for silence and, shockingly, they complied.

"If you don't know the details, you can honestly tell Luke you don't know who helped him out. And you can honestly tell him it wasn't any of you."

"But if we know it was you..." Mattie trailed off.

"I outsourced the problem to people smarter than us." Not technically a lie. "People who know all the ins and outs of New Zealand real estate laws and tricks and financial stuff. I don't know. You know I don't know much about all of that. It's a miracle NIPL is still chugging along, with me at the helm."

"I don't think trains have helms," Daphne said quietly. Cinnamon shushed her.

"Point is," I continued, "the people who know how to get out of this type of mess are currently taking care of the problem, and in a way that none of us could have done."

They eyed me, searching for the lie, and I'd never been more grateful for the haze of jet lag. They weren't seeing past my exhaustion for shit.

"What did we learn the last time we were all in New Zealand?" I asked, pulling their attention away from me and Luke and back to a memory.

"That my relatives are assholes," Mattie grumbled.

"That it's possible to eventually end up eating food from the chef that one has been trying to get to for literally years, if one tries hard enough," Daphne answered.

"Yes," I said, pinching the bridge of my nose. "Those are both true. But also: when the going gets tough, and it's up to us soft and lazy people, sometimes it's easier and more effective for the otherwise gung-ho Honest Mischief Alliance to delegate the tasks to the appropriate authorities. All I did was hand the problem off to someone else."

The three women nodded sagely.

"So it's really done, then?" Mattie asked. "Luke keeps his house? Just like that?"

"He really keeps his house." I nodded. "It seems easy now because we're not involved anymore, but I assure you, there are several people in Auckland juggling some financial and real estate stuff I don't even know how to describe."

Daphne thought for a minute, then raised her glass.

"To the lazy solution," she said. "And outsourcing problems when they're not fun anymore."

"To laziness and outsourcing," I said, the girls following suit.

And to my savings account, my big, dumb heart, and Luke, for being such an incredible person that I hardly thought twice about sacrificing almost my entire savings so he and his family would be safe.

Chapter 19
October 2022
Rin

I didn't have the energy to mourn my lost time in Edinburgh. The list of things I had wanted to do and see was too long, and I would have been happy with any of them. That I got to exactly zero of them was devastating, but in a strictly cerebral sense. My body was already dealing with the aftermath of the better part of a night spent between the toilet and the floor, and my mind was occupied by whatever it would take to feel better. I simply didn't have any human capacity left to think about what might have been.

Despite the regrettable condition of my body, I was feeling better emotionally. There was a kind of relief in having plans canceled. Usually, my perfectionism won out, but sometimes, it was nice to not have to do anything, and not to feel bad about not having done something.

Then there was texting with Luke. Christ, I was so embarrassed. Diarrhea in the next room over from your ex, where he can hear everything? What a nightmare. I felt bad that the food poisoning got to him too. But I felt worse that I was glad he was in the same boat. For one, he had to leave the hotel room, and therefore could no longer hear my struggles in the toilet. For another, the shared experience definitely brought us closer together.

I'd emerged early in the morning and was able to sleep for a few hours in the bed. Thankfully, I hadn't felt the need to return to the toilet since then, which meant I slept in much later than

I meant to. The alarm on my phone went off at ten minutes till eleven, a final warning to gather our things and check out. There was nothing to pack, since we didn't have the chance to settle in before the petrol station food betrayed us, as Luke so succinctly said. He wasn't in his bed, and I started to worry he hadn't made it through the night, so I called him. Woke him up.

We checked out a few minutes late, sore and hungry, though wary of eating. Stowed our bags in Mr Bean and went to have "breakfast" nearby. Toast and tea. I found a dairy and bought some safe snacks, salt biscuits, Starbars, plain crisps. Drinks with electrolytes. Leeds was four hours away. We needed something in our bellies and something for the road.

"I feel inside-out," Luke mumbled, settling into the car seat with slow and deliberate movements. "Like that song. A blender. You take the insides in the blender. The heart. And the blender—"

"Luke, if you don't stop saying 'blender,' I'm going to throw up on you."

"Fair enough." He buckled his seatbelt and I followed his lead. I felt hungover and dead, and between our sunglasses and bonelessness, we reminded me of the vampires in *Only Lovers Left Alive*. Awake when we didn't want to be and lifeless.

"Decision time," he said.

"Oh no," I groaned. "Wasn't I just saying I didn't want to improvise?"

"No improvisation. Confirming plans. First on the list is the park, yeah? Then the distillery? Do you still want to make those stops, or do you want to get to Leeds as quickly as possible and hunker down in a dark room?"

Dark room. Dark room with toast. And tea. But that park was supposed to be beautiful, and the liquor from the distillery tour would settle our stomachs. Was that a thing that happened?

"There's no wrong answer," he assured me. His head tilted back against the seat and his arms hung loose at his sides. He looked how I felt. A little grey and fuzzy.

"A walk in the park," I said. "Being in nature. Which is restorative, right?"

"For most things. I'm not sure food poisoning is one of them."

"Is alcohol restorative?"

Luke thought about it. "I think it also depends on the circumstances."

"To the park, then. If we get there and the sun starts to shine and the smells make us sick, we can get back in the car and drive to the distillery. And if alcohol becomes more of a bane than a blessing, into the car and onto Leeds. Then dark room, toast, nap."

Luke didn't answer for a moment, and I wondered if he'd fallen asleep.

"I can drive," I said, eyeing the ancient dashboard. "If you're not feeling well enough."

He sat up with a sharp inhale. "Naw. I've got you. I feel responsible for making us sick, so I'll be responsible for getting us to the next location. Then I can focus on something besides my angry stomach."

***

Tweed Valley Forest Park was only an hour out of Edinburgh. We passed more farmland and forests to get there, the land showing signs of preparing for winter, with sparse branches and browning grass. It was a quiet ride, and I almost fell asleep. I don't know how Luke stayed awake, but I could hear him popping gum over in the driver's seat. It would usually bother me, but I liked being able to close my eyes and know he was close and awake and paying attention to getting the two of us to the park without incident.

My original plan was to do the treetop obstacle course. As much as we wondered about the effect of the outdoors on our currently poor, broken bodies, Luke and I were usually very athletic and loved a good hike in the woods. He'd done a lot of training for the *Knuckletracker* movies, and I—well, I was regularly at the gym. I loved a good rock wall as much as anyone, and the treetop course looked like fun.

Until I got a look at it from the other side of an all-night puke party.

"Yeah, that's not going to happen," I said, willing my cramping stomach to calm down. "I can barely sit here doing nothing. You're not getting me up on those platforms."

"No argument here," Luke said. "Though I guess doing a bike trail as an alternative isn't really in the cards, either?"

I pictured biking the ups and downs of the trail at speed and my face suddenly got very cold and somehow damp.

"No. Maybe a perambulation to one of the scenic ponds? Take our time? See some nature?"

Luke put a hand to his stomach. "Not sure I can do a perambulation. Best I can do is a shuffle."

I laughed, just a short little chuckle, but even that hurt my ab muscles. "Ug. Ok, let's do a little shuffle through the woods."

Taking a walk in the woods was the best decision we'd made in at least a day. It was quiet and gentle, unrushed. The air was a little chilly but clean. Hardly anyone was out there, and we heard birdsong as we walked. Luke would stop, cock his head, and announce what bird it was. The park wasn't "Blue Spring" pretty—few things were—but it was still lovely, and I think both of us felt better for it.

One of the dark ponds we stopped at had a little dock, and we walked out to the end of it. It was nice to feel isolated. Like the problems of the world wouldn't reach us there, and if anything tried, we'd see it coming. While the park would be vibrant in better weather, the grey clouds hemmed us in and fit our mood. Luke took off his sunglasses and breathed deeply.

"I think I might be cured," he said. He turned to me with a smile, the one that lit up his face and every room he was in, and was lighting up the whole damn forest now. Why couldn't I kiss him, again? What was stopping me?

"Ready for some haggis, then?" Jesus, what was wrong with me?

His smile turned into a grimace, but a playful one. "Oh, you've somehow found vegetarian haggis?"

I'd forgotten. Continue joking, then. "How would that work, do you think?"

"I imagine it comes from the vegetarian sheep. British folklore has a sheep that grows on a bush or something, you can pluck it off the stalk like a cob of corn or an artichoke."

"Is that true?"

"It's one of those things I heard about in passing but my mind was somewhere else and I never found my way back to it. We could look it up if—" Luke broke off and grabbed my shoulder, his eyes going wide.

"Osprey," he whispered.

"What?" I turned around to see. On the opposite shore, in one of the barer trees, a white-and-brown bird of prey sat, watching us.

"Osprey," he repeated, fumbling for his phone. "Oh, the girls will love it." He started taking photos and sending them. I got out my phone and took a photo of him taking photos. The joy in his face was too endearing not to.

My stomach twinged, not from any remaining bacteria or whatever spoils egg sandwiches, but regret. I could have witnessed Luke's complete and luminous happiness nearly every day for the past two years. It made him more handsome than even a formal suit, which made everyone more attractive and made him specifically forget-your-own-name gorgeous.

"Who's really the bird person though," I asked. "You or the girls?"

"Me," he answered quickly. "Obviously me. I'm forty. That's just what happens. You get into birds. Did you know there's a Shazam for birds? You should download it."

"Sure," I said. Probably not going to happen.

Grin on his face, he sent the last few pictures and shook his head. "I feel so much better. From one bird! God, I am a huge nerd, huh?"

I don't know how what happened next actually happened. Luke had his phone firm in hand, then suddenly it was slipping, like in slow motion, as though either of us could have grabbed it back from whatever invisible force was pulling it away (I mean, gravity, right?). I saw the horror creep over his face, and we both leaned to snatch it from the jaws of the water, our hands colliding with each other and the phone and sending it out to land about two metres farther into the pond, with a *blurp* that was inappropriately satisfying.

He stared after it, his face a study in pathos, his arm reaching out as though he could somehow still prevent its early demise.

After a moment, he laughed, an absolutely deranged laugh, and sat down on the dock.

"Shit," I said, kneeling next to him. "Fuck."

He didn't stop laughing. After another minute, he shrugged and started taking off his shoes and coat.

"Um," I said. "What are you doing?"

"Well, Rin, I'm going to pick up my phone."

"Bro, it's in an unspecified depth of pond."

"Exactly," he said, pulling his white jumper over his head. "It could be less than a metre away from the surface."

"Or it could be six metres down."

"Can't know unless I try."

He took off his glasses next, then jeans, then his socks, and I meant to say something about catching giardia and the potential for more diarrhea, but he was already down to his boxers and I forgot how to form words. I wanted to touch his stomach, which looked softer than it had two years ago. I wanted to reacquaint myself with his body and map how he'd changed. I closed my eyes, thinking that might halt the surge of desire, but my mind helpfully offered me memories of his body in all kinds of situations, in various levels of undress.

Before my imagination could get anywhere with those images, the cold droplets from Luke's jump into the lake surprised me out of my daydreams, and I opened my eyes in case another disaster struck and I had to jump in after him.

When he resurfaced, it was without his phone.

"I can't see anything down there." His voice was tight with frustration.

"All the silt," I said, as though knowing it would help somehow. "How deep is it?"

Luke slicked back his hair and exhaled through his mouth like he was trying to calculate something. I could tell he was treading water.

"No idea. More than three metres, I'd wager."

"Luke." God, what would I do without my phone? How did humans get to the point where something so niche a few decades ago became unimaginably important to our day-to day-lives? That's where I kept all my people, all my memories, all my work. "Luke, I think it's gone, love."

He shook his head and looked back to the osprey, which was watching us with a detached interest. "I'm going to look again." And then he was underwater.

He went back a few more times. I didn't have the heart to stop him. Even if he found it, I doubted it would work, so I texted Cass and Lena and told them their dad dropped his phone in a pond but he was ok. Told them to tell their mom to text me to get to Luke. I sent them the last photo in my album, Luke beaming as he took a picture of the bird. Cassidy replied with an lol and Mia's contact information. For a tween, she was incredibly mature. Must have inherited it from Luke's mom.

Next was the group text with the squad.

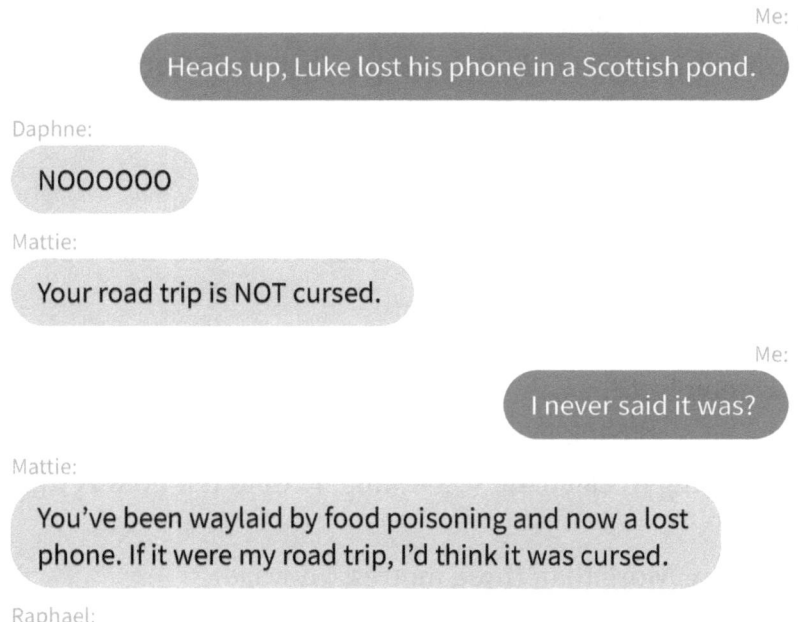

Is he ok?

Me:

He's currently swimming in said pond but can't find the bottom of it, let alone any devices that might have fallen to the bottom of it.

Cinnamon:

Aw, that sucks, Rin. Anything we can do from here?

Me:

Nothing I can think of. All the reservations and everything is on my laptop, which is safe. He's going to miss texting with his girls, though.

Raphael:

Tell him not to worry about it, I'll have a new phone for him when he gets to London. Or I could drive up and deliver it to him in…is it Leeds tonight?

Me:

Normally I would say don't trouble yourself.

Raphael:

That bad, huh?

Mattie:

NOT CURSED

Daphne:

you have no imagination, Mats

Cinnamon:

Both of you have an abundance of imagination. Rin, do you want us to come up too?

Daphne:

> **Party in Leeds! Whoop whoop!**

> Me:
> **NO party in Leeds, please. But a new phone would go a long way, I think.**

> Raphael:
> **No worries, I'll get it now and then we'll leave here and meet wherever you like up there. Send me your hotel info so we can be close by.**

> Daphne:
> **Raph gets a Leeds party. >:(**

> Me:
> **No, dear, he doesn't. Luke doesn't even want to see him.**

Ah, fuck. Wasn't there supposed to be an option to un-send a text? How quickly could I look that up?

> Raphael:
> **Wait, what?**

> Daphne:
> **ooo, gossip**

> Mattie:
> **What's going on?**

> Me:
> **He's having a bad day after a bad night, I'm sure he doesn't want to see me either.**

> Raphael:
> **That's not the save you think it is.**

Me:

> Look, I don't know. He doesn't want to talk about you at all, and he doesn't want to talk *to* you either. Hasn't told me why. I'm trying to get him to open up about it, but there's a lot going on. So I don't know more than that, I'm sorry. I shouldn't have said anything.

Mattie:

> He has been pretty distant lately.

Raphael:

> His mom said as much, too. I'm all for giving people space that they need, but sometimes with Luke, you have to corner him and remind him that he's not alone, and he has people he can be vulnerable around.

Cinnamon:

> This is a problem with everyone on this chat.

Me:

> Aw shit, he's going to see this, isn't he? When he uploads texts to his new phone?

Daphne:

> Not necessarily. Without a place to land, these messages may be lost in the aether.

Mattie:

> Ok but just in case: we love you, Luke, and we're sorry you didn't feel like you could talk to us about whatever's bothering you!

Daphne:

> I love you Luke!

Cinnamon:

> I love you, Luke.

Raphael:
> Love you, bro. I never meant to upset you. I hope when you read this we've already talked it through.

After a few more dives, Luke swam back and put his arms on the dock. I reached out to push the wet hair out of his eyes.

"Had enough, love?"

He set his mouth in a firm line and nodded.

"I'm sorry." I kept playing with the hair behind his ear. "I already let everyone know to text me if they need you. The squad, the girls, Mia. Is there anyone else I should contact?"

He pushed himself out of the water with a grunt and turned around, legs dangling into the pond. I shivered to look at him, but he didn't seem to feel the cold. "Everything is saved in the cloud," he said, waving his hand in the air to indicate the cloud.

"We'll get a new phone in Leeds." No need to tell him *how* we would get a new phone in Leeds. One disappointment at a time. "Come on. I didn't bring any towels. Did you?"

He shook his head and picked up his sunglasses. "I'll spot-dry myself with some other clothes, and hang everything up when we get to the hotel."

"Sure," I said, standing up and hearing a bunch of joints crack. That couldn't be good. "Do you want to go straight to Leeds, then? Skip the distillery?"

"Hell no." He stood next to me, stinky pond water dripping down his broad chest, and I remembered how good his body felt when I could run my hands over him. *Eyes up, Butcher.* He squeezed out his hair and brushed excess liquid off himself. "I just swam in a cold Scottish pool. I need whatever alcohol I can get."

"Your stomach not bad?"

"It feels much improved. This place must be magic. Care for a dip, to cure your own ills?"

I took two steps back, out of his reach, in case he was about to throw me in, too. He smiled slyly.

"It was only a suggestion. Besides, one of us has to have a working phone, and mine has been donated to the fishes."

Back at Mr Bean, Luke dried off with a pale-blue turtleneck and put on dry clothes. By the time we got to the distillery an hour later, we were both ready for whisky and actual food, and ended up having a great time. We laughed and joked around, and Luke fed me some of his chocolate strawberry cake. I drifted into a comfort so complete that the trials of the past day were absent from my thoughts, replaced with a surprising satisfaction. We left in high spirits, never doubting that the rest of the trip would go smoothly.

We were so hopeful, in fact, we didn't notice how dark the afternoon sky had become, or the smell of petrichor on the autumn air.

Chapter 20

June 2020

Luke

It was a warm day for June and we hadn't had any rain all week. Mum had taken the girls to the park for a change of scenery for them and a break for me. We'd been doing well, with the lockdown. Not quite at each others' throats yet, but I credited that to our ability to escape into nature in different ways whenever we needed to.

I'd just had a video call with the producers of our documentary—tentatively titled *Shutdown*—and I got a thrill seeing Rin's face there too. The reason I'd agreed to do *Broke* was, specifically, for the chance to work with Raphael and other good friends. Realizing our friend and director meant for us to make a propaganda film that our reputations would never recover from could easily have shaken my faith in the industry.

But Mason Schilling, a renown player in film production, had scooped up me and Raph literally minutes after we walked off the set for good, and within the hour, we had come up with the idea for the documentary. Mattie and Rin had come on as producers, and for people who had never worked on this kind of project, they certainly seemed to have a knack for it. Then again, making a documentary in real time about the trials and solutions and tragedies and happiness that New Zealand filmmakers experienced while in lockdown because of a pandemic was a novel idea requiring thinking outside the box.

Working on something with most of my new friends was sure to wash away the bad taste that *Broke* had left in my mouth. Daphne had already flown home to San Francisco and her wife. She could have tapped in remotely, like the rest of us, but as much as she followed celebrity gossip, she wasn't about to participate in the day-to-day labor of a documentary. Not when she could be home with her spouse.

I couldn't blame her. I had to work to support my family, and I was lucky to be able to do it in a way I loved. I would act either way, money or no, but it turned out, little girls had to eat regularly? More than once a day, even. And until those freeloaders got a job in the mines or wherever children worked nowadays, I was the one that had to feed them.

Things they don't tell you before becoming a parent, am I right?

But that June afternoon, the hungry monsters were with their Grams, chasing weta or poking anthills or whatever other mischief they could imagine, and I was at home, wondering when Rin would stop by.

They were only a twenty minute drive away, staying at one of their rental cottages with the Redgrave sisters and Raphael. After the producer call, they had actual job-related work to do, phone calls and emails and I'm not sure what else. No worries. I didn't have the luxury of sitting at home waiting for my lover to return. Plenty of chores needed my attention, and they'd take a fraction of the usual time without the children knowingly or unknowingly following in my footsteps, undoing whatever I'd done as soon as I turned away.

First was the laundry. I was hoping the weather would hold, since I preferred drying clothes on the line in the backyard, and it looked like it would. I gathered the wet linens into two baskets, grabbed the cassette player, and went outside.

The sun felt more like a summer than a winter one, blinding and hot, and as I set down the baskets and tape deck, I wondered if I should have put on sunscreen. I already had a beach vibe going, with a light-blue tee shirt and shorts, and barefoot of course. But I didn't want to put another layer between me and the warming rays.

I pushed the "play" button, the familiar resistance and click taking me back to my childhood. The cassette had belonged to Mia, something she had left behind and didn't care enough about to want back, something from the late 90's when cassettes were already on their way out. I hadn't liked it at the time, but the girls would remember it every few months and it would be the only music they played for a week straight every time.

I bopped along to it and tackled the linens, smiling to myself that I would find so much happiness in such a mundane and solitary task. When I finished, I moved to the little greenhouse and cut a few flowers for the vases in our bedrooms and dining room. Winter didn't give us a lot of options, and I didn't know the names of them (bird guy here, not a flower guy). The pinkest one for Lena. Cassidy was on a blue kick, but the best I could do was a blue-ish spiky one that was almost white. Orange for mum, and a delicate purple one for Rin. As I walked back to gather the now-empty baskets and cassette player, the song swept up into a climax I stopped to sing along to, using the flowers as a microphone.

Beyond the music, I heard a sharp sound, and I let the lyrics fall from my lips as a mumble.

"Hello?" I called. A bed sheet snapped against the wind that had picked up. I'd seen this movie before. The victim hanging laundry can't see past the bath towels and nightgowns and knickers to the deranged killer, ready with a knife, poised to strike.

Before I could shake the thought from my mind, the laundry parted and a figure rushed at me, and I screamed and threw the flowers in the air, the exact opposite of what I wanted to do, exactly what the over-dramatic victim would do.

"For the love of Christ, Rin." I let it out in one breath, holding my racing heart in my chest with both hands. They giggled, their phone between us pointed at me. Ah, footage for the doc. Got it. I ran a hand through my hair and laughed.

"How long have you been out here?" I leaned down to pick up the flowers. They, at least, were unscathed.

"I've been here the whole time," Rin said innocently.

"Is that so?" I asked with a grin, darting out to grab their mobile.

They shrieked and danced back, so I dropped the flowers again and chased, and they ran, and we were both very good at it because we both loved running and games. From the backyard to the front yard, me barefoot, them in sturdy boots. Rin had been spending enough time at my house to know the layout of it, and while they didn't have the seemingly photographic memory of Daphne when it came to maps, they already knew all the short-cuts and dead ends, and was able to keep a respectable distance between us as we chased each other.

They kept the recording going, holding the phone up over their head as they ran so we'd both be in the shot. From my angle I could tell we were both smiling like idiots. As we passed through the front door, through the living room, heading out the back, Rin stopped recording and threw their phone into the pillows on the couch. Then we were outside again, and I wondered what their end game was, caught up in the competition. We didn't even realize the weather had turned until the first few raindrops fell on us and Rin came to an unsteady halt.

"The laundry!" They said, wheeling towards the clothesline. But I had closed the distance and wouldn't be distracted.

"Nope," I said, grabbing them and pulling them into a breathless kiss. And it was breathless. We'd both been running flat out and needed a minute to recover, but their skin glowed like sunlight through honey, and their usually perfect bun was a disaster, and not a worry in the world crowded their eyes and I had to kiss them like that. Had to drink them in, the joy of them, the physical space they occupied. I would settle for my lips on theirs.

And Rin kissed me back, just as enthusiastic, their hands grasping at my shoulders and in my hair. *This* was the secret hack to getting them focused, I thought, and if I was any good at it, they would forget that the laundry was left out in the rain. I pulled them closer, running my hands up their back. They wore a tank top, maroon and sleek. It felt too expensive to let it get rained on, and possibly muddied up, but I wasn't going to let them back in the house yet. Hell, I'd buy them a new one.

"Luke," they murmured between kisses, "we have to take in the sheets."

I held them tighter. They were strong. They could get themself out of my grip. If that was what they wanted. The rain got going then, cold and abundant, and when Rin shied away again, I let go of them long enough to pull my tee up and off.

Lucky for me, that was sometimes all it took.

"Ok but the *linens*," they whined, running their hands over my chest. I grinned and knelt down, taking Rin with me. The dirt would churn into mud soon enough. The bedsheets might have to be washed again, but we definitely would, too.

I pulled their tank top over their head and tossed it in the direction of the open back door, not bothering to look where it landed. "You gotta learn to let things get a little dirty."

They shivered and glanced from my lips to my eyes. "But do I have to let things get so cold?"

"I'll keep you warm," I promised, suppressing my own shiver. Shit, it was sunny only ten minutes ago. And cold rain didn't normally get to me. The nice temperature must have tempered me, made me unsuitable for a sudden change like this. Rin had a point.

But, then, they were kissing me again, and I forgot one comfort to indulge in another. I trailed my fingertips down their arm, from their wrist, caressing the sensitive inside of their elbow, and following the definition of their triceps up their shoulder to cup and hold the base of their head in a light grip.

"Any requests?" I murmured. "Anything off limits?" Sometimes, if they were having a more masculine day, they wouldn't want me to touch their chest in a certain way, or be in a certain position, and that was all fine by me. However I could experience Rin was a gift I wouldn't take for granted. They wore a regular-looking bra today, something with a couple hook-and-eye closures, which usually signaled a femme-leaning mood, but I knew better than to assume.

"Everything," they sighed into me.

"Wait, what?" I lifted my hands a few inches away from where I'd been holding them. "Everything is off limits? Are you ok? Do you just want to snuggle in front of the screen and watch something that isn't *Frozen*?"

Rin groaned and laid their head against my chest. "Sorry, no, that's not what I mean. I was requesting everything."

"Don't be sorry."

"I'm sorry for the miscommunication," they clarified, lifting their head to meet my eyes. "But I do appreciate that you don't want to cross any lines."

"Never." I smiled. "No fun that way. But you've told me you want everything, and I'm eager to provide."

They gave me a grin. "Oh, yeah. I can tell."

"Well, I'm not trying to be mysterious about it."

"No," they said, then leaned in close to my ear. "Your shorts are very, very thin, love."

Their breath caressed my ear and neck, followed by the lightest touch of their lips, and I was only too aware Rin would be able to feel the immediate effect of it, which got me even more aroused, and I smiled at being trapped in the best kind of cycle.

I'd never made love outdoors before. But Rin was a force of nature and it felt right to be out in a storm with them. Dramatic and driving, but it was still just us. They held my focus in a way most things couldn't, and I could worship them for that.

It felt right to be anywhere with them.

Chapter 21
October 2022
Luke

For the only person in the car with a mobile, Rin didn't use it much. They hadn't, since we started our journey, and I suspected it was a way for them to show me respect, which sounded mad in my head. When we dated, they spent a lot of time answering emails and making calls, and the Redgrave sisters were sorry to inform me that that was par for the course. That was how seriously Rin took their job in normal times, and it wasn't much mellowed by the pandemic's havoc.

It was looking more and more like they had lost the business. Or sold it, or something like. I toyed with the idea that they had stepped down from their leadership role, but I think they would have rather died first. That thing about the captain going down with the sinking ship? Rin lived by that code.

Raphael hadn't said anything about it. Daphne hadn't either, and if there was anything to know, she would, and would tell me about it first thing. Like when NIPL was doing poorly at the end of 2020, and Daph and I worked together to launch a marketing campaign to drive business. But she hadn't said a word. So Rin hadn't told her.

And despite saying they would, Rin hadn't told me either. Whatever the problem ended up being, it broke my heart to know they were hurting alone. All I could do was be physically available to them, which I would have done even if I was still in possession of my phone. In fact, if it meant getting closer to Rin, I might have thrown it into the lake on purpose.

To be clear, I did not throw my phone in the lake on purpose. Like everyone else, that was where I kept my stuff, and at the very least, it was my only method of communication with my girls. God, I was dumb. I'd taken pictures over countless bodies of water. None of them had demanded the sacrifice of my mobile. Had I stumbled upon a Scottish curse? Offended a lake spirit?

Naw, bro. Just some bad luck and butterfingers.

Story of my life.

The distillery had been sweet as. Especially after my dip in the swamp. The heat in the car didn't work, and anyway, it would have warmed me from the outside in, if it did. Whisky warmed from the heart out, and my heart needed the hug. The food had been choice, too, and the lingering effects of food poisoning had dissipated before we got there, so we were able to enjoy the meal. It was a good feeling, to be warm and dry and in good company with good food and drink.

A half hour away from the distillery, Rin interrupted my reverie with a grunt. "I don't like the look of that sky."

Dark, and grey, but it was getting into winter and both of those were normal for this time of year. We were on a very rural road that should have been intersecting with a slightly less rural road in about fifteen minutes, and then we'd be in Leeds two hours after that. It was foolish to think we could stave off the rain by willing it so, but it had worked thus far and I hadn't given any thought to what we would do when it inevitably caught up to us.

"Uh," I said, knowing I sounded dumb, but there was nothing I could do about it. "Any ideas?"

A fat raindrop splatted against the windscreen, and we jumped like we had been bitten. Rin turned to me, eyes wide with panic.

"Drive," they whispered.

I floored it. Well, not floored. The gas pedal didn't reach that far, and even if it did, the part of me that was the most responsible encouraged me to not. I didn't know what happened when Mr Bean got wet, but I knew that pushing it faster shook the damn thing to the point where I imagined pieces flying off as we drove. And those two things combined seemed not ideal.

Another splat on the glass, and another, then a hundred at once and coming faster. Rin flinched from their window and for a wild second I thought they had been struck by a piece of the car, some metal or plastic torn from the frame by our speed, but it was just the rain getting in past the makeshift window. They grabbed for the plastic sheet to hold it in place.

"This isn't so bad." They shouted over the loud drumming of the rain. If there had ever been insulation beneath the metal roof, it was long gone, and we were basically in a tin can being blasted by a hose. Rin's hands were already soaked and tiny beads of water formed in their hair and on their glasses. "It's cold, but workable."

"Is that tarp even doing anything?" The rest of the car, despite amplifying the noise, seemed to be holding up, though it had only been a few minutes.

"Marginally. It could be worse. I can stay like this for a while, as long as I get a hot shower at the hotel."

"I will personally draw you the hottest bath. I owe you." I glanced over at them again. "I'm sorry. We should have taken the bus."

Rin laughed. "Then you would have missed the osprey."

My heart paused in its wild, adrenaline-fueled gallop. They were willing to brave the cold rain in a recklessly speeding shitbox of a car just so I could see a bird? How the fuck had I ever let them go?

And what could I do to fix that mistake?

A spot of cold pinpricked my neck on the side facing my own window. I slapped at it like a mosquito, but more speckled my cheek. *No, the window is closed*, I thought, and squinted at the years-worn rubber between the top of the glass and the door. As I watched, water dripped again, but from the crack between the door and car frame, not the window.

"Um," I said. More water leaked through. "Do we have an extra tarp for my side? Did you happen to bring any duct tape?"

Rin looked at me and I looked back at the road. I slowed down a bit, thinking that driving into the rain faster might be causing it to enter the car faster. We were alone on the road, so I didn't mind making daring moves. At least the headlights worked (one at a weird angle, but I'd take it), and so did the passenger's side windscreen wiper. Rin was right, it could have been worse. Getting a bit wet would be annoying but not life-threatening.

"Shit," they said. A stream poured from my door, like someone forgot to turn off a sink faucet. A droplet hit my hand from yet another new angle and I saw beads of water forming where the top of the windscreen met the roof. Another drop fell from the rearview mirror, rivulets from above snaking their way down it and onto the console.

Ok, crisis level amended. Water getting into the electronic dashboard would be significantly worse than arriving in the city a little cold and wet.

"Luke."

I hadn't ever heard them use that tone before, and it scared me enough to slow to almost a stop. I followed Rin's gaze to the backseat, where, somehow, it seemed to be raining *inside* the car as heavily as it was raining *outside* the car.

"What the fuck is happening?" My voice had gone up an understandable octave.

"We have to pull over," Rin said.

"And do what?" We didn't bring enough duct tape and tarp for this.

"Get the car cover over Mr Bean, with us in the car, and call for help."

"I can't drive with the cover on the car."

"Yeah, no shit, pull over and stop and we can wait it out."

That might work. I pulled off the road into a patch of grass and shifted into park. The one windscreen wiper flew back and forth, but the downpour was far too strong for one of a pair, and the rain was a blurry layer against the glass. I turned off the headlights, turned off the car, and pressed the button above me that turned on the tiny overhead light. The low wattage cast us in a glow so dim, Lena wouldn't have accepted it as a night light.

"Oh no," Rin said, as the valiant and final bit of tape lost its grip on the plastic covering their open window, and the sheet—little more than clingfilm—fluttered to the ground.

"Stay here," I said, opening my door. I stepped out into the storm and immediately slipped in the mud, landing against the soggy earth on my leg and ass and back and narrowly missing cracking my head against the car.

"Luke!"

"Fuck. I'm ok." I could feel the sludge seeping into my clothes, colder and thicker than a puddle. It was all grass, no hard or sharp rocks beneath me, but I could already tell that my ass would sport a glorious bruise. I laid there a minute, looking up into the censored sky, face pelted by the precipitation that had finally thwarted us. It felt right to take a moment to understand how truly fucked we were. For the first time since seeing Rin again, I wished I had a cigarette.

I heard Rin open their door and a moment later, they kneeled beside me.

"*Are* you ok? Damn it, what's the emergency number here? Is it 999?" They shielded their mobile with their body, trying to make the call.

"Rin," I said with a sigh. "I'm fine. I didn't hit my head. The ground is soft. I'm just wallowing. 'Doesn't like rain' and 'has a complete breakdown due to disintegration of its more important components' shouldn't be equal phrases by anyone's estimation."

"I don't have reception," they said, sliding the phone back into an inner coat pocket.

"Of course you don't. I think I must have angered some kind of spirit or minor god. I'm sorry you got caught up in it."

Rin rolled their eyes. "Don't be so dramatic, you egg. If you're honestly ok, get up and help me with the car cover. Our bags are getting soaked."

They leaned into the car and brought out the cover. I stood to help, only slipping in the mud a little.

"Skip the bonnet," they directed as we unfolded the cloth. "Get the boot, roof, and windscreen. We'll have to figure out a way to persuade the doors to work with us however we can."

The doors were a problem, so I left mine open and jumped in. The cover draped over the opening fine and gathered at the bottom of the windscreen, as planned.

"Um. Luke?" Rin stood outside, holding their door in a weird way.

"Leave it open," I said, wiping my hands off on the front of my jeans. Most of the mud had come off between the rain and wrangling the car cover. "It'll fit better that way."

They pushed it a little, staring at it. "No, there's something wrong. It feels...soft?"

"The metal door feels soft?" I asked, frowning. This car was even more tin-arse than I thought. The cover seemed to be working, though. It was still raining inside the car, but slowly enough that it was probably residual droplets from what had gotten in before.

"The hinge feels soft," they said. "When I open and close it. Like, pliable." I could hear the curiosity in their voice. Not a good sign. They would be out in the rain all night if they thought there was a puzzle to be solved.

"Ok, gross? Stop messing with it and get in."

They stepped back and tilted their head. "Does it look uneven to you?"

"Rin, get in the fucking car." It took a demand to puncture their focus, and they slid into their seat and pulled the cover down the rest of the way to the hood.

Soaked to the bone, both covered in mud, no way to drive anywhere, no working phones, and only a vague idea of where we were on the map. The cloth cover muffled the rain somewhat, so the volume was down from a shower of nails on metal to a stampede of a thousand cats. Which almost made up for the fact that it also smelled like a thousand cats. A thousand wet cats.

I wanted to ask Rin what to do next, because they were usually prepared for most eventualities, but something told me this specific catastrophe had no precedent. Besides, I had a working brain. So far, my ideas included sitting in the car shivering until another car passed by and helped. That was it. That was my one idea.

It must have been Rin's only answer too, because they asked if I knew whether there was a road flare in the car. I didn't. I leaned my seat nearly flat and twisted around to reach through the big hole in the backseat into the boot.

"Hey, the boot's dry," I told them. "Give me your phone. Unless you have a stand-alone torch."

"The one time I don't pack it," they grumbled, handing me their mobile.

Shining the light into the velvety, dark space was scarier than it should have been. I played too many video games in my day, had seen too many horror movies. But there were no alien larvae or reanimated pieces of people or my doppelgänger. No road flare, either. Just our two bags, my carry-on and their duffel, safe and dry and cozy. My unease turned to jealousy.

I unearthed my messenger bag from the floor behind me. Damp, but nothing inside was damaged. Rin shook their backpack over the back seat, and the flying droplets were more numerous than the ones still dripping from the ceiling.

"Waterproof," they said smugly, swiping at the little pools of water on the material. "When you're traveling, you have to pack smart. Scotland. Rain. Waterproof backpack."

I turned around in my still-reclined seat and closed my eyes. The mud on my clothes squished beneath me and I could feel it seeping onto my skin. I already had plenty in my hair and on my neck, working its way down the back of my shirt. Suraj said I could leave Mr Bean wherever he had his last stand and it looked more and more like that was exactly what I would have to do. I still felt bad getting it so dirty.

"Waterproof coat?" I asked.

"That, too."

"Waterproof car?"

I couldn't see their face, so I couldn't gauge whether it was an appropriate time to joke around.

"Knew I forgot something." I heard a smile in their voice.

The smell of wet-cat car cloth, wet-dog car seats, wet-human clothes, and mud was becoming stronger. I sat up with a groan and opened the glove box, thinking there might have been a road flare in there. Nope. But I did find an atlas.

"Hey," I said. "Great news. No need for GPS. This pre-internet treasure shows all the roads in Scotland, Wales, and England. See, a bunch of different maps are printed on something called *paper*, and the paper is gathered and bound in what was once called an *atlas*—"

Rin took it out of my hands with a huff. "Give it here. We're basically the same age, I don't need you to explain to me how a physical road map works."

As they flipped through it, I thought about how we could get out of this situation with only what we had in the car and in our heads. I got sidetracked for a while thinking about the word "brainstorm" and how we had an abundance of storm but not an abundance of brain and shouldn't "brainstorm" describe something more violent than just getting ideas? Or was the creation of ideas inherently violent, like the Big Bang?

"Ok," Rin said with a sigh. "Ok. Based on the last time I looked at the map on my phone, and this map here, I'm pretty sure I know where we are."

"If I'm remembering my *Winnie the Pooh* correctly, knowing where one is is a very good place to start. How close to the nearest outpost of civilization?"

"The nearest house is about one kilometre away." They pointed out their door to the left without looking up. "I saw it on the hill before all the chaos and thought it looked creepy up there all alone and dark. We could go there and ask for help."

"Excellent," I said with a shake of my head. "Petrol station? Friendly farm? Hotel?"

Rin gave me a look. "Farther."

I blew out a breath to get my hair out of my eyes, but the rain made it too heavy. I swiped at it with my hand instead. "Back to the distillery, then?"

"That's a half hour behind us. If we drive at speed." They bit their lip, eyes asking the unvoiced question.

"Doubt I could drive it so fast, bro. Although—" Waiting in the cold, dark, smelly car for who knew how long, hoping someone would pass by, see us, and stop to help. Tramping in the cold, unrelenting rain to a darkened house and hoping there were people there willing to help. Or driving back the way we came, unable to see out the windscreen, rain pelting us as though we were in a top-down convertible, for at least an hour, praying all that water wouldn't find its way into the electrical system, and hoping there was someone in the distillery who could lend us a hand.

"My vote is for the house," Rin said, filling the pause while my mind did a lap.

"We could hold the cover on in a way that I could see out the windscreen without water getting in. It's almost a straight shot back to the whisky. There's nobody out on the roads. We could go as slow as we need."

"Our arms would cramp from holding the cover for that long," they said, pinching their bottom lip. They did that when they were thinking, and I was so glad they were invested in finding a solution.

"They have that awning in front like a hotel," I reminded them. "Even if they were closed, we could park beneath it without worrying we'd be flooded out. Sleep all uncomfortable if we could, and then ask them to call for help when they come in tomorrow morning. Or, not even. Once we get close enough, you should have reception again. Call for a tow, or a cab, or whatever, leave the car where it is, and get to a B&B. Figure out what to do next over breakfast tomorrow."

Rin considered it, because I had said all the right words to spark longing. In this case: mobile reception, sleep, leaving the cold and wet car, warm shelter, and breakfast.

"It would be dicey driving like that," they said at last.

"Dicey-er than sitting here all night? Or tramping a half mile in unknown terrain and mud to a stranger's house?"

"Fuck." They rested the atlas against their forehead and took a deep breath. "Yep. Ok. Fuck it. Let's drive."

I beamed. Rin chose my idea. And they were brilliant, so if my idea was the best, I might be equal to them. I knew this evening couldn't be all bad luck. I was able to lever my seat back to its upright position—so that was one thing going right—then pressed the overhead light to off and the headlights back to on, and turned the key in the ignition.

The car's sputtering reminded me of old cartoons, but I didn't think anything those characters tried would work for me in real life. I had no dynamite, for one. I also didn't think Mr Bean was sentient and could be coaxed by the promise of higher-grade petrol, an oil change, or a petite yet curvy bombshell of a potential passenger. It went quiet without the engine turning over, and I tried again, to the same result.

"Know anything about cars, mate?" I asked Rin.

"Enough to say we're not driving anywhere tonight."

Again I tried and again, a grinding, then silence.

"Don't think it's the battery," I said. "One more time."

This try, the headlights dimming in time with the cyclical effort was the only difference. When I tried it the next and last time, the car didn't even make a sound.

The car's final silence permeated the space. It felt like that part in the movies where the team in the broken spaceship or submarine or the regiment cut off from the rest of their people try the only option left to them, and fail. Rin was right. I was a dramatic muppet.

As we sat there listening to the drumming pattern of the storm, the inside drips that had slowed to almost nothing picked up again. The car cover was failing.

Rin and I looked at each other. This wasn't a spaceship lost and isolated, or a submarine fighting against time and the pressure of the ocean, or a war of any sort. We'd get cold and wet. Might catch an illness. Some of our stuff might be ruined. But it was unlikely it would cost us our lives.

I took in a breath to ask if running to the nearby house was the best course of action, but before I said anything, we heard a high and haunting moan, then a thud that reverberated through the car. Of all the things I worried about, attack by ghost hadn't even been on my list. I imagined my face looked much like Rin's: pale, wide-eyed, frozen in fear. How would I even fight a ghost?

"Oh my god," Rin whined, putting their head in their hands. Much too loud. Ghost would definitely hear.

"Did you bring any weapons?" I whispered.

They lifted their head long enough to give me a pitying look. The one that said, "maybe he's too dumb to try to explain this to." Which I wouldn't mind, if it meant no ghost. I'd rather be wrong than plagued by an undead spirit.

They reached over and lifted their side of the car cover so we could see outside. The open passenger door, which Rin had previously noticed was somehow uneven, was now at a forty-five degree angle to the ground, the bottom edge of it embedded deep into the mud.

Yeah. We should have taken the bus.

Chapter 22

October 2022

Rin

After all my time causing mischief with the Redgraves, I had well learned that some plans just fail. Some fail quietly, like when North Island Pinnacle Leisure could no longer be salvaged and had to be sold. Some can be adapted and improvised on the fly, like when Daphne followed Big Douchey McTechbro to his yacht. Some get too big and complicated and have such wider possible repercussions, they have to be abandoned in favor of passing the info to the proper authorities and hoping they do the right thing, like at Mattie's brother's wedding two years ago.

Rarely had I seen a plan fail as spectacularly as this road trip with Luke.

And for once, I was too fucking exhausted to examine why. We'd both tried our best. It was a fun idea. But neither of us had the resources we needed to pull it off.

"Leave the bigger bags in the boot," I instructed as I put on my backpack. He had already reclined his seat to grab his luggage from the trunk, and when he tried to move it back into an upright position, the lever broke off in his hand.

He sighed, dropped it onto the now forever-reclined seat, and draped his messenger bag's strap over his shoulder. "You're right, there's a chance they'll keep dry if they stay."

"Plus, muddy hill," I added. "Let's not make it more difficult than it has to be."

"Any other instructions?" He asked. He looked beat. After a night of food poisoning and an early afternoon of dropping his phone in a goddamn lake, I was surprised he hadn't given up. Now I was asking him to trek up a slippery hill in nearly pitch black to an unknown location while leaving a bunch of his belongings and his friend's busted car to brave the elements without us.

"Run like hell," I advised. "Also, first one there gets first dibs on shower." A little competition could cheer him up.

He smiled through his exhaustion, and even looking as knackered as he did, he was still beautiful. "You're on," he said, and ducked out of the car.

By the time we made it to the house, I had forgotten how we got there and had no way of gauging how long it had taken. A kilometre in the daytime, regardless of elevation, was pleasant. A kilometre at night, up a rain-slick incline, in a storm, was less pleasant, and my mind made the executive decision to erase it from my memory. I stepped onto the covered porch first, barely noticing how dark the house looked or how old and unstable it might be, but thinking only about getting out of the rain. Luke was right behind me, slowed by his one-strap bag.

He walked straight to the door and pounded against it, yelling a greeting far too chipper for the situation. I was glad to be out of the rain and hadn't thought that far. I checked my mobile to confirm I still had no reception. By the light of the screen, I saw the layers of dirt on the floor, piles of cut wood and other, unrecognizable things in cobwebby corners. Dry, but dirty. I wondered how many weeks or months it had been since somebody had taken care of this place. After a few minutes of no answer and no lights, Luke turned to me.

"Well," he said with a huff, hands on his hips. "This roof isn't leaking. So we'll be dry for the night. First light, I'll try the car again. If it's carked, we'll collect our bags and start walking. It'll suck, but we'll have a better chance of somebody seeing us."

"Oh, fuck that," I said, pulling out my lockpicking kit. I shuffled to the front door and used my mobile to light the lock.

"Oh, we're doing this? Also an option." Luke took the phone from me and steadied it so I could see. It took me longer than it should have. I was exhausted and amped up and scared and miserable and those are terrible conditions when trying to do something delicate like picking a lock. After a few minutes, I had it, and we pushed together into the house.

The door stuck a bit, bloated from decades of moisture in the air. It led into a kitchen, dusty but tidy. Beyond staleness, I didn't smell anything rotting or mildewy, either animal or food or wood or cloth. The torch on my phone illuminated a small table with four chairs, appliances easily thirty years old, and two doorways leading farther into the house. One opened to a hallway, and the other to a family room with a fireplace. Luke tried the light switch, but nothing happened.

"You never answered whether you brought any weapons," Luke whispered.

"No, bro, I did not bring any weapons on my holiday to the other side of the globe."

He made a disapproving grunt. "Me neither. Ok let's remember for next time. You stay here. I'll check it out. Make sure it's safe."

"How are you going to do that without a torch?"

He thought about it, then stuck out his hand.

"Oh, no," I said. "You're not leaving me in the dark. Let's go together."

"Should we take off our shoes? If we can stay, we don't want to track mud everywhere."

"And if we have to leave in a hurry, we'll have lost our shoes in addition to everything else," I countered, but he had already set his bag on the table and was removing his sneakers to better navigate a crisis for the second time today. As he stood up straight, a look came over his face, and he took off his coat and let it fall to the floor. Then he pulled his jumper over his head...

"What is this, now?" I asked, taking a step away as though my soaked clothes might somehow get wet from him shaking his around. "What are you doing?"

"Well, I don't just have mud on my shoes, do I? It's all over my clothes, in my hair." He used his wet jumper to clean the back of his neck and head.

"So if the homeowner has been very quiet, they're going to encounter a dripping, strange man who broke into their house, and you will be chased out into the rain without even the clothes on your back."

"No one is here, Rin." He made a quarter turn away from me and stripped off his socks and jeans. Streaks of mud ran down his back, rolling and dipping where his muscles bunched and stretched. I hadn't gotten a good look at him in the afternoon light, because I was trying to behave (stupid me), but his entire body had changed a lot in two years. He'd lost the bulk of his superhero physique and was narrower, but less lean.

My mouth went dry as I imagined my hands on his hips, sliding up his back, over his chest and stomach. How he'd be softer now, and how his flesh would have a little more give beneath each kiss, and I'd have to press my mouth harder against him to find resistance but I'd want to kiss softer, to tease him. How I would have his whole body to explore, again, anew...

"If it belongs to anyone," he continued, "they're gone, and we're not going to run into them. But that doesn't mean I want to leave their place a mess." He held out his hand again, indicating my phone. "If I scream, you run. The least you can do is leave me with is your mobile."

I only half heard what he was saying, but his tone was sure, and his breath held the aroma of the local whisky we'd been enjoying before the rain ruined everything. I wanted to lick his lips to taste it again. In that moment, I wasn't sure I could have denied him anything.

I handed him my phone. "But to be clear," I said, keeping my grip when he tried to pull it away, so he would pay attention, "if you scream, I *will* run. Towards you. So I can punch whatever's threatening you. Got it?"

His gaze flickered from my eyes to my mouth and back again, and in those few seconds I realized we were utterly alone together with nothing and nobody to interrupt us if anything were to happen, and by the look on his face, the anything he wanted to happen was us. I saw him swallow, the movement directing my sight downwards. He brought his other hand up and ran his fingertips down my fingers, the back of my hand, and grasped my wrist.

I wondered if he could feel my pulse racing, if he could tell it was more from him standing so close to me in so little clothing than it was from the adrenaline of our predicament. Or that my shivering was from the same thing, and not the cold rain.

"I will be right back," he said softly, plucking the phone from me. He turned away with a wink and strode out of the room with the confidence of a man fully clothed.

Maybe this would be the year of saying "fuck everything." Fuck my job, fuck my career, fuck my company and family legacy. My parents, who willed me a broken business and no knowledge or skills to improve it. Fuck borders that kept me from the people

I loved, fuck this lingering pandemic. Fuck being afraid. Being anxious and paralyzed by it.

And maybe, if I was being very bold, and if I was very lucky, fuck Luke Maston.

Because it wouldn't kill me, right? Except in a very monkey's-paw-freak-accident way, like somehow getting electrocuted or the building falling down on us or getting bombed or something. What if I decided to not care about the consequences and did it anyway, and what if, in deciding to fuck up my life as much as possible, I ended up somewhere better that I couldn't have reached in any other way?

I listened to Luke's footsteps as he sauntered through the house. Floorboards creaking in a well-used but not dangerous way. The driving rain was muted, with actual walls and insulation between us and the storm instead of a worn-out piece of metal and a thin cloth. I heard Luke opening closets, running a faucet, and trying the light switch in each room, and each room remained dark. The house was little more than a cottage. While I couldn't keep my eyes on him as he moved from room to room, the glow from my phone was never out of my sight.

My feet squished in my shoes. I hated it almost enough to take them off before Luke returned. But his rounds didn't take long and he came back with a shrug, setting my phone on the table, torch side up. He carried several towels with him and put all but one on the table, too.

"Two bedrooms, one bathroom, a living room and a kitchen," he said, drying off. "No attic or basement or, if there is, no access to it from inside. Closets are clear. No to electricity. Yes to running water. One fireplace, status unknown. I didn't find any torches or candles but I didn't look in every drawer."

I nodded and realized I hadn't even taken off my backpack. I pulled out one of the chairs and set it down, then emptied my pockets next to my phone so I could take off my jacket.

"So we'll stay here tonight," I said, adding my coat to Luke's pile of clothes.

Luke smiled. "It is infinitely preferable to anything outside right now."

I sighed. "I know. We'll dry off, dry out, try to sleep. If anyone shows up, they'll have a car and we could persuade them to bring us somewhere else."

"Unless they, too, have broken down."

"Banish the thought, mate."

He ran the towel over his chest and gave me a smirk.

"Torches and candles are priority number one," I said. "I have a power bank in my bag, but let's not needlessly run down the battery if we don't have to."

"Looks like we'll have to make our own fun," he said. He wouldn't catch my eye, but he was grinning like he knew what he did to me. That was fine. We had a whole night if I wanted to take him up on it. After we got the survival stuff out of the way.

***

We split up the tasks. I'd stepped onto the porch first, so I took the first shower. Contrary to what I'd believed my whole life, cold water did fuck-all to douse my raging desire for Luke. It did wash away the mud, though, and that was the primary goal.

There was a still-working wind-up torch in a kitchen drawer, and Luke used it to hunt down some dry clothes. He brought me an armful as I finished wrapping a towel around myself.

"Dresses and nightshirts. A couple robes. Fuck if I could find pants."

He pulled out a wide sleeveless nightgown in a blue flower print. "This one's for me," he said, holding it up to himself.

"Love it," I said, picking through until I found a similar one in pink.

Luke got in the shower next, and after changing into the nightgown, I went to inspect the fireplace. I had plenty of practice with NIPL's luxury cottages, some of which started out as dirty and unused as this one. It still took a while, and when I realized Luke was done showering and had been going in and out the front door, I asked him to bring in some dry logs I'd seen outside.

"What are you doing out there, anyway?"

"Brought all our wet clothes to the porch and wrung them out. I found some twine in a drawer and made a very sus clothesline across the porch ceiling and hung up what I could. I wouldn't mind making our way tomorrow in this or a similar nightgown, as long as it was dry, but I would love for my own clothes to be up to the task."

When we'd done what we could, we pushed the smaller couch in front of the growing fire, jumped onto the stiff cushions, and burrowed under what smelled like clean blankets. We split a Starbar and sat side by side in quiet for a while, listening to the gentle crackle of the burning logs, our knees touching.

"I don't have another job lined up after this," Luke said.

I paused, mid-chew, wondering where that came from. Whether I missed something he said earlier or if he was continuing a conversation we'd only had in his head.

"I've got pick-ups from something I finished earlier this year, and whatever else they need me for at the Stromness project. But after that? Nothing."

I picked up the sadness in his voice, but I didn't know where he was going with it.

"Sounds like that isn't what you would have chosen, if you had a choice," I said. I dared a glance at him out of the corner of my eye, not wanting to scare him out of being vulnerable just because he was seen. Luke stared at the fire, head cocked to the side, like he was listening to someone else telling him the story of himself.

"No, it isn't," he agreed. "To be honest, it's been difficult to find work ever since *Broke*."

Even though we had all been there when Raphael and Luke had quit the film adaptation of the nationalist propaganda book *That Scarlet, Beating Heart*, none of us talked about it anymore. There was no need. Saying yes to the project had been a mistake, and leaving it had been necessary. Of course they'd been brave to do so. We lived in a world where people often had to compromise their morals simply to survive. The boys knew their careers and reputations might take a hit, but the people worth working for would recognize what they did as the right move.

Or, they should have.

"I'm sorry, Luke," I said. "That sucks." I wanted to say more. Ask him a thousand questions. Ask if he was ok (he definitely wasn't). Ask what he was going to do about it (he didn't sound like he had any idea) or if he was going to move on to something totally different (unclear if he was frustrated enough to make such a big change).

"Also. I, um." Luke cleared his throat. "I haven't really dated anyone."

He shifted beside me, his bare knee knocking into mine. "I'm trying to talk to you about something without saying anything," he grumbled.

"No, no, I got that. Loud and clear."

He laughed. Subdued. I missed the little giggle he did when he was delighted.

"Raphael," he said, catching my eye.

"You haven't gotten work since *Broke*," I said, talking through it aloud so he could guide me. "And you haven't had a romantic partner since..."

I flushed, not wanting to involve myself in his misery.

"Since a few months after *Broke*," he helped, with a half smile.

Oh god. Had he really not dated anyone else in the two years since we broke up? He said something about it the other day, but I thought he was trying to get a rise out of me. Was I the one that got away? Or did I break his heart so badly he didn't want to risk it again? I wanted to ask, but this wasn't about me. Not when he framed it that way. So the subject of Us could wait until after, and I set it aside.

What he was trying to tell me clicked, finally, and I felt stupid. "And in that same time, Raphael got himself a solid partner and his career has been better than ever."

"Bingo."

Jealousy. That made sense. Luke was only human. Of course he'd get jealous sometimes.

"You can't compare yourself to other people, though," I said. "Especially Raph because—"

"Because he was born lucky and talented and rich?"

"No," I huffed. "And I wouldn't say he's had an easy time of it, either. He has his own demons, his own bullies, and his own shortcomings."

"Ah, but none of those led to his career tanking and two years of solitude."

I looked into the fire. If it weren't for doubting my own worth, I might have been able to help with one of his problems. Sometimes

I felt like nobody deserved me because I was meant to be seduced by elf royalty and we could forget about Earth's problems and run naked in the moonlight surrounded by forest creatures and never feel pain or regret ever again. The rest of the time, I felt like nobody deserved me because no mortal should be burdened with my countless neuroses.

"We walked off *Broke* at the same time. The same exact moment. Arm in arm, for fuck's sake. And it affected Raphael wildly different than it did me, if it affected him at all. He met Mattie a few days before I met you, and they're partners now, and I—I fucked up and lost you." His voice broke and he shook his head. I reached for his hand and squeezed. "I know it shouldn't bother me, so I feel even worse about it. More and more, I've found myself unable to celebrate any of his wins. Every little thing makes me so irrationally angry. Like I'm watching someone else live my best life. Which I know is ridiculous."

It was and it wasn't. He had considered Raphael an equal, but his success where Luke had failed created an imbalance.

"And him paying off mum's house made it even worse, and I know that makes me sound like an ungrateful knob, but it's hard to argue that he's not 'living *my* best life' when he's the one literally keeping *my* family housed."

I willed my body's rising heat back down and kept my face as impassive as I could. A year later and he still didn't suspect me. "Raphael's the one who did that?" I asked innocently.

Luke cocked his head and gave me a superficial smile. "He won't admit to it. But he's the only one capable of it. Rather, he's the only one capable of both affording it and being a good enough actor to be believable when he says he didn't. Daphne has the money but she would never *stop* telling me it was her. And with NIPL's slow decline, you couldn't afford it."

His turn to flush. "I didn't mean—"

"No, no," I chuckled, relieved I was still off his radar. "You're absolutely right. Raph is the logical assumption." I turned my gaze to the fireplace's gentle flames because I couldn't look at him. I'd effectively directed Luke's blame away from me, which was great for me, but he'd landed on the guy who already made him feel inadequate, which was not great for Luke. "Do you want solutions, or are you looking for a sympathetic ear? Because the latter, I can do. The former, you know what I would suggest."

"The therapy is in progress. But it takes time, and even though I'm working on all these things, it doesn't mean they disappear." He paused and ran a hand through his hair, still damp from the shower. "I guess I'm tired. Tired of watching others succeed where I try and still fail. Tired of being alone. Tired of not having a friend to talk to about it."

"Because usually that friend is Raphael," I guessed.

Luke nodded.

"This might be a dumb question, but—have you talked to Raphael about it?"

"That's not a dumb question, and I have not. Because he's going to be understanding and wonderful and offer me roles on his projects and friends of his to date and solve all my problems, and I want him to be spiteful and gloating so I can continue hating him more than I hate myself."

Oh that hit, like, way too close to home. But in my case, I wanted my friends to remain in the dark about losing NIPL so I could tell myself they could have helped me, so my fault wasn't in driving a business into the ground, but in not trusting my friends enough, because I hated myself more than I loved them. See? Therapy worked.

"This is all totally relatable," I told him, giving his hand another squeeze. "It's easy to imagine injustice when someone succeeds at something you're striving for."

"Yeah, plus he's gotta be so bloody handsome. Nobody has a right to be that handsome. Have you seen him in a tuxedo? Illegal. Banned. Censored. How many casualties must we suffer before him-in-a-suit is forbidden?"

I laughed. "You're pretty bloody handsome, too. I remember you in a suit. Irresistible."

Luke puffed up at that. "You think?"

"Yeah, mate." I looked at his lips and bit my own. "Way out of my league."

"Naw," he said, squinting at me. "You're just trying to make me feel better."

"I am," I admitted with a shrug. "Doesn't mean it's not true. And, you know, what would be wrong with letting Raph put in a good word for you?" I had to move the subject away from romance.

"I know," he said with a sigh. "And not telling anyone about it was eating away at me. Tonight, I've barely said anything to you about it and I already feel more capable, like I could talk to Raph. How did that happen? Did you do that?"

"If I did, I don't know how, so don't ask me to do it again."

He smiled and settled back into the couch. The very poster boy of how cathartic it could be to talk about one's problems instead of holding everything in.

It was going to happen now, wasn't it?

"Ah, fuck," I said, bowing my head. I felt the burning behind my eyes and squeezed them shut, felt the tightness in the back of my jaw, and I hadn't even said anything yet. That sort of pre-breakdown when the next thing you said was going to be the bad news that changes everything. When you thought you might be able to hold yourself together if you said it fast enough. Prepared to be the paragon of stoicism. And then the mere breath taken to say it was enough to push you over the edge.

Luke could sense it. I hadn't released his hand since I'd grabbed it before. He was as much a comfort to me as I tried to be to him. He took it in his other hand now, with his closer arm snaking around my shoulders and pulling me to him. He didn't say a word, but let me get in a couple deep breaths before I said anything.

"I had to sell NIPL." I made it all the way to the last syllable before the sob took me. For a fraction of a second, I wondered if he could even understand what I said, but he held me tighter and let go of my hand to stroke my hair.

"Oh, sweetheart, I'm so sorry."

I couldn't speak after that. Two years of frustration, working and suffering alone, making decisions and knowing I was the only person to blame if it failed. Then: failing. It was one thing to have a therapist to talk to about it. But I couldn't talk to my friends, and that cut me off from the support they could have given. Saying it aloud, being vulnerable with Luke, broke the dam.

He didn't ask any questions. He knew I couldn't answer, through my flood of tears and all the snot bubbles I was sure were seeping through his ladies nightgown. When, what felt like hours later, I thought I could talk coherently, I did.

"I pivoted, and pivoted, and pivoted," I said thickly, sniffling through it. "So much that I was dizzy from it. I implemented every viable suggestion and even some outlandish ones. Hell, I even took your money. Yours and Raph's and Daphne's and Cinnamon's. I took government money and private money and my own savings and retirement. Sold properties. Fired people. And I still couldn't save it."

The last time I told Luke I was having problems with the business, he basically said it was my fault. That was the way I interpreted it, and I lashed out at him at the time. Blaming me wouldn't help. It made me feel like shit, and that was the first time I knew it wasn't going to work between me and Luke.

This time, I *hoped* he would tell me it was my fault. Then I'd know for sure I was incompetent and could stop wanting to try it again and do it right this time. I could move on.

"It sounds like," he said slowly, "you did everything you could. And you can grieve the loss of an important piece of your story. But you can't beat yourself up over it. You never told the Redgraves, did you?"

I shook my head. "They'd already given me money. They'd already been my cheerleaders, we'd already put our heads together dozens of times."

"That isn't why you didn't tell them. Rin, you and I are alike, in this horrible way. We want to make our loved ones comfortable, but don't want to accept comfort."

"I should be stronger than that," I said, my voice cracking all over again.

"That's bollocks and you know it."

The rain hadn't let up, but it had become white noise at this point, and the part of my brain still trying to protect me tried to focus on the storm. But I needed to tell the rest of the story aloud, and I needed Luke to hear it.

"That's not the worst part," I said. I didn't know if I believed it, but the next part, if not the worst, certainly made things worse overall. "I sold it to an international travel and tourism company, and they hired me on as a consultant. But they wouldn't keep me in New Zealand because I'd fucked up so badly. They have me on an international rotation. I have a *boss*—" I spat the word, still angry, "and a budget I don't control and I need permission for everything and it's awful. I hate it."

I started crying again, though technically I hadn't stopped. Luke rubbed my back and held me close, planted a kiss in my hair. I'd been afraid that letting him take care of me would lead to something more intimate, but I was wading too deep into embarrassing emotions to worry about that now. So I let him comfort me, that thing that we were both pretty bad at.

"You know you have to quit, right? Like, for your mental health?"

There hadn't been a day since I sold NIPL that I hadn't thought about it. The only training I had, in anything besides my hobbies, was in tourism. Even then, it was very specific. I'd taken certification training and other classes as needed, but they were geared towards the company's niche offerings and not the wider industry. I knew a little about flights, as much as anyone who booked a lot of their own travel, so I hired someone to focus on that. I knew more about real estate, but Lizzie was a wizard at it, so I paid her to get it done for NIPL. When I stepped up to take over after my parents passed, my role was more overview than hands-on.

It was too big a job for one person, and the company was so bloated. I spent my time adjusting little things when I should have been overhauling the big things. I didn't know.

"Luke. I only had one job my whole life, and I was so bad at it, I had to sell it to get out of debt. After I paid all the employees, all the severance, all the debts, all the loans, do you know how much I had for myself? Six thousand dollars. A forty-two year old business, the lifeblood of my parents, bringing in millions of dollars a year, and at the end, it came down to six grand."

He was silent a moment, letting his fingers trace light circles against my arm. "First of all, your job isn't your life."

"You can't say it unless it applies to you, too," I countered.

"It applies to me too. My family comes first."

"So if it came down to it, you'd abandon your dream of being an actor to take a job that would keep your family afloat?"

He sighed. "Just because I'm as stubborn about my career as you are doesn't mean I'm wrong."

"I swear, if you tell me to ask Raphael for a job, I'm going to steal all of the clothes in this house and leave on my own so you can wander the countryside naked and lost."

"That's what you told *me* to do!" He jostled me affectionately, and I burrowed into his warm body. "I'm trying to say you have other skills, other interests, other options. Losing the company was a heavy blow, so I'm going to repeat your advice back to you for, like, the third time, by saying therapy is an effective tool to manage the mental and emotional toll. But working for the people who bought you out is effectively killing you, and you can't move on until you leave them behind, too."

I'd wanted Luke to tell me some hard truths. And he was right. Talking about it, even if it didn't lead to any solutions right away, made me feel better.

"Also," he said. "I want to tell you that this, here, holding you and talking with you about these things? Feels right." He took a breath, and spoke even softer. "It feels like we never left."

I sniffled again and pulled away from him, knowing my face was gross from crying, but there wasn't anything I could do about it.

"I don't want to make you uncomfortable," he said, whispering now. His eyes were locked onto mine, alert and intense and trying to say something that didn't need language. "I wouldn't—"

I didn't find out what he wouldn't do. I leaned into him, grabbed the back of his head, and kissed him with the hunger and longing of two entire years without him, with a desperation so needy, I forgot to be embarrassed.

Chapter 23
October 2022
Luke

Starling.

I winced at the thought, shooing it away like it was an actual starling, but once I pictured it, I heard its birdsong too clearly, and I struggled to shake off the last cobwebs holding me to sleep and tried to remember where I was and what happened in real life.

On a couch, beneath blankets, Rin curled against me. Warm. Air a weird but comforting mixture of staleness and fireplace. I took a breath through my nose and stretched, opening my eyes to the dusty living room, the windows on either side of the fireplace bathing the room with bright sunlight. Without the ticking of clocks or humming of a refrigerator or other electrical appliances (or, thank heavens, the driving patter of an unrelenting downpour), the bird's call and Rin's light snores were loud enough to wake me.

If I dreamed, I didn't remember them. It felt more like I had walked in a memory, but there was no way to know which one. A nice one, I think. Something as comforting as waking up beside Rin without an alarm clock spurring us out of bed.

I caressed their bare arm and made note of every place our skin touched. Fingertips to triceps. Armpit to shoulder. Nose to chest. Knee to thigh. A thousand strands of hair to shoulder, neck, face. A hundred more points of contact. There were a lot, because we hadn't bothered to re-clothe ourselves with the borrowed nightgowns after making love. Too much exhaustion and a total lack of shame.

Their hair smelled (inexplicably, as usual) of chocolate, and I wondered how long their shamelessness would last. Forever? Perfect. But unlikely. Sex wasn't a mistake, but we were in the middle of a crisis and if I knew Rin at all, they'd consider it a distraction at best and another bad decision in a long line of them at worst. Until we were safely back in civilisation, I would have to act casual, even though I hoped it meant as much to them as it did to me.

And I hoped they'd acknowledge it instead of running away or making excuses for why we couldn't or shouldn't try a relationship again.

We were supposed to be in London today. By the angle of the sunlight, I guessed it was already noon or close to. We had been a few hours away from Leeds when Mr Bean disintegrated and abandoned us to the elements. So our final destination was about six hours away by car, which we didn't have. I ran down the list of other things we didn't have. Luckily, I still had my naturally optimistic attitude, or our predicament might have driven me to despair. And I was with Rin, so I had a team I could count on. And they motivated me to keep them safe. It was a vicious cycle of love and tenderness.

"Hey, love. Wake up." I hated to rouse them. Besides the trials and tribulations of Mr Bean and the rain, Rin had shared a lot of themself last night, and I wished I could let them sleep off the physical and emotional knackerment for as long as they needed.

They woke up slowly, their eyelashes fluttering their dark hair, which was draped over their face and my chest. A yawn and a stretch, and a pause.

"It stopped raining," I said softly.

"Fuck," they whispered. They jolted upright and made a face and clicked their tongue like something tasted bad. *Me too*, I thought. I guess we'd both left our toothbrushes in the bags back in the car.

"Haven't checked our clothes," I continued. "I was about to, but I would have had to wake you up either way."

"What time is it?" They looked around for their phone, which was on the kitchen table and out of reach.

Hard to tell if they were putting distance between us because of sex the night before or the day and night before the sex. *Casual, Luke. Don't scare them off.* "Noon, I'd guess. Ready to get this party started?"

Rin put a hand against their cheek, and I watched the memories of what happened last night play across their face. A shy smile, the huff of an almost-laugh, and they glanced up at me with a smirk before a frown settled into place like the quick-moving storm clouds of the night before.

"Do you regret it?" I asked. I shouldn't have. If they said yes, it would make the next few hours and days very awkward. If I didn't know, I could act like everything was fine.

"Not you," they grumbled, clearing their throat. Rin reached over to grasp my hand, and the thing causing the tightness in my belly relaxed. "I needed this. You. But I'm going to fall back into emergency mode soon, and I don't want you to think I'm trying to forget what happened last night. We need to be safe and in the company of the squad before I can think of anything beyond that, but I promise that's exactly what I'll do the moment I can."

I brought their hand up and brushed my lips gently over their knuckles. "Well, I'm going to continue being whatever you need, and those terms are acceptable. Do you want a moment to orientate yourself?"

They nodded. I swung my legs over the side of the couch, gave their shoulder a quick kiss, and started getting ready to leave. Outside, most of our clothes were still damp. My boxers were dry, thanks to their thin material, and so were Rin's underthings and all our socks, for the same reason. My sneakers were still soaked through, but Rin's boots had held up. I imagined the unique discomfort of walking for who knew how long in wet jeans and compared it to walking the same path in a soft nightgown. The decision was easy. Besides, we weren't that far from Scotland. Everyone should have been desensitized to men in skirts.

Inside, Rin rifled through their backpack, and I put the few dry clothes on the table.

"Mobile is fully charged," they said, unplugging it from their power bank. "Still no signal. I searched for a landline but didn't find one. I looked in the cabinets again for food but there's nothing."

My stomach answered on its own, a long and angry growl.

"Hush," I told it. "The rest of the clothes are still wet," I said to Rin. "I don't have any other clothes in my bag, so I'm going to have to wear the nightgown or, ideally, several. It's warm and soft and covers most of my legs. I'm going to look for something else to wear as a top. I can't imagine a home having a dozen nightgowns but no other clothing."

"Good idea. I'll wear my nightgown too. My leggings might be dry enough. We can bring the wet stuff with us in a plastic bag, I have a few with me." They took the box of salty crackers out of their backpack. "Can I offer you some breakfast? My water bottle is still full, too. There's more to eat and drink back in the car, but this is it for now."

"Don't mind if I do."

It didn't take long to get everything together, put the furniture back where it belonged, and leave a note and some money on the table. Maybe nobody would find it for years. Maybe it would be found by future travelers in the same situation we had been in. If that was the case, I wished them luck. We left the door unlocked to help those fictional trespassers.

Out on the porch, we gathered the wet clothes and stuffed them into a plastic bag the best we could. We'd found more socks in the dresser, so we doubled up on them. Rin found and took a long-sleeved shirt and tucked it into their leggings, which they judged dry enough. I had taken the nightgown Rin wore and put it and a third (in green) over my blue one, for warmth, and a moth-eaten but clean hand-knit sweater made of weird rainbow yarn that made the garment look brown. There were coats in another closet, and I took a beige trench coat that fit me poorly.

Rin stood a few metres beyond the porch, hands on their hips, pack on their back, looking in every direction. I had done the same when I first came out here, and I knew what they saw: nothing. Hills. Fields. We heard animals, definitely sheep, but couldn't see them. Back towards the road, a tall hedge blocked our view of where Mr Bean should have been. There weren't even any other buildings out there, no homes or sheds or barns. We couldn't have chosen a worse spot to break down if we'd tried.

"Shit," Rin said.

"What?" I hurried down the porch steps. It had been a while since I wore a skirt, and the draft was distracting. "What do you see?"

They sighed. "No, I just remembered, I didn't cancel the hotel reservation last night. They probably charged me anyway. Fuck."

"Hey, I'll still pay for my half," I told them, giving their shoulder a squeeze. "It's not your fault."

"No, there's something else. I, uh, I sort of kept something from you."

A numbness spread from my stomach, like when you knew what someone was going to say in the moments right before they said they've been cheating on you, or somebody died. Rin had been keeping things from me for two years, because they didn't owe me anything. But they'd shared themself last night, and it meant something to them, but I was pretty sure it meant even more to me.

"Tell me," I said. "Whatever it is, we'll work it out."

They bit their lip and shifted their weight from one leg to another. "Raphael and Mattie are waiting for us in Leeds."

Ok. That wasn't what I thought they were going to say. It was way better than anything I thought they were going to tell me, but also, what?

"What?" I asked.

"I texted them about you losing your phone in the pond yesterday and Raphael said he would get you a new one and drive up to meet us in Leeds last night. It was going to be a surprise. But then, the rain, and the car, and no mobile reception, so I couldn't tell them what happened, which means they've been in Leeds since last night, waiting to meet us, and they don't know where we are and they can't get in contact with me, and they must be freaking out right now—"

"Rin." I grabbed their shoulders and turned them to look at me. "You're spiraling, mate. There's nothing you can do about them right now."

"They probably called emergency services—"

"Good. I hope they did. Then someone will find us soon and they'll have sandwiches."

They still had a look of panic in their eyes, like a spooked horse. "Rin, we can only control what we can control. It sucks. But we're going to collect the rest of our stuff and start walking, and before long, we're going to simply stumble into the radius of a cellular tower or flag down a car that has Wi-Fi somehow, and we're going to contact them as soon as it's possible. Right now, it's impossible. But we have a plan, and we're going to follow it and be fine. All right?"

They didn't look much calmer, but they nodded like a normal person and not—what did Mattie call it?—not like a startled Chihuahua. I slid an arm over Rin's shoulders so we could face the day together. We started towards the hedge, and in the daylight, it was easy to make our way without slipping in the mud or tripping on rocks.

"We'll get rescued soon," I said with an enthusiasm I almost felt. "Because my hodgepodge of an outfit looks like an iteration of Doctor Who that was rejected for unrelated reasons. And everyone wants to travel with The Doctor."

That got a laugh out of them, and they glanced at my bare shins. "Too sexy," they assessed.

"Chur."

Closer to the hedge, we heard the animals from before, louder.

"Sheep?" They asked. They smiled. Good. Yes. Forget the continuing terribleness of this ordeal. Think of it like an adventure. Just The Doctor and his companion out for a stroll. Or, more likely, two hobbitses searching for an unforgivably late first breakfast.

"Could be," I said, returning their grin. I couldn't identify the weird metallicky noise, though it could have been an animal I didn't know as well. "Goats, too, sounds like."

We didn't remember how we got through the hedge the first time. When we found an opening, something marked the ground in front of it, mint green and dirty.

"Looks like a blanket," I said. "Or a towel."

"Huh," Rin said. "Weird. There are buttons on it."

I shrugged and ducked through the hedge to the other side.

And walked in to absolute chaos.

I turned around abruptly and blocked Rin's path.

"Uh, what are you doing?"

"Um," I said. Fragments of excuses rose to my consciousness but never made it to my tongue, because I truly had no idea what to say to make them turn around and walk down the other side of the hedge until we met a road far enough away that they couldn't look back and see the carnage I'd witnessed.

"Um," I said again. *Really making a winning case for yourself here, Maston.*

"Um." Not suspicious at all.

"Luke, 'um' is not a full sentence. What the fuck is going on?"

This was gonna be bad. This was gonna be bad.

"I don't know how to fix this," I admitted, my shoulders slumping. Rin tilted their head to try to look past me, and their face fell.

"I know what that is," they said, their voice small. "That's my purple turtleneck. In the mud. Luke."

"I'm so sorry," I told them, before stepping out of their way. I did feel like The Doctor then, remembering all the times he knew they were fucked and instead of explaining, simply apologized.

We had found the sheep and the goats we kept hearing. We found Mr Bean, too. We also found the contents of the bags we'd left behind strewn up and down the road. Trampled into the mud, torn apart, half eaten. One sheep was prancing around with a pair of my boxers draped over it like a cape, and I wondered if another sheep was like, "Oi mate, this teal would be such a good color on you, oh you'd look so lovely" and the first sheep was like, "Naw, you're just teasing" and the other one said, "Hoof to god I'm not, let's put it on you" and then picked up my underwear with its teeth and tossed it onto the first sheep with a little sheep grunt, and now it was showing off because it felt like a beautiful princess—

"*Fuck* me," Rin shouted, pulling me back to reality. It was a good thing that, between the two of us, one of us was always paying attention when there was an emergency. Sometimes, I took the lead, because I was good at last minute decisions, and other times, I stood around dissociating, daydreaming of sheep while Rin assessed the situation. They picked their way among the clothes, slowly moving closer to the car. I followed, scanning the ground for anything important and salvageable.

"The doors," Rin muttered, eyes lingering on each piece of clothing but never collecting any of them. "We left the doors open, and your seat was still reclined so it made a perfect little bridge to the Vast. Hole. Where the backseat should have been, and they thought it was a game and then they found our delicious and dry and soft-sided luggage and brought it out so everyone could enjoy it."

Yeah, no one we eventually told this story to was going to believe any of it.

"You ever have goat stew?" They pitched their voice low and stared daggers at one of the animals in question, who stared back at them with passive, blocky eyes. That goat did not believe Rin would harm it. I had my doubts, too, but I didn't think I'd ever seen them so close to the edge.

"Yes," I said slowly, "but I'm vegetarian now, so maybe don't murder the goat. Animals are gonna animal. Rain is gonna rain."

"And humans gonna human. I think everyone would appreciate the poetry in it. Eating the thing that ate your stuff. Humans love that kind of symmetry. Also, murder."

I stepped over the tatters of my royal-blue sweater, the one I'd gotten in Scotland a dozen years ago when I was working on my first big film. It was expensive, and I'd kept it in good shape. I couldn't afford to replace it. Not in this economy (this economy but also my personal, embarrassing economy).

Rin might have had a point about the whole kill-the-goat thing.

Our destroyed bags rested against each other, sad and broken, beside the back wheel. I wasn't close enough yet, but they both looked empty from a distance. The car cover had been pulled off the car completely. I could have easily mistaken it for a weird-looking pile of mud that the rain and wind had shaped behind the car, if I hadn't known what to look for. Two goats chewed at its edges. One stood by the broken passenger side door, chomping on the filling inside the seat. Another goat jumped onto the bonnet, and I realized that was the metallic sound from before. Sheep milled about. None of them were aggressive or even cared that we were there. They mostly just stood or wandered around, nosing at the treasure they'd pulled from the carcass of Mr Bean.

As we got closer, the smell got worse. Of course, a smorgasbord of the caliber we'd left for them would lead to necessary pissing and shitting, but they had a fucking field day doing it all over the clothes they unearthed from the car. Add to that the smell of wet farm animal and all the odors of the car. It was an absolute disaster.

Rin had been quiet. I didn't know how to react, either. It was too serious for jokes. Now that I looked back on the entire thing—no mobile reception, car disintegrating, zero food, our belongings ruined—I shouldn't have been joking at all.

I shooed away the goat eating the passenger seat. Well, I tried to. Gestures and exclamations of "off with you" had no effect, so I was reduced to physically pushing it away with my hands. Both wet and dry mud tangled its coarse hair, and I came away smelling as fresh as a barnyard. Rin had hand sanitizer. I could find a piece of clothing not totally disgusting, wipe my hands off. Not seeing any, I shrugged and wiped them on the back of the passenger seat, and finished the job on the back bottom part of my new old trench coat. It didn't have to be pretty. It only had to be warm.

The reusable shoppers bag and snacks we left behind had been split open by hungry goats, of course, but our drinks had been left alone. I had most of a bottle of water remaining, and Rin's cola was half full. They'd put the unopened drinks on the floor of the back, and I gathered them, too, fitting them as best I could in my already overstuffed messenger bag. Could my bag from the car be saved and used to carry this stuff? Or could Rin's?

I extricated myself from the corpse of Mr Bean and shuffled the few feet to where my carry-on and Rin's duffel had fallen by the back wheel. Rin's had been torn almost in half, with bites taken out of it. The front panel of mine had been ripped clean off. They looked like they'd been victim of some kind of werewolf attack. I don't know why I thought either of them would be intact, as if the animals had gingerly unzipped them before ravaging their contents.

At least I'd kept all my important things in my shoulder bag. Passport, extra glasses, my phone when it wasn't at the bottom of a lake. I'd packed the little suitcase with only shoes and clothing, and while it would suck to have to replace it all, I hadn't lost anything incredibly precious to me. The blue sweater was only slightly precious. I wondered if Rin had been looking for something specific when they made a noise, like a strangled gasp, and picked something up off the ground. They lifted the remnants of a clear garment bag that contained a mangled, muddy twist of dark cloth.

"What is it?" I asked, walking over to them.

They shook their head, but I couldn't tell if they were responding to me or the destroyed ensemble. After staring at it for another minute, they dropped it back to the ground and walked away.

"Rin?" This was not good. They headed in the direction we'd originally been going, and I doubted we'd return this way again. I turned back to the car and tapped my fist against my chest. *Goodbye, Mr Bean. You left us in the second most terrible situation you could have, but at least you didn't explode with us in you. Flights of angels and whatnot.*

I caught up to Rin and fell into stride beside them. A couple sheep followed us, but I couldn't worry about that. In fact, if their owner tried to track them down, we would be found, too, and the nightmare would be mostly over. So let them come along. It would be a parade of fools.

We didn't need to speak. Thanks to the atlas, we knew which way to head. It was easier without having to lug our additional bags. Just the two of us and a handful of destructive but beautifully dressed sheep and the packs on our backs and the open road. Like wanderers, or the stereotypical hobo. If only there was a train we could jump on—

Focus, Luke. No more wandering off. Rin needs you.

After an hour of walking without any cars passing us, the sheep lost interest and left. The sun did, too, though it tagged a bright cloud cover to take its place. Rin still hadn't said anything, but I knew they were deep in Emergency Mode, full of emotions, and didn't want to interact with the guy who convinced them to go on a four-day road trip in a foreign country in a vehicle made of little more than rust and dreams, instead of a dry bus with Wi-Fi and dozens of other people who could work together if anything even remotely inconvenient happened, let alone the breakdown to end all breakdowns.

They needed the time to think, and process, and since all we had to do was the repetitive work of one foot in front of the other until we hit an intersection, it was the perfect time for them to let their mind do its thing while their body didn't need it.

When we did hit the crossroad, Rin stopped, and I stopped with them.

"That was my outfit for the premiere," they said softly. They had their eyes closed, as though seeing me react to them with empathy or pity or sympathy would be too emotional for them. "I bought it when it looked like NIPL was starting to turn around. Cost way too much money, more than I would ever spend normally, but I had been passing it in the store window every time I walked to work, and I wanted it and wanted to celebrate so I bought it."

"I'll buy you a new one," I said. Not the point, I knew, but the point was much bigger than I could fit in one expression of the emotion Rin was trying to avoid.

"With what money, Luke?"

Oh that emotion, I could name. Passive aggression. Deserved, but still.

"Rin, I am so sorry. So, so sorry. I know I said before that my plans might not always turn out right but they weren't shit. I'm going to admit now that they are, usually, shit. But I was excited to spend time with you, and I thought a road trip would be fun, and there's no way I could have expected it to turn out like it has."

Rin hadn't moved, eyes still closed, and I started pacing. "Dozens of things went wrong," I continued, "and we could have abandoned this whole thing at any time. I didn't because I'm stubborn, yeah, but mostly, I just wanted to be with you. Impress you. In fact, I welcomed the little setbacks, because they gave me the chance to show you that I can be a good partner when things go tits up. But why didn't *you* walk away from this? The moment you saw that shitbox of a car, your self-preservation should have kicked in. A short walk to the ferry, then catch the bus from Scrabster. But you didn't."

I stopped pacing in front of them and let out an exhale loud enough that they knew where I was. They looked up at me. The cloudy sky and the dark trees and earth made their eyes look more grey than blue. Maybe their sadness also affected it. That's what I saw there, beyond tiredness and disappointment. Just plain old sadness.

"Luke," they said, like I was asking something I already knew, that they had explained to me a hundred times.

But I didn't know it. I *wanted* it. I imagined it and fantasized about it. I would go to the greatest lengths to find out if it could be possible, even borrowing the shambles of a car and embarking on a doomed road trip. After everything that had happened, if Rin told me for sure, it would have been worth it. Even losing my phone and getting lost.

"Rin, I don't know. I can only guess, until you tell me, and I know better than to assume with you. That's not a criticism. I know how important communication is."

They tipped their head back and looked at the sky with a huff. When they did an about-face and started walking away from me, it was the first and only time I ever thought Rin was truly out of my reach. Then they stopped and looked over their shoulder.

"I missed you," they said. They'd said it before, a couple times in the last few days, but the extraordinary thing was that this time, it sounded like "I love you."

I felt tears in my eyes. My throat swallowed what could have been a shaky breath or could have been the beginning of my own breakdown. I lifted my hands to let them fall against my sides in a gesture I hoped they would know meant "yeah."

"I missed you, too." *I love you, too.*

"You can't take all the blame," they said, turning their whole body back to face me, and I closed the distance in a few strides.

"I will if you want me to." Of all the mishaps of the last few days, nothing got my heart rate up as much as thinking we could be together again.

Rin sighed, a lonely sound. "I don't want you to want me to want you to take the blame and yes I know that's a clumsy sentence but you know what I mean."

"I should want you to think the best of me."

"To do right by me, yeah." They shuffled their feet in the browning grass. "This all sucks, and I know there's nothing we can do and, no matter what happens—grrrr—" they growled into the woods and turned in a circle. "I'm glad to be with you."

I couldn't help myself. "'Here at the end of all things'?" My grin was way too maniacal for such a serious situation, but if you give me a *Lord of the Rings* opening, I'm damn well going to take it.

"Jesus I hope not," they said, thankfully unaffected by my creepy smile. "I'm hungry and swiftly approaching hangry, but if we walk long enough, we *have* to come across something or someone that will help us. Even if it's the mere fringes of a goddamn mobile tower."

Obsessed with food, a very long walk ahead, and the mention of a tower? It wasn't my fault. They'd started it with Frodo's line, and now my brain was in nerd mode. And under these specific circumstances, that was not helpful. I handed them their soft drink, forgetting it until now, and they drank it immediately. I glanced around, hoping to notice something that might help us, praying to Galadriel to light our way.

Not far into the trees, I saw something white and flat and eye height. I couldn't read the faded sign until I was right next to it, but it sounded promising. I sent a silent thanks to the Lady of the Wood.

"I don't know about a mobile tower," I said as Rin stepped up beside me. "But how do you feel about a world-famous private garden?"

Chapter 24
October 2022
Rin

"That sign was erected the last time someone cleaned the cottage we burgled," I said, trying for the hundredth time already that day to act normal even though half my mind was celebrating like we'd landed on the moon, and the other half was panicking like we'd run out of gas on the way there.

Sex with Luke hadn't caused such a divided reaction from me in the past. Then again, we hadn't been in the middle of a new breakdown after dealing with a full two years of life-wide breakdowns before. He was as considerate, as creative and enthusiastic, as beautiful and generous as ever, and my body still responded to him like a goddamn instrument.

And in the middle of this crisis, that was a problem.

I put my empty cola bottle at the bottom of the sign's wooden stake and tried to push the memory of his lips and hands and moans further into my subconscious. Tried to replace it by dredging up some guilt about leaving trash in the woods. My DNA was all over it, so if we ended up as a Netflix true crime documentary, at least someone would know we'd been here. *Yes, murder, pivot from the weight of him on you and the coconut smell of his warmed skin and think about murder.*

"After all this time, the garden must have changed hands or been bulldozed over for a tennis court or something."

"World famous!" He repeated, pointing to the sign, making an expression of incredulity.

"It can't be world famous if it isn't on the internet, and believe me, I looked up every attraction between Edinburgh and Leeds, from the number one tourist trap on everyone's lists to the most obscure roadside shed selling meat pies, as you may remember."

Luke glanced between the sign and the forest beyond, hands on his hips and one foot up on a fallen log. Somehow, between his stolen trench coat, sweater, and nightgowns, his athletic posture, and the unmistakable desire for mischief in his eyes, he reminded me of every bard in every roleplaying game Cinnamon made me play. If whatever he had in mind included singing or bullshitting, I wouldn't be surprised. "Is it in the atlas?"

Hmm. Ok, good point. I put my backpack on the driest part of the ground and pulled out the atlas. The pages were a little wavy and damp, but it was still readable.

"And if it *is* on private land, they'll catch us trespassing. And maybe they'll have sandwiches." Luke's voice got kind of wistful as he mentioned his imagined sandwiches.

I pinched my lower lip as I scanned the map. "I'm not sure I'm 'get arrested' level desperate yet. Ok. You were right, it's here, but..." I flipped forwards and back a few pages. "There aren't any details, it just says 'Richelieu Gardens and Labyrinth'."

I glanced up at Luke, whose posture reminded me of Lena and Cassidy so much, I barked a laugh. His arms hung at his sides, and his jaw had dropped and his eyebrows were nearly to his hairline. He was begging to go there with his whole body. "You want to go, don't you?"

His eyes widened and he nodded his head.

"Even if there aren't sandwiches?"

He shut his mouth and stared into the distance, considering. "I don't think any of our current possible choices would include sandwiches. It was wishful thinking. But a world famous attraction is bound to have resources to get us back on track. And a labyrinth would be fun. The girls would love to see it—"

Remembering he no longer had a way to communicate with his daughters, or take or send photos to them, his level of joy visibly diminished. I put my pack back on and patted his shoulder.

"It's ok, mate. As soon as even half a bar appears, I'm calling Mattie to get us out of here, but right after that, you're calling Cass. And I'll take plenty of photos. Our primary goal is to find either a mobile signal or a person. Your brain might not remember, but I'm counting on your stomach to remind you regularly."

As if in answer, his stomach whined, and I felt bad for him. I felt bad for me too. My belly had been quieter but crampy.

"Well," I said, gesturing in the direction the arrow on the sign pointed. "Lead the way."

Luke literally leapt at the chance, launching himself through the woods with the energy of someone who'd last had a full and satisfying meal more recently than twenty four hours ago. He didn't keep up that level of intensity for long, though. I asked if the rest of the drinks had been destroyed, and when he said he brought all of them, I urged him to have one of the carbonated ones. The caffeine might cause a crash later, but the salt would do him good now.

Ninety minutes, one soda, and half a water bottle later, we arrived at the wooden gates of the gardens. Grey brick walls extended in either direction, taller than either of us, too tall to climb (though I expected Luke to try anyway). They'd either been left to nature or the crumbling blocks and crowding vegetation were part of a deliberate wild aesthetic. Iron filigrees held together the rotting wood of the double doors, and the top band of metal spelled out "Richelieu."

After all that work to get there, once we arrived, we both hesitated to open the doors. It wasn't scary. The day was bright enough for a cloudy one, the trees didn't give weird vibes, and plenty of birds sang in the branches. But the wood looked on the verge of crumbling if we pushed it, and the iron latch likely to disintegrate to dust in our hands. There were so many stories about mysterious doors in lonely forests, and we were reluctant to start yet another adventure without finishing the one we were already in, especially without eating something first and in Luke's case, specifically, sandwiches.

"Oh, wait," I said, which was silly, because neither of us had made any sort of motion to move. I brought out my phone and took a photo of the door, then stepped back and took a wider shot of Luke at the door to show how tall the walls were.

"I want to think you're doing that to send to Lena and Cass," Luke said, "but it also sort of feels like you're trying to get a record of where we've been for when we're murdered."

"A thing can be two things at once," I said with a wink. "What happened to the enthusiastic Luke of two hours ago?"

"Two hours of walking," he said with a sigh. Yeah, I couldn't blame him.

"Still want to explore?" I asked, turning to take a selfie of us.

"I do." He made a face for the camera. "But now that I see it, I'm afraid you might be right. It looks like it was abandoned before we were born."

"So," I said, grabbing the door handle, "let's get arrested for trespassing."

In my experience, few people were spurred to action by a call to get caught doing something they weren't supposed to, but in my defense, those were somehow always the people I befriended.

Beyond the doors (which didn't fall apart or turn into a portal, though they did stick a bit), we stumbled into a rectangular, traditional garden, untended for decades. The inner walls were made from the same material as the outer ones, though not as high. The doorways in every side had no doors, but we couldn't see much down those paths without getting closer. A round fountain occupied the middle of the garden, with three massive sculpted fish dancing up the centre and unsupervised weeds twining up the statue and overflowing from the pool, which was half filled with rainwater and smelled like swamp. Square raised beds—one in each corner—were overgrown, and each with a Grecian-style statue enveloped in the same leafless, untamed bramble as the fountain.

"Like *Sleeping Beauty*," I murmured.

"Like Weeping Angels," Luke answered with a shudder.

"I know that's Doctor Who, but I haven't seen it."

"For the best," he said. "Don't look them up. We'll watch it together when we're safely back in civilization." He cast a glance towards the nearest statue, gave another shiver, and made his way to the doorway on our left.

In its heyday, the Richelieu Gardens and Labyrinth must have been spectacular. We'd gone through several doorways into different styles of gardens before I had the idea of making a map so we wouldn't get lost. On a blank page at the back of the atlas, I penciled in a rough sketch of what we'd seen so far.

Each section was set up differently, some more traditional, some more modern. One thing they had in common was the overgrown plants. As we made our way farther from where we'd entered, I simultaneously hoped we would come across some sign of recent activity (so we wouldn't be lost there forever and die) and hoped we *wouldn't* come across any recent activity (bringing the chance of being murdered down significantly).

Besides the occasional birdsong and Luke muttering the names of those birds under his breath, the only sounds were our breathing and our footsteps, brushing across years of leaves and unattended tendrils, over paths of dirt or pebbles or stone or, in some cases, what looked to be concrete, cracked and pale.

"Ohhhh," Luke said, drawing out the word. He turned in a circle, shaking his head. "*This* is the labyrinth. All these gardens, linked up together. The whole big garden is the labyrinth."

"You'd better hope not," I said, finishing the outline of our current garden, "or else the only way out is the door we came in."

"No, there'd be a way out at the other end, right?" His voice carried a frown. And a bit of worry I'd heard too many times the last few days. I was all for adventure, but honestly, this was ridiculous.

"If the designers used the words 'labyrinth' and 'maze' interchangeably, then sure."

"What a time to indulge in pedantry."

"Hell, I hope I'm wrong." I looked up from our makeshift map to catch his eye. "I, too, would love another exit. Preferably something leading directly into a posh little hotel, or—" I checked my phone. "Literally anywhere with a signal."

Two gardens later, still no sign of an exit or a directory or recent human antics, Luke let out a growl, followed by a feral scream. I dropped the atlas and pencil and rushed over to him, thinking he'd stepped in a bear trap (totally reasonable) or found a dead body (less reasonable, but after the days we'd had, unsurprising).

"What's wrong? Are you hurt?"

He stumbled back, laughing. I didn't see anything on the ground where he had been, no traps or carcass.

"Luke?"

"I'm tired," he said, still smiling, throwing his hands up in exasperation. "We wanted to find someone. Why are we being so quiet? HELLOOOOOO!"

Part of me cringed against the noise, and it was the part that still parked my car beneath lampposts or with the carriage return on the driver's side, and walked with my keys between my fingers like Wolverine in case I had to defend myself, and worried about going golfing with three strangers at a remote course and my *god* was that only four days ago?

But Luke had a point, even if he was delirious from fasting for a day. We would have to luck into a mobile tower signal, but finding people to help us required initiative.

"You're right," I said, turning back to pick up the things I'd dropped. "But let's walk and yell, and hopefully we'll find some success one way or another."

So we yelled as we walked. The birds kept talking, too, which Luke thought was a good sign. If they weren't too scared by human noise to stop singing, that meant they were used to it. And soon, we did find something.

This garden was L-shaped, with stone benches around what was once a koi pond in the longer side of the garden. In the shorter side was another raised bed, but the brush had been cleared away and new plants installed. To one side, there was a black wheelbarrow and gardening tools, and two small bushes in green plastic buckets, ready to be planted.

I grabbed at Luke's sleeve, but he was reaching for me at the same time, and we ended up slapping our hands together a couple times before I grasped the front of his coat.

"I see it," he said, gripping my hand that was gripping him. "Hello?" He projected his voice towards the fresh plants and the doorway beside it, and we made our way to it slowly. "I know it sounds cliché, but our car broke down in the rain and our mobiles don't have a signal and we need help—oh, Rin, it's *Rocky Horror*!"

It wasn't just the hunger and anxiety making his brain jump to stories with similar situations, but they certainly didn't help.

"And a hundred other films, most of which are actual horror." My strength was in unarmed combat, but that trowel looked nice and sharp, and the long-handled thing resting against the wall would make a good ranged weapon. We could throw the potted plants if we had to, or push the wheelbarrow ahead of us like a shield—

"Oh, sweet," Luke whispered. The gardening tools/weapons were still out of reach, but we'd come close enough to see through the doorway into the garden beyond it, and Luke changed our heading. I cast another glance at the trowel. Without more training, it wouldn't be as effective as my bare hands, and I sighed that practicality won out over the false security that holding a sharp object would give me.

From the doorway, we had a clear view of the next garden, and Luke was right. It was sweet. The dead leaves that had littered every walkway were swept aside, and the dove-grey paving stones lay bright and intact, curving a path past corner beds and giving the space a circular feel. Accumulated plant matter had been cleared out of the beds and replaced with fresh bushes and, come spring, what would be flowers. I wondered if someone had brought in a power washer for the stones, and if so, that meant there was power nearby, and that meant we had an in back to our modern lives.

Where previous plots had statues of angels or Greeks or animals, or interesting focal points made of boulders or other natural materials, this one had six stone thrones sitting sentinel beside outer doors, and another six surrounded a table-like structure in the middle of the garden. The round table was another raised bed, with a narrow opening between two of the chairs so someone—presumably the gardener—could stand in the centre and tend to the flowers from there.

It was a safe assumption, since there was, in fact, a person standing in the centre of the table-bed, shears in his gloved hands, wide-brimmed hat on his head, and a very alive baby badger perched on his shoulder. After everything we'd been through, nothing about this tableau felt out of place.

"Oh," the stranger said, seeing us. A small noise, surprise and disappointment, though I might have been projecting on the latter.

Luke and I should have coordinated how we were going to handle this ahead of time. I had decades of experience in customer service, and Luke was charming in an everyman sort of way. But we both looked like shit, hungry and undomesticated, me a slightly shorter version of She-Hulk with less green, and Luke's outfit was basically what happened when a cartoon character ran through a bunch of clothes hung out to dry. So it was hard to say which of us would have a better chance at earning this stranger's confidence.

"Hey, mate," Luke said with a wave and a smile. "We're so sorry to bother you, but as I'm sure you've guessed, my friend and I are incredibly lost and any help you can spare would be most appreciated."

He leaned in to his Kiwi accent, even more than when it was just the two of us. We must be going for 'bumbling tourists,' which wasn't even a lie, but it didn't hurt to play it up a bit. I gave the stranger a chagrined smile and shrugged a little. *Yes, we are very dumb tourists. Look how dumb we are.*

The stranger stared at us, frozen with his shears mid-snip. The badger on his shoulder was either oblivious to the situation or assessed and dismissed it as beneath him, turned around in a circle like a cat, and curled up against his human's neck.

"My name is Luke. Luke Maston." He took a step into the garden, walking the line between appearing scared and being respectful. The gardener was fifteen or twenty years older than us, not quite the demographic that would immediately recognize Luke's face or name, so the chances he wouldn't care or that we'd walked into a *Misery* situation were about equal.

"And this is Rin," he continued, gesturing to me, and I gave a little wave too. "Could you direct us to the closest...uh...well, anywhere, really. Anywhere within walking distance where we could find a mobile signal, or a bus stop, or sandwiches?"

In a moment of what I can only describe as quintessential Englishness, the man shook off the shock of unexpected and probably unwanted visitors and stepped into the role of host.

"Of course," he said gently, "where are my manners?" He dropped the shears and gloves into a basket, set his hat atop it, and came around the table to greet us. There must have been a step inside the table, because up close, he was far shorter than both of us. He wore dark tan trousers and wellies, a white-and-blue shirt reminding me of Luke's nightgown, a gold ascot that looked out of place for someone digging into dirt, and a dark-pink, velvet overcoat that looked even more out of place. Hair a little darker than Luke's, a little longer, and curlier—Luke would say he had 'hobbit hair'—light-blue eyes, and delicate features beneath very pale, papery skin.

"I'm Andrew Bell-Nixon, but you can call me Daisy." We shook hands, and he gestured to the badger. "This is Lady Stephanie."

Lady Stephanie didn't seem in the mood to shake, so we waved to her.

"So sorry to hear about your troubles," Daisy said, nodding for us to follow him. Luke and I exchanged a look that was part relief and part wariness and trailed the strange little man across the garden. "Like the Greeks of old, I shall endeavour to make the weary travelers feel at home. And if your home turns out to be Mount Olympus, I hope upon your return you can tell your fellow deities that that Daisy chap was a welcoming fellow, and that he and Lady Stephanie saw to your needs in your hour of despair."

We passed through a round doorway into another well-kept garden, this one in a traditional arrangement, at odds with Daisy's more eccentric clothing style and manner of speaking. I almost felt guilty knowing I could easily defend myself from him if the encounter did fall more in the way of a horror film and less like a lighthearted episode of Doctor Who, now that Luke got it in my head. Between him and Daisy, it felt like a special with Six and Eight, and Lady Stephanie and I were their companions.

"I hope we won't be too much trouble," Luke said. "All we need is to get in touch with our mates, or find a bus to take us into the closest city. Or sandwiches."

"Well," Daisy said with a sigh, "there will be sandwiches. It's tea time, after all. But I'm afraid the closest bus stop is quite far, and in your state—" he glanced back at us with an apologetic look. "I imagine you'll need sustenance first. I do have a telephone and you're welcome to use it, but we're off the beaten path, as they say, and it may take a while for someone to come to collect you. Please do allow me to offer you tea in the meantime, even if my humble abode is but a short stop on what I'm sure is a journey for the ages."

After all the open doorways Luke and I had walked through since entering the maze, we finally arrived at another closed door, a twin to the first, though this one was in perfect condition. It shouldn't have made me as emotional as it did, but after the day I'd had, seeing the clear demarcation between being lost in a remote wilderness and finding refuge with more help on the way overwhelmed me. I could see the end of our trials, and my mind threatened to abandon emergency mode for the crash of exhaustion that always immediately followed it, but I still had work to do. *Hold it together, dear, just a little bit longer.*

I don't know if Luke saw me, if my face changed, or if he could sense my tension subsiding, but he reached out a hand and squeezed my shoulder. We weren't out of the woods yet, but we'd gotten to this point together, and we'd get to the end together, too. Even if the end turned out to be violent and in the basement of a murderous eccentric.

Chapter 25
October 2022
Luke

Daisy's house was a literal castle. I should have suspected as much. This far into the English countryside, out of range of any mobile service, grounds that included a labyrinth of countless adjoined gardens (countless only because we didn't visit them all; I'm sure they were able to be counted and didn't occasionally disappear or something). And that shiny new door might as well have been a magical portal, with how eager Rin and I were to go through it.

Instead of a fae realm, we walked onto a vast and surprisingly maintained lawn and a hard-packed dirt path winding its way from us towards a huge stone building with towers and turrets and possibly crenelations, if I had known exactly what those were. I'd seen plenty of castles throughout the U.K., but for some reason, this one reminded me of the Billingstead in New Zealand, where we stayed to film *Broke* and where Mattie's brother was supposed to have his wedding. Since our stay had ended with a fire alarm, a health emergency, a cancelled wedding, a bomb threat, and arrest (not me), I hoped this crenelated construction would bring us better luck.

Then again, I'd also left the Billingstead with the person who would be the love of my life, so it wasn't all bad.

And Daisy had promised us sandwiches. At this point, that was all it took to gain my trust. He seemed cool, too. I mean, he had a pet badger and wore a velvet blazer to garden. I wanted to tell Rin to take his picture, but that seemed kind of rude, considering we had already trespassed on his property and crashed his afternoon tea. Nobody would believe us about him otherwise, but maybe that was for the best. Maybe this part of our adventure was meant to sound unbelievable to anyone who wasn't there.

Rin was hesitant. I couldn't blame them. Potentially dangerous situations had always turned out fine for me, but I was a cis white guy who looked it. If they had been worried about being alone with three strangers on a golf course, they had to be feeling anxious about being alone with one very odd stranger on his remote estate with no mobile service.

Daisy had spent the walk to his home talking about the history of the grounds and his role in it (loved the gardens when he was young and spent decades thinking about it, then bought it when he got his inheritance even though it was derelict), how he got his nickname (Bell-Nixon, bell, cow bell, coo, Daisy), and how he and Lady Stephanie spent their evenings together (watching old episodes of shows from the BBC that a friend had given him on DVD). Friends would visit for regular get-togethers and to bring him to his appointments and whatnot, since he didn't own any kind of vehicle. Daisy seemed happy, but to me, it sounded like a lonely way to live.

The side door was unlocked, of course. Who would be out here to break in?

"Now, the phone is in the den, I believe. I can point you in that direction while I go get us tea."

"If you need a hand, I'm happy to help," I said, giving him my most disarming smile.

"No need, no need." Daisy waved me off. "The den, there. Please make yourselves at home. Lady Stephanie and I will return momentarily."

The room he waved us into was two stories of dark panels, bright chandeliers, and musty furniture. Hunting trophies hung from every wall artlessly, like whoever had hunted them only cared that they were displayed, not arranged. The exception was a huge stag head, classically positioned above an unlit stone fireplace. Books lined shelves around the room, as disorganized as the taxidermied animals, and I could guess at a glance we wouldn't find anything published in the last thirty years.

"We should leave after tea," Rin said. They wandered around the room, arms crossed over their chest.

"Yeah," I said, "after we eat, and call Mattie and Raph, and figure out if they want to pick us up here or down the road or something."

Rin nodded, eyes scanning the tables and shelves. "Sure. Yeah. But there's just one thing, Luke."

"What's that?"

"Where's the phone he was talking about?"

I turned around, looking where they already had. Nothing. "Drawer or cabinet?" I ventured, opening a pair of doors beneath a bookshelf and finding more books.

Rin checked their mobile. "Still no signal, and there isn't any Wi-Fi in range."

"Ok," I said, moving to the next cabinet. "When Daisy comes back, he'll point it out."

"I don't feel comfortable here."

I knew better than to dismiss someone's unease. I wasn't picking up any red flags, but that didn't mean they didn't exist. But here, now, it was complicated because where would we go? Abandoning my search for a phone that may or may not exist, I went to stand with Rin.

"Is it something specific?" I asked under my breath. "Because I'm pretty sure this place is real and not something we imagined, or an illusion of the fair folk, or a fever dream. The isolation is creepy. All the animals staring at us is unsettling."

"I don't know," they said, pinching their bottom lip. "You're right, though, it feels like a dream. Hunger's getting to me. Dehydration. I'm anxious."

I reached out to rub their upper arms and pull them in for a hug. Their hair still smelled good, like a salon, despite rain and mud and musty blankets, and my mind immediately served up the memory of sex the night before. I sighed against them and let the thought fade. They needed security, not Horny Luke. "Water, food, rest," I listed. "The only way to be sure if there's anything worth getting anxious about is to eliminate the usual culprits."

"Yeah, but in the meantime, if there is something we should be on the alert for, we'll miss it, because we're busy drinking and eating and sleeping."

I let go of them to swing my bag around and fish out one of the unopened water bottles. "Drink this whole thing. Now. We can refill it from the tap here. No need to ration anymore."

"Tea time!" Daisy announced from the doorway, and Rin and I jumped apart. Lady Stephanie had taken up on his other shoulder, and he slid the large tray of tea and snacks onto the low table between a couch and two chairs in the middle of the room. "I made a few cheese and pickle sandwiches, and some jam sandwiches. I also found some biscuits. And of course, the tea. Cream, and the sugar is here. A proper afternoon tea with guests. Bon appétit!"

I won't lie. I tore into those sandwiches like I hadn't eaten in a week. Rin was just as hungry, but they'd been instilled with a sense of what was proper etiquette, and between that and their general wariness about the whole situation, they were able to pick up the slack of convincing Daisy we weren't terrible people when I dropped the act to shovel snacks into my mouth.

"Thank you again for your hospitality," Rin said, settling into the chair next to me. "Did you say you had a phone we could use?"

As Daisy poured the tea, Lady Stephanie waddled down his arm onto the table to sniff at the food, and then me. I reached out to pet her, and she leaned into the scritches and I fell in love. Daisy straightened and looked around the room.

"Why, yes, it's here." He frowned. "Somewhere. Oh, now where could it have gotten off to?"

"Does it have legs?" I heard the sarcasm and hoped Daisy hadn't. Rin was sitting too far away, or I would have nudged them. Their anxiousness could have been stomach-related, but I would keep an eye out for any suspicious behavior on Daisy's part. So far, he seemed like a guy who liked his solitude. Lady Stephanie investigated Rin next. They tried to ignore her, but the badger's little nose twitches were undeniable, and they gave in to petting her with a sigh.

"I don't use it much," Daisy continued, abandoning the tea to launch a search for his elusive telephone. "My friends stop by every Saturday, and there's nothing so important that it can't wait. And I rather like being 'off the grid,' as they say."

Rin took a tentative bite of biscuit. "Yeah, we noticed there isn't any Wi-Fi, either. Do you have internet access?"

I didn't see how a good old-fashioned landline phone could have been hiding beneath a pile of books, but Daisy picked through a stack of titles as though *he* believed there was a chance it could.

"No, I never went in for that. I prefer the caress of delicate leaves or flower petals, and the soft fur of my animal companions to the cold, dead plastic of a keyboard."

He was making a lot of sense. Didn't sound like a serial killer at all. Rin squirmed in their seat and I successfully refrained from eating the rest of the biscuits.

"So no phone," Rin said.

"We'll have to dig for it. It's terribly gaudy, you shouldn't be able to miss it. Unless I couldn't stand it anymore and put it out of sight. Yes, that sounds like me."

He turned to us with an embarrassed smile and smoothed the front of his coat. "I do apologize. As you can see, I'm woefully unprepared to host anyone who isn't part of my predictable fraternity."

"No worries, mate," I said, taking one more biscuit and swearing that this was the last one for me because Rin needed to eat too. "You've already done more for us than we ever expected. We're out of the rain, we're dry, and you've fed us. You've been an admirable host, Daisy, don't get down on yourself because you couldn't predict that two uninvited strangers would need a phone."

I looked to Rin to get some backup, but they were playing with the badger, who had crawled into their lap and was showing off her belly like a particularly affectionate cat, and nobody could resist petting it, not even Rin Butcher.

Well, no phone didn't put us in a *worse* place than we were before. Daisy had said he could direct us to a bus stop, and as long as we ate what we could and took a couple sandwiches for the road and filled our water bottles and used an actual bathroom instead of a tree in the woods, I think we'd be fine.

As if on cue, rain pattered against the high windows in a quick whoosh. I hadn't realized how dark it had gotten outside. Maybe Daisy had extra rain gear he could lend us, too.

"Oh," he said, looking up at the noise. "Bother. I had hoped to send you out in better conditions." He cocked his head like he'd thought of something. "Please allow me to extend an invitation for you to stay here for the night."

Rin's head snapped up from playing with Lady Stephanie, first watching Daisy, then turning to me with a question in their eyes.

"We might not have as modern an amenity as the internet, but I assure you, we have hot water, clean, soft beds, and I can certainly provide you with dinner and breakfast before you go on your way. It feels awfully rude to offer you a couple of biscuits before sending you back into the storm. And if you need clothing, I have trunks full. I can't guarantee their condition, and it will take some time to discern what's useful, but I will open them to you."

I already knew what Rin would say. They were already saying it with their whole face, their whole body, even, hands frozen above Lady Stephanie who, at the lack of petting, picked herself up and waddled across the table and back to Daisy, who scooped her up like a baby.

But I was already plotting. What did I tell Rin? Water, food, and rest. Here was the opportunity to get all of that done and start fresh tomorrow. Plus a hot shower and the possibility of better-fitting clothes? All my underwear had been in my luggage. And now it was being worn by sheep for fashion. We could pick a room with one bed on purpose, lock ourselves in. I'd keep Rin safe.

"Daisy, that's so generous," Rin said, recovering from their initial surprise. "I'm not sure we can accept. Do you mind if Luke and I have a minute to discuss it first?"

He bowed, then eyed the now empty tea tray. "In the meantime, I shall gather more biscuits for you. If you require my assistance before I return, simply shout."

The moment he left the room, Rin leaned over the arm of their chair and stage whispered, "Are you serious?"

I popped the last bite of the last cheese sandwich in my mouth. "I havven even fed anyfing yeh."

"Exactly. You're considering it. Even after I told you I didn't feel comfortable here."

I shook my head and swallowed before responding. This wasn't a conversation I could have with my mouth full. "Rin, we need to eat. We need to sleep. If the closest bus stop is a three hour walk or whatever, that's three more hours in the rain today, plus however long it takes for the bus to get there, and by the way things have been going, who's to say it's not a defunct stop from twenty years ago?"

"We need to contact our friends," they said. "They don't know where we are."

"Not the most pressing issue right now, mate. They're not the ones who are lost. We can find our way to them, but we need to be in a condition to do that. I will stand guard while you take a shower. We'll stay in the same room and put a chair against the door. Hell, if you want, we can sleep in shifts. Get up early, eat as much as we can, then head out, rain or shine."

They got up to pace the room. I thought I was being the logical one, and Rin probably felt they were. Most likely, neither of us could claim it, after surviving the harsh conditions of the past day. But that was why we needed to stay.

Hands on their hips, they turned to me, scrunching up their lips like they were trying not to say something, and I felt a pang of guilt. Were they stopping themself because it might upset me, and they were sacrificing their own comfort to make sure I wouldn't make the situation worse? Of all the times I wish I could have read Rin's mind, this might have been the most important one. I also wished I could read my own mind, but there was too much static.

"I don't feel comfortable here, and I don't think I should have to detail for you the past bad experiences it reminds me of for you to believe me."

"You absolutely don't have to do that," I said, getting up. I longed for a bed, for a little bit of comfort, even if it was just theater, but not if it triggered something so upsetting to Rin. "It's dangerous to continue walking in the rain, pushing our bodies like this. But I understand it's also dangerous to stay, not knowing who he is or what his intentions are. But I'm here too, and I'm not going to let anything happen to you. My choice is to stay, because I'm willing to risk being murdered for a bed, I know, I'm a simple man and possibly a stupid one. If you'd rather take our chances on the road again, that's what we'll do. Easy as."

Their stare was so intense, it felt like a door shutting when they turned away. All our ideas were rubbish. Our guts were compromised, thanks to food poisoning then emptiness for so long, but our ability to reason was, too. All those trials to get here, the fear and panic, the uncertainty and disappointment. Being cut off from our friends.

"We can stay," they said. "But we're doing everything you said. You guard the door while I shower, share a room, chair under the doorknob, the works. Neither of us gets murdered tonight."

The promise of a clean, warm bed drove most of the tension from my body. All but the small knot of worry that could have been stomach cramps from eating a dozen sandwiches and a whole sleeve of biscuits in under ten minutes. "Don't do this just for me."

"I'm doing it for both of us."

"Why does it feel like you're sacrificing yourself for my cock-ups?"

"I'm getting us out of this situation," they said, putting a hand on my chest. "And you're right about what we need to be able to do that. I'm not comfortable with the details, but as long as you remain vigilant, I'll be able to deal with it."

I put my hand over theirs and smiled. "We're in this together."

They rolled their eyes. "Well, let's get out of this together, too."

Chapter 26

October 2022

Rin

Nothing that happened the rest of the afternoon or evening gave me any more insight into whether we were safe, but worrying over it didn't leave me any time to think more about sex with Luke, which was good. Survival first, sex later.

He convinced me to stay. Luke could convince me of almost anything. He was enthusiastic and insistent, and his heart was in the right place, even if his logic was flawed. That was the theme of this road trip as well as his usual personality. And as much as I saw the holes in his plans, I wanted to rest, too. I wanted that hot shower and dinner and bed and breakfast. Luke's plan was my plan, if I had only listened to the "soft animal of my body."

Daisy was delighted we were staying, but it was hard to tell if he meant it or if he was doing what Mattie did when she was overwhelmed and just going through the motions of what was expected and giving canned responses. Lady Stephanie was unreadable, but I imagined she would welcome the many new hands to pet her.

We still couldn't find the phone (if it even existed), but Daisy took us on a tour of the castle and I made a point to look for the old device in every room, to no avail. The building was bigger on the inside, and I couldn't help but think of *Beauty and the Beast*. The library wasn't as impressive, but was any? Daisy said it used to be some sort of museum. I asked if I could take pictures, and he hesitated a long time before acquiescing, with the caveat that I wouldn't take any photos of his personal items. Everything that had come with the house was fair game, since they were already documented in coffee table books and postcards and brochures from nearly fifty years ago. The books weren't curated by him, strangers' portraits lined the halls, most of the closets contained the clothes of people long passed.

It would have been incredibly interesting if I wasn't trapped there.

One thing did catch my eye: a hand-drawn map hanging at the top of the stairs, yellowed with age, the castle (called Richelieu, like the gardens, though the map predated it by I would say a century or two) and its position in the county sketched in fine detail. It showed a town about twenty centimetres to the southeast. I had no idea what that translated to in kilometres, or if it was even close to accurate, but I made a note to compare it to the atlas once we were settled in the room we'd have for the night.

If Daisy had any problem with me and Luke sharing a bed, he didn't say anything. Too polite, or was he holding it all in until he could murder us later? We had taken a roundabout way to get to the guest bedroom, so he gave us directions to the dining room, where we would have dinner in a few hours. He said we were welcome to any of the clothes in any of the rooms he'd shown us, and when he left us to tend to his own things, Luke was ready to explore the possibilities of a new outfit that wasn't three nightgowns and a tatty jumper.

We took our bags with us instead of leaving them in the room. We might have been the ones crashing Daisy's place, but trust worked both ways and I wasn't there yet. Luke had a field day raiding wardrobe after wardrobe, gathering a new wardrobe's worth of clothes. I had some luck too, though I would wait until after my shower to try them on.

True to his word, Luke kept guard outside the en suite bathroom, after a thorough search to make sure there weren't any cameras or peep holes. Daisy's aversion to technology could have been an act. I'd been fooled before.

"Thanks for that," I said as I stepped out of the steam and into the bedroom, drying my hair with a towel. "The water is nice and hot. You'll fall asleep as soon as you get out."

"And miss dinner? Naw, bro." He turned in a circle. "What do you think?"

Between his rummaged clothes, modern haircut, and blocky glasses, he could have stepped directly out of the 1970's. A brown-and-orange button-down shirt, tan slacks with a significant flare, chocolate leather dress shoes. The outfit made me cringe, but he looked really fucking good in it.

"Groovy, bro," I said with a smirk. He beamed at me and turned towards the full-length mirror mounted on a stand in the corner.

"Fits well," he said, running a hand down the buttons, looking at the garment with a critical eye. Fuck yes it did.

"But can you run in it?"

"Why would I—Oh. Murder."

I laughed. "That too, but if we're going to be hiking for hours longer, I think you need to focus on comfort, durability, and warmth."

He nodded, unbuttoned the shirt, and threw it in one of the two piles to his right. A larger, single pile on his left contained the items he hadn't tried on yet.

"You'll guard the door for me now, right? That's how it works?" He unzipped his fly and I turned my back to him, adjusting the towel around my chest. Too close, too naked, too much desire bubbling up in me. And sex was always when the people in the haunted house got stabbed.

"That's how it works." I heard the bell-bottoms swish against the other clothes in the pile, and Luke shut the bathroom door behind him to within an inch of the door frame. Even when I was guarding him, he had to leave it open to hear if I shouted for help.

He'd said we were in this together. He meant it, and I knew it was more than guilt that drove him. Slowly, reluctantly, and despite the confusion of the last few days' extraordinary circumstances, I was starting to form a conclusion.

Luke was still in love with me.

And I wanted him to be.

The idea of having a partner I could count on, who would problem-solve on their own and listen to me, who I was as ridiculously attracted to as Luke, had somehow become the number one thing on my life's wish list. I sat on the bed, a big and comfortable affair that could have been leftover from the same era as Luke's most recent outfit, and wondered how he had finally usurped "career" as the thing I wanted most.

Career blowing up had been a big factor, I would guess. Made me rethink what I wanted out of life, even as I went through the motions and agreed to work for the people who bought us out. That had been a mindless decision that had finally made it back to my mind to be scrutinized, way after the fact, but better late than never. My parents had both passed. My best friends lived an ocean away. I was lonely.

And, well. He was Luke. I'd always been in love with him.

The timing was unfortunate, but when, in the last two years, would I have thought, "yes, now is the time for love"? The issues I'd carefully cultivated in that time had grown into beautiful, monstrous shrubs, abloom with red flags. I wondered if Luke was too hyperfocused to see them. Or maybe the man was colorblind.

From the shower, Luke started singing, and I was startled back into the moment. I would have said it at any time since we broke up, but I had good reason right now: I had to focus on the immediate emergency before I could give our relationship the attention it deserved. And when we were safe again, hopefully soon and hopefully in London with our friends, I would be bold and tell him how I felt.

After we had both showered and found appropriate clothes (Luke went with his orange-and-brown ensemble, and I found a pair of work pants and a pale-blue linen blouse that, while I wasn't a fan of the color, felt heavy with durability, like a shield), we made our way downstairs to dinner, which was, as expected, odd.

Daisy expressed his pleasure and gratitude that he was able to share a meal with people. Half the time he spoke, I thought he might prefer to be alone, and the rest of the time, I was convinced he was starving for company. Though if I had a castle and a garden and a fortune, I can't say I wouldn't also retire to the woods with only a baby badger as my companion.

Still, my anxiety persisted. It could be that the old-fashioned, upper-class guy didn't want to be bothered by riff-raff. Or maybe he was involved in something he didn't want discovered, but wasn't necessarily nefarious, like those tableaus of taxidermied rodents. Or it could be Daphne's favourite guess whenever there was something secretive going on: sex parties.

Or maybe I just didn't sleep well for two nights, didn't eat for almost twenty-four hours, and the thousand other things that had been working against me for—a conservative estimate would be, oh, five years. And if that was the case, Daisy didn't deserve my suspicion. That was why I needed Luke to be a partner in this, and I had to take his mundane view of it into consideration.

Our host didn't cook for us, but heated up a few frozen dinners, which we ate on heavy china plates. Lady Stephanie had her own place at the table, and she was the reason I hadn't run out into the rain yet. If Daisy cared for animals that much, it was less likely he was a murderer.

The conversation stayed light. Luke took the reins, talking about his career. Safe and simple, and with his natural charm, he made everyone feel at ease. Daisy had seen one of his movies, a World War I story that was mostly about horses. It came out before *Knuckletracker* and was one of the few I hadn't gotten a chance to see. The conversation went so well, Daisy invited us to retire to the cigar room for a brandy and a smoke.

Luke looked to me, and I tried to figure out what I could say or what look I could give that would make him understand that, one, I wasn't interested, two, I didn't want to insult our host, and three, as Cinnamon often said, we shouldn't split the party. As I was trying to think, I don't know what face I ended up making, but Luke made his own confused face, turned to Daisy, and accepted the invitation.

"If you don't mind," I cut in. "I'm so sorry. But I'm knackered. If you'll both forgive me, I think I'm going to go to bed. Luke, didn't you say you wanted to retire early tonight?"

"I think I've found my second wind," he said, smiling. Ok we needed to work on the whole working-as-a-team thing. "But if you're tired, by all means. I'm sure Daisy understands. I'll keep him company—" Luke waggled an eyebrow out of view of the man in question, and I was glad one of us could effectively nonverbally communicate. "And you get a head start on a good night's sleep.

If that's acceptable to you, Daisy?" He turned to him with another easy smile.

"Oh, quite acceptable, of course," Daisy said. "You've had an ordeal, and you certainly have no obligation to stay awake to entertain me, I can do that well enough on my own."

Luke stood and started gathering the plates. "I won't be long, Rin," he said. "You'll relax with a soft pillow and warm bed, and I'll relax with a soft smoke and a warm brandy."

"That only half makes sense," I mumbled, standing up. "Thank you again for your hospitality, Daisy. Good night, Lady Stephanie."

I should have gone to bed. Luke was keeping Daisy busy, so I didn't have to worry about that. But I was a snoop at heart, and I needed to do the bare minimum to convince myself the source of my anxiety was in my head and not in the house.

So I snooped.

Chapter 27
October 2022
Luke

When I got up to the bedroom, Rin was still awake. My first thought was that they had waited up for me to seduce me, because I was full of brandy and my mind was ripe with every bad idea. Not that seduction was a bad idea. But if I thought being intimate the night before, in a stranger's cabin, in a highly emotional and unstable state, might make the situation worse, certainly being in a stranger's castle, in a highly emotional and unstable state (Rin) and slightly giddy from a tipple (me) would cause even more problems.

I had no regrets about what had happened between us. But for tonight's very specific situation, I was sober enough to recognize the wisdom of abstinence.

Still, it only took a moment for Rin's actual purpose to become clear.

"I think we should leave." They were dressed in their clothes from dinner, and their few belongings were out of sight. In the backpack again, I assumed.

I locked the door behind me and dragged the heavy armchair in front of it. Rin watched.

"Let me guess," I said, struggling with the old furniture. "You found bodies in a freezer." They crossed their arms over their chest and gave me their best no-nonsense stare. "Ok, no bodies. Where did you go and what did you find?"

They came right up to me, animated in a way that made me wonder if they'd found coffee wherever they'd been, and spoke at the lowest volume they could, like they were afraid of being overheard.

"Locked doors," they said, eyes wide, like that was supposed to mean something.

"Locked doors," I repeated. They nodded. "A rich man who lives in a former museum locks some of his rooms. Rin." I rubbed my forehead. The bed was so close. My eyes were already shut. I didn't need to see to make it to those comfy blankets and mattress that wasn't a couch or the floor of a toilet. My hands could find and undo my shirt's buttons on their own. The only thing stopping me was an almost-six-foot-tall Amazon of a person telling me the guy whose castle we crashed had the foresight to lock his valuables away from us strangers.

"Nope," I said, heading towards my "keep" pile of clothes. I'd have to sort through them and decide what to wear when we left and what to pack. "If that's all you have, you don't have anything. I spent a pleasant hour with the guy, and I think he's just a nerd like the us, neurodivergent like us, and rich enough that he can indulge in both of those things away from people who would judge him for it."

"There's more."

I unbuttoned my shirt anyway. If they were going to make me leave this nice and cozy house, I'd be wearing one of the jumpers we found.

"I found weird stains," they said. "And I heard something. Like moaning."

"Gross."

"Luke, I'm serious. You said if I didn't feel comfortable, we could leave."

I did say that. But I wasn't expecting to have to entertain Rin's paranoia. Usually, they were the levelheaded of the two of us.

"I'm sure you looked," I said, switching the dress shirt for a long sleeved one that might have been long underwear. "Are there any secret doors in here? Secret panels, where someone could sneak in without coming through this main door? Eyeholes cut out of paintings, so someone could watch us while we sleep?"

They exhaled through their nose and I thought of a bull.

One good reason to leave, beyond vibes, and we'd go. "So why aren't we safe in this room tonight?"

"Because we aren't safe in this house!"

"Rin, that's not—" God, I didn't want to argue. I didn't want to argue, but I also didn't want to leave in the dark, in the rain, in the cold, several brandies in with only the vaguest idea of where we were going and no clue how long we would have to be walking for. "We'll sleep in shifts."

"Luke."

"It's the best I can do, Rin." I finally got the shirt on after struggling with one of the sleeves. "My body can't go out there like this. You've got energy. I'm dead on my feet. Set your alarm for five hours and wake me up then. I'll take over the watch and we'll make it to morning. Pack, eat, and leave. I promise."

It wasn't fair. I couldn't see any way to compromise, and if Rin did, they didn't suggest it. Staying meant they were anxious, possibly debilitatingly so. But at least they were sheltered and fed and clothed. Leaving meant pushing myself beyond what I knew I could handle at the moment, again, possibly debilitatingly so. Without a car or a phone, there was no other option: it was one or the other.

They stared at me, and I could feel them searching in my eyes and soul. No, nothing would change my mind. Nothing short of an actual and immediate emergency. Yes, I felt like shit about it, but that was a later problem. I knew I was being selfish but suspected I was the one with the more logical plan. And I was hoping that, once this whole ordeal was over, Rin would be able to look back when they weren't in a panic and see I'd been right.

"You said we were a team." They spoke slowly, making sure I would understand. I did. "You said we were in this together."

"We are and we are."

"So how are you going to do your part if you're drunk?"

"I'm not drunk." I almost was. It was hard not to keep chasing comfort once I had a taste of it. Once I was out of the storm and being taken care of.

They pressed their lips together and nodded. "Yeah. Sure. It's ok. I see. We teach people how we want to be treated, so it must be my fault that you're unreliable."

"That's not fair."

"No?"

"There's no compromise. We can't half leave, and we can't half stay. You emotionally can't handle staying, and I physically can't handle leaving. I promise you—I *promise* you—I am your partner in this, and sleeping in shifts should satisfy both of our needs. Wake me in five hours, then you can sleep while I keep watch." I turned down the sheets and shimmied beneath the covers. "Or you could leave on your own. Save yourself. Leave me behind for Daisy to sacrifice to his badger gods or bury me in one of the many gardens or turn me into another sculpture. Too bad he didn't catch me mid-*Knuckletracker*, I could have fit right in with those Olympic statues."

The bed was very cozy, and I would have fallen asleep immediately, but I was waiting to hear Rin agree to my plan. Which they did, with a grunt of frustration, and I let my eyes close. I would make it up to them. Once we escaped the not-a-murder-house.

"*Luke.*"

The room was dark. My eyelids were sticky, my tongue plastered to the roof of my mouth. I must have been asleep for a while.

"S'my turn?" I mumbled, stifling a groan as I stretched and rubbed at my eyes. Five hours hadn't been enough.

"Get your stuff," Rin whispered. "We have to go."

That didn't sound good. "What happened?" I asked and cleared my throat. I needed another minute to wake up before I tried doing anything. "What time is it? Is it my turn to keep watch?"

By the faint light coming from the bathroom, I could see Rin wore the same castle museum clothes they had on at dinner, with a red jumper we'd also found, and their coat. Their backpack sat at the end of the bed and looked stuffed.

"A little before three a.m. We have to go," they repeated.

"We have to go, but you're going to take the clothes Daisy gave you. That doesn't seem very nice."

"There's something going on here." They picked up a green jumper and stretchy dark pants from my pile. "Put these on. I don't know what else you want to take, but pack up quickly."

"We talked about this." I got up anyway and started changing into the clothes they'd picked out. "Rin, I'm going to need more than—"

Somewhere in the house, something thumped, hard, like a piece of furniture being dropped on the floor, and it was followed by a sound between a moan and a whimper. More force behind it than the house settling. More human than the wind or a creaky door. An invisible breath whispered against my neck, and goosepimples bloomed down my arms.

I stared at Rin and hurried to dress myself. My heart had jumped to my throat and was beating in an increasing tempo. "The fuck was that?"

"One of the many things I haven't woken you up for before now. You want to stick around to find out?"

"Maybe Daisy is hurt," I said, zipping the pants. "We should investigate."

"Cool, yeah, fine," Rin said, shouldering their pack. "We can do that on our way out."

I couldn't argue. Instead, I handed Rin the drinks from my messenger bag and stuffed the space with socks and pants.

"Wait," they said. They grabbed the clothes out of it and started rolling them into compact shapes that would let me fit more. Out in the house, a growing whistle died down. I recognized it as a teapot, but that didn't do anything to calm my nerves.

Outside clothes on, bags packed, chair returned from its protective position, we opened the door quietly and listened. The light from the table lamp at the end of the hall didn't reach very far, but my eyes were accustomed to the darkness, and I didn't see anything out of place. And there were no more noises to direct us where to go. Or where to avoid.

We moved into the hallway, Rin first, cabin-torch held aloft, and they turned to grab a decorative dagger off the wall with their free hand.

"That can't be a good idea," I whispered.

Rin took a breath to give me what I could tell, by their face, would be a sarcastic response, but before they could speak, we heard a series of barks from deep in the house.

"The hounds?" I asked. Sleepy brain trying to make light, but in truth, I was on edge.

"You don't think he would have mentioned having dogs?"

And that's when the organ music started.

Look. I loved Rin as much as I could love anybody, and that was a lot, but without seeing any of the things they thought were suspicious, or feeling any of the vague discomfort, or—until now—hearing whatever weird shit they were hearing, I wasn't prepared to blindly trust them. Not when my senses were telling me everything was fine and I could have a brandy and a good night's rest.

I could hold my own in a fight, but not against something supernatural. In that instant, Rin became my expert, guide, and savior. Whatever they said was gospel.

I looked around the hallway for a weapon, but Rin had taken the only sharp object, and my choices were crumbling paintings, a thick phone book from probably 1988, or the lamp that was our only light besides the torch. Phone book it was.

Rin took the lead and we walked slowly, careful not to make a noise, even though the music would have concealed it. In their explorations the evening before, they must have mapped this part of the castle pretty well. The only hesitation in their steps came from wanting to make zero noise, not a question of direction.

"I think it's coming from the wing with the locked doors," Rin said. "We should be able to avoid it if you want to go through the kitchen and take some rations on our way."

I nodded, but their focus was ahead, so I said, "Yeah."

At the bottom of the stairs, Rin pointed at the dark wood floor. "See? Stains." Dark and old and unidentifiable, partially hidden by a thin runner of a rug. I didn't look closely, in the hopes that having only one piece of information would allow it to sail under the radar of my imagination, but I was thwarted again.

"Haunted house," I mumbled, trying to make myself feel better.

"What?"

"What if Daisy is developing a haunted house and we're here in the early stages of production?"

They spared me a glance. "Yeah, I know," I said. "I can't help it."

We turned a corner and I traded the phone book for a candelabra that looked much heavier than it turned out to be. The organ music was still going strong, louder than upstairs, and a tune I'd heard before but couldn't name. I sniffed at a new smell, something oily and faint, like an old car.

As much as I kept trying to put the clues together into a shape that wasn't our dead bodies, Rin had gotten in my head and I couldn't think of anything else. Another thud, and a clap like wood falling against wood, and a shorter moan. I had no fucking idea what it was, but even with a mundane explanation, it was unacceptably unnerving.

Rin was doing remarkably well, standing tall between me and whatever it was ahead, legs apart and floating on the balls of their feet. I couldn't hear their breathing, but I saw their shoulders rise and fall slowly and I knew they were consciously controlling their breath as much as they were the rest of their body. I could hardly feel my own legs, and my breath was raggedy, which I tried to fix by copying Rin. Apparently, all that boxing training gave them the skills and confidence to handle the same situations as the Scooby Gang. Far away in my brain, I wondered why they'd taken the knife off the wall for a weapon when they would be more effective with their fists.

One hallway until the kitchen, and the music was stuck on a discordant cluster of notes. So it wasn't a recording. Someone was out here practicing the organ. Down the hall, metal clashed against metal, like someone shaking a silverware drawer, and we paused. How many other people were in this house?

I adjusted my grip on the candelabra, feeling my pulse in my fingers. Rin motioned for me to walk closer to the wall and they shut off the torch. A faint light glowed in the kitchen, and as we approached, there was more clattering and an animalistic grunt. Rin put up a hand for us to stop. Heavy footsteps trailed to the other side of the kitchen, then came towards our door at a fast pace.

Rin shifted their weight and held the knife in front of them, and I set the candelabra and my bag on the floor and moved up next to them. Drowsiness had totally left my system, and now that the threat seemed to be less ghost and more human, I was ready to act. Rin might have had the formal training, but even without my occasional film prep and combat coordination, I knew how to fight.

A figure flew out in front of us, and Rin swiped at them with a yell. It happened quickly, their arm lashing out, the figure jumping back with its own scream and dropping the box they carried, me reaching to pull Rin back all at once. I had a glimpse of Daisy a split second before Rin did and saw his hands were full. He wasn't a threat. Even if he was, Rin would be using a damn knife to attack someone who couldn't defend himself, let alone attack first.

The box clattered to the floor, and Daisy let out a yelp, clutching at his breast with one hand and the wall with the other. Despite Rin's rooted stance, I was able to sway them back a few inches by pulling on their backpack, hopefully enough that they hadn't caused damage with the dagger, which they held in front of them with a shaking hand.

"Whoa, whoa," I said, raising my free hand in a gesture of peace. The overhead light came on, and I clearly saw Daisy at the switch. "Daisy, I'm so sorry. Rin, he's not a threat." I rested my forehead over their ear so they could hear my words without distraction.

"Drop the knife, love. He's unarmed." They did as I said, their breath slowing as the adrenaline subsided and we were left with embarrassment.

"What?" Daisy said breathlessly. "What?"

"Are you ok?" I asked him. "Are you hurt?"

Rin took a step back to lean against the wall, and I let go of their backpack. Daisy had kept a hand up by the light switch, the other still on his chest, pinching the low, silky collar of his robe. The front of it didn't look damaged, no cuts, no long slashes blooming with blood. The falling cardboard box had sounded like a drawer full of silverware, but in the light, it held a number of tools, most of which I couldn't identify besides the odd screwdriver, a pair of pliers, and a mallet.

"What is *wrong* with you?" Daisy shrieked.

"We heard noises," I said. "And after a day of walking, and no food, and the rain, our emotions got the better of us. We weren't thinking clearly. I'm sorry, Daisy."

"Get out!"

Rin nodded, hand to their heart, mirroring Daisy. They hadn't looked up from the box on the floor.

"This is just a misunderstanding." If there was a chance I could make things right, where we would be allowed to stay the rest of the night, I had to try. Now that I knew there were no ghosts. "We heard loud noises and were worried. Then the organ started playing, but there was someone in the kitchen..."

"I live here! Who did you think it might have been?"

"Well," I said, "you couldn't be in two places at once. And then those loud bangs."

"No," he said, finding his composure. He was livid, and rightly so. "I'm restoring the organ, and it's loud. I let Lady Stephanie ramble across the keys when I have to retrieve something so I know where she is and do you know what? I don't have to explain myself to you in my own home. You're no longer welcome here. Gather your belongings and go." He gave our outfits a disdainful glare. "You may keep those clothes. I don't want to see them again."

My cheeks and ears flushed with shame. Rin had been quiet this whole time, and I wasn't going to argue with the man we'd nearly stabbed in, as he said, his own home. I nodded to him, picked up my messenger bag, and turned Rin to face the way we'd come.

"I'm so sorry, Daisy," I repeated as we walked away. He simply stood there, chin up, looking defiant. It must have taken a lot of courage for him to stand up to us, and I felt terrible for being the cause of his distress.

We left out the front, through a wide, wooden double door that matched the ones in the garden, though this was bigger and heavier. It was recessed into the castle, so when we stepped onto the front entryway, we were shielded from the weather. The rain that had teased and threatened and doomed us for so many days was visibly waning in the light of two lampposts on either side of the entryway and two more farther down the stone path, by the circular driveway. Rin looked out onto the grounds, but even if it had been day, I didn't think they would have seen what was in front of them.

"Rin," I said gently, reaching out to touch their arm with the back of my fingers. Their face was blank, like when they were jet-lagged and lost in a mental fog.

"Sorry I fucked things up," they said quietly, not meeting my eyes.

I should have ignored them. Changed the subject. Said something like, "Which way should we start walking?" Instead, I said nothing. It wouldn't help anything if I pretended they hadn't been the cause. Besides, I was getting angrier by the moment, and I didn't know how to direct it, but I knew I didn't want to take it out on Rin even if they were the reason I had to start walking again in the rain at three o'clock in the morning without the first fucking clue of which direction to go.

They burst into tears. And I knew I had reached my own breaking point, because I didn't care.

"Rin," I said, putting a hand on their shoulder. "We've got to go."

"I'm such a fool."

"Blame won't help us get to where we need to go. I assume you made a plan for this exact situation."

"I already feel like shit," they said, wiping their eyes with a sleeve. "I don't need you to comment on it."

"I didn't realize my words meant anything to you," I said, taking my hand from their shoulder and adjusting my bag. "They didn't mean anything to you last night. Or yesterday afternoon, when I asked you to trust me and you went rogue playing spy instead."

"My gut was telling me something was off."

"Our guts had been empty for a full day, of course it was telling you something was off!"

"I'm sorry I asked you to trust me and that I ended up being wrong," they said, turning to me and throwing their hands in the air. "But I'm not allowed to make mistakes, am I?"

"For fuck's sake, Rin," I said, and laughed sharply. "Your anxiety was so bad, it was contagious. We could be sleeping in a regular bed right now, but no, you got into my head. Told me *my* gut was wrong, because, what? I don't know what it's like to be in danger? My most persistent fans call themselves Mastondons, do you think I've never been afraid of being stalked and murdered?"

"And if we'd ended up in a castle owned by one of them, you wouldn't want to stay there, either."

"How was Daisy a threat to you?"

"I couldn't be sure he wasn't. But I can't afford to make mistakes anymore." Rin's face scrunched up and they took a step back, quickly looking down at the stones beneath our feet, and I wondered if they thought one of those mistakes was sleeping together the night before. "I have to think about every little thing that might go wrong because when I don't, I end up losing my goddamn family business."

Ah, fuck. Rin.

"And," they continued, "one of those little things was how trustworthy you would be. You said you had a car, but didn't check if it was even road-worthy. You didn't make a plan in case we broke down, and I'm pretty sure if there was a mobile signal right now, you *still* wouldn't call Raphael for help, but that's hypothetical anyway because you dropped your phone in a lake. You've been irresponsible and unreliable when I needed a partner—"

"That's all I ever wanted to be," I interrupted. "Your partner. From the moment I met you. But I can't feel like a partner if I don't feel needed, and instead of being vulnerable and letting yourself be supported, you double down. You cut yourself off from the people who love you out of some desire to appear strong and all it's ever done is hurt you. And me." My voice cracked as I broke off. Three in the morning while fleeing a stranger's castle was the wrong time to have this conversation, but the curdling in my stomach was telling me I not might get another chance. "I'm clearly useless in some emergencies, and so are you. But besides outlying disasters, we are really, really good together, Rin."

They stared at me, their head cocked, lines of worry between their eyes. They pressed their lips into a line and glanced out across the lawn.

"Well," they said. "For the last five years, my life has been nothing but disasters. So yeah, tonight, I followed my intuition instead of trusting yours. And now I'm going to follow it about twenty kilometres that way—" they pointed behind them and away from the castle "to a village that has a bus stop and pray that I pick up a mobile signal along the way. I can't say you're welcome to join me, but I can't stop you."

They turned on their heel and stomped down the path, adjusting their pack as they went. The rain had mostly let up. Between their waterproof jacket and waterproof pack, they'd be mostly dry by the time they got to that village.

It would have been impossible to talk to them in this state and I didn't want to. They had a plan and a map and their anger and I had one of the three and it wasn't the one that would take me anywhere. So I sat on the dry walkway, put my back against the stone wall, and waited for morning.

Chapter 28
July 2020
Luke

Rin was at their office up in Auckland for a few days, going over financial records and trying to solve the puzzle of how to make money in a tourism business when the pandemic had frozen travel in New Zealand for who knew how long. It had been four months since the announcement that the country was going into a shutdown. Everyone worried about getting sick and nobody traveled. Certainly not for holiday. Certainly not for a posh, in-country holiday. And entering New Zealand was restricted, so no foreigners were renting Rin's baches, either.

I could tell they were stressed about it but pretending not to be, around me and the girls. I thought working in the office would help them focus. Plus, they'd be closer to Tessa's boxing gym, which reopened a few days ago, and I was sure Rin would appreciate working out there instead of my busted shed. This scheme to get them out of the house should have been foolproof. I hadn't counted on the master schemer outmaneuvering me.

First workout of the day, done. I was between filming *Knuckletracker* movies but had to keep the physique for my next project. I couldn't fucking wait to be done with them and let my body go soft. Eat an enormous bowl of pasta with the creamiest, buttery-est sauce I've ever had in my life. Huge slice of cake. No—tiramisu. Use the former gym time to take Lena and Cassidy out, or stay in and watch a movie on the couch. If they could sit still long enough. More likely we'd be hiking or playing some outdoor team sport. Rin was good at a lot of sports, and Cassidy made them promise to teach her boxing.

Just what I needed. A mini-me that also knew how to fight. I would never win an argument ever again.

To be honest, between Lena, Cassidy, Rin, and my mum, I couldn't win an argument already. Four to one. I smiled like an idiot, thinking how fantastic that was. A real team. *Team Maston, Now Including Rin*!

With my mind full of the fantasy of a virus-free and unsustainable-work-schedule-free future, I left the makeshift gym-shed and entered the house, heading to the fridge to snack on boiled chicken directly from the container while I made my high-protein, no-carb, no-taste lunch.

A bang came from the dining room, and I jumped, nearly dropping the chicken. Rin in Auckland, mum and the girls at their aunt's through the end of the week. We didn't have any pets, despite what the girls would say about the weta they tried to keep in the lidless and lizard-less lizard tank we kept outside. I wondered, briefly, if I, too, should have asked Rin to teach me boxing.

Another thud. I slid my food back in the fridge, silently closing the door. I looked around for some kind of weapon. Knife was too much. I needed something with bludgeoning damage. All our sports equipment was in the shed...there, on the counter. I pursed my lips, thinking how Cinnamon would laugh if one of our RPG characters tried it as an improvised weapon. But it was the best I could do.

I grabbed it and twirled it with the confidence of someone who'd been trained to do so with a prop sword and creeped towards the noise. As I was psyching myself up to rush whoever was there, I heard another thud, and a loud "Fuck!"

"Rin?" I stood up straight and turned the corner, doing my best to look normal while drenched in sweat, bits of chicken stuck to my shirt, and holding a pink and sparkly tasseled baton over my head like a club.

There they were, at the huge, rectangular wooden table mum used for her tailoring projects. She had cleared it off before she left with the girls, saying I never knew when I would need a big, flat surface like that. I tried to forget that she might have meant it as a sex thing, but I'm sure she never would have guessed that Rin was going to use it for what looked like all the paperwork their office had accumulated over its entire half century or so of existence.

"Sorry," they said, barely glancing up from organizing the stacks of folders they pulled out of a box. Several empty boxes were stacked together by the living room chair, the top one filled with folded cloth tote bags. "I didn't mean to scare you. I texted you I was coming back, but I knew you were in the shed and might not see it."

I lowered the baton and approached the table cautiously. Not because Rin was a physical danger to me, but because it looked like they were in the middle of being an emotional danger to themself.

"No worries, bro. You're free to come and go as you like. I was just startled."

"And Lena's baton was the best weapon you had at hand?" They paused and looked at me again, smiling, and I knew I could bring them back down to calmer levels. Keep it light, that's what always worked.

I twirled said baton again, this time like it was a baton and not a weapon. Thanks to Lena, I was pretty good at it. "Sometimes the best way to defuse a situation is with pizzazz!" I ended my routine with jazz hands, the sparkly streamers making hushing noises, like a crowd roaring its approval.

Rin laughed, genuine, a loud and sharp sound they hated and called a bark, but I loved and called a caw. They wouldn't mind being compared to a dog. They valued loyalty and were a fierce protector and a true friend. But a crow had a streak of intelligent mischief about them. You could befriend them and they would remember it for life, but if you did something to make them hate your face, you were fucked.

Also, Rin had pretty gothy tattoos curving from their back over their shoulders. Trees and vines in silhouette, black leaves blown from an invisible wind, birds soaring. With a low enough neckline, the tips of branches on their chest poked out. A tee shirt would cover most of it, except for a cluster of black lines up their neck that looked more delicate and Celtic than tribal. So. They cawed a laugh. Exactly what I wanted.

"Well." I tossed the baton across the room onto the couch and put my hands on my hips. "I'm very glad you're back, but I'm suspicious that you're not here early to seduce me, or it would be me sprawled across the table and not the physical representation of every email and text message you've sent and received in your life."

Rin sighed. "I started going through paperwork and ran out of room at the office. Your mom's sewing table seemed perfect. It'll work." They nodded, like they'd just decided it.

I walked around to stand next to them. "What are you looking for? Is it something I can help with?"

"Financial stuff I have to figure out. I'm hoping that spreading it out so I can see everything at once will make it clearer."

Almost four months with no income. Yeah, I could see how Rin might need to figure out some "financial stuff."

"Wait, isn't Daphne an accountant?" I asked.

Rin frowned. "Technically."

"Did you text her to help? I bet she'd be glad to."

They pushed up their glasses, squinted at the papers on the table, and started rearranging them. "If you couldn't get any more work because you walked off *Broke* with Raphael, would you ask Raphael to get you roles? Or would you try to do it on your own, to assure yourself you had the talent and skills to achieve your career goals without relying on the favors of others?"

Rin's questions cut right to the heart of me, pinpointing both my fear of being blacklisted for doing the right thing and having to rely on a friend being in-the-know instead of getting it done myself.

"So." I cleared my throat, leaving their questions unanswered. "It's a stroke of luck that mum didn't have any tailoring projects in queue and took the girls to visit relatives for the weekend. What would you have done otherwise?"

Rin glanced between the two papers they were holding, then gazed into the distance. "Probably had a nervous breakdown."

They weren't joking. But voicing the problem was their way of telling their friends it was ok. Putting it out there with a wink, because if it were an immediately serious issue, it wouldn't have been spoken aloud at all.

I had a similar approach when something was bothering me. I put on the show of being carefree because otherwise, anxiety and loss of control would drive me mad.

"Put me in, coach." I opened my arms wide to indicate how open I was to receive whatever they wanted to throw at me.

"Slow down, you eager muppet. If you can focus, I wouldn't mind another set of eyes. But your eyes don't know what to look for yet."

I pulled out a chair and sat up straight, trying to indicate with posture that I was ready to work. "Tell me what to look for."

Rin explained what had been happening at NIPL since early March, what they'd tried and what they needed both short- and long-term.

"What you sell requires people to travel there," I summarized when they had finished. "And nobody is going anywhere right now."

"That," they said with a sigh, "is the biggest and most long-term challenge." They laughed without humor. "How to make money from empty houses."

One idea after another pinged in my brain, from "sell the houses" to "rent them to the government for larger family quarantines" to a dozen other outlandish and impractical things, all of which Rin already thought of.

They pulled out the chair they'd been leaning against and sat down, resting their chin in their hand. "Whatever we come up with is going to take a lot of work. The Redgraves don't know the full extent of what's been happening. If they did, Daphne would offer to become an investor, confident that we'll turn everything around and be better than ever." They pushed one of the documents around with their finger. "I can't take her money. Not when I know it would be the same as throwing it into the campfire we had a few weeks ago."

"It wouldn't be like that," I said. If Rin wouldn't take Daphne's money, they weren't going to take mine, and that was going to be my next suggestion. "But if it could keep you afloat for a while, a few months—" I didn't know how wealthy Daphne was.

Not Raphael-rich, I'd guess, but if all of us invested what we could..."—or even a year, that might be enough to keep you open until things get back to normal. Either way, it sounds like something that will take a while to figure out and longer to put into action."

"Yeah," they said. "Meanwhile, there is a more time-sensitive problem."

"Money."

"Money," they agreed.

"What are you looking at?"

They ran their fingers through their hair, and I caught the scent of their shampoo and wanted a hot chocolate. They shuffled through some papers and pulled two folders closer.

"I'm going to be ten thousand dollars short this month."

I sucked in my breath with a hiss. It was involuntary, and when Rin glanced up at me, I wished I had been able to stop myself. "What about savings?"

They picked up one of the pens from the table and twirled it around their fingers absentmindedly. "How about I give you all the reports and statements and everything. If you read it cold, maybe you'll find a solution I didn't."

I made grabby hands for the papers, and Rin laughed. "Give me the reports. I love puzzles, and I'm good at math."

We worked side by side for a few hours. I retrieved the girls' oversized pink and purple calculators so I wouldn't get distracted trying to use the app on my phone, and I found blank notebooks for scratch paper. I made us tea once, and Rin made the second round.

When I'd come to the same conclusion the sixth time in a row, I tossed my pen across the table in defeat. "Rin my dear, I'm afraid

North Island Pinnacle Leisure needs about ten thousand dollars to break even this month."

They sighed, gravelly and ending with a growl. "Fuck," they said, the word clipped. Rin put their head in their hands. "I pay the employees first," they mumbled. "Then the main office rent and utilities..." They kept talking, but I couldn't understand, so I figured it was more a list for them than for me.

When they surfaced for air, their face pink from smothering themselves, they said, "I can't figure out how to not lose at least one of my properties."

"Well," I said, "you won't lose it immediately. It'll go into default, and there are a whole bunch of steps after that."

They laughed again, crossed their arms, and looked at me. "Zero income this quarter, Luke. I have four properties already in default."

I looked across the table at the hills of paperwork, and it suddenly seemed insurmountable. Twenty-six properties was too many properties. The main office was too expensive, when they could fit everyone at a smaller location. Too many employees. Too many gift baskets. The excess paperwork was a metaphor for how bloated the company had become. And why wasn't there enough money to cover even a month of bad luck?

"Can you take out loans to cover your loans?" I asked.

Rin grimaced. "I hate this," they said, pushing their chair back and pacing again. "I hate it. In almost fifty years, my parents never had this problem."

"Your parents never competed against a pandemic."

"Don't try to be cute."

"It's the truth, Rin. I know everyone's saying it, but you can't compare this pandemic, in these times, to anything anyone else has gone through in recorded history. So why not make a decision you wouldn't usually make in normal times and let your friends help you out? Call it an investment, or loans, or gifts, call it whatever you want. But between the five of us, we can give you the time you need to figure out the more long-term stuff."

They took off their glasses and pinched the bridge of their nose. "Skip that part."

I laughed. "Rin, you can't skip that part."

"Chronologically, I know," they said. "But that's not a solution for how this business remains viable. There's no money coming from the thing I'm supposed to be selling. So skip the you-all-banding-together for now, because that's an idea, and I have no ideas for what to do long term. Other companies have been talking about 'pivoting,' and I'd be open to it, if I knew what to pivot to."

I picked up one of the pencils and tapped the eraser end against the table. One of the multitude of ideas I'd had when Rin had asked how to make money from empty houses hadn't been half bad, but now I had to search for it.

"Wait," I said, a possibility forming. "Wait. Wait."

Rin cocked their head, whether intrigued by my swift problem-solving or silently wondering how they were attracted to such a dummy, I had no idea. My thoughts were moving faster than I could catch them.

"Hear me out," I said. They raised an eyebrow. "Switch marketing tactics. At this point, parents have been trapped in their house with their kids for weeks. Making food at home. Cleaning the house themselves. Living on top of each other. I love my daughters, but I understand how parents would crave a break from all that."

I leaned forwards, the idea taking shape. "Market the houses as an escape. Partner with house cleaning companies, private chefs, babysitting and caretaking folks. The parents can rent these cottages that will be cleaned by someone else. All their meals will be prepared by someone else, the dishes cleaned by someone else. The laundry, everything. Set them up with a babysitter for however long they'll be gone. They get a break, come back feeling recharged and refreshed, remember what luxury feels like, tell all their friends, and remember you when they want to do it again."

I waited while Rin considered it, but I knew I'd figured it out.

"I..." they started, pinching their bottom lip. "I like that idea."

Rin was right that I was a bit of a muppet, even if they said it affectionately. But they were brilliant. They ran their own business. They apparently partook in regular schemes with their friends, and had since grammar school. They liked my idea? I'd never felt so smart.

"I'll bring it up at the meeting tomorrow," Rin said, a little distantly. As the seconds ticked by and they didn't say anything more, their face closed.

They felt like a failure. That was the heart of the matter. They felt like a failure and were embarrassed to admit it by asking for help. I had no training and was bad at keeping money, but even I could tell that the main problem was the company's lack of savings. A multi-million-dollar business like NIPL, that'd been successful for so long, should have had significant funds set aside for exactly this kind of emergency. According to the records I looked through, they didn't.

From what they'd told me about themself, Rin never went to business school. They learned everything from their parents and they were comfortable with that because NIPL was successful. As long as Rin kept doing what they did, the company would survive. They didn't know they should have had a wider profit margin because they'd never operated that way.

"I think I know what happened," I said. "And you didn't do anything wrong."

"Covid happened," they said, looking at me like I was an idiot. "I know covid isn't my fault."

"No. I mean, yes, you're right, covid isn't your fault. But here, look." I separated a few pages from the pile in front of me and laid them out across the table. "The profit margins have always been slim, and very little, if any of it, went towards building an emergency fund. That's the way it had always been run, that's the way you inherited it, and that's the way you continued because it had always been a successful model. But not a sturdy one. Literally any catastrophe would have sent it into exactly the situation you have now. That it happened when you're in charge is coincidence.

"I know you're overwhelmed, partly by trying to figure out how to save the business, and partly because you feeling like a failure because this happened on your watch. But you don't need to feel embarrassed or shitty. The business would have become insolvent as soon as any misfortune happened, because of the way your parents ran it and taught you to run it."

Rin stood very still, staring at me, unblinking. Letting it sink in, going over the details to find any weak spots. I'd learned that when they got into their head like that, and decided that they were the bad guy, I had to hit them with a dose of cold logic. The trick was to—

"Are you fucking serious."

It wasn't a question. It was a statement, level, spoken from the depths of their gut. Their mouth barely moved, and they still hadn't blinked.

Not good. Very not good. I sucked in a breath, about to explain how it was a good thing, but they shook their head, a tiny amount, like their subconscious part that liked me was trying to keep me from digging the hole any deeper. A numbness spread from my lower back, fear making pins and needles in my stomach and legs. I'd said something wrong, and it was the most wrong I'd ever been, and it hurt them.

"The company that my family built for decades is in danger of failing. You say you want to help, and I accept because I'm that desperate. And your solution is that I shouldn't worry about it because my parents didn't know how to run a business."

When they put it that way, it sounded awful.

"Not only that," they continued, cheeks flushed, "but if they had taught me how to run it correctly, I wouldn't be in this situation right now."

"That's not what I said. It's not what I meant to say. I was trying to comfort you because if you knew it wasn't something you could control, that means it's not your fault."

They breathed deep, about to speak, then sighed quickly and smiled. But tears were forming in their eyes and they raked their fingers through their hair in frustration and I knew it was much worse than they were letting on.

"It *is* something I can control, and it's something I *have* to fix. This is my livelihood, Luke. And it's the livelihood of all my employees."

"Of course, I understand—"

"But beyond that? It's my legacy. And when you criticize it—" they pointed a shaking finger at me. "You're criticizing the legacy that my parents left me, and it's all I *fucking have left of them*."

In the whirlwind of everything that had happened since we met, I had forgotten that Rin had lost their parents so recently. Their dad the previous year. Their mom the year before. They didn't talk about them, besides the one night we mapped out our families to each other, and they seemed so well-adjusted to life in general that I never thought about it. I knew they were deeply hurt by the loss, and dealing with work had become their number one burden, and they were still exploring gender stuff that, if not as traumatic, still demanded time and patience and asking questions whose answers had to be built from scratch.

Did the other people who loved Rin know all that? Was I the only one who happily took them at their word that none of it was a big deal?

They'd been waiting for a response, and I didn't have one. They were hurt and scared of losing another pillar of their existence that they'd come to rely on. I had mistakenly taken their masking at literal face value so I could pretend I didn't have to do any hard work in the relationship, but that was a separate issue for another time. Important, extremely important, since I loved them, but the present state of things wasn't about me.

Rin had started gathering everything on the table, shoving papers into folders without looking. Trying not to cry. I wanted to reach out to them, stop them from leaving, but I knew better. I stayed seated. Standing up would create a chaos of movement, and they didn't need more chaos.

"Rin," I said softly, "you're right. I was out of line. I can't imagine how stressful all of this has been for you, and I'm sorry I made it worse. I can explain myself, but I know now isn't the time. Right now, I want to help you, however that may be. I think that means I don't stop you from leaving, because my face is going to make things worse."

They paused but didn't look at me.

"You can stay, and I'll go visit Raph to give you some time alone. Or I can carry these boxes to your car once you fill them, so you can continue your research somewhere else. Send me a text when you want to come over or talk."

Don't leave me. Let me explain. I didn't mean it. We can fix it. I promise I won't be so thick-headed in the future.

"I'm so sorry," I repeated.

Rin nodded and resumed packing. "You can take the boxes to the car. I'll stay up in Auckland. It might take a while."

A while was fine. I just didn't want it to be the end. I could talk to Raph, or Mattie and Daphne, see what they had to say about it. What meaningful thing I could do to make amends. But for now, all I could do was nod, and carry the literal weight of Rin's burden to their car.

Chapter 29

October 2022

Rin

My anger didn't last the walk to the village. It didn't even last to the end of the driveway. The only thing stopping me from turning around and gathering Luke up and apologizing was my overwhelming embarrassment and my near-constant belief that I was too much of a mess for him or anyone to have to put up with. A belief that, once again, was proving correct.

I could blame it on the day we'd had. The two days. Luke would tell me, as always, that I was put under extraordinary circumstances and how I acted wasn't how I would normally act. Except the past five years had been nothing *but* extraordinary circumstances, and if that was normal life now, then this was my updated, normal reaction to things.

I was tired of living in unprecedented times. I yearned for precedented ones.

Luke was right about everything, especially when he said the answer was therapy. That and quitting my job and starting over. At the very least, I was sure I could get a job at Tessa's. Not a full-on boxing instructor, but something more entry-level might be humbling, and maybe that was what I needed.

Regardless, I wasn't going to get therapy or a new job between Daisy's castle and the bus stop twenty kilometres away. But the tramp would burn away some shame. It would be a few hours, but according to the atlas, I'd only have to change direction for three different roads on the way, and the last was a pretty straight shot into town. And there was a good chance my mobile would pick up a signal before I got there.

If I called Mats first, I'd have to do so much explaining. But Daph could look up the bus schedule if my signal wasn't strong enough, and I could ask her to pick me up in London when I got there, without her demanding the entire story first. *Then* I could call Mattie and tell her where to get Luke. I wasn't going to completely abandon him, but if I couldn't handle walking with him for another three hours, I couldn't handle being in a car with him for the six hours or however long it would take to get to London.

Luke and I needed to talk. Like, serious, sit down, no distractions, talk. Outside of catastrophe and attempting to survive. As much as I loved him and as much as he might love me, I wasn't a good partner for him. I needed to do so much work on myself, and it wasn't fair to ask him to tolerate me in the meantime. Which was the same reason I gave two years ago when we broke up. That was depressing. I hadn't made any progress in two years.

Best to be upfront about it, let him know he's going to have to move on. If my actions at Daisy's didn't make that already abundantly clear to him.

The lightest of rain drizzled against the hood of my jacket, tapping lightly against the waterproof material. I heard it in the woods, beyond the meaty footsteps of my boots on the fine gravel driveway. Larger drips of water accumulated in the late October leaves and fell to the dirt with an intermittent, heavy bass to accompany the rest of the chorus singing against bark, leaves, and forest floor.

I kept the torch low, and when it finally illuminated the closed iron gate and brick pillars at the end of the driveway, I took a breath and looked behind me, half expecting Luke to have followed.

He should have stayed, if he could. I deserved to be awake and trudging through the countryside at this ungodly hour in this exact weather. But Luke hadn't done anything wrong besides trust my broken and hungry intuition. There was a chance he could charm his way back inside the castle. It wouldn't take much. Honesty would get him pretty far. And he wouldn't have had the chance if I hadn't left.

Sure I was alone, I opened and slipped through the gate, surprised at how smoothly it turned on its hinges until I remembered that Daisy said he had friends over frequently. The man had a whole life and people who loved him, and here I was, crashing into it and ruining everything. I seriously needed to take a good, hard look at my life and decide who I wanted to be, because this wasn't it. This was a nightmare.

In the three hours I spent walking—in the middle of each road, torch in hand—I encountered no cars, no people, no wildlife. The rain had stopped but residual drips sounded throughout the forest, and when the land changed from woods to farm, I had only my footsteps to keep me company. I saw no houses or other buildings, but the torch only reached so far, and the sky wouldn't lighten for a few hours yet. Adrenaline and emotional turmoil kept me awake when I might have fallen asleep while walking—I'd be pulling an all-nighter, which had become increasingly frequent, with proportionally worsening consequences. It would be a kindness to pass out on the bus.

I stopped once and ate a sandwich I'd taken from the kitchen while the guys were having their post-dinner drinks, but for the most part, the solitude, the repetitive walking, and the physical activity created the perfect environment for me to consider how to fix the situation with Luke and also my life. It was also the perfect opportunity to have a good cry where nobody could judge me for it.

When I saw the first street lamp, I checked my phone. No signal yet. Ten minutes later, I picked up the faintest half of a bar, but I still couldn't get through. Getting closer to town, I passed a large building with Wi-Fi I didn't have time to guess the password to, but a few metres past it, my phone started dinging and chirping and vibrating with notifications of the dozens of ways people had tried to contact me in the past few days. Instead of looking at any of them, I immediately called Daphne.

"Rin!" The phone had barely rung before she picked up, and it was all I could do not to start crying again. Cinnamon mumbled in the background, and their voices felt like coming home.

I wanted to be casual, let her know I was ok and it wasn't a big deal, but something must have cracked in me between Mr Bean's demise and almost killing a perfectly lovely man, and I heard myself telling her, "I need help."

"We've got you, Rin-Rin. You need us to pick you up? You need an ambulance? Where are you? Is Luke ok?"

I told her the name of the village I was walking into. "I need a bus schedule, could you look it up for me?"

Daphne set Cinnamon to that task. "Is Luke ok? What happened? Mattie said she was going to meet you in Leeds two nights ago, we were so worried."

"Luke is back at the house we stayed in, and he's fine. I'm going to call Mattie in a minute and tell her and Raph to pick him up."

"Then why am I looking up a bus schedule for you?"

"Because," I said with a sigh. "Being in a car with him for that long would be too much. I need to be alone for a while. We had a fight. Me and Luke. The car broke down. Like, *broke* down.

We were lost, and there was no service for me to call or text. I freaked out and started walking. I have a map. Figured I could get transportation from here, and let Luke ride to London with Mattie and Raph."

There was a silence on the line, and I knew Daphne was figuring out what I hadn't said. That was the problem with being friends with smart people.

"You don't deserve to be alone," she finally concluded.

"Fuck, Daph." At this rate, I'd never stop crying.

"Look, it just sounds like a bunch of unfortunate events out of your control put you in a highly emotional situation, and I think you should show yourself some grace and take the soft way out instead of punishing yourself."

"Well, you would say that."

"Obviously," she said, undeterred. "Because I just did. I have the info for the nearest bus stop, and I'll give it to you, but let me urge you one last time to let yourself accept help—even though you're very bad at doing so, I know—and let Mattie and Raph pick you up and take care of you. Tell them you don't want to talk about the details and then pretend to be asleep in the back of the car. It's what I would do."

I loved Daphne like a sister, but she was definitely the youngest sister. Of course she would expect other people to take care of her. She never worried about whether she would have a safety net, a support system to help her, because she made sure to offer the same to the people she loved.

And I may have been an only child, but I grew up with the Redgraves and if anything, I was the eldest. It was hard for me to expect or accept help, and if I did, I felt like a failure. A failure at what? Who could say. Life? Only offering help but never being a burden that needed it?

"I need to be alone," I said. "How early can I get into London by bus?"

Daphne read me the information and we made plans for her and Cinnamon to pick me up at the station a little after noon.

"I know this can't be in your top twenty things to think about right now," Daph said, "but do you still want to go to the premiere tonight?"

Part of me felt like Scrooge on Christmas morning, delighted I hadn't missed the only event I'd been excited about for months. Another part felt blindsided. It had been weeks since I had food poisoning in Scotland, so I should have missed the premiere, but now I had to get dressed up and presentable and go to a theater? Where I'd see Luke?

"I don't know," I told her. "I lost all my clothes. It's a long story. I don't have anything to wear."

"Oh, Raph took care of that. Not *all* your clothes—dear god Rin, I need to know every single detail right now about all of this but I know you're busy but it's destroying me. Raphael got a stylist and they brought, like, a rack of clothes for each of us. There's a black dress you would just kill in, if you're in a femme mood. And a three-piece silk suit in a super dark red, like dried blood, god it would be fabulous on you even without the jacket—"

"Daph."

"Right. Sorry. Not the time, you have to call Mattie. You need anything else from us before I let you go?"

I smiled. I needed the reality check that some people saw the same problems I did but their solution was simply a gorgeous outfit.

"No, no. I'll text or call if there's a problem."

"Text and call even if there isn't a problem. There's a bakery near the bus stop that opens soon, so text me when you eat breakfast. Then text me when you get on the bus. Then send me pictures of cows or sheep or whatever you see out the window on the way. Then call me—" Cinnamon cut in and said something I couldn't hear. "Cinnamon says she's glad you're safe but I have to let you go now so you can finish your quest. Text me, is all. I love you, Rin-Rin."

"Love you too, Daph. And Cinnamon."

I ended the call and looked around. I'd entered the village proper, and it was, if nothing else, cute. My phone buzzed with a text. The newest of dozens I still hadn't read, this was, predictably, from Daphne, and showed the location of the bakery she'd mentioned. My stomach growled reading the word "bakery."

After Mattie, I told it. *As a reward.*

Mattie also answered the phone before the end of the first ring. "Rin? Is that you?"

"I'm fine, Luke is fine, we're not hurt, I'm so sorry to worry you." With Mats, it was best to get all the important information out as soon as possible. "I'm safe, and Luke is safe. I already talked to Daphne and she helped me, and now I'm calling you for a very specific favor."

There was a pause on her end, and I knew she was stopping herself from asking the questions that I already answered.

"Where are you?"

"North of Leeds. I need you and Raph to go pick up Luke. He's not hurt," I emphasized. "We had a row and I walked away and he let me and it's for the best. I'm taking a bus into London. But he's back at a house we stayed at last night and doesn't have any way to get in touch with anyone and doesn't have a way to get out of there. I sort of took the only map we had."

"Where is he?"

I gave her directions as best I could, with this little town as my point of reference. She relayed it to Raphael and told him to start packing.

"You know I need more information," Mats told me with a sniffle.

She received a very abridged version of the past two days' events.

"Don't take a bus to London," she begged. "We can pick you up, too."

"I don't want to see him. Especially not for so long, trapped in a car again."

Mattie sighed. "That bad, huh?"

"That bad and my fault." My voice caught on the last word and I cleared my throat to try to cover it up, but that never worked with the Redgraves.

"You know he never stopped loving you, so whatever it is that happened, I doubt it'll change how he feels about you now."

"It should," I mumbled. "Daphne pointed me towards a place where I can have breakfast, so I'm going to eat now. I promise I'll fill you both in on everything when we're all in the city."

"You can start now. You can eat and talk at the same time."

"I need some alone time."

"Sounds like you had a lot of that this morning."

"I need at least another half day of alone time. I need to think."

"Are you sure I can't convince you to let us get you?"

If I didn't let her rescue me personally, it would stay in her voice until she could finally embrace me and check me over for bruises and missing limbs that afternoon. I thought of being trapped in the car with Luke and having to answer questions. No. No, I'd made the right choice. And Mats would be fine.

"I'll text you," I said. "You'll always know where I am."

She sniffled again. Oh, my soft Mattie. So sensitive and caring. "I'll text you too. You're going to tell me everything."

"I'm going to tell you everything," I agreed. "In London."

"No more disasters. I love you."

"I love you too, muppet."

Ahead, I could see the bakery, and their open sign illuminated. The bus stop was down the street a few blocks, its clearly marked signage perfectly positioned beneath a street lamp. I had almost an hour to wait for the bus. Plenty of time for breakfast. As much as Daphne might disagree, croissants couldn't fix everything. But I was game to see just how much they could.

Chapter 30
October 2022
Luke

The door creaked and I woke with a start. The damp October night was unmistakable against my exposed face and hands, and the world smelled of wet earth and stone. My shoulders ached, my neck hurt, and my butt was fast asleep from sitting on the unforgiving entryway. I shifted my feet and opened my eyes. The front lawn and driveway and misty air looked the same as when I drifted off, the time between immeasurable from where I sat.

Rin.

I could have spent the rest of the night staring at the spot where they disappeared, when the beam of their torch was swallowed by the dark woods and I just had to have faith that they weren't swallowed with it.

But the door. There'd been a noise.

I glanced up to see Daisy, arms folded and standing in the middle of the doorway, looking down at me with an unreadable expression.

I breathed deep through my nose and rubbed my face. "I know, mate," I said with a nod. "I'll be gone. For what it's worth, I'm sorry. You were nothing but kind and you didn't deserve our nonsense."

He glanced between me and the yard. I didn't want to leave. Rin had showed me on the map how to get to the town, and my confidence in being able to remember it was hovering at thirty percent and dropping with each minute I wasn't actively trying to recreate that path. I knew I had to. Get to a phone, call Raphael, let him rescue me like he was always trying to do. Wrestle with the uncomfortable knowledge that letting him do it earlier in the week would have prevented this whole situation.

Maybe Daisy wanted to watch me go. Make sure the threat of us had truly passed. But I didn't want to move in a way where he might feel even more threatened, so unless I wormed myself away from the wall and rolled my body far enough away from the house that standing up couldn't be mistaken for an act of aggression, I had to wait for him to go back inside.

"I saw her leave," he said.

"Them. Yeah."

"You didn't stop them."

I laughed. "There's no stopping Rin. Which is great when they're confident and brimming with ideas. Not so great when they're dehydrated, exhausted, paranoid, and too embarrassed to be perceived anymore. Even by someone who loves them." I fiddled with the strap of my messenger bag. "I could have followed. Tagged along as they figured out how to get rescued. But they didn't want anything I offered, and it seemed selfish to impose myself on them."

If storming off alone into the night was an extreme reaction, so was staying behind with no possible exit. But things usually worked out for me. And I needed the time alone to consider why it hurt so much that Rin couldn't believe me, and why I couldn't just believe them.

Daisy heaved a world-weary sigh. "Well, come on back inside, Luke. You won't be doing anyone any favors shivering at my door or getting lost in the woods. If nothing else, I have people coming over tomorrow night, and I'm sure one of them can bring you wherever you need."

I looked up at him, this slight man in his dressing gown and slippers, inviting me back into his castle in the middle of nowhere, after what we'd put him through.

"Can I help with the organ?" I gathered myself and stood up, trying to stretch the stiffness out of my limbs.

He raised an eyebrow. "Do you know how to repair one?"

"No," I said. "But I can follow directions and I'm an extra pair of hands."

Daisy considered it for a moment, then shook his head and gestured me inside. "No. No, it's kind of you to offer. But you should rest." I followed him, and he closed the door behind us. "I should have told you both about my unconventional sleep schedule and hobbies."

"Absolutely not," I said. "It's your house, we were uninvited. You didn't owe us anything."

"Perhaps. It would have saved a lot of bother, though."

I thought back to Rin pointing out the lack of a phone in the den. "I'm not sure it would have. Rin and I have had a hell of a week."

The thought of it triggered a renewed tiredness in my bones, and the bedroom where I'd been sleeping earlier in the night seemed too far away for the effort it would take to get there. "Do you mind if I crash on one of the couches nearby?"

He showed me to a parlor near the kitchen and a washroom, and my desire to be helpful and kind and a good guest was abandoned for the first comfortable couch I saw. I settled in and was asleep immediately.

Later, after I didn't know how long, a softly chirping animal roused me back to consciousness. I'd been woken up by dogs before. Cats, too. The badger was new to me.

Lady Stephanie's soft fur tickled my cheek as her little cold nose nudged my own. Her diminutive paws patted my face in exploration, claws tapping against my skin, and her little breaths sniffed me out.

"G'morning my lady," I mumbled, raising a hand to pet her. She made a sound like a purr, and I wondered if Mia could somehow get a domestic badger for Lena and Cassidy to keep in California. New Zealand would never approve it. And the girls couldn't appreciate her vicariously since I didn't have any way to take her picture.

At the thought of my kids, my heart sank. They must have been so worried about me. And I didn't know when I'd be able to tell them I was ok. Rin could have found a mobile signal and told everyone what happened, where I was. They were angry with me, but they weren't malicious. I bet they called the cavalry and I would be rescued at any moment. Depending, of course, on what time it was.

I reluctantly opened my eyes to a still-dark room. The light level didn't tell me anything. Between the shortening days and the normal cloudy skies, it could be five in the morning as easily as noon. And my tiredness level was also useless, for obvious reasons. By the soreness in new places, I was pretty sure I'd slept for a bit. Long enough for the couch flaws to imprint upon my flesh and my mouth to grow that thin film of phlegm, like dust on a disused organ.

"Oh good, you're awake."

"That's a generous interpretation of my state," I told Daisy, clearing my throat.

"I found the telephone."

He found the telephone. I froze for a moment while my mind absorbed it, then struggled to get out of the deep couch. Lady

Stephanie jumped to the floor with a grunt, and I apologized to her under my breath.

"You found the phone? Does it work?" I successfully pulled myself up into a standing position, a little dizzy.

"Oh yes." Lady Stephanie had made her way to her person, and Daisy picked her up from where he stood just inside the door. "I forgot I moved it into its own room beneath the stairs. In my pursuit of collecting history about the castle, I had come across a diary entry from 1942 when they installed their first telephones in the building. They repurposed the little room beneath the main staircase for it. Added some lush seating. A perfect closet of privacy."

My shoulders drooped. "So it's a phone from 1942."

"No, dear, it's a *room* from 1942. The telephone itself was replaced several times. It had never occurred to me that something was beneath the stairs, but once I read that diary entry, I renovated the space and put my phone from the den there. It's adorable."

"But it works."

"It works."

"I need it."

Daisy inclined his head and led me to the phone closet. He was right. It was adorable, with walnut paneling and raspberry-red velvet cushions. One flower-shaped sconce illuminated the little desk built beneath it and the crystal and gold landline phone that nearly fooled me until I saw the buttons were press and not rotary.

"There's a phone book on the shelf beneath, there." Daisy pointed to the desk and cradled Lady Stephanie like a baby in his other arm. "If you require any additional assistance, I shall be in the kitchen making tea."

Daisy shut the door as he left and I lifted the receiver to my ear.

I never thought I'd be so relieved to hear a dial tone.

I punched in Cassidy's number first. She didn't answer, and I remembered they'd gotten to London the day before from California, so it would feel like bedtime to her, not awake time. And I was calling from an unknown number, so I should be proud she wasn't answering calls from people she didn't know.

Mia was used to changing time zones pretty frequently, and she picked up on the third ring. I gave her a bare-bones summary of what had happened. Her practical and measured responses were less from her being practical and measured and more from her general attitude of genuine ambivalence towards me. She worried about my safety as the father of Lena and Cassidy first, and as a human being second, and that was the end of the list of ways she thought about me. I told her Raphael was nearby and I was going to get him to retrieve me, and she told me she'd tell the girls I was safe and loved them, and if I ended up needing a ride, to call her back.

Mia's disinterest set the tone that nothing was insurmountable, everything had a straightforward solution, and there was no need to panic. It was what I needed. But it still would have been nice to know someone had cared enough about me to worry.

Enter Raphael.

"Hello?"

I took a deep breath. "Hey, mate. Wondering if you'd like to meet for some brekkie or whatnot."

"Jesus Christ, Luke." He let out a sigh that sounded like he'd been holding it for two days.

"Is that a no? No breakfast? What about second breakfast?"

Maybe Rin was on to something, when they said I deflected difficult situations with humor and it made me seem like I couldn't take anything seriously.

"I'm ok," I quickly added. "Safe and sound, but without a car, a phone, or direction."

"Glad to hear it," he said. "Now put Daisy on, we're about a half hour out at most and we need more specific directions now that we're getting closer."

"Rin," I whispered, my whole body flushing with warmth. Of course they didn't leave me behind to rot. Of course the first thing they did was send someone to my rescue. My throat tightened and I tried to swallow around it. Here I was, dry and rested, just waiting for someone to pick me up, while Rin had trekked through the cold, wet night to find help. I should have been with them. Every stroke of bad luck we'd had was my fault, yet they were the one to fix it, on their own.

I'd spent the last week fantasizing about having a relationship with them again. But what would I bring to it? Sarcasm and the smarmy privilege of not having to think about the number of ways any given situation could go catastrophically bad for me? A joke for every occasion? Unemployment, depression, a lack of direction and an unclear future? If they still believed they were a mess, they definitely didn't need me adding to that chaos.

Raphael had been talking while my mind wandered and I caught up with him again as he said that "Daphne will pick them up in London, they'll get there around noon—"

"What?" I asked. "Who?"

"—I know you lost all your clothes, so it's a good thing I told the stylist to make a rack for you anyway, and obviously we can go shopping tomorrow to replenish your wardrobe—"

"Stop, wait. Who's Daphne picking up?"

"Rin."

"They're not in the car with you?"

Silence on his end.

"Raph, where the fuck is Rin?"

Noises like someone was handling the phone, then Mattie's voice came on. "Hey Luke, sorry. Rin took a bus into London. They're safe, I promise. I'm texting with them as we speak." She chuckled. "I'm torn between keeping up a steady stream of communication and letting them sleep. I should let them sleep, though."

I rubbed my forehead. "Mats, why is Rin on a bus to London and not in the car with you? How far did they walk?" I mumbled the last part, mostly to myself.

"They weren't in the headspace to be around other people for a while," Mattie said.

I could read between the lines. I should have expected it, and on some level I did, but on a much more conscious level, it was a punch in the gut. Walked that far then got onto a fucking bus instead of finding comfort with their best friend. Because they didn't want to see me.

"Um," I said. There had to be a response to this. "Um," I repeated.

"Luke," Raph said, an edge of demand in his voice, "go get Daisy and ask if he can give us directions. Get him now."

I nodded and set the receiver on the desk. *Raphael needed directions. Get Daisy. Rin didn't even want to be rescued with you.*

Daisy returned with me to the phone room and let me hold Lady Stephanie while he talked to Raph. It wasn't long before Daisy was laughing and carrying on a conversation with Raphael like they were old friends. That's usually how it went. I could charm people more down-to-earth, Raph could charm the upper crust. Together, we were unstoppable. There was a reason we were voted Most Powerful Bromance three years in a row.

"Why didn't you tell me you knew Raphael Callan?" Daisy set the phone receiver aside and took the baby badger from me. "I'm good friends with his uncle on his mother's side. We were fast mates, all through school. I'm afraid I've been a poor host indeed, to drive his nephew's own best mate into the night. I do hope you forgive me."

"There's nothing to forgive, Daisy, truly." The last thing I needed was this man we had wronged believing that he had done anything to earn it. "If the scales aren't balanced yet, it's because I owe you for your hospitality."

"You're a good man, Luke. Your friends are about twenty minutes away, at my estimate, and they're still on the line."

He left me again, with a pat on the shoulder, and I sat in the telephone room.

"Do you know the entire goddamn gentry?"

"Unfortunately," Raph said wryly. "Though, in this case, fortunately. Once our internet search produced his name, I remembered it. Funny you ended up with him."

"Hilarious. Twenty minutes, then?"

"Twenty minutes. But I think Daisy wanted us to join him for breakfast before we left."

I nodded. Yeah, that sounded like him. "I've behaved badly."

"Sometimes we do that."

My irritation with him returned. Saying "we" as though the consequences of our mistakes were equal. I tamped it down. He was my ticket out of here, and if nothing else, I could count on him to pick me up and dust me off and set me up any time he found me struggling, even if he didn't share in my suffering. As much as I needed to sit down and have a serious conversation with Rin, I also needed to do the same with Raphael. Might as well make the whole list now, get everyone out of the way.

We hung up. They arrived. Daisy invited us to have breakfast, and we stayed. Mattie cooed over Lady Stephanie, and so did Raphael, and I envied the ease with which he conducted himself. But he had been raised in this world, and he hadn't spent the last three nights awake and suffering food poisoning, car disintegration, goat attacks, a labyrinth, or delusions of being murdered.

There was no malice in Raphael, and it was unfair of me to assign it to him to feel better about myself. We'd talk in London, then. Mats would go see Rin, and Raph and I could talk. Not that it wasn't something I wanted Mattie to overhear. But he and I had as much history as she and Rin, and all of us knew it was important to give our relationships proper focus without involving other people.

By the time we left, Raphael and Daisy were making plans for Raph to visit and bring his uncle, and Mattie had won Daisy's heart by adoring Lady Stephanie. Honestly, though, who wouldn't?

We said our goodbyes and I slid into the back of Raph's black Mercedes, the smell of clean leather and the luxurious sound of the shutting doors an assuring sign of the civilization I'd missed. I set my bag on the seat and used it as a pillow, feeling exhaustion overtaking me, creeping up from my toes and fingers, a heaviness in my chest and head. Raph turned in his seat to look at me, raising an eyebrow that was the equivalent of all the questions he wanted to ask.

"Sorry, bro," I mumbled. The answers were on the tip of my tongue, but my eyes were already closing and none of me was light enough to move again, and I slipped into a comfortable and dreamless sleep.

Chapter 31

August 2020

Rin

"It's because I said your parents were shitty business owners."

We sat on the hood of my car, the red SUV I'd bought earlier in the year, before I even suspected that covid would forever change my business, my savings, my relationships. I was trying to downgrade everything in my life today, in one day, so I could wake up tomorrow with the drive and focus I needed to save my goddamn company. Later in the morning, I'd be trading in the car for a used EV, and if my calculations were correct, it would only cost a couple thousand dollars to own it outright. Cheaper than four more years of expensive car payments. That was second on my list of things to streamline.

First on my list was breaking up with Luke.

My eyes followed the roof line of his house, a contemporary ranch built in the sixties and added onto as the Maston family grew. Single car garage attached and expanded for two cars. Large shed in the back, the garden, the greenhouse. The new in-law apartment and the expanded and remodeled kitchen.

And I knew the story behind every one of them. Every addition to the family, every birth, when someone moved out, when someone moved back in. The hobbies that spurred a new growth at the property and whether the hobbyist kept up with it or the room was eventually repurposed. Luke had told me some of it. Ann had told me much more, presented to me like a gift. Like I had passed some test I didn't remember taking and I could now know the history of the Mastons as a way of becoming part of that history. She saw how Luke looked at me and simply adopted me into her family. She knew her son that well.

I choked up thinking about it. Of all the things I was going to miss about not being with Luke, feeling like part of a family was high on that list.

"I was angry when you said that," I admitted, flicking a burr off my boot laces. "But I needed time to think about what you meant, and I know you weren't trying to hurt me. Hell, you weren't even wrong. It wasn't a personal attack, but I couldn't think straight in the moment." I paused, considering. "I guess that *is* what prompted me to do this, but not in the way you think. Not because you said something wrong, but because I reacted to it so...horrifically."

"Of course you did," he said, taking my hand. His was warm, and soft, and the pulse of his grasp reminded me of comfort. "I could never prove myself to you. The desire was there but the execution failed. You're amazing, and you need someone on your level. No amount of pranks or sex or distractions would have convinced you. Plus, look at what you've had to deal with this year, while I tried to focus you on me. I was thoughtless."

And I had too many thoughts. "I'm not punishing you," I said, my voice close to a whisper. If I tried to speak any louder, my voice would crack, and it would all be downhill from there. "*I* don't feel steady. *I* don't feel solid. And that's something I need—and want—to learn how to do on my own so I'm not always reliant on another person for it." I held up my other hand to stop his inevitable interruption. "You or anyone."

Luke shifted beside me. Restless and struggling to say the right thing? Me, too.

"Rin." His voice darkened. Like he was bringing up a secret from the depths of his being to share with me. Time slowed and I tensed, thinking he would say he loved me, to try to get me to stay. What he said was just as bad. "You feel like home."

I ducked my head and let my breath out in a shaky stream. I hated this. I wanted to stay. Our hearts wouldn't be broken and I would learn to cope with all the pressure of my shaken-up life without shaking the Mastons apart too.

"It feels like you belong here," he continued. "In this place and with me and in my family. When you're around, I can focus. Everything becomes clearer, and I don't notice what would otherwise distract me. And that's the kind of person I've always wanted to be. You make me happy to do it."

"Yeah," I said, wiping my eyes. "I know what you mean. Because you see me. In the way I've wanted to be seen. And you did it right from the start." I laughed and sniffled. "I've never felt more comfortable. But I don't know how to...commit myself to saving this business *and* commit myself to you. I don't know how to do it. And *learning* how to do it would be a third thing I would try to focus on and it all feels like too much."

Luke brought my hand to his mouth and kissed it, then wrapped his other hand around mine, holding it in his lap like a caught bird.

"I can wait." He smiled and glanced up at me. "That's what family does. Even if you have to go away for a while. To figure things out. But I need you to know that I wish you would stay with me." He took a breath and glanced towards the house. "I'm not saying this to guilt you into anything. I should have said it a month ago. Two months ago. I should have said it the moment I knew instead of keeping it for some vague better future time.

"I love you. Whether you go or stay. Whether we break up or dive headlong into our chaos together. You're resilient and compassionate and considerate, but you also laugh at my dumbest jokes because you're always on the verge of making the same ones. You have a sense of justice that's unbelievably hot, and despite you trying to convince everyone that you're capable of handling everything and anything, I want to take all your problems and do it myself. Give you all those pre-solved puzzles to make your life easier, to make you happy. And that isn't going to change just because you're not actively in my life anymore. And besides. I can wait for you."

My cheeks were wet with tears, and I could feel my nose running, threatening to turn into a snot bubble that Luke would find endearing and wouldn't make him love me any less. I squeezed his hand, hard, and he squeezed back, sniffling himself. I cleared my throat and turned it into a laugh.

"The timing. The timing is messed up. Not us."

"It's the timing," he agreed softly.

"Fucking timing."

"Hate it. The worst."

I sighed and glanced around at the blurry world. It wasn't fair.

"I love you, too," I told him.

He let go of my hand to pull me close, his arms wrapped around my shoulders, kissing my hair as I cried against him.

I was tired of losing every thing I loved. Year after year, like dominoes, one precious thing after another fell. Out of my reach. Out of my control. Mother, father, world without a pandemic, the business slipping through my fingers faster the more I tried to hold it tight, like sand. The one person who made me feel less anxious, less hopeless, and more like myself than ever before.

He said he'd wait. He said I could come back. I wished I could believe in myself like that. Wished I could believe I'd get my shit together quickly enough, completely, to be the kind of partner

Luke needed. And the kind of parent Lena and Cassidy needed. But the smallest setback seemed insurmountable, and cutting myself off from everything but the problem at hand had always been the most effective approach.

"It's ok if you don't come back," he whispered. "You can't escape me completely. Our best mates are soulmates now, so we'll still see each other. And if you ever get to the point where you can ask for help, I'll answer. I'll always answer."

"Stop saying such nice things!" I moaned.

He breathed a laugh against the top of my head and pulled away. "I know you're going to beat yourself up over it later, and I don't want you to. I can't stop you, but if you know I know, you'll feel bad about it and stop."

"Your logic is flawless," I said with a laugh.

I didn't want to leave. And I couldn't right myself if I stayed.

"Timing," I whispered.

"I'll wait."

"It could be a while. It could be too long."

Luke smiled again, full of sadness, and full of hope. "Rin. You're worth waiting a lifetime for."

Chapter 32
October 2022
Rin

The cessation of movement woke me. I lifted my head from the cold bus window with a quick inhale, breathing in the scent of the heat registers trying their best, sweat and hair product from a thousand bodies in the cloth seats, cigarette smoke on the clothing of the people behind me. The engine had been shut off, and the driver was announcing our arrival in London over a loudspeaker that reminded me of the adults in a Peanuts movie. People around me stood up, stretched, gathered their belongings. I only had my backpack, resting on my lap.

Wi-Fi had been spotty on the bus, but I had been able to contact everyone I needed to while I ate three sausage rolls and a chocolate croissant at the bakery. I tried to keep up the stream of texts with Daphne and Mattie once I boarded. Instead, my body chose sleep, and I was grateful for the four hours of rest. I'd been so exhausted, not even the usual bus-related discomforts could pierce my slumber.

I retrieved my phone from my pocket and pulled my backpack around, preparing to stand up and leave once the rows in front of me emptied. A bunch of notifications flashed on my screen. Work, asking for a log and receipts I didn't have because neither the cottage we'd broken into nor the castle I'd fled in the middle of the night had supplied them. Mattie, saying she and Raphael had picked up Luke and stayed for breakfast with Daisy (unsurprising), and would be back in the city around the same time as me. And Daphne, directing me where to go when I disembarked, because she and Cinnamon were already waiting for me at the terminal.

The station was busy for a weekday afternoon, and I took my time getting to where Daphne said she would be. My mind was loud. Four hours wasn't enough sleep. Not after being awake for almost 24 hours. Not after all that physical and emotional turmoil. And I wouldn't have time for a nap before the premiere, which I still wanted to go to. It was the only thing I'd accomplished in the last two years. No way was I missing it.

But that meant everything I was thinking would remain an intolerable cacophony until I slept or solved it. Mattie and Daph and I needed to have a conversation about me losing NIPL and how depressed I was, and that would have to wait until we got to the hotel. Luke and I needed to have a different conversation, but I wasn't sure I wanted to do that before the premiere. Then there was work.

I stopped short in the vast hall. I'd been walking slowly, half paying attention to my surroundings, sticking close to the wall so others could pass. Snippets of phone conversations washed over me, families talking as they walked by, footsteps everywhere in all directions, moving. Everyone had somewhere to be. Was it easier for them? Did they know where they were going and how to get there? How? How did they know? What map did they receive, did they find, did they stumble into, that I had somehow missed completely? Why did I feel like I was always in the dark, having to create my own roads? Why, when I thought I knew the way, did the path disappear?

Numbness spread through my stomach, and I couldn't feel my legs. I could see my legs. I could see all of me, like I was looking down from above. And the people around me moved. In straight lines, in wobbly lines. Some doubled back. But they all made progress. They chose, and went, and changed if they needed. There were no rules. Everyone was making it up.

It was a terrifying thought, and a tantalizing one. The more I considered it, the more I felt something shifting, sliding, and finally, aligning.

Maybe I would be great at making it up. Maybe I would thrive with no rules.

Feeling returned to my body in a wave of heat, a flush, a blush, and I saw from my own eyes again, though I still felt floaty. Giddy, even, as I began typing on my phone, even if the emotion wasn't mirrored in my frown. I sent the email, double checked Daphne's text of where to find her, and slid the phone back into my pocket. The rough, unfamiliar material reminded me I'd technically stolen these clothes from Daisy, and I laughed aloud. I was a fool, and he was a sweetheart, and I would do my damnedest to send him a heartfelt apology, a professional organ repair person, and a truck full of treats for Lady Stephanie. All I had to do was make it through the day.

"Rin-Rin!" Daphne crashed into me with the force of a Redgrave, and it would have knocked anybody else off their feet. She'd let her platinum hair grow long enough to style it into a shoulder-length butterfly cut, and her inky-blue eyes shone with genuine and intense joy before she buried her face in my neck. Her outfit was uncharacteristically subdued—a belted navy trench coat, white silk shirt with a bluebell pattern, and what appeared to be at least knee-high black leather boots.

I held her tight, breathing in the scent she'd been wearing since she was a teenager, a perfume that reminded me of night-blooming flowers. Familiar and comforting, it became an anchor in the sea of my sleep-starved consciousness.

Cinnamon was only a half step behind Daphne and didn't wait to make it a group hug. I made room for her, shifting my arm so I could embrace the both of them properly.

"I need to know everything!" Daph shouted into my neck. In case I couldn't hear her, I could still feel the vibrations of her volume against me. "I was so worried. Mattie and Raph were already up there but I almost stole a car to track you down myself—"

"My Starlight here wouldn't be reasoned with," Cinnamon said. She smiled up at me from where her head rested against Daph's. Her dark eyes saw right through me, their almost-reddish tint mesmerizing. I'd known Daphne for decades, but I still wondered how she was able to pull a woman who was possibly the most beautiful person in San Francisco. "She could only be distracted. And she made it very difficult."

"I'm here now," I said, even though it felt redundant. "But I'd rather not be *here* here."

"We have a car." Cinnamon left the hug first. Now that she stood farther back, I could see she wore a cranberry turtleneck under a lightweight black puffer jacket, black leggings, and sneakers.

My cheeks flushed. Good that they had a car and I wouldn't have to feel embarrassed by my outfit in front of thousands of strangers on the way home.

"We're glad you're back," Cinnamon continued, as Daphne reluctantly let go of me. "And not just because it'll stop her from attempting illegal or dangerous things."

"I doubt anything would stop her from attempting illegal or dangerous things," I said with a smirk.

Daph sniffled and moved a strand of hair out of her face. "Your safety and presence are all I required."

Cinnamon tried to hide a smile. "We'd better be on our way, before she goes full formal."

"I'll have you know I can be quite formal whenever I desire!" Instead of walking beside me, Daphne took my hand and led me out of the station behind her, head held high and defiant, and I was enveloped in a deep and satisfying joy. I could get through just about anything as long as I had people who loved me.

The lot of them were staying in a hotel a few blocks away from the theater hosting the premiere of *Shutdown*. Raphael owned a flat in the city, but the cluster of rooms at the hotel would give us each our own private space, and there would be enough room for the clothing racks and the hair stylists and makeup artists he'd hired on our behalf.

Daphne showed me where I could find her and Cinnamon before leaving me in front of my room with my key card and a kiss.

"Meet us in a half hour," she said, gently tugging on a strand of my hair with a sad smile. "I know it's not much time, but I figured you might want to get a little settled first. Or take a shower. Not that you smell. But. Well. Bus." She shrugged. "We'll try on outfits for tonight and you can catch us up on everything. Mattie will be back soon. The boys' clothes are in her and Raph's room, so you don't have to see Luke right away."

She hesitated. "You...don't want to see Luke right away, right?"

I didn't. And I did.

"You did good," I said, giving her an equally sad smile. "Don't worry, I'll explain the best I can. In a half hour."

My accommodations were downright stately. And I'd been given the smallest of the four suites. I put my bag on the dining table and felt uncomfortably out of place. This was a room designed for a whole collection of luggage and steamer trunks and hat boxes. Not one dirty, overstuffed backpack. I had a suspicion it was a metaphor for my own impostor syndrome, but that was something that didn't need to be unpacked yet.

The shower was a godsend, the water just this side of scalding, the shampoo a designer brand, the dirt and grime and tension in my shoulders washing away with deceptive ease. All of my clothes were dirty, and I had planned to shuffle over to Daph and Cinnamon's room in the classic hotel fluffy robe and slippers, but I found an entire closet full of hotel-branded clothing. The expected bathrobe of course, but also jackets, scarves, polo shirts, gym shorts, loungewear, and pyjamas. It was beautiful and exactly the kind of thing I would offer my clients.

Well. Former clients.

My heart stuttered, remembering what I'd lost. I loved working in hospitality and tourism. And I was good at it, even if I didn't have any talent for running a tourism business. Under different circumstances, I could be satisfied with my job at The International Travel Source. Emphasis on the "under different circumstances."

I chose the pyjama set. Long pants and a button-down, long-sleeve shirt, in a thin flannel the same cobalt blue as the rest of the hotel's branded items. It was soft enough that I almost didn't believe I deserved it. I did have one clean pair of underwear and one sports bra, tucked into the bottom of my bag for situations like this. I'd made a lot of mistakes, but preparing for the worst by bringing an extra set of undergarments would never be one of them. I slid my phone and key card into a pyjama pants pocket, put on the traditional fleece-lined hotel slippers, and made my way over to Daph's.

Raphael had given Daphne and Cinnamon the largest suite. It was easily three times the size of mine. Knowing the youngest Redgrave sister's penchant for fashion, I could imagine that

Daphne would have brought her own clothes enough to fill the space. Instead, four large racks of clothing took up the four corners of what I would call the living room. I could tell at a glance whose was whose. Neutral colors well-cut in timeless silhouettes would be Cinnamon. Daphne's would be the opposite of her wife's conservative wardrobe, the rack with wild colors and pieces whose shapes required alternatives to hangers. The corner that looked like it belonged to a more modern Sophia from *Golden Girls* was unmistakably Matalina's.

And then there was mine. Where the girls' choices were organized by color and shape, mine ran the literal spectrum from feminine to masculine. I'd never be one to wear a ball gown, but one end of the rack started with cocktail dresses in dark colors. One of them was black, and I remembered Daphne telling me about it when we spoke on the phone. She'd also mentioned a red suit, which I found near the other end. The color was so dark it was nearly black, and it called to me. It was silk, as she said, and I let the soft sleeve of the jacket slip through my fingers, a fluttering growing in my belly when I touched the material.

"What did I tell you?" Daphne asked with a sly smile. In one hand, she held a flute of sparkling wine, and she reached the other towards the jacket. "The color is gorgeous, and there are so many ways to style it. If you wanted to do something more feminine, you could skip the vest and shirt altogether and go bare underneath. It would make a daring neckline for you, but dear god you'd look hot. With the ends of your tattoo visible on your chest? Fuck, Rin."

"Don't start until I'm out!" Mattie called from the bathroom, opening the door a crack. "It's not my fault I've had to pee for the last three hours!"

"Wouldn't dream of it, darling," Daphne answered. "Anyway," she continued, turning back to me and lowering her voice. I shook my head. Sisters. "Another option is the full three-piece suit, with or without a shirt. Or everything but the jacket. Or just the vest and pants. You'd look stunning in literally anything on the rack, to be honest. You could take the whole collection, if you wanted. Raphael says it's a gift. I, myself, am taking half my rack, and Raph's stylist to boot. I have the taste to do it myself, but not the access, and I wants it, precious."

"I can hear you still talking! Give me a second!" Mattie sounded desperate.

Across the room, Cinnamon laughed. I'd missed this, all of this. The Honest Mischief Alliance. Being caught up in silly drama, being part of a family. Being comfortable and feeling safe. I had been stupid to avoid it because I didn't want them to know about my failures. If anyone would understand, it would be them. I stroked the red jacket with the back of my hand and swallowed past the emotion caught in my throat.

"A goat ate my binder," I mumbled. Daphne stared at me for a moment, mouth open, before closing her eyes and taking a deep breath.

"Jesus Christ, Rin." Not shock or concern. Daph was trying to stop herself from asking the thousand questions such a statement inspired in her. She was doing a fantastic job, for her.

"Did you say a *goat...ate...*your *binder?*" Mattie shouted.

"Ok." Daphne nodded and opened her eyes, then walked to a tall set of drawers on wheels next to my clothing rack. In the rush of joy of seeing all the new and beautiful clothes, I hadn't noticed each rack had a similar supplementary dresser. Daph patted the top of mine like she was showing off a new truck. "Any underthing you can imagine needing has been provided for you. You didn't think we just half-assed this, did you? We got all the clothes, jewelry, shoes, accessories, everything we'd need to step out onto the red carpet. Mattie and I made sure the stylist knew your array of possibilities."

Of course they did.

Arms encircled my waist from behind, and Mattie squeezed me tight.

"I'm so glad you're ok," she said, her voice wavering.

"Aw, Mats, me too." I spun in her arms so I could wrap myself around her just as securely. "I wasn't ever in danger, though. Merely waylaid with no Wi-Fi."

"Exposure," she spat. "Starvation. Car explosion or collision. Drowning. Murder. Wolves!"

"Wolves, Mattie?" I said at the same time Cinnamon asked, "Drowning?"

"You all know Luke would never let them succumb to such a fate," Daph said, her eyes full of mischief. "He loves Rin too much to let them drown or be murdered."

"Oh, are we doing this now?" Mattie asked. She let go of me to wipe her eyes with her sleeve. "Come to the couches, Rin. Time to spill the beans."

I sighed and followed the Redgraves to the centre of the living room, where we joined Cinnamon. My stomach rumbled when I noticed the array of snacks on the coffee table, but I had a feeling I'd be talking for a while, and if my mouth was full, I'd have to repeat myself. I settled into a cushion on the other side of the couch from Mats. "I would argue that *I* would never let myself succumb to such a fate. That I don't need saving."

"We all know that's a lie. That's the problem." Mattie gave me a sympathetic look as she loaded up what looked like a real china plate with fruit and cheese. Daphne checked the tea in the teapot and poured each of us a cup. "Not the lying, but you thinking it's ok to offer help without needing any in return."

"So you'd better fess up," Daph added, handing me the steaming cup of tea. "Tell us what's been going on. You won't regret it."

I snorted. "How can you be so sure?"

She looked at me like I was the dumbest person in the world. One side of her mouth curled up in a confused, dopey look. "Because it's *us*."

Few things in this world could compel me to admit, to anyone, my problems, my failures, my emotions, and my hopes and fears. But Daphne's sincere confusion over why I wouldn't trust the three of them like the best friends they obviously were to me was one of those things.

I started at how hard it had been to keep NIPL going. Told them about selling it and taking a job with the company that bought it. How I felt like a failure. Why I had actually been in Scotland. How I felt about Luke. Why I feared I was still too much of a disaster to be with him. Our entire, doomed road trip. Mr Bean. The cottage and goats. The labyrinth and Daisy.

By the end, all of us were crying, and all of us were on one couch, piled together in a group hug, high on the catharsis of tears and emotional bloodletting. They hadn't even made more than one snickering comment about how I went from NIPL to TITS. They felt like my sisters again, and for the first time since I broke up with Luke two years ago, I felt like I had a real family.

"Oh," I said, taking one of Mattie's tissues she kept up her sleeves and blowing my nose. "And I quit my job at The International Travel Source."

"What? When?" She asked.

"Between getting off the bus and finding Daphne."

"That was like. Four minutes," Daph said.

"I sent an email. All that no sleep was good for one thing: not giving a fuck about things that seemed important a few days ago."

Beside me, Cinnamon rubbed my back and said, "I think that was the most important thing you could do for yourself right now. I have no doubt you could do the job, but the emotional baggage that came with it was completely out of proportion. It was brave. I'm proud of you, and I'm also excited for what comes next for you."

"What does come next for you?" Daphne asked.

I shrugged. "I was thinking of working at Tessa's, if she'd hire me. Not as a boxing instructor, not yet, anyway. I wouldn't mind starting at the bottom there. Really start over. With something gentle, something that didn't require my total body and soul. I liked being a part of *Shutdown*, but I'm not sure being a producer is what I want to do. Although…"

Thinking of the documentary reminded me of Stromness and meeting Luke's coworkers on his current film. Will had thought Luke and I knew each other from work.

"What would it take to be a stunt performer?"

I'd been talking to myself, but that didn't stop the girls.

Daphne squeed. "Holy crap, you'd be so good at that."

"Raphael could put you in contact with the right people literally today," Mattie added.

"It was just a thought," I said, shying away from their attention. "But I should set something up soon. I still need to make a living."

"Raph and I could float you—"

"If I may," Daphne interrupted, "Cinnamon and I would be delighted to fund this next stage of your career. We have a grant we're offering called the Rin Butcher Second Chance Career Change Grant, and I'm pleased to inform you that your application was approved—"

"Raphael can get you a job on his current film."

"Redgraves!" I shouted with a laugh that for all its joy, ended in a choked sob. "I love you to death. All of you. And, in a break from traditional Rin-ness, I will be sincerely entertaining any ideas you have regarding my continuing to be housed and fed. And happy and fulfilled."

"And Luke?" Cinnamon asked softly. She'd been quiet, and her canny gaze had looked into me, found the thing I wasn't saying, and plucked it out into the open.

My eyes stung, as though I were crying from scratch and hadn't been sobbing out all my problems to my friends all afternoon. I blinked fast, but not fast enough. "I can't see how being with me would be better for him than what he has now. I have nothing to offer him besides, I don't know, additional money problems and contact anxiety. Another mouth to feed, another whole person's entire fucked up life to handle."

Cinnamon huffed. "Did you ever consider that Luke is willing to take on the responsibility of you if it means he gets to experience your extraordinary love?"

"I can't let myself believe that," I whispered, my tightening throat threatening to cut me off at any moment.

"Why not?"

"Because it doesn't balance, what little I'd add to his life versus what I would take from him."

"He was behind the viral campaign to book NIPL baches in the end of 2020," Daphne said.

I startled.

"Daphne Ebenezer Redgrave," Mattie scolded.

"They should know!" She shouted in exasperation. "Luke is as bad at feeling deserving of love as Rin is, which means that, most likely, neither of them know what the other has done in the name of love. My fealty is to Rin-Rin, I can't keep Luke's secrets from them! *We* know how much they both care and what they're willing to do, and if they don't see it, it's our responsibility as lovers of love and them to tell them both before it's too late!"

"I wondered," I murmured, wiping at my eyes. The flood of bookings in November that year was an unexpected miracle. It had single-handedly kept NIPL going for months.

"Fuck it." Mattie sighed. "He kept Tessa's open, too."

"What?"

Mats nodded. "He convinced some production company to contract her for personal trainers."

I frowned. "She never told me about it."

"Why would she? Besides, she signed an NDA. But Luke didn't. He read an article saying that they might have to close, confirmed with us that that was the boxing place you went to, next thing we knew, it wasn't in danger of closing anymore."

"And he admitted it was him?"

Mattie gave me a look. "As much as you've admitted to settling the debt on his mother's house."

"Me getting the right people involved in his mortgage problem isn't the same as Luke personally getting involved in my business."

"No," Mats said, glancing away and acting shy in a way that was very suspicious. "You're right. The only way it would be equal is if you, let's say, covered the amount from your personal savings."

I felt the tips of my ears burning. Ok, I thought I had been way sneakier than this. "Which we all agreed none of us could do."

"The jig is up, Rin!" Daph burst out, with a relatable exasperation. "We tracked down the paperwork ourselves. Admit it."

I sighed dramatically. Nothing got past these people. "You caught me! Congratulations! Are you going to tell him? Like you're telling me all the crazy things he's done for me?"

"Crazy?" Mattie laughed. "Sure, sure. But you know. It seems like he has no problem asking for help from his friends when it's in service to someone he loves. He only has a problem asking for help if it's to help *him*. Sound familiar, dear?"

Too familiar. I grimaced.

"Don't let us pressure you," Cinnamon said, which was also manipulative, considering she was the one who brought him up. "Ultimately, only you can know what your relationship is like, if it will work, if it's worth fighting for. We want you to see what we see. The things he might have kept from you, for whatever reason. And from where we are, he loves you very much. And if I'm not mistaken, he's also ridiculously in love with you."

Mattie and Daphne nodded furiously. Cinnamon looked away and asked, "Will you tell us you're not ridiculously in love with him, too?"

She was giving me space, and the Redgraves followed her lead, Daphne looking at her hands, Mattie playing with a button on her sleeve. God, how did they ever let me join in their subterfuge, if I was so completely transparent? Did *everyone* know I was still in love with Luke? Fuck, did *Luke* know I was in love with Luke?

"I...don't think you're the people I need to admit that to," I said slowly. They let me sit in silence for a while. With my work problem sort of solved but set aside for now, I had space to focus on Luke and what we could mean to each other. The girls stood up, one by one, and gravitated towards their clothes, calling to each other from their personal corners, trying to coordinate across their vastly different styles.

I didn't need an answer right away. I'd see Luke tonight, and there was no pressure to tell him how I felt, except that I wanted to know what would happen. But I already felt like I had room to breathe, and that extra space could be filled with all sorts of possibilities.

Chapter 33

October 2022

Luke

It was quiet. And still. Too quiet and still. I lifted my head with a snort, twisting my neck wrong in the process.

"Ow," I gurgled, clearing my throat and rubbing the muscle I'd tweaked.

"Old injury?"

Raphael. I opened my eyes. We were parked in a garage, engine off, Mattie nowhere to be seen. Raph stared at me from the front seat with a look of obvious concern.

"Old body," I explained, not entirely joking. I rubbed a new pain in my back. "Where's Mats?"

"Up in the room with the others."

"Rin?"

"They're there, too."

I let out a sigh of relief. It had been so stupid of them to go walking off into the night like that, in that condition. And it had been just as stupid of me not to follow them. Mattie had said she was in contact with Rin, and with my phone at the bottom of a random Scottish pond, all I could do was trust they were ok.

I launched myself upright. "I need your phone. I have to call Cass."

"I can do you one better," he said with a grin. "Ta da!"

He presented the brand new phone opened in its box like a guy presenting his girlfriend with a set of jewelry. That's right, Rin had told me that Raphael and Mattie were in Leeds to bring me a replacement for the phone I'd lost. If Mr Bean had been able to make it another two hours on the road, I would have had a phone this whole time.

"It's already programmed," he explained. I took it and tapped the screen, and my usual lockscreen photo of Cass, Lena, and mum popped up. "Everything downloaded from the cloud."

"How?"

"Your mum is a very good guesser of your passwords."

The sound that escaped me was so embarrassing, I didn't realize it was me until Raphael was climbing over the front seat to join me in the back.

"Hey, mate, you're all right," he murmured, pulling me close to him as another sob left my lips. "You're all right."

Once I knew I was crying, I just let myself at it. There was no point in putting in the effort to try to stop. Not when it had been building up for days—for years, if part of it was losing Rin the first time. And besides, I was with Raph. There was no one I was closer to, or trusted more, and if nothing else, I could count on him to support me no matter what. So, for a while, I let him.

"Ah," I said eventually, lifting my head and trying to pull the snot back into my nose. "I fucked up. A lot."

He kept an arm around my shoulders and pulled a handkerchief out of his pocket for me. Of course.

"We all fuck up sometimes."

"Yeah but I fucked up like, five things at once."

"That's not so many."

"They were big things, Raph."

He shrugged. "Arson? Murder? Kidnapping? Sexual assault?"

"No. What? No."

"Well, those are the only unforgivable ones I can think of right now. Which are you talking about?"

I thought back, to this morning, then the night before, chronicling all my cock-ups in my head before I said them aloud. By the time I had gotten to seeing Suraj's shitbox of a car that early morning a lifetime and less than a week ago, I had been quiet for so long, Raph decided to interrupt me.

"Do you remember Berlin?"

The question came out of nowhere, and I had to take myself out of my tangled mind to understand what he was getting at.

Raph and I met each other for the first time in Berlin, over a decade ago. It was the first time we worked together. Raph was a rising star, his breakthrough film with Payton had come out about six months before and it was impossible for him to keep a low profile. Besides being handsome as fuck, he was kind, professional, level-headed, and charming in a way that was frustratingly sincere.

I thought he was a total wanker.

It was jealousy. I knew it at the time, but I was young enough to pretend it was something loftier. He wasn't better than me. I treated him just as professionally, just as kindly. But as soon as I didn't have to be in the same place as him, I bugged out.

I wasn't as subtle or clever as I thought. One night, he invited a bunch of us out to a club. Said he could get us in easy. Trying to make himself look cool. Sure, we said, and we went. He opened a tab for us, winning over a couple of our coworkers, but not me. Later in the night, I found him in the bathroom hallway, standing between a girl so drunk she couldn't get up off the floor and a guy so angry I thought he was going to pop an artery. Raphael had his hands up in the universal symbol of "I don't want to fight," but he wouldn't let the guy near her.

"Hey bro," I said to Raph with a nod. All casual. "What's this, then?"

"I don't think it's a good idea for her to go with him," he said, never taking his eyes off the guy, who was pacing and mumbling and occasionally spitting. "She was here with some girlfriends. I saw something." He glanced at me then, quick, and a shiver ran down my spine. Whatever he'd seen, it was enough for him to suspect, and that was good enough for me.

"Why are you holding your arms like that?" I asked.

"I don't know how to fight. And I don't know any German. So I don't know how to tell him to fuck off."

"Ah. No worries. I speak his language."

And I clocked that German motherfucker right in the face.

It wasn't a pretty fight, but it was a quick one, and my opponent scampered off after getting his ass kicked. Meanwhile, Raphael protected the girl. Her friends eventually found her and took her off, and Raph turned his focus to me.

"I've got to learn to fight," he said, frowning at my bruises. Nothing broken, no blood, so it wasn't bad.

"Naw," I said, rubbing my jaw. "You might bust up your money maker."

He looked past me, down the hall where the group of girls were making their way out. "Some things are more important."

In the back of Raphael's car, in London, thirteen or fourteen years later, I said, "I remember Berlin. I fucked up then, too. I was a dick to you."

"You were a dick," Raphael agreed. "But when you had to set aside your pettiness and help me with something more important, you reassessed the situation. And how did that turn out? Are we enemies, or are we best mates?"

I shook my head. We had been best mates, but again, I fucked it up, more recently.

"I'm trying to tell you that, even when you fuck up, you can find a way to set things right again." Raph shifted in his seat. "You've been distant lately and I don't know why, but you can't get rid of me." I thought for a minute that he'd read my mind, but more likely he could read my face and body language and silence after so many years of friendship.

I'd told Rin my problem with Raphael. The thought of telling him about it was embarrassing. I felt like a bad friend. I felt like a failure. Failing at a friendship with Raphael Fucking Callan, a man so effortlessly befriended and generous and compassionate, felt like starting a beef with Santa Claus or Mister Rogers. It said way more about me than about him, and I didn't like what it said.

But the only way to get over it was to tell him. So I did. My jealousy of every aspect of his life, and the ways mine had fallen apart. That I had no jobs lined up. That I had driven Rin away for good. He listened. Part of me thought he was giving me too much benefit of the doubt. I wanted him to be angry with me. It would have justified what I was feeling. But another part of me thought...maybe this man just loved me. And if someone like him could still love me, maybe I still had a chance with everything else. Maybe I hadn't fucked up *everything*.

When I'd finished, Raphael sighed and looked at the car ceiling. Through the ceiling, it seemed. Probably struggling with how to respond.

"I know it's not fair," I told him. "It's not your fault you're successful. I've been stupid about it, and I'm sorry. If you don't want to be friends anymore, or you need some time away from me and my nonsense, I get it. I won't—"

"Rin paid off your mum's house."

"—bother you if you don't...what?" His words caught up to me. I knew what each one meant individually. Rin. Paid. Off. Your. (My?). Mum's. House. "What?"

"You thought it was me." He smiled at me from beneath his thick lashes, grin like a fox. "That was part of it, wasn't it? Why you were angry with me. You thought I had one-upped you by bailing you out. But you told me not to, and I respect your wishes, even if they're damn foolish. That didn't stop me from posing the problem to the rest of the Honest Mischiefs. Daph was going to do it herself, but Rin told her it was taken care of. Said it was some New Zealand loophole she wouldn't understand. It wasn't."

"No," I said, my voice sounding far away. "No. It was a charitable organization."

"It was a shell corporation," he said gently. "Rin works in real estate. They know people. Months later, Daph was bored at work and had her own contacts track it down. It may have been charitable, but it wasn't from small donations or some billionaire philanthropist. It was most of Rin's savings."

"No," I said again. Why would they do that? Their company was struggling.

Oh god. If they hadn't used their money on that, on me, they might still have NIPL.

I was the reason Rin lost their family business.

"Why would they do that?" My voice cracked. "Fuck. Fuck."

"Because Rin loves you, Luke. They try to hide it. Best we can tell, they think they're not good enough for you."

"They saved my mother's house and prevented me and my children from becoming homeless, and they think *they're* not good enough for *me*? Be serious."

Raph shrugged again. "It makes sense to me because that's exactly something you would do, and you're basically the same person."

"I owe them. I owe them so much." And I repaid them with the horrors of this past week. Is this what my daughters meant when they called someone "cringe"? "One of us is certainly better than the other, and mate, it's not me."

"Do you love them?"

Obviously. Enormously. With my entire soul. With every thought. Did he even have to ask?

"Yes."

"Do they know that?"

They knew it two years ago. But our last day as a couple was the last time they could have known for sure. The first and last time I'd said it.

"Call who you need to," Raph said. "Come up to the room when you're done. Eight oh five. Shower and dress for the premiere. There's no time to talk to Rin before the show. But you're in it, you know. Together. As it should be." He clapped my shoulder and left the car.

I might have fucked up five times over, but Raphael was telling me all was not lost. A hope that had been flickering, doused, and relit innumerable times over the past two years kindled to life again. Rin loved me. And maybe the timing was never going to be right. But I wasn't going to let them go this time. I would fight for us. As long as they loved me. I would make it right. I would. I would.

Chapter 34
October 2022
Rin

Attending the premiere was nothing like I expected. I'd watched plenty, their highlights covered on entertainment news channels. Especially over the last few years, whenever I knew Luke or Raphael would be there. Mattie had said this one would be different. It was a documentary, for one, so there weren't any celebrities to attract attention besides our boys. But our boys did attract a lot of attention.

Daphne, Cinnamon, and I left the hotel first. There was a small cadre of fans waiting outside, and much to Daphne's delight, they mistook her for someone famous. An easy mistake, especially when she wore a delicate copper dress with off-the-shoulder sleeves and a mini train. Cinnamon wore a floor-length black gown with jacquard chevrons and a copper belt in the same v-shape. Simple and stunning.

They, and Mattie, had chosen outfits with copper in them to match the waistcoat they'd all known I was going to pick from the start. I couldn't resist the dark-red suit, though I ended up opting for no jacket. The color alone had swayed me, but the material was comfortable and soft, and I wasn't sure I had ever felt more at ease in any clothing since I was a kid. The waistcoat was the same color, "dried blood," as Daph said, and embroidered with copper leaves. The stylist had paired it with an almond-colored fitted shirt and fixed a puffy black ascot (that reminded me of

Daisy) with a copper pin in the shape of a lily. I'd taken a chance with the hair stylist and took off a few inches of length, then a few inches of width in the form of a significant undercut on the right side of my head. The makeup artist was a magician who did something to make the watercolor blues and greens of my eyes pop.

I had never looked so good in my whole life. And despite the trials and setbacks of the past week, I was grinning like a fool. When the squad saw my final look, they all fangirled. Daphne even got flustered, and I marked it down as a win that I made the most lesbian lesbian I knew blush over the most masc-presenting I'd ever been.

"You look like you're filled with joy," Mattie explained. "I can't remember the last time I saw you this happy."

I brought her in close and kissed the top of her head. It felt good to feel good and look good.

"The clothes are a minor part of it," I said. She smiled up at me. She knew.

A black SUV brought me, Daph, and Cinnamon to the theater, where there was a decent-sized crowd waiting, I guessed, for Raphael and Luke. The three of us walked the red carpet anyway, following the directions of the nice people there to guide us, and we got more compliments than I expected.

As we were about to enter the theater, a cluster of screams rose up by the street, and I turned to see Luke starting his slow walk down the carpet.

Sometimes I forgot he was an honest-to-god movie star. When he did things like drop his phone in a lake or check his blind spot before switching lanes or make a dad joke that had his kids groaning with embarrassment, he was just...Luke. I'd seen him fold laundry and cook a mediocre dinner and snore his way through the night.

Other times, I would remember. When he would turn his charm up to eleven, trying to coerce me into whatever wild plan he had in mind. When he played pretend with Lena and Cassidy and decided to channel the dedication and drama of a Shakespearean actor.

When he wore a suit.

The stylist had made sure we all looked amazing in our own right, but she knew the six of us were a team and carried the copper theme to Luke and Raph's outfits as well. Luke's suit was black, mostly a matte material, with lapels the same shiny fabric as my vest, blood red with copper embroidery. Same color tie and pocket square, his own copper tie pin, and his black plastic glasses.

I didn't think I'd be able to tell if seeing him had any effect on me, since I'd had a fluttering in my belly since we left the hotel, and I was high on my own comfort. But oh, I could tell. And he did.

He waved and nodded to the cameras and took selfies with fans, smiling and laughing and in his element, and I felt the first seeds of self doubt. The feeling arrived attached to a memory from two years before. Mattie and Raph started writing letters to each other before they even knew who the other was, but when Mats suspected that the guy signing his letters "R" might be someone famous and talented as well as handsome, she suddenly thought she couldn't be good enough for him. At the time, I'd called her a muppet. Reminded her of her self-worth. It simply didn't make any sense to me that this incredible woman would do a complete about-face at the thought of her love interest being famous.

But now? Yeah. I understood. Luke was the guy who packed me snacks even when I said I didn't want them, because he knew I'd get hangry and was trying to look out for me. He was the guy who trusted me with his kids. And if the Redgraves were right, he was also the guy who used his connections to bring in enough business for me to keep NIPL going and to keep my favourite gym open.

He also had admirers around the world. They didn't know he couldn't tie a shoe to save his life, or that he needed nine hours of sleep or he'd be cranky. But how could I be sure I was a better partner for him than anyone else? When he had so many people to choose from? When I broke his heart and told him he was thoughtless and, more recently, abandoned him in the wilderness without a phone or a map?

"Rin," Daph whispered, grasping my elbow and gently tugging me away. "I could watch him all day, too, but they're telling us we have to go inside now."

I nodded and let her lead me away. It wasn't like I could talk to him now anyway. After the movie, then. After the dinner after the movie. Tomorrow.

In the lobby, I put on the face mask that matched my waistcoat. Raphael had pushed for the premiere to have a mask requirement. He didn't want to risk anyone getting sick, but especially Lena, and everyone agreed. I wished it were that easy everywhere else.

There was too much going on to concentrate on any one person. I shook hands and nodded, recognizing many of the Kiwis that made up the bulk of the people followed in the documentary. I saw Lena and Cassidy the same time they saw me, and Lena shouted, "Rin-Rin!" and ran to give me a hug.

"Hey, Lena. Long time no see, huh?" I hugged her back fiercely, but made sure not to muss up her pink dress. Her hair was already a lost cause, half of the up-do sagging to the side, loose strands everywhere. Affection flooded me. She was still young enough that she didn't care about her appearance, only chasing after every thing that made her happy.

She gave me a big squeeze, stepped back with wide eyes, and whispered, "Did my dad really drop his phone in a lake?"

"She thinks he faked it so he wouldn't have to answer her texts anymore," Cassidy said, stepping up behind her sister. "Hi Rin."

They'd both grown up, in the two short years since I last saw them in person. Cass wore a bright-purple pantsuit that only looked a little ridiculous on the twelve-year-old, but I understood what she was trying to do, acting all mature.

"Hi Cass. His phone is definitely at the bottom of a lake. Why would you think it wasn't?"

Cass cleared her throat and thumbed towards her mother, who hadn't moved from talking to two people I didn't recognize, though she waved when I caught her eye.

I didn't know Mia well, but from what I did know of her, it most likely wasn't malicious, making the girls think their father didn't want to talk to them. That was just something Mia would do herself, and didn't see the point in trying to sugarcoat it for the girls, who never hid the fact that they loved being with their father more.

"Well," I said, crouching down to their level, "he can show you his brand new phone when he gets here. And I can show you the texts between me and Raphael, where he said he'll buy your dad a new phone. And I have pictures of him swimming in the lake to try to find it. We stayed there a long time looking for it. He was very upset that he wouldn't be able to text or call you, especially since he dropped it taking a picture of a bird for you—"

My mind blanked on the bird. Cormorant? Some kind of hawk?

"The osprey," Cass said. "He told us earlier. That man loves birds."

"'That man?'" I repeated. "Are you sure you can talk about your dad like that?"

Cass shrugged. "He'd think it was funny."

Yeah. He would.

The girls saw someone else they knew and were off before I could say anything else. I socialized a bit more, finding Daph and Cinnamon and sticking with them as we made the rounds. Mason Schilling, the executive producer and the person who made the documentary happen in the first place, greeted me warmly. It was the first time we'd met in person, and he was boisterous but kind. He introduced me to other people I wouldn't remember the next day, or even later that night, despite my years of training in social situations. Since I quit the tourism industry a few hours before, it seemed like every skill I'd honed for it had immediately deteriorated.

Cinnamon made up for my lack of social savvy. Part of it was being a therapist, part of it was growing up in a family whose business required it, like mine, and part of it was that Cinnamon was a naturally inquisitive and compassionate person. Daphne was shockingly well behaved. She hadn't even brought her slingshot or pebbles "just in case." I noted when Luke walked in, though we hadn't made eye contact yet, and Mattie and Raph weren't far behind him. Mattie wore copper jewelry and a cream-colored dress with the same jacquard chevrons as Cinnamon's, and Raphael's suit was similar to Luke's, but with a cream-colored shirt and pocket square and no tie. A few minutes later, they caught up to us.

"Hey," Luke said, sidling up to me. "You look absolutely stunning."

I'd been trying to avoid looking at or talking to him directly. I wasn't sure what to say yet, but I knew I had to say something, and I knew the four minutes before we went to watch our documentary together wasn't the right time to say it. I turned to him and caught his eye. He was breathless, and I could tell by his eyes that he was smiling, his face as open and earnest as a puppy's. I could read the hope in it, but also the briefest of frowns that disappeared as the momentary doubt was swept back up into his general optimistic outlook.

"Thanks," I said, trying to remain calm in the face of his handsomeness and his obvious affection. "So do you."

He leaned in to go through the motions of kissing me on the cheek despite our masks, or hug me, I wasn't sure, and I turned my body and face to receive one, but he'd meant the other, and we ended up stepping back from each other, embarrassed. We couldn't even get a hug right. He ducked his head sheepishly and I winked, letting him know we were good.

"At least something positive came from our disastrous road trip," he said, gesturing to me as his looked me over. "You would have never worn this if your other outfit hadn't been breakfast for sheep."

It was the wrong thing to say. He had a knack for that. But for some reason, it didn't bother me. I wasn't quite at the place where I could laugh about it yet. I should have complimented him, too. On the suit. On the documentary. On how great his kids were.

"I'm sorry I left you," I blurted out instead, at the same time he said, "I'm glad you got here ok."

"Oh," I said.

"Naw, don't be sorry." He crossed him arms and nodded. "It was the right move. I would have slowed you down." He cocked his head at me and I knew he was giving me his best grin.

"No," I said, shaking my head. The lights above us dimmed and brightened, and everyone around us started towards the theater doors. "You would have kept me upright. And sane. I was stupid and impulsive. I would have loved for you to be with me."

He took a breath and held it, his eyes searching mine. I thought I'd been talking about leaving him at Daisy's. It wasn't until I heard myself aloud that I knew I was talking about leaving him two years ago.

"Rin, I—"

"Daddy, our movie is starting!" Lena came barreling out of nowhere, jumping for the crook of her dad's crossed arms and hanging like a little monkey. "We don't want to miss the previews!"

Luke put his hand over Lena's, keeping her grip on him so she wouldn't slip, but he didn't take his eyes off me.

"Sit with me," he demanded, leaning forwards so I knew he was talking to me. "We made it together. We should see it finished together."

I'd spent several days sitting beside him, close enough to touch. I could do it again for a few hours. Just because he looked devastatingly hot and smelled like summer and we were about to watch home videos of when we were together didn't mean it had to be awkward. Or emotional. There was plenty of time later for both those things.

I nodded, and let him lead me into the dark theater.

Chapter 35
October 2022
Luke

That had sounded suspiciously like regret. Looking back, Rin wished I'd been with them on their journey. They could have been talking about leaving the castle this morning (dear god was it just this morning?), but how they said it made me think that the path they'd wanted to walk with me had been the one they'd been walking alone for two years.

And Rin showed up in that suit. I knew they didn't wear it for my benefit, but it had far too effective an effect on me. And their haircut. And they looked so goddamn *comfortable* and happy, like when we first met, when they still thought they could save their business without sacrificing everything else in their life.

It was good I was wearing a mask, and that it was dark in the theater, because I could feel the flush in my face from my chin to the tips of my ears. We would talk after. Rin would sit beside me and this time, I wouldn't let them leave again without telling them how I felt. Without fighting for us.

Seating was trickier than it should have been, since all of us wanted to sit next to everyone else. In the end, it went Cinnamon, Daphne, Lena, Me, Rin, Cass, Mattie, and Raphael. There were no previews, of course, much to Lena's disappointment. The lights dimmed until we were in darkness, and it was like a switch flipped in my brain along with it, the simple ritual getting me in the mindset of watching a film, focusing my attention on the story I was about to watch.

It was a story I knew. One I had helped create, both behind the scenes and in front of the cameras. Raphael narrated it, which was weird. He had a great voice for it, but hearing him talk about what we all went through in those first few months of the pandemic, knowing one of the people he was talking about was me, made it weird.

Within five minutes of Raph and I quitting *Broke*, Mason Schilling also left, and stopped to ask us if we wanted to work with him instead. Mattie came up with the idea for the documentary within an hour. A day later, we were already taking video for it.

We didn't know what it would be, eventually. The concept was interesting and the scale of the pandemic unseen for a century. We knew plenty of people in our industry who would be out of work because of it, but if they documented how it affected their daily life, that could be their work, they could be paid, and maybe we'd even get something profound from it.

About thirty people participated, and of that, eight households became the focus of the final cut. I knew mine was one of them. My wild daughters and our adventures in lockdown were simply entertaining, but my celebrity status would also help to boost the appeal. We all sent in our recordings and let the creative, narrative people figure out how best to present them. I had no idea what the final version would look like.

Watching it for the first time, I thought it might be the best film I'd ever made.

Each household had unique problems and solutions, but there were a lot of universal trials, and footage from the other twenty or so people were added to make montages: cleaning mail with bleach wipes, coming home from the grocery store with substitute items because the shelves were so empty, trying to set up a work space next to kids who were remote learning and having video meetings with screaming babies in the background. Through it all, the uncertainty.

I tried to watch from a distance. With an objective and critical eye. But that was Lena and Cassidy up there, making a cake with my mum, flour streaking their hair somehow and chocolate chips strewn across the counter, with Lena sucking them up into her mouth like a vacuum cleaner. That was me converting my shed into an exercise room so I could stay in shape for the next *Knuckletracker* movie. Another scene: Rin and I slow dancing in the living room, and in present-time, I felt a twinge in my chest. We watched one of our sing-along nights with the girls. Rin bringing over groceries unasked because they found the only brand of biscuits the girls liked that month.

A lot of video from the squad, of me simply watching Rin, a smile on my face.

There were also confessionals. One of Rin's came up first. I recognized the bed as the one from their cottage down the street from me, and they looked like they just woke up. The light was dim. They talked about how worried they were, how unsure they were that NIPL could survive, how they hoped the pandemic would peter out quickly without taking any more lives and without destroying their business.

Beside me, Rin shifted, and I wondered if they had forgotten about that night.

I had forgotten about most of mine. In one, I was on a walk in the woods behind my house, worried for my family and our health, especially Lena.

"But I think I'm lucky," I huffed on-screen, stepping over a fallen tree. "I love spending time with them. And Rin. This has been a very strange way to start a relationship, but I wouldn't change it for anything. With all the turmoil in the world, and the uncertainty, it feels like Rin has always been a part of our family. They're a stabilizing influence. I hope they know it. You know what? I'll tell them tonight." I stopped walking and held the camera closer to my face. "Tell the people you care about how you feel," I urged the audience. "Tell them they're appreciated. Don't let them leave just because you couldn't get over yourself enough to be vulnerable."

My heart skipped a beat. It skipped two. I sat still and waited for the wash of adrenaline to pass. Without looking at them, I reached over and took Rin's hand, and they let me. I wanted to stand up and shout to stop the film so I could tell Rin I loved them. But they weren't going anywhere. I had them in my grasp now. I only needed to make it through the rest of the movie, which apparently would be a lot harder than I expected it to be.

Near the end was another clip of me and Rin that I hadn't known anyone had filmed. It had happened a week before we broke up. I remembered it clearly because it was what I remembered when we broke up, and it was the reason I knew Rin was being honest when they said that leaving me was about them needing to focus on their business and not something I had done wrong.

It started with Cass and Lena, chewing gum and blowing bubbles and clearly watching themselves do it on the phone screen. Raphael and Mattie spoke in the background, and *Frozen* was playing on the TV. We heard the front door of the house open, its creak familiar, then Rin's strained voice asking where I was. Cass looked up. Raphael said, "His bedroom, I think." As Rin's footsteps faded, Cass switched the camera around and followed, frame bouncing as she tip-toed down the hall after Rin, snapping her gum as she went.

When my sneaky child got to the bedroom, she stopped chewing and hit the floor, quietly maneuvering the phone into a position that peeked around the door frame and into the room. Rin was pacing in a small circle, one hand on their hip and another at their forehead. I had stopped folding the laundry on the bed and was reaching a hand out to them.

"I didn't expect it to happen so soon," Rin said softly, a tension in their voice that meant they were trying not to cry. "I didn't expect it to happen at all."

"Whatever it is, we'll get through it," I told them. They weren't staying still long enough for me to grab and hold them. "But you seem to be alive and whole, and I know the girls and Raph and Mats and mum are out there alive and whole. So nobody important is dead and that's the big thing."

Rin sniffled. "That bar is so low."

"Of course it is," I said with a grin. "How else do you think I'm so satisfied all the time? Low bars."

They paused in their comforting motion and I put my arms around them, pulling them tighter once they unfolded their own arms to wrap around me. I stroked their hair and rocked with them.

"Do we need to bury a body?" I murmured. "Easy enough. Lots of woods back here. Fake your own death? Flee the country? Sue somebody? We've got resources, love, let me know what you need."

"I don't know," Rin said, their voice cracking. "I don't know, and that's the problem. I decided today…we had a meeting. Went over everything. There's only one way out right now, and that's to sell thirty percent of our properties. I told them to do it. A third of my parents' business, Luke. A year after I took over. Just…gone."

A sob swallowed whatever else Rin was going to say, and I stopped our swaying, so they would feel steady. Anchored. I let them cry without answering, for a long time, rubbing their back and hair and holding them so close and tight it could have shattered my heart.

My heart was breaking for them then, and again now, watching and remembering. Despite the gravity of that moment, I had felt seen, accepted. Rin had allowed me to take care of them, and I felt like a good partner. Beside me in the theater, Rin shuddered, and I grasped their hand tighter. Let them know I was still here.

"I believe in you," on-screen-me told on-screen-Rin. "That doesn't mean I expect you to keep doing hard things. Especially not alone. If you do choose the hard path, I'll be there beside you. And if you choose an easier path, I will gladly lead you down that road."

Rin huffed a laugh. "I know you will. But we don't know which is which. Not when the world is all upside down like this."

"Fucking pandemic," I spat. "Ruining everything."

"Not everything," they said. "It gave us time to be together."

They looked up at me, and I kissed them.

I remembered that kiss, too.

It wasn't the most passionate or the most desperate. It wasn't a promise or the fulfillment of a promise. It wasn't a question or an answer. But it was the most honest. The most intimate. The most terrifying. Two souls laid bare, vulnerable, and accepted.

We rested our foreheads against each other and stayed that way, without talking, while the screen faded to black.

In the theater, Rin stood up in such a sudden motion, I thought they had somehow fallen up out of their chair. They let go of my hand and shimmied past me and out of the row of seats so fast, I didn't have time to understand they were leaving. As the screen brightened with the next scene, Daphne turn to me in tears.

"Go to them," she ordered.

I didn't need the encouragement.

The lights in the lobby were blinding, and I stumbled into the atrium with a hand blocking the brightness like a sailor at sea.

"Which way did they go?" I asked someone dressed like an usher. They pointed down a hallway that ended with a set of doors.

"Out, then left."

I followed. Where on earth were they going? I wasn't sure they'd ever been in London before. I had no doubt they had studied a map of it in preparation for coming here, but if they weren't just blindly trying to get far away from their emotions and the theater, I'd be shocked.

The sun had set while we were watching the documentary—our documentary—and the temperature had also set. As I exited the theater, peeling off my mask and shoving it into a pocket, a cool breeze reminded me it was autumn outside, and passing cars made shushing sounds as they drove through the wet streets. It had stopped raining, for the moment, but lingering water reflected the bright lights of the busy road, and I couldn't see Rin anywhere.

I turned left and started jogging, scanning the sidewalk ahead of me and across the street. I couldn't imagine they would have ducked into any of the stores along the way. Not if they were overcome and overstimulated. But if that were the case, they wouldn't likely be on the sidewalk, either. At the end of the block, I craned my neck to look down the intersecting street on the left and saw what appeared to be a park, its greenery dark in the growing dusk.

Bingo.

While it wasn't empty, the park was certainly quieter than the street, and it didn't take long to find Rin, who had stopped in front of a statue of a family of badgers, lit by a yellow-tinted lamppost.

It stopped me in my tracks, too. The smallest looked just like Lady Stephanie, rolled onto her back to paw at her mother's snout. Rin stared at it, head cocked, mask gone, arms crossed in front of them, looking pensive and chilly. Their shirt was luxurious but thin, crafted for the privilege of indoors and warmth, a status symbol meant to be the antithesis of practical, and Rin was the paragon of pragmatism. My suit jacket was fitted to my current bicep size, which was smaller than Rin's at this point, so I couldn't even give them my coat.

I walked up behind them. Either they hadn't heard me or didn't care who got this close, but they must have known it was me. I couldn't mistake them for anyone else: beyond their rich cocoa scent, their boxer's build, dark hair that sparked in the light like embers, and eyes the color of the clear and ancient river of Blue Spring, beyond all that, their presence was palpable, an energy effortlessly drawing me closer no matter how far away I was.

The trees and the darkness reduced the city noise to static, my breath the loudest sound, Rin's sniffles the next, followed by...

"Nightingale," I whispered, my eyes darting towards the impromptu birdsong in the nearest sycamore.

Rin turned to me slowly. Every feature of their face gave away their secret. Watery eyes, flushed cheeks, running nose, swollen lips. The telltale signs of a good cry.

"This is going to sound vain," I said, my voice as tight as my heart in my chest. "But you don't have to cry over me."

They snorted—a feat, through all that snot—and wiped their eyes.

"And yet here I am," they said, glancing me over. "How did I know you would find me?" Their voice was thick, the question genuine, like they honestly didn't know. Like they didn't know I would always find them.

So I answered the best I could. I kissed them.

All of my memories slipped away, into the cold, the darkness. My lips pressed against theirs and it was the first time, and every time, like I had never left. I had never stopped kissing them, so there was no comparison. They were soft and warm and pressed back, and I held Rin against me, feeling the smoothness of the silk waistcoat and the relative roughness of their thin dress shirt. I let my left hand caress their jaw, up to their ear and the soft fuzz of their new undercut.

And Rin kissed me back. They ran their hands around my waist and up my back, clutching at the fabric of my jacket. The tip of their tongue grazed my lips and I met them with mine, slowly, savoring the feeling of intimacy and trust. They pulled away enough to plant kisses around my mouth and on the tip of my nose, and rested their forehead against mine, mimicking the scene we just watched.

"I love you," they whispered with a sniffle, moments before I said it myself. My whole chest filled with warmth, and whatever doubts I had about us melted away. "I'm so sorry for what I put you through. It took me two years to get my priorities in order, and I thought it was too late."

"Don't apologize," I said, smiling against them. "It's not too late. We must have needed that time to find our way here. I love you too, Rin."

They let out a sob, and we held each other tighter.

"Even after everything?" They asked.

"Even after what, love? You keeping me in your heart for two years? You settled the debt on my mum's house. You didn't have the money to do that. Should I not love you for that?"

"There's plenty you did for me, too. That doesn't excuse all my nonsense."

"I love nonsense. And I told you I would wait for you. Did you not believe me?"

"I didn't believe I deserved it."

I lifted my head and used my finger to tilt their chin up to look at me. A remnant of their tears, pooled beneath my fingertips, left an air-chilled trail as it rolled down and across the back of my hand.

"Do you still believe that?" I asked.

They frowned, sniffled again, and glanced into the sky and branches behind me. This was how I knew I would get an honest answer.

"I don't know. But I want to start pursuing what I want. I'm tired of starving myself of affection and connection and saying it's what I deserve. I think I feel a slightly hedonistic era taking over now."

I laughed aloud. "Rin as hedonist is something I could get behind. And if we're talking about the ways we've changed? I want you to know you can count on me." A breeze picked up and ruffled Rin's hair, and I reached up to smooth it back into place. "I want to be the someone you count on. I know this whole road trip was the exact *opposite* of that, and I can only blame my eagerness to spend time with you again."

They nodded. "I want you," they breathed, a tremor of vulnerability in it. "And I'm so sorry for everything I've done to make you feel like you weren't worthy, when the truth is, I want you and I need you. Not someone like you, but you, Luke Maston. Your all-encompassing heart and strong hands and optimism and humor and sometimes-scattered mind that means well. I want to give you space to grow without worrying I won't be there while you do. Because I would love to be there while you do."

I felt something break in me, then, but I knew it was the wall that had been keeping me from feeling everything I knew I felt about Rin. Something I had built subconsciously to protect me if they said, definitively, that I was neither wanted nor needed. The flood of joy, so light I was dizzy with it, blinded my senses, and all I could do was hold Rin tighter and nod against them until I could speak coherently.

"I don't know where to go from here," they said with a sniffle. "I'm good at following directions but something like this...I feel like I have the map in my hands, but I don't know how to read it. Or I follow the roads but, in reality, they don't go where the map shows they do. Or they don't exist at all. Or maybe they just don't exist for me."

If anyone could understand what that felt like, it was me. The difference was that Rin would do their best to prepare for any unforeseen obstacles to the point of inducing anxiety, while I would forget to prepare for anything and cover up my ensuing dimwitted panic with an ease and confidence I didn't feel.

But Rin knew. They saw through all of that to my soft and chewy centre, and loved me anyway.

"I don't know where to go from here, either," I admitted, finding my voice again. "I'm terrible at following directions, and I haven't had much luck trying to wing it on my own, either. And if you'll forgive me continuing your metaphor—when I'm with you, I don't need a map. It wouldn't do me any good, when my compass always points to you."

Rin's face crumpled, and they rested their head against my chest with a sob. A brightness grew within me. Despite the cold and the coming night. Despite the love of my life crying in my arms. Despite the wake of destruction we left between here and Stromness. All I saw was the future. All I saw was us.

"I've got you," I told Rin. "You're home."

Epilogue: November 2022
Rin

As my breath came faster and the hits harder, my brain began shutting down peripheral senses to focus on the much more important task at hand. The quick punch-and-clank rhythm of the speed bags, snap of a jump rope; the grey dawn light finally overtaking the indoor fluorescents; the sweat and bleach wafting up to the ring; a tinge of metal on my tongue, hopefully from the smell of weight training equipment and not my own blood—all of these things filtered out of my attention. Even the soreness in my ankle, and the otherwise indelible stress of my first day at my new job: blessedly redirected, to be forgotten or collected when I wasn't trying to bob and weave and land a few hits of my own.

I was there for a workout, not a win, but Tessa had insisted on being my sparring partner anyway.

"I want you to focus on technique," she'd said. "They're going to start you with the building blocks, and I don't want you embarrassing me with bad forms."

So she ran me through the exercises that would do just that, and pushed me hard. I might have been excited to start studying with professional stunt performers, but I also needed all that extra anxiety beaten out of me. Hopefully in buckets of sweat and not bruises.

When I was on the verge of tipping out of high energy and into exhaustion, Tessa called it. We bumped gloves and I climbed out of the ring to the bench where I'd put my stuff and a very sleepy Luke, who handed me my water bottle without opening his eyes.

"Is it morning yet?" He mumbled.

I shot a stream of water into my mouth and swallowed. "You're missing Cassidy."

He cracked one eye open and turned to look at his eldest daughter before snuggling back down onto the bench. "She's doing footwork. Again. I saw that last week. And the week before. Wake me when she's got a bout."

"You could probably stand to practice a bit too," I teased.

His eyes opened enough to squint at me. "Are you insinuating that Wisdom Connor, the Knuckletracker himself, has lost his edge?"

"No, of course not," I scoffed. "I'm straight up saying it, bro."

Luke feigned a lunge at me, but I knew his style by now and stepped into it, so he ended up hugging me around my waist, which cracked him up. His laugh rang through the open space of the gym, and it made me so happy that I couldn't help grabbing his face and kissing him.

"Rin-Rin and Daddy, sitting in a tree..." Lena stuck her head out from under the blanket she was curled up in beneath the bench, and we looked down at her.

"Where'd you learn that one?" Luke asked her.

"Auntie Daphne."

"Of course," he grumbled. "What else did she teach you?"

Lena gave him a disappointed look. "Snitches get stitches, Dad."

He looked at me and I shrugged. "You know the rule, Luke."

"But I'm too young to be The Man," he whined. "I'm the one with the secrets to take to the grave. I can be included!"

"In some things," I said gently, running my fingers through his hair. His hands were still on my lower back and threatening to move lower. "You have to let your daughters have their own squad that doesn't include you. I promise, you don't want to know all their secrets. You think you do, and that's because you love them. But you don't. You'll have to be happy with your own core squad." I leaned over and whispered in his ear, "It's me. I'm your core squad. Tell me all your secrets. I'll never snitch."

"I'm yours, too," he whispered, and nipped at my neck. "What's the plan, then?" He asked louder. "Shower here? Breakfast? You're meeting them at eight, right?"

"I would like waffles," Lena said politely, sketching a colorful drawing on her tablet.

"One vote for waffles," Luke said.

"Waffles!" Cassidy yelled from the corner, slightly out of breath.

"Waffles," I agreed. "But also eggs and yoghurt and beans and veggies. I had a big workout and I'm going to do more physical work today. I need my protein."

"But not meat," Lena added. When we returned to New Zealand after the documentary premiere, me going vegetarian was one of many changes we made. Luke and I had spent the first week back at a bach. After our disastrous trip in Scotland, Luke wrapping up his last bit of work, and me unemployed for the first time in my whole life, we needed a break, and we took advantage of it to make up for lost time.

After that, I spent the weekdays at their house and the weekends at my Auckland flat, and the three of them came with me. The girls thought it was like camping, making a pillow-and-blanket fort in my living room while Luke and I took the one bed. Cass started taking lessons at Tessa's, and we made a fun weekend of it. The first time we had dinner and the girls saw the meat on my plate, clearly uncomfortable but not sure how to say anything about it, I caved. As Luke had said, it wasn't a big sacrifice to give it up, and it made the girls disproportionately happy, so I was glad to do it.

Our current arrangement couldn't last long. Raphael had gotten both of us work, and Luke only grumbled about it a little. He'd have to be in Wellington for it, while I was training with stunt performers up in Auckland, and his house was between the two. I didn't have much else keeping me up here, besides Tessa's, and I had a feeling I'd be selling my flat in the next year.

We didn't have a strategy yet. Beyond breakfast with my family, the entirety of my plan was to stay with Luke and build a life together where we and the kids and our larger squad of friends were the number one priority, and everything else could remain as unorganized as the piles of clothes on the girls' bedroom floors.

And as long as Luke and I faced it together, I was, surprisingly, gratefully, totally ok with that.

Acknowledgements

This is a long one because I've been gathering more help as the months pass and my authorly responsibilities grow.

First and always, I'm most grateful to my readers. That includes you! That also includes my beta readers, Donna, Ámá, and Adam; and my sensitivity reader, LJ. Editing requires reading and rereading, too, and May is always a gentle guide through the thicket of what I meant the story to be.

Amanda kept telling me she wanted to help in any way possible, but I'm sure she never anticipated getting emergency-tagged-in to make my entire damn book cover. It may have ended up being a team effort (especially with the formatting, always my nemesis), but her incredible artistic talent is what saved the day. There's a reason most of my tattoos are her handiwork. Check it out for yourself: @veggiesaurus on Instagram.

My parents hosted me for a month while I wrote *Paper Roads*, giving me the time and space to focus on the work without being distracted by the responsibilities of home. My thanks to them and my husband, who took care of those responsibilities while I was away. Jerome and Rachael also hosted me, this time in Aotearoa New Zealand, as I immersed myself in the culture to make my characters as authentically Kiwi as possible (as always, any mistakes on that front are mine and mine alone). I will visit again soon. You'll never be rid of me.

They're not around to read this, but Mormor and Morfar supported me financially and that's made a world of difference. I hope these novels would have made them proud.

Lastly, I would never be able to do this without my street team. My Dad, Sal, and Joan somehow end up distributing my books everywhere and to everyone, like book-specific Santa Clauses. Adam and Donna talk my novels up so much, I have strangers telling me they found my books through them, which is still wild to me. When Pete heard I was writing my first novel, he immediately offered to host its eventual launch event at Bell, Book & Comic—before I even finished writing a chapter, when my whole career as an author was just a whisper of an idea—and he continues to support and promote me.

I couldn't have done this without all of you, and I love you all.

About the Author

Jem Spears (she/they/he) is a queer, neurodivergent writer who was raised in New England, educated in Los Angeles, and embraced by Cincinnati. Somewhere in the Midwest, when the sun dips below the horizon, if it's not too humid, you can find her in her natural habitat: napping beneath a pile of cats. The rest of the time, she's at her computer, making characters kiss. She also writes poetry and nonfiction as Jacquelyn Merrill Ruiz, and fanfic on AO3 under yet another pseudonym. *Paper Roads* is book three of the International Love and Misadventure series.

***

Find out more about the author online at www.jemspears.com.

www.ingramcontent.com/pod-product-compliance
Lightning Source LLC
LaVergne TN
LVHW091702070526
838199LV00050B/2248